D1809490

The Glory Girls

By the same author

The Iron Master
When Tomorrow Comes
The Jealous Land
To The Ends of the Earth

The Glory Girls

June Gadsby

ROBERT HALE · LONDON

© June Gadsby 2007
First published in Great Britain 2007

ISBN 978-0-7090-8244-6

Robert Hale Limited
Clerkenwell House
Clerkenwell Green
London EC1R 0HT

The right of June Gadsby to be identified as
author of this work has been asserted by her
in accordance with the Copyright, Designs and
Patents Act 1988

2 4 6 8 10 9 7 5 3 1

Typeset in 10/12¾pt Sabon
by Derek Doyle & Associates, Shaw Heath
Printed and bound in Great Britain
by Biddles Limited, King's Lynn

For the late Mary Lambert, a real heroine,
and FANYs everywhere

With grateful thanks to the following for help with research: my husband, Brian Gadsby; Hugh Popham (The FANY in Peace & War); Pat Beauchamp (Fanny Goes to War); Sarah Helm (A Life in Secrets); Sir Winston Churchill (The Second World War) and the Casa Guilla, unique hotel of St Engracia, Lerida, Spain.

Any errors regarding the FANYs in this fictitious tale are uniquely my own.

PROLOGUE

1914

T HE wind blowing across the land between the battlefield and the British Army Hospital camp carried with it echoes of bullets fired and exploding shells. The pretty white clouds on the horizon were not caused by weather changes, but were puffs of smoke arising above the battle sites. Frances Emily Croft imagined she could hear the cries of the soldiers falling to enemy bullets and bayonets. Or was it their tormented souls she could hear drifting over the mud-flats?

When she joined the First-Aid Nursing Yeomanry in 1913, searching for a worthy aim in life, she had not expected to end up like this. At first, it was so jolly with such good camaraderie and a vigorous and healthy life style. It left no room for regrets and fits of the miseries that so often attacked young women who wanted more out of life than simple domesticity. She loved the marching, the parades on horseback, the rigid routine of their lives in train-ing-camp. And later, the feeling that one was doing something useful, learn-ing to drive motorized ambulances, the exhilaration of taking an engine apart and knowing how to put it back together again in working order.

On the down side, perhaps, was the actual nursing element. It wasn't too onerous learning how to roll bandages, clean and dress wounds – imaginary ones, of course. The trouble was she wasn't good with people, so she had to learn how to be sympathetic too, rather than be impatient and irritable, which came far more naturally to her. No doubt, she had thought, she would muddle through, if she ever had to do it for real.

Reality came sooner than expected with the outbreak of war. Frances was among the first of the FANYs, as they were affectionately known, to be shipped out to the Flanders fields, where it was her unending task to take supplies up to the trenches and transport sick and injured soldiers back to the hospital. The Belgian Tommies were very grateful for the service she and her fellow FANYs provided, but what they appreciated even more was the fact that these women, some of them mere girls, could communicate with them in their own language.

Now, the unit was in northern France. It had been a thrill to receive her posting here. The excitement was short-lived. When she saw the devastation of this much loved land she feared that it had been a wrong decision to commit herself so profoundly to the cause. Had she been a man – how happy her father would have been – it might have been the making of her. As it was, day after long day was wearing her down, and proving that she was not, after all, made of such stern stuff.

Frances gnawed on the end of a pencil stub and let out a long sigh. The wind suddenly changed, pummelling the canvas of the makeshift field hospital behind her. It whipped her hair out of its neat bun and bit into her tear-stained cheeks. There was a rattle of paper as the pages of her personal journal turned, going back like a time machine. She put out a hand to arrest their journey and the book fell open at a place she would rather not have revisited. However, the temptation to read again what she had written was too strong to resist. Strangely enough, it was like reading the account of a total stranger, in another life, another world.

How little I knew back then of life, she thought. How little I knew of me! I thought I was courageous and bold. Instead, I have found my feminine side. Why, I'm just a silly flibbertigibbet with a girl's fragile heart, so easily broken. Whatever happened to brave, daring old Frances?

She scrubbed again at her smarting eyes and read the words before her, tracing them with a fingertip, not to miss a phrase or a nuance that would give a hint of the real Frances.

England, after so many years of living in France, is so cold, so drab, so boring. My prospects of marriage would appear to be nil – not that I'm the marrying kind; my prospects of an interesting life are even less. How lucky to find an organization such as the first-aid Nursing Yeomanry. It is all thanks to the incredibly romantic dream of one man. A sergeant-major by the name of Edward Charles Baker, who served under Lord Kitchener. The idea, or it may have been a hallucination, came to him when he was wounded during the Sudan Campaign. At that time he thought that there was a missing link and that a troop of young women would do the job (How droll!). So here I am. One of Mr Baker's 'Missing Links', and proud to be part of the vision he had as long ago as 1907. I'm sure that every one of us is now more useful than we have ever been in ordinary life. One has to be a volunteer, of course, but what price that, set against the excitement of riding out into the fields of battle to bring aid and succour to the poor wounded soldiers? If there were any, that is.

The training is rigorous, carried out in camps around the country. We march, we train, we tone up our bodies, but most of all, we ready our minds for the fray. Whatever that means. However, it is more than a little exciting and the amicable rapport between the girls is incredible. We come from all walks of life, but mostly from the middle classes. There are, inevitably, one or two rather snooty individuals – they take some getting to know, but after a couple of weeks the ice is well and truly broken.

Being a good horsewoman is essential, of course. Not sure that I approve of the red tunic we are obliged to wear. It's a little too gay for my quiet personality and too vivid for my rather drab complexion, but one cannot have everything.

Anyway, I have got this far and still have no inclination to surrender the flag. Goodness, what an adventure!

Frances turned the pages, her heart heavy with nostalgia for those early days, and for the hopes and ambitions she had carried with her.

By 1914, the diary entries became more erratic. One page stood out, alone and void of any description, but Frances experienced the same breathless squeezing of her heart as she had the day she had made the entry:

5 August, 1914: It seems that Britain is at war with Germany. Perhaps now we will see some real action. It will be FANYs to the fore from now on. I can't wait.

31 October, 1914: Today we embarked for Belgium, heading for the battlefields with our trusty vehicles. My father's beloved old Ford Model T has been drawn into the operation, converted into a small sitting ambulance or transport for generals, I suppose. He would be so proud to know that his car is to be used for saving lives. My poor father! I wonder what he would be doing now, had he not died so tragically of that silly heart attack? I'm sure they will never again have an Ambassador as loyal as he, not in the whole of France, or indeed in Europe. Mother, of course, thinks that I am totally absurd to continue with the FANYs in times of war. I cannot imagine why.

There is no way that I would want such a sedentary life as she enjoys. I have an overpowering need to 'give' and this silly little war will prove that I stand for something. Thank goodness they have done away with the red tunic. Khaki is so much more practical.

Frances started to close the journal, thinking to put it aside. It was late and she ought to get some rest before it was her turn to rush up to the trenches with a fresh supply of bandages, morphine, dry biscuits and tea. However, the wind seemed to have a say in things and mischievously turned the pages again, making them fall open this time to the less frequent entries during her time here in France.

The handwriting was erratic and unsteady, like that of an elderly person, and indeed, that was how she so often felt, so weary was she of the daily dose of danger and bloodshed. Days when there were just too many suppurating wounds to be drained and re-dressed, when morphine wasn't enough to kill the pain, and she went to sleep with the screams of the patients in her ears.

The France I used to love so much is not the France that surrounds me now. I have swapped the idyllic countryside with its sleepy farms and flower-strewn meadows for trenches running with blood, disease and rotting flesh. I have to grit my teeth and hold on to the contents of my stomach. It would never do to show the other girls how weak I am, though Penelope Freeman fainted clean away at the sight of her first dead body, so I know I'm not alone.

Today I pulled up the sheets on three more of our dear boys in uniform, not one of them above the age of twenty. John, thank God, still holds on. It is our conversations, long into the night, that keep me going. We talk of golden dawns, birdsong and the love that one person has for another, imaginings of the future and our own dreams of a life without all this carnage.

I do not think of why I joined the FANYs. It is no longer worth a thought. Only in my weakest moments do I weep into my pillow and wish I were back in England – but it is only a fleeting wish and best buried among other impossible frivolities of my mind. My days are spent behind the wheel, taking out what first aid I can and pick- ing up the injured, bringing them back here to the field hospital. We do what we can. It is never enough. But I have been able to spend time with my lovely sergeant. Long after the others are asleep and the guns and cannons are silent, I sit with him, holding his hand. It seems right, somehow. I have never felt such love for any human being.

Something inside Frances's heart twisted cruelly. She stuffed the journal into her knapsack, stood up and took a deep breath before returning to the dormitory where FANYs and registered nurses alike fell in and out of the low pallet beds, so exhausted that they did not worry about who had slept there before them. When the weather was wet and cold, as it often was, they were glad of the heat still lingering in the folds of the rough army blankets. Nobody cared any more about fleas or bedbugs. The greatest worry was trying not to contract dysentery or typhoid, which seemed to kill as many poor souls as did the German bullets.

Tonight, however, Frances was not ready for her bed. Sergeant John Temple was to be shipped out at first light in the morning. She had prayed for his recovery from his serious injuries, then she had prayed that he would not recover too quickly. Now, he was going to leave her and she did not know how she would cope without him, for they had enjoyed a very special relationship that she was sure she would never find with any other man.

'Ah, dear sweet Fanny!' John was the only person she had allowed to call her by that name. 'You came!'

His face lit up at the sight of her as she walked between the beds of the surgical ward where he had hovered between life and death for so long.

'How could I not come to see you?' She smiled, feeling her lips quiver emotionally.

He reached out to her and they clasped hands as she sat down on his bunk beside him.

'They say I'm going home tomorrow, Fanny,' he told her, his kind and loving eyes searching her face. 'I may not see you again.'

'Please . . . John, don't!' Her throat was tight, the words strangled. 'I can't bear to think of being separated from you, but . . .'

He pulled her hands up to his face, kissing her fingers with light, feathery touches of his lips. She could see that he, too, was emotional, though she was sure that he would also be happy to get out of the war. Who would not be relieved to see an end to such horrors as these men had been forced to live through day after day, without pause?

'Don't forget me, Fanny, will you? And . . . and when this is all over. . . .'

Frances nodded and felt tears sting her eyes. She did not cry often, but today she had been unable to hold it back. She kissed his forehead tenderly, then briefly touched his lips.

'We'll find each other,' she said in a croaking whisper. 'I'll wait for you, John, even if it takes for ever.'

'Oh, Fanny, I do adore you!' It was a heartfelt cry and then they were clinging together.

If they thought of a future together, neither of them spoke the words, yet there was a wealth of feeling in the silence they maintained.

By tomorrow he would be gone. Tomorrow she would be driving again to the trenches in her ambulance without a windscreen for cover, the wind and rain blinding her. There would be other soldiers needing her help. It would be hard, but the thought of going home, one day, to John, would be all she needed to keep her going.

CHAPTER ONE

1939

'Hey, what a picture! Let me get some of that!'

Mary West couldn't see what the workmen across the street were enjoying. She was unaware that the sight of those shapely hips of hers undulating, bobbing and dipping in time to the sound of Jack Langley's band playing *An Apple For The Teacher* had set them off whistling and whooping. At first she ignored them, until she realized that she was the cause of the commotion, then she whipped around, her cheeks burning with embarrassment, eyes flashing with indignation.

She was not the kind of girl that went in for making a public spectacle of herself, but dance-music always set her off. It was as if it touched a hidden switch and she just couldn't keep still. At least she hadn't sung the words out loud, which she was quite likely to do, for singing was as much a part of her as dancing and she couldn't wait for December when the whole of Felling would gather in the Palais de Danse for a grand benefit ball and talent contest.

Well, not the whole town, perhaps, but a good many well-meaning and fun-loving people would be there, lending their support to the war effort, even though some believed the war would be over before it really got going. There had been so much scaremongering and propaganda for years, it was no wonder they called it the phoney war.

It was only twenty-one years since the end of the war that was supposed to end all wars. They had said it would never happen again, but on 3 September, 1939, the Prime Minister, Mr Neville Chamberlain, announced that Britain was once more at war with Germany. It was almost a relief. At last, there was something definite to get their teeth into. Action, instead of the endless waiting that wore people out.

Still not convinced that it would ever come about, they had been encouraged to dig trenches, build shelters, donate scrap metal to the government. And still they waited, wondering if it was all in vain.

However, like the rest of Great Britain, the inhabitants of the small mining town threw themselves into the war effort with commendable vigour.

The place already looked like a war zone with trenches where there had once been green grass and pretty flower-beds. Anderson shelters were springing up everywhere, in front gardens and back yards. And concrete tank-traps were placed in ominous rows all the way down The Bankies to the River Tyne. German tanks were going to have a hard job getting past those if they ever dared invade this far north.

People were already issued with gas-masks, with egg-shaped cocoons for tiny babies. Everybody laughed through their fear and made jokes about how ridiculous they looked wearing the things. There was propaganda everywhere: films, leaflets and broadcasts on the wireless. Young men, hungry for adventure, had flocked to join up even before the government started issuing conscription orders. The very air they breathed seemed electrified with suppressed anticipation to the point of madness.

'Hey, pet, ye gannin' to the dance Saturday?'

More catcalls and whistles. The young workmen were intent on bothering Mary.

'Save a dance for me, sweetheart!'

Mary had been looking forward to the Saturday evening dance with mixed feelings. A part of her loved the idea of dancing to the new music that was coming over from America. The music was exhilarating; it made her whole being come alive. The other part of her wondered if she would actually get to dance at all. She had done very little dancing since meeting Walter. Her fiancé of two years was digging in the heels of his two left feet and claiming that he would rather join up than make a fool of himself on a dance floor. If it was left up to him he would choose a night at the pictures any time, especially if the film showing at the Corona was a swashbuckling adventure or the comic antics of Laurel and Hardy. Mary preferred musicals and love stories that made her snuffle into her hankie.

'Mary?'

She heard Walter's voice now, calling her from the pork-butcher-shop doorway, where he was standing regarding her from halfway down the High Street. He was like that, was Walter. You just had to think about him and up he popped. Just look at him, Mary thought fondly. Big, soft and rosy-cheeked. Nervous as a rabbit he was, which he proved on many an occasion, jumping a mile every time anything went pop, bang or click near him. She hoped, for his sake, that if he was ever called up he would be turned down by the medical board, like Mrs Johnson's big, brawny son who had flat feet and couldn't see further than his nose, even with glasses.

Mary smiled and gave Walter a wave. Inside the back room of the pub, the band was starting up again with another practice number. This time it was *Jeepers Creepers*. She hesitated, because it was one of her favourite tunes, but then the smell of stale beer wafting through the open window started to get to her.

She glanced about her, ignoring the continuing whistles from the lads laying bricks across the way, and went to have a word with Walter, even though she was in a bit of a hurry, it being her lunch-time.

'Were those louts whistling at you?' he asked, his expression darkening into one of jealous anger, though she knew he was too gentle to take anybody to task, even if it meant saving her honour.

'Oh, they're just having a bit of fun. Take no notice. *I* don't,' she said with a grin as he bent down to peck her on the cheek: 'Haven't you any customers, then?'

'Nah,' he replied, rubbing the back of his broad neck. 'Things have gone from bad to worse since this ruddy war started. Meat's in short supply these days. And there's talk of things being rationed, too. Let's hope it gets sorted out soon.'

Walter had been running the family business since his father's heart attack two years previously. The only competition in the town was the Co-op and both the shops had recently seen queues forming right down the street. Housewives were stockpiling general groceries as if there was no tomorrow. The fact that it was the coldest winter on record for about half a century didn't deter the housewives of Felling. They wore extra layers of clothing, woollen headscarves and gloves and stamped their booted feet to keep warm as they waited.

'They say it'll get worse before it gets better,' Mary said and winced, thinking that she sounded just like her mother, who was a bit of a Job's comforter at the best of times.

'Aye.' Walter cast about him, a sure sign that he was about to change the subject. 'Any chance of you helping out on the deliveries tonight, Mary? Kevin's joined up, the idiot.'

Kevin was Walter's delivery boy. He wasn't highly intelligent, but he was a good worker and his absence would be sorely felt. Mary sighed, wondering just how long it was going to be before towns and villages would be emptied of every male who wasn't too old or too infirm to fight for his country.

'As long as I get to drive the van.' She smiled, dimpling and waiting for the usual frown, for Walter didn't have much confidence in women drivers, even though she had passed her test a few months ago.

'Sorry, no chance of that. Not with petrol being rationed.'

Mary blew out her cheeks and pulled a face. 'I suppose I'll have to use Kevin's bike, then.'

'I don't know what you want to drive for, anyway,' he told her grumpily and glowered at her beneath lowered brows. 'I don't know any other women, except those Beasley females, who drive. Them and the vicar's wife.'

'Oh, there are quite a few of us around these days,' she said. 'And you watch what you say about Mrs Beasley and her daughter. They were like family to me when I was growing up.'

It was true. Brigadier and Mrs Beasley had 'adopted' Mary as a companion to their daughter, Anne, when the girls were only six years old. They had enjoyed a unique education in the capable hands of a private tutor, Miss Frances Croft who, although English, had been born and raised in France, where her father had been something important at the British Embassy in Paris. It was very rare that a girl like Mary, who came from a very different background, could have such an opportunity, though she wasn't always happy with the arrangement at the time.

Anne had been a strange girl, quiet and moody and often rebellious. Left alone with her studies, she was lazy and uninterested. With Mary at her side, she became competitive and enthusiastic. Mary's mother had not been too happy about handing her daughter over to this wealthy, influential family, but could not turn her back on the financial remuneration, and the fact that her youngest daughter might possibly make something of herself at the end of the day.

'I saw Miss Beasley the other day,' Walter said, twisting his face and sucking air through his teeth. 'She came into the shop here and demanded that I keep her a pound of the best steak. I told her, I said, you come and take your chances like everybody else. I don't go in for keeping things under the counter for customers who think they're privileged. Aye, that's what I said to her. She didn't like it.'

Mary laughed. 'No, I can imagine the look on her face. Poor Anne.'

'There's nowt poor about that family, as you well know.' Walter stuck his hands in his pockets and rocked on the balls of his feet. 'Now, are you going to help me out th' night or not?'

'I suppose so,' Mary said. 'Look, Walter, I'd better get on. Mr Harper will have one of his tantrums if I'm late again.'

'You're heading in the wrong direction, aren't you?'

Mary shook her head. 'I've got to pick up a prescription for Gran. She's got bronchitis again and she can't seem to shift it.'

'Does she still sleep in the back yard?' Walter rolled his eyes. 'Can't you persuade her that yon Adolph Hitler isn't coming to bomb her out of her bed?'

'You know my gran,' Mary said with a laugh, picturing her grandmother wrapped in eiderdowns and with a woolly hat pulled over her eyes and ears, down in the reinforced concrete shelter, which was how she had been every night since war had been declared. No wonder she had bronchitis.

Mary glanced from side to side and, pleased that there was no one looking, stepped up to Walter and gave him a quick kiss. 'I'm off. See you later?'

She hurried away, knowing that Walter's wistful eyes would follow her all the way up the High Street. But she dared not linger. Time was ticking on. Over at Harper's Drapery Store she could picture the boss keeping a mean eye on his watch.

And there lay the biggest problem in Mary's life. Mr Harper lived up to his reputation of being a slave-driver and a lecherous individual, who went through his female employees like a hot knife through butter. Mary longed for the day when she could say goodbye to brassières, corsets and camisole knickers, though her mother liked her daughter serving fancy underwear to the more genteel ladies of the town. It was better than Woolworth's, or slaving all day in a factory like so many of her school chums had ended up doing. Still, she was prepared to wait until something more stimulating came along.

Dr Gordon's surgery was packed with coughs, streaming noses and fretful children. Mary's heart sank. If she had to wait more than five minutes she really would be late getting back to her post. Mr Harper would take great pleasure out of hauling her over the coals and he was still smarting from a blow she had orchestrated to his tender regions with the aid of the metal cash register drawer. He had been a little too free with his hands under cover of the counter. With a surreptitious press of the right key, the drawer had shot out and found its mark, bringing tears to the poor man's eyes and great satisfaction to Mary's heart, though she went through the motions of being "dreadfully sorry" for her carelessness.

Mary's thoughts of Mr Harper and the cash register were interrupted by the loud discordant whirring of the practice bell, indicating that Dr Gordon was ready to see the next patient. There was a bit of a scuffle between two women as they argued over whose turn it was. By the time they had calmed down, a man with a flat cap pulled over his eyes, a white silk muffler about his throat, and a cigarette attached to his bottom lip as if it had been glued there, had taken advantage of the situatin. He muttered something about *ruddy women* as he left the green-painted walls of the waiting-room and entered the brown-painted walls of the passage leading to the consulting-rooms.

Mary glanced anxiously at her watch and decided to leave, but the doorbell gave a sharp jangle and everyone looked up, surprised to see Dr Gordon himself step in from the street. He looked flustered and red-faced from hurrying, as he squeezed through the crowded room, pushing his black doctor's bag before him.

'Sorry, sorry!' he said to the mournful eyes and curious glances that followed him. 'Today's my day for emergencies.'

'If I have to wait here any longer,' said one fat woman whom Mary could smell across the room, '*I'll* be a bliddy emergency.'

She set off cackling with toothless laughter. Some of the other patients joined in. Others looked more embarrassed than amused.

'Och, Mary,' Dr Gordon said, getting his eye on her, for she was standing directly in his path. 'What are you doing here? You're not ill, are you?'

'No, Dr Gordon. It's not me . . .'

'Well, you soon will be ill if you wait here with all these germs being breathed into the atmosphere. What is it? Your grandmother again?'

'Yes, I'm afraid so. She needs a new prescription to get her over the weekend. She's not worse, but she's no better.'

'Aye, it's this blessed cold spell we've been having that does it. I'll give you something stronger for her. Come on through.'

'Oh, but. . . .'

Mary's voice was drowned out by protests about her jumping the queue. Dr Gordon held up his hand and addressed them all with a soothing voice and a winning smile.

'No need to get upset,' he said. 'We have two doctors dealing with your needs now. I'll just write a prescription for this lassie's poor old grandma and then we'll go through you all like a dose of salts.'

'If you're not in the surgery, Doctor, who is?' asked one heavily pregnant woman with her arm in a sling. Two small children clung to her coat with sticky fingers, emanating a sickly sweet aroma of raspberry gum-drops and minty black bullets.

'Aye,' said a fellow with a huge red boil on the back of his neck. 'I hope it's a proper doctor you've got in there and not one o' them locum types what don't know their arse from their elbow.'

'I think you'll find that Dr Craig, who happens to be my nephew, is very much a proper doctor, Mr Albertson. All right, Mary. Follow me, my dear.'

As Mary followed the doctor she heard mutters of surprise behind her at the news he had just imparted. She knew that Dr Gordon's nephew had worked for a while in the infirmary in Newcastle, but she hadn't heard that he was now in this practice.

The man who had gone before his turn passed them in the narrow corridor, grumbling with heartfelt disdain about newfangled doctors with daft ideas.

'Something upsetting you, Mr Dobson?' Dr Gordon called after the patient.

'Aye, there is. It's a raw deal when a doctor signs ye off afore ye're ready,' Mr Dobson told them. 'I'd go to another doctor, if there was one.'

'Come now, Mr Dobson. You know better than that. If Dr Craig thinks you're ready to go back to work—'

'I ain't ready!'

'Tommy Dobson, you were more than ready last time I saw you, but I gave you an extra week anyway out of the goodness of my heart. However, I hear you've been moonlighting, masquerading as a rag-and-bone man. If the authorities catch you, my lad, they'll come down on you like a ton of bricks and you won't have a job to go back to.'

'I won't anyway when they starts drafting fellas like me into the war. What'll happen to the wife and bairns then, eh?'

With a look of disgust he marched out of the practice and Dr Gordon shook his head after him, his kindly eyes full of sympathy.

'He's right, of course. It's not just the men who go to war who suffer.' He gave Mary a wan smile, then ushered her into his consulting-room, just as the other door opened and a youngish doctor appeared in a crisp white surgery coat, a stethoscope around his neck and a brooding expression in his dark eyes.

'Ah, there you are, Alex,' Dr Gordon placed an avuncular hand on his nephew's shoulder and drew him into the room. 'You look as though you need a break.'

'Too damned right I do.'

Mary watched closely as the younger man paced the small square of parquet floor in front of her. He looked disgruntled, his bad mood marring what she suspected could be a rather nice face.

'Mary?'

Mary blinked at Dr Gordon, realizing that she had drifted off into her own private world while the two doctors had a short exchange of words.

'I'm sorry?'

'My nephew here will take care of your granny's prescription while I go and prevent mayhem breaking out in the waiting-room.'

'Oh, that's very kind.' She let her gaze flicker over to Dr Craig, who was already installing himself behind the desk and pulling a prescription pad towards him.

'Blast!'

The sharp explosive curse erupted from Dr Craig as his uncle left the room. Mary looked at him with raised eyebrows, thinking that it had been a mistake to arrive at what was obviously a bad time for everybody.

'I'm sorry. I didn't mean to cause a problem, but Dr Gordon insisted,' Mary apologized, and a pair of surprisingly intense eyes met hers. 'Maybe I can come back later, when you're not so busy?'

'I wasn't swearing at you, Miss. . . ?'

'West . . . Mary West.'

'Yes, of course. Sit down . . . please.'

Mary sat on the hard wooden chair in front of the cluttered desk and watched him search among the jumble of papers and general miscellany that was characteristic of Dr Gordon, who always seemed able to find what he was looking for. Not so his nephew, she thought.

'Try the vase on the windowsill,' she suggested, guessing what it was that he was missing.

'I beg your pardon?' His eyes were on her again, his forehead creasing deeply.

She indicated the short fat porcelain vase to his left, which sat in front of a tiny window of four opaque glass panes. 'Pens and pencils. He usually keeps them in there.'

'Ah!' He picked up the vase and peered inside. 'You're quite right. Other people's consulting-rooms . . . Thank you.'

He continued to stare into the vase and at its contents, but it was obvious that he was not actually seeing anything. There was a faraway look about him that suggested he had more pressing things on his mind than a pen or a pencil, or indeed the prescription she was so urgently waiting for.

'Gran's name is Henrietta West and Dr Gordon usually gives her—'

'What?' He looked startled, then recovered himself quickly. 'That's quite all right, Miss West. I'll get the details from her notes, if I can find the blessed things . . .'

'They're in the small drawers on top of the filing cabinet,' Mary said, hoping he wouldn't bite her head off again for helping him out, but she really couldn't hang about much longer. 'The one on the right, at the back – W for West, H for Henrietta.'

He gave her a sharp glance, then got up and went to the drawers indicated.

'I do know my alphabet,' he said, then the irritation became an apologetic smile. 'And you are W for West, M for Mary, I believe.'

'That's right.' She smiled back at him and his eyes lost some of their hardness as he looked at her properly for the first time.

'Here we are,' he said, pulling out two buff packages, hers slim, the other, belonging to her grandmother, bulging. 'Is there anything I can do for you while you're here?'

'Not a thing, thank you,' she told him, suddenly feeling shy and gauche because his stare had been one of appraisal and the light that came into his eyes was full of curiosity and interest, though respectful, unlike the workmen she had encountered in the street a short while ago.

'By the feel of your notes, you are rarely ill,' he said, checking the details on the outside of the packet before replacing it in the drawer.

'I suppose I'm lucky.'

'You are. Very lucky. And young, of course. Obviously fit. And cheerful, I'd say.' He said all this, pronouncing these short, snappy phrases, while he inspected her grandmother's notes and wrote out the necessary prescription. 'Is there ever a time when you don't smile, Mary?'

She blinked at the use of her Christian name, but then he was pretty young himself, not above twenty-eight or thirty, she guessed. Of course, his uncle, Dr Gordon, called her Mary, but then he had known her all her life, had even brought her into the world and given her that life-awakening tap on her bottom before handing her over to the midwife.

'I suppose there must be times when I find things to frown at, but not often,' she said. 'I've never really thought about it.'

'I would think it's almost physically impossible for you not to smile,' he said, handing her the prescription. 'How lucky for your fiancé.'

She did frown at that remark, for she couldn't think how he could have known that she was engaged.

'How did you. . . ?'

His laugh was pleasant and she thought that he too would be better advised to keep a smile on his face, since it transformed him from an apparently discontented person to a rather good-looking young man.

'I noticed the ring,' he said and she looked immediately down at Walter's tiny, diamond-chip engagement-ring, which he had pressed upon her so long ago that she was no longer conscious of wearing it.

'Oh, that! Yes.' Was her smile rueful, unenthusiastic? Part of her hoped that it was neither, yet another part of her experienced that sinking sensation that comes with disappointment tinged with guilt.

'Will the happy day be soon?'

'No . . . oh, no!' Goodness, Mary thought, feeling her cheeks burn as he went on scrutinizing her in a most disturbing fashion. 'I mean . . . well, there's nothing planned, really.'

'I thought perhaps your fiancé might be going off to enlist in the forces. Such a lot of couples rush into marriage in times of war.' Dr Craig sighed and tapped his pen methodically against the fingers of the other hand. 'It's not the wisest of moves. We already have quite a few very young pregnant ladies left to cope on their own.'

'That's sad,' Mary said, eyeing the door and thinking of the time that was passing, but she didn't want to leave until he dismissed her and sent for the next patient.

'Don't let it happen to you, Mary,' he said, throwing down the pen as if it offended him. 'Now, where are you going? I have a call to make so maybe I can give you a lift?'

'Oh, it's really no distance . . .' she began to say, but he held up a hand and waited for her to tell him where she was headed. 'Well, actually, it would help. I must try and get Gran's medicine before I go back to work. She's really struggling with this last bout of bronchitis. The thing is, I'm already late and my boss is a stickler for punctuality.'

'Well, let's not get you a black mark.' He looked briefly about him, picked up a well-worn doctor's bag and indicated to Mary to precede him out of the door. 'Shall we go?'

Heads were raised and curious eyes followed them as they made their way out to the street. Mary felt she ought to apologize in some way to the poor folk still sitting waiting to be seen, but she decided that a proud posture, with eyes to the front was more advisable. She had wasted enough time already.

The doctor's small black Morris looked as if it had seen many miles, though it was clean inside, and was surprisingly comfortable. It smelled of leather and polish rather than the stale cigarette smoke she had to put up with in Walter's delivery van.

'You work at Harper's Drapery Store, don't you?'

Dr Craig turned the key in the ignition and the engine throbbed into life. He eased the car away from the kerb, waiting for a black-and-gold Rington's tea van to get clear before turning and heading towards the High Street.

'You seem to know a lot about me, Dr Craig,' she said, smiling broadly.

'You didn't find those details in my medical notes.'

'Ah, yes, well . . .' He hesitated, slowing down to allow an old lady to cross the road in front of him without looking to left or to right of her. 'I bought a lace tablecloth in Harper's for my wife a few weeks ago and I saw you behind one of the counters. You wouldn't have noticed me. I got in and out as quickly as I could. It's not a shop that men feel at ease visiting.'

She gave a hiccup of laughter, but she knew what he meant. Men were embarrassed at being seen within a mile of lingerie counters, even if they were as fine as Harper's.

'No, I must admit, we don't get many male customers. Those we do get are usually dragged in screaming by their wives.'

'Hmm, yes. The manager, however, seemed quite at home there.'

'That's Mr Harper.'

'I'd watch him if I were you. I don't think I would trust him with *my* wife.'

'That's one of the problems of working there,' Mary said, her smile fading somewhat.

She recalled the number of times she and the other sales assistants at Harper's had found it necessary to dodge the owner's wandering hands. No young woman, it seemed, was safe from the surreptitious gropings stolen in dark corners of the stock room or wicked pinches when he thought no one was looking. Not to mention the insidious remarks that were far from gentlemanly and often threatening.

Dr Craig stopped the car outside the chemist's. Harper's Drapery Store was only two doors further down, so there was no problem, as long as the chemist's wasn't also full of customers.

'Thank you so much, Dr Craig,' Mary said, dimpling shyly.

'Not at all.' His forehead creased as he glanced at an address scribbled on a scrap of paper. 'Before you go, you couldn't put me right for Elsdon Street, could you? A Miss Croft?'

'Oh, you're going the wrong way!' Mary exclaimed. 'Elsdon Street is right at the top end of Split Crow Road. Is it Miss Frances Croft you're going to see? I hope she's not ill.'

'Yes, it is, as a matter of fact. Do you know her? I'm afraid I can't discuss details of any of my patients, but I believe she is quite poorly.'

Mary nodded, chewing on her mouth, memories of her childhood flooding back. 'Oh, I'm sorry to hear that. Actually, I was a pupil of hers, but that was a long time ago.'

'She's a teacher?'

'Yes . . . well, no . . . not exactly. She does private tutoring and I used to attend her classes with Brigadier Beasley's daughter. She taught us French and German, but we went to the grammar school for everything else.'

'Really? I never thought I'd hear of that kind of thing in a small mining town. Felling is full of surprises.'

'We're not all peasants, you know, Dr Craig.' She didn't mean to make it sound scathing, but Mary was very protective of her home town and didn't take kindly to people who ran it down as though it was in the back of beyond.

The doctor did a double take and combed long fingers through his hair, clearly disturbed by her response to his careless words.

'Sorry! I didn't mean to sound condescending. Actually, I quite like the place . . . and its people. I just wish my wife would . . .' He pulled himself up short. 'Anyway, I'd better be off.'

'Goodbye, doctor . . . and give my respects to Miss Croft.'

'I will. Goodbye, Mary. Take care.'

Then he was once again turning the car in the road and driving off in the opposite direction, leaving her staring after the smoking exhaust as he climbed back up the High Street.

Fortunately for Mary the chemist shop was nearly empty. The only customer was a rather horsy-faced girl in military uniform, which was a surprise, because most people in uniform were men, either home on leave or just about to embark for parts unknown. This girl looked smart in khaki jacket and skirt, peaked cap, and stout leather brogues.

She didn't take long with her purchase of Aspro and a bottle of eau de cologne and, as soon as she left, Mary had the attention of the pharmacist, Mr Morrell.

'Mary! What can I do for you, dear?'

She handed over her grandmother's prescription. 'More of the same I'm afraid,' she told him and heard him sigh.

'Ah, poor Mrs West. I'll just get this for you. You all right, Mary, dear?' The pharmacist studied her closely, peering over his spectacles. 'You look blooming, as usual.'

'I'm fine, Mr Morrell, thank you. Fighting fit, actually.'

He laughed and said, jokingly: 'In that case, maybe you should join the FANYs. I hear they're looking for girls like you.'

'The what? The Fannies, did you say? What on earth is that?'

'Well, didn't you see that young woman just now? It's a voluntary organization. Been going for more years than I care to remember. Started long before the Great War.'

'Are they soldiers of some sort?' Mary was more than a little interested, though she couldn't imagine herself wearing a uniform of any kind.

'Yes and no. They've changed over the years. Used to be auxiliary nurses and helped with the wounded out in Flanders and the Somme. I had a cousin in London who was a FANY – that's short for First-Aid Nursing Yeomanry. Brave women, the lot of them. Brave or brainless. I never could make my mind up on that score, but then who am I to judge?'

'And now they're back at war?'

'Yes, but it's not just bandages and bedpans these days, apparently. They still drive ambulances, but now they're expected to be mechanics and wireless operators. It's all a bit masculine, but we'll need all the help we can get when most of our boys are involved in the actual fighting.'

'Yes.' Mary nodded. 'I hear there are quite a lot of women already working on the docks and in the shipyards.'

'So much for a woman's place being in the home bringing up the bairns and giving succour to the husband, eh?' Mr Morrell chuckled and handed Mary a packet containing a bottle of tincture and some tablets. 'There you are, dear. Tell your grannie to take this little lot three times a day and not to miss. She'll be as right as rain in no time.'

Clutching the package to her, Mary hurried back to Harper's, her mind buzzing with what she had just heard. The shop was busy with lunch-time shoppers. Iris Morrison was looking harassed as she tried valiantly to cover both her counter, where she sold woollen garments, and Mary's. When she saw Mary the look of relief on her face could be felt right across the shop floor. Unfortunately for Mary Mr Harper also saw it and turned on his heel just as Mary threw off her coat and slid behind the ladies' underwear counter.

'Miss West! You are five minutes late back from your lunch and I will not tolerate it.'

Mr Harper was almost purple with rage and he displayed it in front of a host of shocked customers. One or two women decided to make a hasty exit rather than witness the embarrassing spectacle of the young sales assistant being dragged out from her post and marched back to the door, the owner ranting and raving at the top of his voice.

'I told you last week that the next time you were late you would have to seek employment elsewhere and that's exactly what I am telling you to do right now.' Mr Harper gave Mary a push and she collided with a customer before she bounced painfully off the doorframe. 'Out! I will have your wages sent out to you, if anything is owing.'

He slammed the door in her face and Mary stood in the freezing street, shivering and not sure what to do. She didn't like the idea of going back inside, but it was cold out and she had no coat. Not only that, her grandmother's medicines were also in there, sitting on the counter where she had left them.

She took a deep breath and started to push open the heavy glass door, but Mr Harper saw her and raised an accusing finger in her direction, his face as black as thunder.

'Out, I said!'

'But Mr Harper, I . . .' Mary stamped her foot and gritted her teeth, no longer caring whom she embarrassed. 'Is this because I won't let you molest me? You, a married man?'

Her loud words drew shocked gasps from the customers inside the shop and a string of women passing by.

'Out!'

She glared at him through the glass, then saw Iris grab her things and rush forward with them.

'Miss Morrison, back to your post at once. I will not have you fraternizing with Miss West at any price. She's a very bad influence and I won't put up with it any longer.'

There was a murmur of guarded conversation passing among the ladies queuing up to buy their lisle stockings and stays and bloomers. There were sympathetic comments, for Mary was well liked by all of Harper's clientele.

At the risk of losing her own position, Iris ignored her employer, though it would have been more unfortunate for Mr Harper had he fired her too. The shop was already functioning on reduced staff.

'Here you are, Mary, love,' Iris said, thrusting Mary's coat, bag, and old Henrietta West's medicines at her. 'Mind how you go, now.'

'Thanks, Iris. See you later.'

As they exchanged smiles the air all around was ripped apart by the air-raid siren and the peaceful town of Felling instantly erupted into action. Feet slapped on the pavements as everybody rushed to get under cover. Had Mary been behind her counter at Harper's she would have joined the rest of the staff in the stock-room, padded liberally with sandbags. Today, that wasn't going to happen. Happily, the warning had been announced on the wireless and in the newspapers. It was just one of the many practice drills that were essential to keep everyone from getting too blasé about the war that was taking such a long time to get going and, therefore, never seemed real.

'Hey, you. . . !' Mary saw the khaki-clad girl from the chemist's looking her way and beckoning frantically. 'Come on. This way.'

She hesitated, but behind her there was a kind of explosion and muffled screams. The noise spurred her on and she sprinted over the road, almost falling into the girl's arms, tripping in her haste and thinking that the air-raid was real after all.

'Steady on!' said the uniformed girl in Mary's ear as she pulled her firmly inside a makeshift shelter between the bicycle-shop and the ironmonger's.

'Was that a bomb?' she said, disbelief making her want to laugh, but she didn't think it would go down well.

'Don't be ridiculous,' the girl said, then she bellowed towards the entrance of the shelter. 'Come on, you lot. If that had been a real air-raid, you might be dead by now.'

Mary saw the small band of Harper's employees staggering towards them, shedding clouds of dust and coughing fit to burst. Dummy bomb or not, something serious had happened over there.

'That *stupid* man!' Iris said, spitting out dust as she came to join Mary. 'He'd moved all his blooming antique furniture into the room above the stock-room. The whole lot came crashing through the ceiling. We were seconds away from being buried alive.'

Mary smiled sympathetically, glad that no one had been hurt. She turned her attention back on to the girl soldier through the gloom of the shelter. There was something familiar about her. She ought to have recognized her in the chemist's, but she had been too busy with her thoughts, worrying about her gran, agitating about getting back to work, and wondering curiously about Dr Alexander Craig. There were far too many distracting things going through her head these days.

'Good heavens! It's Anne Beasley, isn't it?' she exclaimed. 'I've only just realized that it's you.'

'Oh, hello, Mary. Didn't recognize you either. It's been a while, hasn't it?'

'What on earth are you doing in that uniform?'

'Goodness, didn't you know? I'm in the FANYs. It's jolly good. So much more exciting than life with Mummy and Daddy.'

'Really?'

'Mm. I was always so envious of my brother being in the Army. Well, now I have my own little army life and it's wonderful.'

Mary had thought that Anne was the very last girl in the world who would do anything that involved being part of a regiment and answering to orders. She had been such a quiet, withdrawn child, then a rather unlikeable adolescent with snobbish tendencies. However, she did remember how Anne used to be jealous of her brother's adventurous life, free of parental restrictions. He had followed willingly in his brigadier father's footsteps and became a professional soldier. He was very much his own man.

'How is Alfred?' Mary asked, feeling that there was a need for some polite conversation.

'He's a captain now and quite important. Daddy's very proud of him, of course. I think he's quite pleased with me too, in his own peculiar way. One can never tell with parents, can one?'

Anne had spent two years in a Swiss finishing-school. It had left its mark on her accent, which had been a little plummy at the best of times, and which the snob in her always emphasized when speaking to people she considered beneath her.

Mary watched her childhood companion organizing the people in the shelter, then went to talk to Iris, who looked as if she was in need of some moral support.

'Come on, Iris,' she said to the shaking girl with whom she had worked for the past three years. 'There's more room further inside. I hope you won't lose your job too because of me.'

'Oh, don't worry, Mary.' Iris squeezed her hand and gave a wobbly smile. 'I was going to leave anyway. I told you about the interview with the War Pensions people, didn't I? Well, they've told me I can start right away. It means I won't get drafted if they start pulling us women into the war. You should think about it.'

Well, thought Mary, it was certainly time to do some thinking and make a choice. Good Lord, the world was her oyster now that she was free of old Harper. She could get a job driving a truck at Reyroll's, become a riveter in the shipyard, or a clippie on the buses. However, she thought that she would try for an office job, like Iris. She had often dreamed of being a secretary, ever since she had taught herself to type on Brigadier Beasley's old Imperial typewriter when she was fourteen.

Or, she thought with an amused smile, she could join the FANYs like Anne over there and look important in khaki. Anne had always liked uniforms, but usually when there were men inside them. It was so strange seeing her now, taking charge and being so efficient.

Anne turned and caught her looking. She gave a half-hearted smile tinged with curiosity; the kind you gave to people you didn't know very well. It was a long time since they had been friends and Mary wasn't sure that she wanted to be Anne's friend again.

CHAPTER TWO

Dᴿ Alex Craig parked his car outside the redbrick Victorian terrace house in Elsdon Street. Although there was a certain shabbiness about the paintwork, the house had an air of past elegance about it. The tiny, postage-stamp of a garden had once been full of roses, but was now sadly neglected.

From the street he could look down over the Tyne Valley for miles, and it was possible to see ships' funnels moving up and down the river. With such a magnificent panorama it was no wonder they called the area Mount Pleasant.

'Hey, mister, you lookin' for Gerries, then?'

The scratchy voice of a small boy with dirty, scabby knees and a runny nose made him turn.

'Good heavens, no!'

'Me da says it pays to be on the look-out, like.'

'Does he really?'

'Aye, but me ma says they'll nivvor git up this far.'

'Well, young man, let's hope that your "ma" is right, but we'd better all be on the look-out anyway, eh?'

'Aye.' The boy's eyes slid down to the black bag Alex was carrying. 'You a doctor or summat?'

'That I am.' Alex started down the garden path of number twenty-eight.

'Ye're Scotch, aren't ye?'

'That too.'

'Is the auld witch bad, then?'

'I beg your pardon?' Alex hesitated, struggling to make sense of the lad's guttural Geordie accent.

'That Miss Croft wot lives in there. She's a witch. You wouldn't catch me gannin in hor hoose.'

'I'm sure she's a perfectly nice lady. You mustn't believe all you hear about people.'

'She's a witch, I telt ye. Me grannie says.' The boy nodded sagely. 'Nivvor smiles. Just stares doon hor nose at folks and doesn't say a word.'

Alex glanced at the patient's packet of notes, which he had at the ready in his hand, convinced that he must have come to the wrong house. The lady in question was purported to be fifty. Hardly the age to be taken for a witch, he thought. However, to a twelve-year-old that could seem pretty old.

'Here!' he said, delving into his pocket and drawing out a penny for the lad. 'Start saving for your old age.'

The boy gave the penny a round-eyed look, grabbed it out of Alex's outstretched hand, grinned cheekily and hopped away down the street.

There was no need to pull the bell-chain, though Alex suspected it had probably stopped working long ago. As he approached the door, it opened a fraction and a long thin face peered out at him.

'Miss Croft?' he enquired. 'Miss Frances Croft? I'm Dr Craig. I was told you weren't feeling too well.'

The face frowned at him. A pair of thin, dark eyebrows knitted together and the sharp nose gave an indignant lift.

'I didn't send for you,' the woman said, her voice surprisingly strong and cultured. 'There's nothing wrong with me, I assure you.'

'I see.' Alex felt irritated, but the irritation soon passed when the air-raid siren shrieked and the woman backed into the hallway with a small gasp and a hand to her heart. 'Do you have a shelter, Miss Croft?'

'Yes, but . . .' She looked rigid with fear. 'I can't go in there. Claustrophobia, you see. It reminds me too much . . .'

'You had a bad experience in the past?'

She swallowed hard and nodded. 'In the war . . . .the *other* war.'

'You were . . . ?' Alex felt the need to tread warily; the woman looked to be on the verge of a nervous breakdown if her facial twitching and jerky body movements were anything to go by.

'I was in Belgium at first,' she said, her eyes glassy. 'Flanders. And later, in France . . . I was raised in France, you see . . . I thought . . . but it was . . . it had changed so . . .'

Alex glanced down at her record with a curious frown.

'Forgive me, Miss Croft, but you were not a child in the nineteen-fourteen war, so . . . ?' All these open-ended sentences waiting for information volunteered were beginning to irritate him.

'No. I was at the front, doctor. I drove an ambulance . . . helped out in the field hospitals. We did everything . . . anything that was demanded of us . . . and more.'

'You were with. . . ?'

'The FANYs.' She gave a minute smile, knowing that he did not understand, then went on to explain. 'The First-Aid Nursing Yeomanry. A voluntary service . . . all women, of course.'

'Aye. I have heard of them,' Alex said. 'Then you must be very proud of yourself, Miss Croft.'

'Yes.' It was such a small, unenthusiastic sound. He thought the subject was best left. 'Though it's not an experience I should wish to repeat.'

Miss Croft flinched afresh as the sound of distant ambulance sirens and the clanging of a fire-engine bell drifted up the valley.

'I believe it's just practice,' Alex told her, 'but best to go inside, Miss Croft.'

'Yes,' she replied, rather vague, not moving.

'And if you wouldn't mind, I'd appreciate being able to come in rather than stand out here in the street.'

'Oh, but . . .' She clasped her throat with the hand that wasn't clasping her heart and looked as if he had suggested something quite out of the question.

'I am your doctor, Miss Croft,' he said softly.

'My doctor is Dr Gordon,' she told him stiffly and her fear could be heard in the quaking of her voice.

'Dr Gordon is my uncle. I work with him in the Crowhall Lane practice.' He gave her an encouraging smile. 'And since I've come all this way, I might as well check you over, just to be on the safe side.'

'Well, in that case . . .' She stepped back even further and motioned for him to enter. 'I'm sorry, Doctor. The place is such a mess. I don't have any help, you see, and lately . . . well, it's been difficult.'

She led the way into a comfortable living-room where the windows were well blacked out behind heavy velvet drapes. The black-out curfew wasn't due to start for another thirty minutes, but Alex suspected that it was like this permanently, cutting out all hint of daylight. No wonder the woman was depressed, Alex thought.

At either side of a wide fireplace glass globes shimmered with flickering gas-flames turned as low as they could get. Apart from an open book, a scattering of papers and a cup of cooling tea, he couldn't see that anything was out of place, but she was, as his uncle had warned him, a very proud lady.

'I'll make a fresh pot of tea, Doctor,' she murmured and left him standing there, his eyes growing slowly accustomed to the gloom.

Alex couldn't help whiling away the few minutes Miss Croft took to make the tea by glancing at the items spread out over the green-baize cloth on the dining table. There were letters and photographs, all of them rather old and well-worn.

One photograph in particular attracted his attention. He could have been mistaken, but it did appear to be a much younger Frances Croft looking not exactly pretty, but certainly striking. She was standing by an army vehicle that was probably an ambulance, though the style was military and very much out of date. Another showed her in nurse's uniform sitting by the bed of a wounded soldier, she with her arm about the young man. Both of them were smiling happily into the camera.

A letter that was lying open near the photographs showed signs of water damage and the ink was smudged, but he could make out what was written there in a bold, sweeping hand.

My dearest, darling Fanny, This is the hardest thing I have ever had to do – not even during those terrible times during the war when I was fighting and, later, lying wounded in that Flanders field, did my heart weigh so heavily. Sweet Fanny, I made you a promise, to come and find you when this was over, but I cannot do it. I cannot break Margaret's heart. How can I? She has suffered more than enough already, as have our children. I must therefore ask you to release me from my promise, made in all sincerity. Please, please forgive me. You will always occupy a place in my heart, Fanny, dear, but. . . .

The all-clear sounded as Miss Croft walked back into the room, proudly erect, carrying a tea tray on which there were two cups of tea and two slices of Dundee cake. Alex straightened quickly and took a step back from the table, feeling a rush of guilt at having intruded into the woman's personal, most private world.

'Oh!' She gave a soft exclamation as she noticed the papers and quickly put the tray down over them before Alex could offer to clear a space for it. 'I'm sorry . . . I forgot I was sorting out some old papers . . .'

'Nostalgia's very good at times, but it can be a little depressing too, don't you think, Miss Croft?'

Alex watched her face start to crumple, then was amazed at how she managed to get her emotions under control without shedding the tears that welled up in her small, sad eyes.

'War is a very depressing time,' she said. 'Even a war where nothing much seems to be happening. Do have a piece of fruit-cake. I made it myself.'

'Delicious,' Alex said after his first bite, thinking that the woman certainly did not partake too freely of her own cooking, for she was painfully thin. 'Now, tell me, Miss Croft. What is it that's troubling you?'

'What makes you think something is troubling me?'

'Well, I can see it for myself, in your eyes, in the trembling of your lips and the shaking of your hands. I wouldn't be much of a doctor if I declared you fit and well, now, would I?'

'I'm not sick. Is that what they told you?' She flashed him a look over her teacup.

'All right, Miss Croft, I think I can be honest with you. A very kind and well-meaning neighbour told Dr Gordon that you had been behaving – shall we say, a little out of character? She's quite worried about you. Looking at you right now, I'd say she has cause, wouldn't you?'

Miss Croft's mouth twisted slightly. She put down her cup and saucer and pushed it away from her.

'It's nothing,' she said, her voice too high, too urgent. 'It's just my nerves. I have suffered from my nerves since . . . for many years. I was there amidst the fighting, the shelling – in those filthy trenches. I was there, Doctor . . . and it's all coming back, like a bad, recurring dream.'

'And you never married?' Alex saw the woman's eyes dart to the open letter that was still showing beneath the tea-tray.

'No. I never married. I . . . he . . .' She gulped and swallowed with difficulty. 'There was someone. Things are different, you know, in wartime. He was among the injured men whom I nursed. There was a time we thought he wouldn't make it, but he pulled through. We . . . we fell in love. It was wrong. We both knew that, but I really thought that when the war was over, he would come back to me. How selfish. He loved his wife, too. There were children – three of them. How could he not go back to them?'

'Indeed.' Alex watched as tears slid down her hollow cheeks. 'It must have been hard for you, Miss Croft. And now, of course, the memories are all flooding back.'

He saw her gulp and nod. He bent forward and picked up a felt badge that had once graced the uniform she must have worn during that horrendous time out in the Flanders fields.

'We rode horses, you know,' Miss Croft said. 'and many of the ambulances were horse drawn too. It was a good life . . . at first. I was useful, speaking both French and German so fluently. I even nursed a German soldier once. A nice boy. So polite. All he could think of was getting back home to his family, to his girl. Just like our boys. He didn't want to be fighting in any war.'

'What happened to him?'

'He died. They shot him when they found him trying to escape.' She looked up with a shrug of her shoulder. 'He was the enemy, you see.'

'Yes, I see.'

'I'm sorry, but I don't like to speak of those times . . .'

'I understand. Look, I'll give you something that will help.' He took out his prescription pad and scribbled something on it, passing it over to her. 'By the way, I met someone today who asked me to send you her regards. Mary West. She said she was a pupil of yours.'

'Oh, dear me! Goodness, yes. Dear Mary. Such a bright, happy-go-lucky child.' Miss Croft managed a smile through her tears. 'I used to teach her along with the Beasley girl . . . yes, Anne it was. Now *she* was a different kettle of fish. Such a difficult, moody child. They were both extremely talented, but I tended to prefer Mary, even though she had a mischievous streak. She was always getting into trouble of one sort or another. Not exactly a tomboy, you understand, but . . . well, she had a way of getting the utmost enjoyment out of everything she did, making the most of any difficulty.'

'She sounds like a wonderful person.' Alex smiled wistfully, thinking of the girl he had met earlier, remembering her calm, gentle face that was like a ray of sunshine after the rain, saw again the upturned mouth that always looked as if it were smiling. She had vitality and an inner beauty that somehow shone through features that could almost have been described as plain.

'Oh, yes . . . yes, she was wonderful. A miner's daughter, would you believe! Her mother must be so proud of her. I know I would be.'

Alex nodded thoughtfully and took his leave of Frances Croft. It was already dark outside in the deserted street. Further down, there was an ARP warden banging on a front door and demanding that they adjust their black-out curtaining so that the 'ruddy Gerries' didn't zoom in on them.

'Good night!' he called out and the man swung his masked torch around to pick him up in its muted beam.

'Aye. Good night, sir! Mind you don't drive on full headlights, eh? Sidelights only.'

'I'll remember.'

*

'What on earth are you doing home at this hour, Mary?'

Mary's mother was on her hands and knees, scrubbing the scullery floor when she arrived earlier than usual. Jenny West's ample rear end swayed to and fro with the rhythmic movements of her scrubbing brush and she didn't stop to talk, simply threw her words over her shoulder.

'I got the sack, Mam,' Mary said, wincing as the scrubbing brush paused, then was dropped with a great splash of dirty water into the bucket next to her mother.

'What did you say, our Mary? I don't believe it! The sack? Well, you just go right back there and ask Mr Harper to take you back, do you hear me? No West has ever lost a job. Not in this family.'

'I'm sorry, but Mr Harper wouldn't have me back, and I don't want to go back. He's horrible, Mam. I feel sorry for that poor wife of his. None of the girls is safe with him. He can't keep his hands to himself.'

'So it's true what they're saying about young Maggie Brown? She won't say who planted the bairn inside her, but the rumours suggest it was some fella at Harpers. I never thought it would be Mr Harper himself.'

Maggie Brown had worked on the haberdashery counter until recently. She left in a cloud of shame to have a baby and there was no man involved, or that was what she tried to tell people. As if they would believe that the pregnancy had happened all on its own.

'And she's not the only one, either,' Mary said and her mother rounded on her, skidding on the soapy floor and sitting in a puddle, untold horror registering in her plump face.

'Eeh, our Mary! He's not had his way with you, has he? You're not . . . you know . . . so-so . . . are you?'

'Of course I'm not, Mam.' Mary bit her lip to stop from laughing, for Jenny West looked so funny sitting there, her eyes popping and her mouth hanging open. 'I wouldn't let any man touch me. Not like that, anyway. And especially not Mr Harper. What do you take me for?'

'Well, this war seems to be affecting everybody. There's no telling what could happen. I just don't want you to do anything that would shame your dad and me. Now, promise me, girl. You'll not do it . . . not even with Walter. You haven't already, have you, please God?'

'No, Mam, I haven't.' Mary gave her mother a grimace. 'I'm saving myself for when the time is right.'

Mary averted her eyes because she could see herself in the mirror above the mantelpiece and something in her expression was a little too honest. The fact was, the time never did seem right when she was with

Walter. This was something that had been bothering her for some time, which was why she had to give some thought to breaking off the engagement.

'Well, I'm glad to hear it.' Jenny heaved herself up by the corner of the scullery bench and emptied the dirty water down the deep stone sink. 'Walter's a nice boy. I'm sure he respects you.'

'Yes, Mam,' Mary said, quickly changing the subject. 'Anyway, I thought I'd go to the employment exchange tomorrow and see what there is. Iris Morrison's just got herself taken on by the War Pensions Office.'

'Oh, goodness, where's that then? In London? I'm not having you go traipsing down there, love. It's too far away from home. And dangerous.'

'It's not in London, Mam.' Mary watched the tense twitching of her mother's back as she refilled the bucket with clean water. 'It's down near Saltwell Park in Gateshead.'

'Is it now? Well, that's far enough. She'll spend half her time travelling to and from work.'

Mary shook her head. Her mother was the limit, she really was, but then her life had been filled with marriage and raising children. She had left school at thirteen and gone into service until she got married at twenty-one, which had been pretty normal in her day.

'Where's our Helen?'

Mary was suddenly conscious that her sister was missing and so was the baby that kept them all busy from morning till night. Helen and her husband lived at home with Jenny and Frank West while they saved for a place of their own. The trouble was, Trevor was expecting to be called up at any minute, him being in the Territorial Army and a reservist.

'Oh, don't ask. She's off somewhere with that poor bairn and I don't know what to tell Trevor if he gets home from the factory before she's back.'

'But where did she go? Didn't she tell you?' It wasn't like Helen to go off on her own and stay out beyond black-out time.

'Aye, lass. She's trying to get herself a job.'

'She's what?'

Jenny heaved the bucket out of the sink, poured in a few drops of vinegar, wrung out a floor cloth in it and started wiping down the linoleum so that it shone bright and clean.

'She's got some bee in her bonnet about being independent. Says she's bored. Wants more out of life. I ask you.'

'But what about the baby?' Mary was concerned for the well-being of her little niece though she could appreciate how her sister was feeling.

'As I say, don't ask. Only . . .' Jenny's backside stopped swaying and she sat back on her heels and heaved a heartfelt sigh. 'She just went off saying she was desperate to do something more than just sit at home knitting. As if looking after her husband and our little Carol isn't occupation enough. I know they're a bit strapped for cash, like, but she says it's not that.'

'Then what is it? Oh, you don't think there's anything wrong, do you . . . I mean, between Helen and Trevor?'

Mary had heard muttered arguments filtering through the dividing wall between her tiny box room and theirs. She could understand the difficulty of their trying to live a full, married life, jammed as they were upstairs in this cramped miner's cottage. That was one of the reasons she had not wanted to rush into marriage with Walter, when the only place they could possibly live in was the flat above Walter's shop, with his parents. Walter's dad was all right, but his mother was a difficult woman. Mary didn't think she could cope with having the woman breathing down their necks twenty-four hours a day, seven days a week. Walter, being their son, couldn't see the problem. He'd have two women running around after him and seemed quite pleased with the idea.

Jenny threw her hands in the air. 'Eeh, I don't know, our Mary? You young people seem to have a lot more complications than people of my generation ever had. We just got married and got on with it, taking the good with the bad.'

There wasn't a lot Mary could say to that. Whatever she said on the subject would probably upset her mother, and everybody avoided getting Jenny emotional, because she did tend to go overboard and make everybody else miserable with her.

'Did you get your gran's medicine?' Jenny asked as they were sitting over a cup of tea half an hour later.

'Yes,' Mary nodded and her mouth clamped tightly shut, because she was about to laugh and she knew her mother didn't like anything that resembled mockery, especially where her grandmother was concerned. 'I made sure she took some straight away and tucked her up as best I could.'

She had called in at her gran's house two doors away and found the place deserted. Fortunately, she had a key and was able to let herself in. It was then an easy business to go through to the back of the house, where she found her grandmother locked in the air-raid shelter that had been built in the yard next to the lavatory. Nothing short of Hitler's army would have winkled the old woman out of her hiding place, even though it was freezing cold and as dark as a dungeon.

There was old Annie, muffled up to the eyeballs, sucking on a precious orange, dribbling the juice down her chin and demanding to know if the war was over yet. Poor old soul, she was as deaf as a post and so scared that she wouldn't hear the siren wailing to forewarn her of an enemy attack, she preferred to camp out in the shelter on a permanent basis, coming out only at meal-times, when she joined the family.

'Dear God,' moaned Jenny. 'It's to be hoped the war ends soon, so your gran can get back to normal.'

'I can't help feeling that she's going to have a long wait,' Mary said, thinking of the long wait they had already had. 'Do you think she's all right, Mam? I mean, in the head . . . you know?'

Jenny gave her a scathing look. She lifted her head at the sound of a latchkey grating in the lock of the front door.

'That'll be your dad,' she said.

It was indeed Frank West, back from making sure the good folk living over the old Cube Pit area of Felling were following all the rules of security. He looked almost blue with the cold, banging his hands together to get the circulation going, but he smiled broadly on seeing Mary.

'By gum, it's parky out there th' night,' he said. 'Hullo, love. Finished early, have you?'

'Just finished, Frank,' Jenny answered for her. 'That rotten boss of hers has given her the sack.'

Frank's eyebrows shot up, then he gave a shrug.

'Oh, aye? Well, I always said you were too good for that place. You'll find another job without too much bother, I bet.'

'Thanks Dad,' Mary said and placed an affectionate kiss on his frozen cheek.

'What did I do to deserve that, then?'

'Nothing at all, Dad.'

He looked at her curiously for a second or two, then settled himself in front of the fire with his *Evening Chronicle* to wait for his tea. Jenny had a cauldron of chicken broth and dumplings bubbling merrily on top of the stove and the whole place was filled with its delicious aroma.

Another rattle at the front door announced the arrival of Helen and she appeared with the sleeping, six-month-old Carol in her arms. She looked worn out, but radiant.

'Well, that's that settled,' she said, collapsing into the nearest chair as soon as her mother took charge of the infant. 'I've got some good news and I can't wait until Trevor gets back, so I'm going to blab it all out now.'

'Oh, aye? What is it then, this news of yours?' Jenny rocked back and forward, her granddaughter clamped tightly to her chest, kissing her until the child stirred, opened sleepy eyes and gave a whimper of complaint.

'I've found us a place of our own,' Helen said, a trifle breathlessly. 'Well, not exactly our own. It's just two rooms in a house at the top of Watermill Lane. Two rooms and a kitchen and we share a bathroom with the owner. She's a widow and the place is too big for her to manage, so she agreed a low rent if I'll help with the housework.'

'You're going to leave us?' Jenny's eyes immediately filled with tears. 'Aw, hinny, you don't have to do that. You know you're welcome to stay here as long as you like.'

'I know that, Mam,' Helen said, 'but it's best this way. And . . . I've found a job. The new munitions factory down on Sunderland Road. I'll be helping to make bits for the aeroplanes. You know, the ones that'll win the war.'

'But you hate the very idea of work,' Mary said, half teasingly. 'What's brought this on?'

'Aye, our Helen. I think you've got some explaining to do, young lady. And what I want to know is what's going to happen to this bairn of yours when you're at work in this munchings factory, or whatever it is.'

'Munitions, Mam, and it's very important. Don't worry about Carol. Mrs Greaves, our landlady, loves children. She'll be more than happy to look after her. Isn't that wonderful?'

'Wonderful,' said Mary, positively bemused by her sister's unprecedented behaviour.

'Well, I don't think it's wonderful at all,' Jenny muttered. 'Did you hear that, Frank? Our Helen's leaving us and some stranger is going to take care of Carol.'

'Oh, aye?' came the reply from behind the newspaper. 'Well, at least you'll be able to get your front room back to normal for Christmas.'

'Oh, men!' Jenny shook her head and dabbed her glistening eyes with the edge of her pinny. 'They never understand. Oh, well, at least it frees the room for you and Walter, doesn't it, our Mary?'

Mary didn't say anything. She curled up on the clippie mat in front of the hearth and stared into the flames that were leaping up the wide chimney. Her eyes found the hole at one side where they raked out the soot. She used to put her Christmas wishes in there when she was a little girl. It was a magic place and, she truly believed, a place where dreams came true. In her imagination, she wrote a short note now, the invisible child in her flicking it into the small aperture.

Then she sat back from the heat and laughed softly to herself. Tomorrow, or the next day, her mother would rake out the soot, not knowing that Mary's dream was there among the powdery blackness. Dreams were for children, after all, and she was all grown up and didn't believe in magic any more.

After a busy evening clinic, Alex Craig was sitting at one end of the dining-room table, bringing up to date the notes of the patients he had seen that day. It seemed as though the war and the gruelling harshness of the winter weather that year were taking their toll on the population. He and his uncle had handed out prescriptions as if they were on some sort of production line. There had hardly been time to write more than a few salient words as he went along.

'Do stop doing that, Alex,' his wife snapped out, impatient with the monotonous drumming of his fingers. 'You're being very irritating this evening.'

'It's been a long, hard day, Fiona.' He glanced across the room to where she was sitting staring into the glowing elements of the gas fire. The book she had been reading was discarded, open and face down on her lap as if she had suddenly become bored with it. 'Why don't you take up something to occupy yourself with? Knitting, perhaps. Embroidery? My mother gets a lot of pleasure out of embroidery . . . oh, and tapestry. Now that's something you could do, surely?'

'I am not your mother, Alex. Please don't patronize me with suggestions that I take up such domestic pursuits. You'll be suggesting next that I should make cakes and jam and I can't think of anything I would rather do less.'

'Well, after all, you are a member of the local WI. Isn't that what they do?'

'Oh, that bunch of old hens. I only joined for the contacts, but apart from Penelope Beasley and, at some stretch of the imagination, the vicar's wife, there is absolutely nobody of any note within their ranks.'

'I hear they're doing an awful lot towards the war effort. Why aren't you down there now with them, helping out? You know, doing your bit.'

'Knitting mittens and balaclavas and making bandages from old sheets? Having coffee-mornings? Really, Alex.'

'Perhaps . . .' He hesitated fractionally, unsure whether or not to broach the subject that had been uppermost in his mind for so long. 'Perhaps things might seem better, Fiona, if we had a family.'

Then he saw it, that same outraged expression, and knew that it had been a mistake.

'Oh, not that again, Alex! There's plenty of time yet. Besides, I'm not even sure I want to be a mother. All that sick and dirty nappies and lost sleep. No, thank you.'

Alex fell silent. He could see that the conversation was going nowhere. In fact, it was most likely to lead to a slanging match if he persisted. They seemed to have more and more heated exchanges these days, neither one of them able to speak without a barb attached.

What the hell had happened to their marriage, Alex wondered gloomily? It had all started out happily enough. Maybe that was the problem. Happily *enough*. He had never felt that great boost of excitement that went beyond the superficial realms of lust. It was Fiona who had made the running, Fiona who pushed him into marriage. Looking back now over the last five years, it was easy to see how it had all gone wrong. She had been too forceful and he had been too young and impressionable. Had love ever entered into the equation? He thought not.

And for Fiona's part, she had quickly become bored with being his wife. She didn't find him exciting enough. He was always working, and when he wasn't nose to the grindstone in the hospital or, as now, in the practice, he was too tired for the kind of social life she would have preferred. He had thought, perhaps, that if they started a family, things would improve. Well, she had knocked that theory on the head more than once, much to his disappointment.

Alex collected the packets of patient-notes into a neat pile, secured them with an elastic band and popped them into his Gladstone bag. His conscience was telling him he had to do something to salvage whatever remained of a relationship that he had sworn before God to protect. He wasn't a religious man, but he did believe in the sanctity of marriage. Even so, it did take two to make any marriage work and Fiona had long ago ceased to meet him halfway. With a sigh, he pushed himself up from the table.

'Why don't we go out for a drink?' he suggested, thinking that being in a public place was preferable to an unfriendly silence here at home.

Fiona gave him a languid look and her mouth twitched in the way it did when she thought he was being stupid.

'I'm not in the mood. Besides, we have alcohol in the sideboard. I can think of better things to do than mingle with pitmen and dockers swilling beer.'

Alex gritted his teeth. Although he was fairly new to Tyneside, he already felt a natural urge to defend the mainly working-class population. They were the salt of the earth, these big-hearted, hard-working

Geordies. He had received nothing but warmth from them since he first put his foreign nose into their midst.

'They're good people, Fiona,' he said, his voice tight but controlled. 'You shouldn't run them down. Good Lord, you don't even know them.'

'Oh, go out for a drink, if that's what you want, but don't expect me to come with you.' Fiona's eyes flashed angrily, then she turned her gaze back to the fire. 'Go and get drunk, if you must. I don't care.'

Alex said no more. He grabbed his overcoat, scarf and the mandatory gas mask, and headed for the pub. It was his uncle's turn to be on call that night, so he didn't worry too much about being absent.

The evening being fine, though the air was freezing and the pavements icy, Alex decided to go on foot up to Victoria Square, where there was a pub that seemed popular with the locals. He felt the need for exercise and to breathe some good, clean air. And to distance himself from the house, which had never truly felt like a home, mainly because Fiona seemed incapable of making it so.

The Jubilee public house was heaving with bodies, quite a few of them servicemen. The young, brash soldiers were intent on enjoying their freedom and filled the place with raucous laughter as they shouted out toasts bordering on the ridiculous and the vulgar, such as 'Up yours, Adolph!' and 'Here's to Adolf in Blunderland!'

One man sat alone in a corner, warding off company with aggressive arm waves. The fellow, Alex noticed, was in his fifties and stared down sullenly into his glass. Like Alex, he was drinking whisky, but was obviously a few shots ahead, for his eyes were clouded and there was a dribble of saliva coursing down his chin from his slack mouth.

'Who's that in the corner over there?' Alex asked the barman as he paid for his second whisky. 'The fellow with the glum expression and the haunted eyes.'

'Oh, that's Frank West,' the barman told him and Alex wandered over to where the man was still sitting staring into space.

'Mind if I join you?' he asked, sitting down anyway. 'It's the only vacant seat.'

The man raised his eyes and swallowed hard, then shrugged his shoulders uncaringly. He ignored Alex and returned to his serious drinking, calling for another whisky as soon as he had downed the last drop of the one before him.

'Hey, Frank, lad. I think ye've had enough, eh? Ye'll nivvor get home th' neet.' The barman hovered by Alex's shoulder, shaking his head. Then he bent down and shouted in Alex's ear because it was too noisy to whisper. 'He's a bit upset, ye see. Got turned down by the Draft Board when he tried to join up.'

Alex looked at the lined face of the miner in amazement. The fellow was slowly sinking down as he muttered something unintelligibly, then his forehead crashed on to the table before him.

'Where does he live?' Alex asked.

'Up Split Crow Road way,' said another miner who had wandered over, clutching his thick pint glass. 'Silly old fool. Fancy trying to join up at his age. You'd think he'd have had enough of war after the last one.'

'Yes.' Alex sighed, then stood up and hauled the slightly built, semi-conscious man to his feet. 'However, there's no telling what goes on in a man's mind at times like these. I'll see him home.'

'It's a long walk, and uphill all the way.'

'It'll do us both good. Split Crow Road, is it?'

'Aye, that's right. George Street. On the right, just past the allotments.'

Alex's eyes narrowed slightly. He couldn't be sure, but the man he was now supporting, and who was almost comatose, was very likely Mary West's father.

It was going to be quite a challenge, getting the drunken man home, but in the square they came upon a horse and cart going in the right direction. The man driving it was Tommy Dobson, the patient who had created such a fuss at being signed off that morning.

'Hold on there,' Alex called out as he saw that Tommy was about to pass them by. 'Can you give us a lift up Split Crow Road as far as George Street?'

The man glowered at him beneath his flat cap and tried to disappear into his coat collar.

'Aye, put him on the back,' he said eventually, his voice muffled. 'I'll see he gets there safely enough.'

'No, I'll go with him, just to make sure.'

'Ye divvint trust us, eh?'

'Tommy Dobson, I know it's you, so there's no use pretending you're somebody different. Now will you give us a lift or not?'

'What's in it for me, eh? Ye ganna give us another sick note?'

'What's in it for you, my man, is my silence if you go back to work and stop all your shenanigans.'

There was a brief hesitation, then Tommy whipped off his cap and scratched fiercely at his greasy head.

'Aye, gan on then. Hop aboard.'

It took them ten minutes. The horse was old and kept stopping to pant and cough, filling the air with steam from its nostrils and a fouler stench from its rear. But at least it seemed to know its way, even in the pitch-black night. The cartwheels mounted the kerb only once.

When Alex jumped down at the end of George Street and pulled Mr West after him, he could see Tommy Dobson hovering expectantly.

'Don't push your luck, laddie,' he said and received a grimace in return. 'My gratitude is all you're getting. Consider this as part of your donation towards the war effort. And get yourself back to work by Monday morning, or I'll want to know why not.'

Without a further word, Dobson clicked his tongue and the horse moved on. Alex looked about him, recognizing the area, even in the dark. That patient he had visited this afternoon – Miss Croft – she lived two streets further up.

'Come on, Mr West,' he said, tightening his grip about the man's waist so that they were almost joined at the hip. 'Let's get you to your bed.'

'Ye're a good lad,' Frank West muttered and patted Alex's shoulder. 'I bet they wouldn't turn you down, eh?'

Frank managed to stay awake long enough to indicate which house he lived in. As Alex rapped on the door with the heavy iron knocker, he saw a flicker of light through a chink in the fanlight black-out curtain. After a few seconds he heard feet coming down the stairs at a run.

'Mrs West?' he spoke out as soon as the door began to open. 'It's Dr Craig. I've got your husband here. He's a bit under the weather, I'm afraid.'

But the person who stood there, her face illuminated by a sudden beam of light as the moon appeared from behind a bank of cloud, was none other than Mary West.

'Dr Craig? Oh, goodness, Dad! What's happened? Mam, come quick!'

'It's all right,' Alex said, stepping over the threshold with his burden. 'He's not hurt. Just the worse for too much drink.'

'He's drunk? But Dad never touches alcohol.'

'Well, he did tonight. Better get him up the stairs and pour him into bed. He'll have a beauty of a hangover in the morning.'

'I just don't believe that your dad would do such a thing,' Jenny West sat with her head in her hands, which is how she had been since Dr Craig left. 'And just fancy, that doctor bringing him all the way home. What must he think of us, eh?'

'I don't know, Mam,' Mary said, putting a cup of strong, sweet tea in front of her mother. 'But it was very kind of him to do that. Otherwise,

Dad might have ended up sleeping in the gutter tonight and they'd have found him all frozen to death in the morning.'

'Oh, but the shame of it!' Jenny moaned. 'What on earth possessed him?'

Mary knew there was no point in struggling with the whys and the wherefores. Her father kept his feelings very much to himself, and although he never spoke of it, he was proud to have served his king and country in the Great War. No doubt he felt that Britain and King George needed him again.

'Poor Dad,' she said, glancing at her sister, who looked as stricken as her mother. 'I thought he was a bit quieter than usual. I bet he'll feel awful when he realizes what he's done.'

Jenny West got up from the table and threw her hands up in the air. She paced back and forward in front of the coal fire that was still glowing in the grate.

'I don't know how I'm going to face people,' she said.

'Oh, Mam! It's not a crime to get drunk.' Mary felt her voice sharpen. 'He must have been feeling pretty bad to drink as much as he did.'

'It's a crime for your father to drink himself stupid,' Jenny said. 'And Dr Craig had had a drink or two as well. I could smell the whisky on his breath. And him a doctor!'

Mary had noticed the smell of alcohol too, and wondered if both men had reason to drown their sorrows. Her dad had been turned down by the Army and perhaps laughed at because of his age and his bad chest from years of breathing in coal dust. What was Dr Craig's reason for drinking a little more than was good for him, she wondered curiously? He didn't give the impression of being a drinking man.

But then, whatever it was, it was none of her business. He had been kind enough to see that her father got home safely and had stayed to drink a warming cup of tea by the fire. And when she had let him out of the house later on he had gripped her hand and smiled down at her, and the smile had reached his eyes. It was such a special smile and she felt it was just for her. His hand was firm and strong, unlike Walter's pudgy grip that lacked substance. She really must make a point of calling in to thank him. They had all been so shocked by her father's state that she was sure they had all forgotten their manners.

'Mary!' She jumped as her mother's sharp voice penetrated her thoughts. 'Stop dreaming and go and see if your dad's come back to the land of the living. There's a drop of broth left in the pan. He probably needs something in his stomach to soak up the alcohol. Silly old fool!'

CHAPTER THREE

It was a few days before things settled down in the West household. Jenny was at last speaking again to Frank, though grudgingly. Mary was glad, in a way, that she had lost her job at Harper's, for she was able to be there for her parents when they needed her most. Although after a couple of days dealing with her mother's obvious depression following her husband's drinking session, Mary was more than ready to start looking for another position.

And that was exactly what she was about to do on Friday morning when there was a furious banging on the front door.

'Oh, that's got to be bad news!' her mother wailed, clamping her face between her hands and looking as if she had frozen solid to the kitchen floor.

'It's all right, Mam,' Mary said. 'Calm down. I'll go.'

She pulled open the door, stepping back sharply when Iris Morrison tumbled in, rosy cheeked and breathless.

'Mary, grab your things and come with me,' Iris said between gasps.

'Iris, what on earth. . . ?' Mary stared at her friend. 'What's happened?'

'Nothing, as yet, but if we don't get down to the pensions office quick you'll lose the chance of a lifetime. Go on . . . coat, bag, gloves, scarf . . . quick!'

'What?'

'There's another vacancy come up for a pensions clerk and they're interviewing this morning. I told them about you and they said if you could get down there by nine they'd see you.'

'Oh, Iris!'

Mary was already rushing back into the house while Iris caught her breath on the doorstep.

'Where are you going?' Jenny poked her head out in time to see Mary wind her scarf around her neck and pull on some woollen gloves.

'Job interview, Mam,' Mary told her. 'I'm off with Iris. See you later. Wish me luck?'

'Oh, aye, hinny. Good luck. It's not at any factory, is it?'

'No, Mam. It's in an office.'

And then the two young women were outside in the crisp November morning, their feet crunching on the ground frost, their faces tingling as the icy wind slapped their cheeks.

It was a treacherous route down the slippery slope of Split Crow Road and they hung on to each other, laughing nervously, their booted feet slithering away from under them at every step.

'Sorry I couldn't come up last night, Mary,' Iris said, wiping the steam from her glasses as they paused to catch their breath at the bottom of the first hill. 'I was late home and I can't see in the dark. And everybody's down with the flu in our house, so I had to do the supper as well.'

'I'm so glad you thought of me, Iris,' Mary said and they started off again, arm in arm, running, sliding, hardly able to stop themselves until they reached Heworth and the tramcars that ran into Gateshead and Newcastle.

'Here it comes,' Iris said with a sigh of relief after a few minutes' wait as they hopped from one foot to the other to keep warm.

The tramcar that rattled towards them displayed the destination of 'Saltwell Park' and the windows were steamed up from the body temperature of the passengers already inside.

They jumped aboard and paid the tuppence fare to the driver, but as he clanged the bell and started off there was a loud yell and the clatter of feet running down the road after them.

'Stop the tram! Hey! Wait a minute!'

Mary peered out of the back of the tram and saw a diminutive figure running hell for leather after them, coat and skirt flying in the wind, skinny sparrow legs working in overdrive, and one hand clamped over a hat that was insisting on taking flight.

The driver must have been in a good mood, for he slowed down, but didn't stop. The girl chasing them never flagged. She got to the boarding-platform and leapt forward and up, arms reaching out. Mary caught her and pulled her inside.

'Bloody hell!' The expletive from the girl under the hat, which had come down over her eyes, scorched Mary's ears.

'What were you trying to do?' Mary laughed. 'Break your neck? There'll be another tram in a few minutes.'

'Aye, but I'm late already and I have to get back by eleven or there'll be hell to pay.'

Mary clamped her lips together to hide her amusement as the other girl went through the intricate business of rearranging her person, which had been more than just a little disarranged by her flight after the tram.

Giving her a friendly smile, Mary hooked her hand under the girl's arm, because she was unsteady as the tram gathered speed. 'Come on inside. It'll be warmer.'

'Aye. This effin' weather's playin' havoc wi' me chilblains.' A pair of small eyes like dark pebbles flashed at her. 'And ye can stop lookin' at us like that. We can't all talk posh like you, ye know.'

'It was just that I thought I'd seen you before somewhere . . .' Mary told her quickly, having no wish to offend the girl, who was obviously touchy on the subject of her broad Geordie accent.

'Aye, mebbe, if you've had somebody in the family die recently. I work for me da. He's an undertaker.' She waved her hands about. 'Oh, damn these chilblains!'

Mary sympathized, glad that she wasn't troubled with the same affliction, but she knew plenty of people who complained bitterly about it. With a smile and a nod, she went to join Iris in the centre of the tram, pulling the back of the seat forward so she could sit facing her friend as they rocked and rattled their way to Gateshead.

'That could have been nasty,' Iris said jerking her head towards the girl from the funeral parlour. 'It's a wonder she didn't fall and break a leg or something.'

'I've never seen anybody run like that.' Mary laughed into the folds of her scarf, wishing there was some form of heating in the tram, for it was nearly as cold as it was outside, and the driver looked a bit blue about the gills too. 'When she jumped I held my breath, but she kind of just flew.'

'Yes, well, those Donaldsons aren't made to break.'

'You know her?'

'Not exactly,' Iris put her hands under her armpits for warmth and hugged herself tightly, her breath coming out in a great cloud and meeting the same from Mary's open mouth. 'The family's well known around here. They're from Elliot Street and you can't get anything rougher, but they run a good funeral service. Four lads and one girl, though I hear tell she's as bad as any of her brothers. Effie, she's called, mainly on account of her swearing.'

Mary stifled a giggle, and then they were both laughing and were glad there were other passengers to hide them from the object of their humour. However, Mary did catch the girl staring at them with a malignant eye when she gave a swift glance over her shoulder.

'She's not the friendliest character in the world, is she? I didn't even get a thank-you for hauling her on board.'

'No, well, I suppose she's more used to dealing with corpses.'

'That's not my idea of fun.' Mary said with a shudder, recalling the strange almost almond smell of the embalming fluid that pervaded everything after they had had her grandfather laid out.

'The mother died or scarpered years ago,' Iris muttered out of the corner of her mouth. 'Effie's the youngest, but they say she's held the family together one way or another. Mam says she's a right little scrubber and no mistake, but she won't stand for any nonsense from anybody.'

'Well, she has to be admired.'

'Yes, maybe, but she's got a right reputation. You just have to look at her the wrong way and she's on you like a ton of bricks.' Iris grabbed Mary as she was about to give Effie another look. 'No, don't look round or she'll think we're talking about her.'

'Oh, Iris, you are funny.'

'I don't mess with any of the Donaldsons,' Iris told her. 'Effie in particular. Come on, it's our stop next.'

They staggered to the exit as the tram pulled in and stopped. There were a few people to get off and Iris pushed her way past them, dragging Mary with her. As fast as they could go on the frosted ground they hurried to the War Pensions Office.

It was a plain, redbrick building with nothing to recommend it as a site worthy of note. Inside it was even plainer, with its starkly blank walls painted cream over heavily embossed Lincrusta wallpaper. It might have been considered fashionable, but to Mary it looked rather as though they'd decorated the place with rice-pudding.

'In there,' Iris said, giving Mary a shove towards a door marked 'Chief Clerk'. 'Mr Hornby's expecting you. I'll pop back and see how you've got on in about half an hour.'

Iris entered another room where there was a buzz of female voices, the sound of a typewriter clacking and the buzz of a switchboard. Already, there was a short queue of customers lining up in reception, waiting for the service window to be opened to them.

Taking a deep breath, Mary knocked on Mr Hornby's door and heard the summons to enter. The man sitting at the large desk in the centre of the room looked harassed, even though it was barely nine o'clock. He had fat, florid cheeks and peered at her through thick-lensed glasses that sat on a fleshy nose, which resembled a piece of bread-dough.

'Mr Hornby? I'm Mary West,' Mary introduced herself.

He glanced down at his diary, stabbed a finger on the top name of a long list of names and blinked up at her. 'Ah, yes. Come in, Miss West. Sit down, sit down . . . and tell me all about yourself, eh?'

Fifteen minutes later, the interview was over and Mr Hornby was accompanying Mary to the door, congratulating her on obtaining the position of junior pensions clerk and shaking her hand vigorously. As she thanked him again and started to walk in the direction of the reception office, she almost bumped into someone hovering just outside the door.

'That effin' does it!'

Mary recognized the girl as none other than Effie Donaldson who had sprinted like a mad thing after the tramcar. She started to apologize for her own clumsiness, but the girl was already being addressed by Mr Hornby.

'Was there something you wanted?' he said, peering down his dumpling nose.

'Aye. I've come about the clerical job.'

'Oh, dear, yes, I see.' Mr Hornby's face twisted as he sniffed the air between them and expanded his broad chest. 'Well, I'm afraid you're too late. It's already been filled.'

Effie Donaldson seemed to sag inside her bones and every line on her thin face turned downwards.

'Bloody Norah! After all the rush. And I did get here on time an' all. Nearly killed mesel' to get here, too.'

'Yes, well . . .' Mr Hornby twitched from head to foot, glanced uncomfortably at Mary, then started to back into his office, his hand ready to close, and possibly lock the door. 'Perhaps another time . . . er . . . Miss . . . er. . . ?'

'It's Donaldson,' Effie pronounced loudly and angrily. 'Effie Donaldson, and don't you look down yer nose at me. I'm as good as the rest. I just wanted the chance to . . .'

The door clicked firmly shut and Effie was left talking to the solid wood panel. Her words tailed off and she slumped, then, remembering Mary's presence, her shoulders rose again and she spun on her heel to face her.

'What ye starin' at, eh? Are you the bleedin' new pensions clerk then? Is that what you was runnin' for – to get ahead of me?'

Mary shook her head. 'I'm sorry. I didn't know you were coming for an interview.'

'Aye, well I was, but then, I don't look like you, or talk like you. I'm not posh, as you well know. I'm effin' common as muck, me. It was daft to even think they'd give us a go at makin' somethin' of mesel'. They probably think I can't read and write.'

'I'm sure you can, as well as anybody.' Mary hastened to pour oil over obviously troubled waters. 'Look, I really am sorry.'

'Like hell you are. Anyway, they don't need good English to hand out pensions, do they? And I can do me sums. I was always pretty good at arithmetic.'

'I don't know what to say, except there may be another vacancy soon.'

'Ye'll be tellin' us next that it was meant to be.'

Effie's face twisted into a wry smile, though it would take a good deal more than that to make her halfway to being pretty. Hers was a roughly hewn face, void of all the usual feminine softness. The dark eyes were too close together beneath thick black eyebrows and there was the hint of a moustache shadowing her upper lip. She had small canine teeth that were white enough, but crooked.

'Actually, I do believe that things happen for the best,' Mary said hastily. 'Even the bad things. Believing that helps me get through life.'

'If ye had my life ye'd not think like that, I can tell ye.'

'No, perhaps not, but we all have to cope with our problems in our own way.'

Out of the corner of her eye, Mary could see Iris poking her nose out of the office door across the corridor. Effie saw her too and rounded on her.

'I suppose I have you to thank for this,' she called out, standing squarely and placing her hands on her thin hips. 'Well, ye can quit worryin' about yer friend here. She got the job.'

Iris's eyes sparkled and she pressed her hands together, ignoring Effie Donaldson and looking at Mary for confirmation.

'I start on Monday,' Mary told her.

'Fantastic! Must go. Fridays are always busy.'

Iris ducked back inside the office and Mary turned to have a final word with Effie, but the girl had already left and could be seen marching resentfully down the street, shoulders slumped, head down. Mary felt sorry for her. Maybe the poor girl would have got the job, though she doubted it, judging by the look on Mr Hornby's face.

With a sigh, Mary took a different route and walked into town rather than cross Effie's path again. She found a small café open and bought a cup of coffee and a currant bun. Well, she told herself, she had a reason to celebrate. She had landed herself a government job, so she wouldn't be called up alongside the men, which otherwise had seemed likely, for there was certainly plenty of talk about it being in the pipeline.

'Are you nervous?'

Iris's guarded whisper from the next desk broke through Mary's concentration. She had been working at the War Pensions Office for three weeks and had not, so far, felt that it was a job she would ever really enjoy. Too much bending over ledgers and filling in forms. She was even seeing columns of figures in her sleep.

'Not right at this minute,' she whispered back, keeping a wary eye open for Mr Hornby in case he chose that moment to stroll through the general office. 'Why should I be?'

'Oh, you daft Clara!' Iris giggled. 'I'm talking about tomorrow night. You know, the talent contest.'

She waited for Mary's reply, ignoring a sharp look from Mrs Shelton, their supervisor, who was a stickler for silence and efficiency, even more than Harry Hornby himself, who could be charmed with a cheeky smile and a humorous remark, as long as he was in a receptive mood. Whereas Mrs Shelton was a widow, never receptive, outwardly full of gloom, but inwardly, so Iris informed Mary, on heat for Mr Hornby.

'I'm trying not to think about it,' Mary said. 'Have you decided yet what you're going to do?'

Iris had had them all in stitches over the past couple of weeks, trying out new routines, as she called them, in the hope that she would win the Christmas Talent Contest, which was to be the entertainment for the war-benefit ball on the twenty-third of December. Singing was out of the question. Iris was tone deaf. Doing a tap dance seemed a better option, but she couldn't remember the steps she had learnt at the age of five and ended up tripping herself up. Then she thought that perhaps she could be a stand-up comedian, but she didn't know any jokes.

'I'd love to win, you know,' she had said to Mary, 'but I'm not much good at anything, really.'

'I suppose we all want to win, Iris,' Mary had told her kindly, 'but it's not that important. At least we'll be doing our bit for Britain.'

'Yes, you're right, as usual, Mary, but I really would like to shine, just once in my life.'

Mary went back to her ledger, wishing she could do something finer for her country than stand up and sing. Sighing wistfully, she continued to fill in figures with a scratchy pen, trying carefully not to splash ink over the pages. She was actually a lot more nervous about the competition than she was willing to admit. She loved singing and dancing, but most of what she had done had been at home in front of her family and friends. The thought of doing it in public before a paying audience was a little overwhelming.

Last week they had held auditions in the drill hall, a big, empty building that was acoustically daunting because of its echo. Mary had felt quite uneasy hearing her own voice coming back at her through the empty void of the high ceiling. Actually, she thought, it sounded much better than it was in reality. The row of judges had applauded her, their smiles wide and encouraging and she couldn't believe her luck when they told her she had been accepted, along with half a dozen other girls, one of whom was Iris, who had recited a sad little poem that brought tears to her own eyes, so she swore she would do something different on the night.

Men didn't go in much for talent competitions. Certainly not the Geordie males, who thought it was pretty cissy to get up on the stage and make fools of themselves. However, old Mr Dolan had been persuaded to play the spoons and there were fourteen-year-old twin boys who played the penny-whistle in duet.

'It's your big night tomorrow, Mary, so I'm told.'

Mary looked up to find Harry Hornby standing at her elbow.

'It's important for all of us, Mr Hornby,' she told him, moving away and leaving a space between them. 'I hope you and your wife are going?'

'Oh, dear me, no . . . I mean . . .' The chief clerical officer looked uncomfortable, scratched his balding pate, then stuck his hands behind his back and rocked on the balls of his very small feet. 'I don't have a wife . . . I mean . . . er . . . I never married, you know.'

'I'm sorry, Mr Hornby. I didn't know.' Mary wasn't quite sure why she should feel sorry for him, but he looked quite sad standing there telling her that he had nobody with whom to share his life.

'But I shall be there,' he said, brightening considerably as the moment passed. 'I'll be in the audience, cheering you on.'

'And Iris, too, I hope,' Mary said, giving him her special teasing smile that had served her well over the years and kept her from landing in trouble.

'Oh . . . er . . . hmm . . . yes, yes, of course. Now, enough of this chatter. Get on with your work, girls.'

Mary glanced across at Iris as Mr Hornby waddled back to his own office. Iris rolled her eyes to the ceiling, then shook her head.

'I think he likes you, Mary.'

'Oh, dear.' Mary sighed. 'I hope not.'

'Lor', what a drip!' Iris muttered. 'No wonder he's not married. Probably lives at home with his old mam. I doubt he'd know what to do with a girl if one was handed to him on a plate.'

'Well, if that's true, you shouldn't make fun of the poor man,' Mary said sympathetically.

'Silence!' The order was snapped out by Mrs Shelton, who had been surreptitiously combing her hair and replacing her lipstick with the aid of a hand mirror in her desk drawer. 'Busy mouths do not get the work done!'

'Are you going in for the talent competition, Mrs Shelton?' Iris asked cheekily and the woman's cheeks flushed a deeper pink beneath the fuchsia of her thickly applied rouge.

'Don't be ridiculous, girl!'

Mary kept her head down low over her ledger and hoped she wouldn't get a fit of the giggles, because if she did she would not be able to stop and she would undoubtedly snort quite loudly. It was one of the things she hated about herself, but it was how she was and she had to live with it.

Next to her, Iris's shoulders were shaking, but they both knew they would have to contain their mirth until the big old railway clock on the wall ticked its last second up to six o'clock when it would be time to pack up and go home.

The whole West family turned out for the benefit. It was the night before Christmas Eve. There was a clear inky black sky, winking stars and a crisp coating of snow underfoot. Even Mary's grandmother had been persuaded to leave her air-raid shelter, having been given the promise that there was to be no raid that night, and even if there was, there was a perfectly good shelter beneath the band rostrum at the Palais de Danse.

'It's a long time since I was at the Pally,' Mary's gran said as she walked breathlessly between Mary and Helen in the centre of the group. 'Eeh, I used to love dancin', I did, but I always got the little fellas askin' me up to dance. And if they wus big, they wus too big and I used to get a creek in me neck lookin' up at them.'

'I bet you were a little belter in your youth, Gran,' said Trevor, who was carrying young Carol in his arms. 'Bet you broke a few hearts, eh?'

'Oh, I did me share, ye know.' Everybody laughed as the old woman's feet went out from under her, but she was held firm by her two granddaughters. 'Eeh, divvint let us fall on me bum, lassies! Them seats are awful hard at the Pally, I'll bet.'

'Who's giving out the prizes tonight, Mary?' Jenny West asked from behind.

'Well, Jack Langley's going to do the judging and Dr Gordon's handing out the prizes,' Mary said. 'They tried to get somebody important from Gateshead or Newcastle, but there are big functions happening over there tonight as well.'

'I'd say Dr Gordon's important enough for Felling,' Jenny said fondly, for in her eyes there was no one better than the big, brusque Scot.

'He does my chest good,' said Grandma West and they all laughed again. 'Now what did I say that was so funny? I've been under that man for years and I always feel better for it.'

'Oh, aye, Mam?' Frank West winked at his wife and that set them all off again, so it was a very merry band that kicked the snow from their boots as they entered through the impressive foyer of the Palais de Danse a few minutes later.

The first person Mary got her eye on was the unlikely figure of Effie Donaldson handing out tickets in the box office. She smiled warmly at the girl as her dad forked out for the entrance tickets.

'Hello, Effie. Remember me? I didn't know you worked here.'

'Oh, it's you, is it?' There was nothing friendly about the dark frown and the knitted black brows that had been plucked pencil-thin since the last time they had met. 'I work here weekends. It makes a change from layin' oot dead people. So, how's the pensions place, then?'

'Not as exciting as you might think,' Mary said, a slow, cautious smile spreading on her face.

'Aw, get her!' Effie remarked, then got busy counting out the shillings and the pennies Frank West had passed over to her. She did so with surprising speed, finding it to be not quite right. 'Ye're a tanner short, mister. Look here . . .'

Before Frank could argue that he had given her the right money, she counted out every coin before their eyes, causing complaints from the people starting to queue up behind the West family.

'Aye, she's right, Mr West,' Trevor said and dug deep in his pocket for the missing sixpence. 'There ye are, pet. Keep the change, eh?'

'Funny bugger!' Effie glowered at him through the glass partition behind which she was sitting on a high stool, made higher for her by two thick cushions, otherwise she would hardly have been able to see over the ticket-machine.

The hall was already heaving with bodies, everybody animated with excitement and high expectations. Tables with crisp white linen cloths circled the big dance-floor, which was waxed to a brilliant shine, and so slippery that some of the girls were rubbing the soles of their dancing shoes with sandpaper to prevent any dangerous skidding when the dancing got lively.

And it promised to get lively all right. The two vocalists of Jack Langley's band were going to demonstrate the new jitterbug dancing they'd come across during a recent tour of America. Mary wasn't the only one looking forward to trying out the new steps.

'Let's find a table near the stage before they're all taken,' Jenny West said, leading the way.

'Where's the lavatory?' Mary's grandmother wanted to know as soon as she was seated, squinting in the bright lights after the darkness of the black-out night. 'I can't settle happily if I don't know where the lav is.'

'It's all right, Gran,' Mary told her, slipping an arm about the frail old shoulders. 'I'll take you when you're ready.'

'Better go now, then it's done,' Annie West said, sticking out her lips in a big pout as she searched the building for the WC signs. 'Then I'll want a cup of tea and a nice bit of cake.'

'It's all right, Mary,' Helen said. 'I'll take Gran to the lavatory. You go and help Mam with the refreshments.'

Mary nodded and followed her mother to the refreshments table, which was being run by the ladies of the Women's Institute, so there was a good chance of the cakes being of the highest quality. The ladies of the twin sets and pearls were so highly competitive with their cooking that they always used the best ingredients available and usually got everything right.

Armed with supper tickets for the whole family, Mary and Jenny filled two trays with food, surprised at how much there was, considering everything was about to be rationed.

'Oh, just look at that chocolate cake!' Mary exclaimed and started to reach out for a piece, but someone stepped in front of her and blocked her way.

'You're only supposed to take enough food for one,' the young woman said with a manner that was so stiff her jaws must have been bonded together with cement.

'I beg your pardon, miss,' Mary's mother said, quite put out at hearing her daughter spoken to in such a manner. 'But there are nine of us, plus my daughter's fiancé, who we've paid for, but he's coming later.'

The young woman with the shoulder-length fair hair and the tight skirt, turned around and they could see she was ready for an argument by the narrowing of her cool grey-blue eyes.

'Let me see your tickets?'

'We gave them in to your colleague over there.' Jenny nodded to the plump, middle-aged woman at the other end of the table. 'Ask her if you don't believe us.'

'This is quite irregular,' the woman said, her mouth tightening into a thin, straight line. 'Stay here. Don't move from this spot . . .'

However, before she herself could move, a familiar figure suddenly materialized beside her, almost as stern, but not quite as formidable.

'Is there a problem, Fiona? Why Mary . . . ah, and Mrs West! How nice to see you.' Dr Gordon greeted them amicably. 'And I see you've got all the family with you, even Mrs West senior. You must take her a piece of apple-pie. My wife made it and, if I say so myself, it deserves a prize.'

The woman called Fiona looked indignant and walked back to mutter something to the lady in charge, but seemed to get short shrift from there too and marched off huffily.

'Have we done something wrong, Dr Gordon?' Mary's mother wanted to know; she was a stickler for doing everything right by the book and would be mortified to be found contravening any rule or regulation. 'We did buy sufficient tickets for all of us and they told us to help ourselves, but that young woman seemed to think we were stealing the food.'

Dr Gordon bristled as he looked after the woman with the blonde hair and the cool manner.

'Och, take no notice. Fiona obviously made a mistake. She's been in a bad mood all day and if I could find that nephew of mine I'd ask him why.'

'Your nephew?' Mary asked, puzzled. 'Dr Craig?'

'Aye. That's his wife.'

'Oh, I see.' Mary looked more closely at the woman, who was now standing in the entrance to the foyer with an air about her of someone spoiling for a fight. It was a pity, she thought, that Dr Craig had such a dragon for a wife, and maybe that had something to do with why he was so dour and preoccupied.

There was a high-pitched scream from the microphone, then a deafening roll on the drums got everybody's attention. Mary's grandmother had to be stopped from donning her gas-mask – and Mary hung on to her in case she decided to duck under a table and embarrass them all by refusing to come out.

'Ladies and gentlemen!' Bandleader Jack Langley was on stage, fronting his twenty-piece dance band, and he was addressing the mass of people who were gathered in the hall. 'Can I ask you to take your seats please, so the show can begin? First, we've got some announcements and, while you have your supper, there's a talk by the Honourable Mrs Benjamin-Smythe of the WVS on how best to cope in times of war. After which, we'll have the talent contest and end the evening with some dancing.'

At that point, Dr Gordon excused himself and the West family found a table that was so near the band the older ladies complained that they would be deaf before the evening was out.

Mary listened to the talk with only half an ear. Her attention kept wandering as she wondered where Walter had got to. He had warned her that he might be late, but she thought he should have been there long before now. She would have liked his support while she was on stage doing her turn, but it didn't look as if he was going to make it. Well, as long as he arrived before the dancing. She would never forgive him if he left her sitting all alone like a wallflower. Of course, there were other men there whom she could dance with, but it wouldn't look right, her being engaged to Walter.

Mrs Benjamin-Smythe, an experienced speaker, took them through the possibilities and the eventualities of war and how to deal with them all. She paid special attention to the economies women would have to make, should the war stretch out beyond the next few months, when everything would be rationed or unavailable. Old clothes would have to be made over or reinforced, meals would have to be tailored to suit the most meagre supply of provisions; paper and scrap metal would have to be saved.

And so on, and so on. Everyone had heard it all before, and it was boring as a form of entertainment, but Mary supposed it was necessary. The war had hardly made a dent in Britain as yet, but constraints were already being felt.

'I won't bend your ears any longer,' said Mrs Benjamin-Smythe at long last and there were audible sighs of relief rippling through the hall. 'Just remember that in war-time there is no waste. Everything must be saved and used over and over and over again.'

'Like us soldiers!' came the cry from the back where there was a small group of newly drafted privates in their crisp khaki uniforms, both men and uniforms lacking in age and experience.

'Aye, man!' came a second cry, this time from a blond, fresh-faced youth in sailor's uniform. 'Three cheers for the red, white and blue and look out, Hitler, here we come.'

'Yes,' muttered Mrs Benjamin-Smythe as the hall erupted into three deafening cheers. 'Yes, yes . . . very good . . . yes. Now, if the contestants for the talent competition could assemble backstage, please. . . ?'

'Go on, then, our Mary,' said Frank West, smiling proudly at his younger daughter. 'Go and show them what you can do.'

Everybody at the table made encouraging sounds and Mary found herself suddenly wishing that she hadn't told everybody she was going in for the competition. Having had time to look around her, she had noticed a good many people there whom she knew, including Mr Hornby from the War Pensions Office and one or two others who worked there, as well as a group of her friends and neighbours who had somehow found out about it. They were all looking in her direction and grinning, one or two of them making remarks behind their hands, which she was glad she couldn't hear.

'Why isn't Walter here?' she said as she rose to her feet uncertainly. 'He promised me.'

'Oh, go on, Mary.' Helen gave her a little push. 'Walter wasn't going to be up there on stage with you, was he? You go and give it your best and never mind Walter.'

'She's right, lass,' her Aunty Bella said, nudging her husband, Arthur, and winking around the table. 'We've all heard you sing like that Deanna Durbin, so get up there and prove it to the rest of the world.'

Mary swallowed with difficulty and followed the stream of contestants backstage, her legs feeling rubbery, her heart palpitating. Jack Langley himself was there to meet them, and making sure the band had the right music at the ready. When Mary told him she was going to sing 'My Own', which was, indeed, one of Deanna Durbin's best ballades, he twinkled at her.

'Singing it to your sweetheart are you, love?' he asked.

'Well, I hope so, but he's not here yet,' Mary said.

'Weren't you the girl who used to come in and listen to us practising? I haven't seen you for a while.'

'No, I don't work at Harper's any more. I changed my job.'

'Hope you got something that'll keep you near the home fires,' he said and wandered off to sort out the rest of the contestants.

The competition got started with a small girl singing 'An Apple for the Teacher', which attracted a loud applause because of the child's innocent, wavery voice and cute lisp. Next came the Beresford twins with their penny whistles and a very slow version of 'Little Sir Echo' with a few missed notes and embarrassed grins all round. Iris came next, with a selection of badly memorized jokes of Flanagan and Allen. She left the stage in tears, but was comforted by a rather good-looking soldier, so she was soon smiling again and wishing Mary good luck. But before it was Mary's turn, there was a barbershop quartet, an Irish tenor and old Mr Dolan playing his spoons, though it was impossible to make out which tune he rattled them to.

At last, it was Mary's turn and she stood in front of the microphone, her knees knocking, her mouth dry. As the band played the introductory notes of her song, her eyes skimmed the hall, desperately searching for Walter, but he wasn't there. She started singing on cue, aware that her voice sounded weak and nervous, then suddenly she saw someone at the back of the crowd. Someone who was giving her his full attention, smiling and nodding his approval.

But it wasn't Walter. It was Dr Craig. Mary focused on him and fixed her gaze firmly so that she could see no other person. Thankfully, her confidence returned, and with it her voice.

'My own . . .' she sang as sweetly as she knew how. 'Let me call you my own. . .'

The hall erupted as the song ended and even the band stood to applaud. It was such an emotional moment she might have wept had she not been surrounded by the other contestants as they waited nervously backstage for the results.

While Jack Langley and his panel of judges conferred, the band played a medley of songs, and cups of tea were passed around each table. Mary caught sight of Helen hurrying her grandmother to the ladies' lavatory and hoped they would be back in time for the announcement. Now that her song was over, her knees had stopped knocking, but she was still burning with excitement. Later, she might give Walter a piece of her mind for not turning up, but right now she wanted to enjoy the feeling of achievement. They had actually liked her singing. Dr Craig had liked it too, she was sure. She didn't know why that should be important to her, but it was.

Five minutes later Jack strode back on to the stage, a sheet of paper in his hand. He placed himself in front of the microphone and waited until a hush descended.

'Well, here we are, ladies and gentlemen. I have the results of our wonderful talent competition here in my hand. Only a slight change of plan . . .' He glanced over his shoulder, nodding to someone in the wings.

'As you know, Dr Gordon was to present the prizes this evening, but there's been a slight technical hitch.' There was a murmur of disappointment. 'Apparently, Mrs Hutchinson has decided to give birth before her time, so the good doctor has been called to assist. However, at no expense spared, we have his deputy on hand and willing to do the job for him. Please give a big hand and a warm welcome to Dr Alex Craig . . . or should I say *Captain* Craig!'

Mary felt a stirring deep within her as hands met in a thunderous applause when Alex Craig walked on to the stage, not in his civilian clothes, but in an Army uniform that bore the insignia of captain in the Medical Corps. He looked very smart and very handsome, standing there, acknowledging the standing ovation. Mary could see Dr Gordon's wife desperately wiping away tears of emotion and something tugged at her own heartstrings.

All the contestants were given small token mementoes of the occasion in the form of a certificate. The children received sweets and a bar of chocolate. Mr Dolan received a bottle of Newcastle Brown ale for his courage and audacity, rather than for his clackety spoons and everybody roared with laughter when he announced that he wouldn't drink the contents of the bottle until the last all-clear was sounded.

'And now, the moment you've all been waiting for,' Jack told them, his face lighting up. 'The prize for the best act here this evening. It wasn't difficult, was it? It goes to Felling's own little nightingale . . . Miss Mary West!'

Mary gulped and took half a pace backwards in her surprise, before eager hands pushed her forward and there she was, the grand winner, but what was the prize? She looked from Dr Craig's penetrating gaze, which she found rather embarrassing, to Jack Langley's smiling face and waited. Jack held up his hands for silence.

'The prize, ladies and gentlemen, is a cheque for ten guineas, generously donated by Dr Gordon, and presented by Captain Craig. Go on, sir, and give the girl a kiss too. It might be your last opportunity before you go and look after the sick and the wounded in this damned war.'

The hall erupted yet again. Mary felt her mouth drop open with astonishment. Well, that was a turn up for the books, she thought, and serve Walter right if he had just arrived and saw it happening. And, oh, what were her mam and dad thinking right now? And what about Mrs Craig, that haughty female with the bad temper and the cold eyes?

'Congratulations, Mary,' Dr Craig placed his hands on her shoulders and she felt the warmth of them penetrating the soft fabric of her dress.

Beneath the warmth her skin suddenly tingled, and as he smiled down at her and lowered his head towards hers, the tingling spread throughout her rigid body.

It was only a chaste kiss on the cheek, but it did something to Mary that no kiss had ever achieved. If only, she thought, Walter's kiss would make her feel like this. She wouldn't be keeping him waiting. She would be marching him down the aisle before he could say Jack Robinson.

'Thank you,' was all she could say, her voice croaking deep in her throat.

For an instant, their eyes met and in that one small passage of time something passed between them that Mary would remember for the rest of her life.

'And now, ladies and gentlemen,' Jack was continuing, 'I'm going to ask all the contestants here on stage to join hands and sing with the band . . .' He shaded his eyes, then pointed in a swinging arc into the crowd. 'And all you servicemen out there can come up and join us. If you can't sing, whistle.'

Mary felt her hand being clasped. Dr Craig was still there at her side, holding her hand so tightly that she could feel the bones of her fingers crunch, but she didn't mind. She didn't mind at all. On the other side of her Iris sidled up, linking arms with her.

'Lucky beggar,' her friend whispered, and Mary guessed that Iris was referring to Dr Craig's kiss rather than her success with the talent competition.

As regimental-issue booted feet clumped up on to the rostrum, the band struck up with the poignant song that they heard so much these days. 'Wish me luck as you wave me goodbye, cheerio, here I go on my way . . .'

Mary could hear Dr Craig's rich baritone voice next to her and although she sang her own heart out with a smile, not a tear, she had a terrible sinking feeling in her stomach mingling with a strange excitement. She found herself squeezing his hand back and wondering again where his wife was and why she wasn't here supporting him, loving him, crying for what he was about to do.

After the last notes of the song died and the audience pulled the place apart with their applause, couples immediately took to the floor and danced the foxtrot. Mary smiled shyly at Dr Craig and made her way back to her table, where the West family were ready to congratulate her with hugs and more kisses.

The evening continued with a full programme of dancing, including some hilarious demonstrations of the American dances they had all heard of but had never seen, other than in flashes on the Pathé newsreels at the cinema.

'What is it they're doing, our Mary?' Old Mrs West prodded Mary with a crooked finger and waited while the laughter died down so she could hear Mary's response.

'It's the jitterbug, Gran,' Mary told her. 'The Americans invented it.'

'Jitterbug! I thought that was a creepy crawly that you stamped your foot on.'

'Well, it certainly has people stamping their feet,' Mary laughed, feeling her whole body react to the fast, cheerful music.

But even the jitterbug couldn't hold Mary's concentration for long. Her thoughts were too distracted, swinging between Walter and Dr Craig, and that kiss. And Walter still wasn't here, as he should have been. And neither was Alex Craig's wife. And Alex was sitting there at the other side of the hall, all alone at a tiny table for two, staring into his empty glass. She looked across at him, her heart thumping hollowly in her chest, her emotions tying themselves into knots.

'Eeh, Mary, love!' Jenny reached across the table and tapped Mary's hand. 'Just look who's here at last.'

And there was Walter, apologetic and flushed, making his way clumsily through the dancers on the floor. She gave him a wave, wondering why she should feel so flat, but put it down to the fact that she was not exactly pleased with him for letting her down like this.

'Where have you been, Walter? The night's almost over.'

'Sorry, pet, but I met up with some of the lads and we got talking, and . . .' Walter took a deep breath. 'I've decided to join up.'

'You've what? Mam! Dad! Walter's going to join up.' Mary turned back to Walter and caught a whiff of stale beer on his breath. 'You've been drinking, Walter Morgan!'

'Aye, I have. Just a couple of pints.'

'Oh, Walter! What's your mam going to say when she finds out?'

'That's the reason I'm so late. I went home first to tell them.' Walter took out his handkerchief and mopped his perspiring brow. 'Dad was all right about it, but Mam nearly had kittens. It's taken us all this time to calm her down. I think she might have liked it better if I'd joined the Royal Air Force, but you know me and heights. Those planes fly very high.'

Mary blew out her cheeks. She wasn't sure what to say, what to think.

'I won the talent competition, Walter,' she said and he looked at her as if she had spoken in Chinese before it registered.

'Oh, I forgot about that. You won it? Well done, pet. What did you get as a prize?'

'Ten guineas and . . .' she hesitated, 'and a kiss from Dr Craig.'

'Oh!' Then his heavy brows came down as he studied her closely. 'Mary, now that I'm probably going to be sent away overseas . . . well, away from the north-east, anyway . . . .how about us getting married? We can get a special licence and . . .'

'What? Oh, Walter, I don't know . . . I . . .'

Mary had never felt so flustered, or so pushed into a tight corner. She stared at him, her tongue flicking in and out, as she tried to moisten her dry lips.

'We can get hitched before I have to go to Catterick training camp. Come on, lass. We've waited long enough.'

Mary glanced around the table, glad that nobody else had heard. They were all too busy watching the gyrations on the floor, laughing hysterically at the antics of some folk who threw themselves around and called it dancing.

'Not here, Walter . . . please . . .' Mary said as the music changed and Jack Langley was introducing the last waltz. 'Let's dance, eh? It's the last waltz and I haven't had a dance all evening.'

'Aw, bloomin' heck, Mary. Give over, will you.' Walter pulled his arm away from her grasp as she tried to haul him up on his feet. 'I hate dancing. You know that. Why don't you get up with somebody else, eh?'

'Who do you suggest, Walter?'

She hadn't spoken the words too loudly, but one or two heads turned and she felt her cheeks burn. However, it wasn't the head-turning that she found disconcerting. It was the fact that Dr Craig was standing right beside her. In fact, she had bumped into him, rather heavily as she stood up. He gave her that enigmatic smile of his that didn't quite reach his eyes. Then he was looking at Walter.

'Would you mind,' he asked Walter, 'if Mary danced the last waltz with me?'

'Aye, go on then,' Walter said, after a moment's hesitation, then he added the word 'sir' on seeing the doctor's army rank.

The short walk between table and dance floor was completely lost on Mary. She couldn't remember how her legs had carried her the distance. It was as if she had been magically transported. One minute she was trying to persuade Walter to dance and the next, well, here she was whirling in the arms of Dr Alex Craig who looked so good in his captain's uniform and danced so well. And she was determined to enjoy the experience, since it might be the last time she would ever see him.

'You dance as beautifully as you sing, Mary,' he said, his warm breath wafting across her forehead, stirring stray tendrils of hair that she had tried in vain to straighten and capture in a blue slide to match her dress.

'Thank you,' she said, thinking that she sounded like a star-struck little girl, and feeling exactly like that. 'So do you, Dr Craig . . . .er . . . Captain Craig . . .'

He threw back his head and laughed. 'I'd prefer it if you dropped all titles and called me Alex, since it's my last night here.'

'Oh, but . . .' She raised her eyes to his, conscious of his arm tightening around her and again the firm squeeze of his hand. Goodness, was he flirting with her? No, she was sure it wasn't that, but . . . 'Shouldn't you be dancing with your wife . . . Alex?'

A cloud came over his face. A dark, unfathomable cloud. She thought she must have said the wrong thing and he was angry with her, but when he spoke, his voice was soft, almost like a caress.

'My wife prefers to be elsewhere, Mary. I'm being selfish, but please, just humour me for the rest of this dance.'

The rest of the dance was too short by far. Mary wished with every step that it would last for ever. And in the same breath, she told herself how stupid it was to feel like this about a man she hardly knew, and could never have.

CHAPTER FOUR

'EEH, when we all stood up and sung 'Auld Lang Syne' I wept buckets!'

Jenny West was chattering merrily about Saturday night's benefit as she and Mary dished out the Christmas Day lunch for the family gathered about the table in the living-room. The old table had been extended as long as was possible and everybody was squeezed in, elbow to elbow, but they didn't mind. It was Christmas and they were all putting the war on hold and enjoying themselves.

'You weren't the only one, Mam,' Mary said, spooning sage and onion stuffing on each plate as her mother sliced off more turkey. 'There were quite a few tears and not all of them were from women either.'

'A bit more stuffing on your dad's plate, Mary,' Jenny said, inspecting the row of plates that were lined up on every available surface in the scullery, which was full of steam and the succulent smells of roasting meat and boiling vegetables. 'And give him an extra roast potato. He needs building up with all the extra work he's doing these days. I don't know. In the pit all day, patrolling the streets at night. He'll knock himself up.'

'He's wiry, Mam. He'll be all right. Anyway, I'm sure it makes him feel better, knowing he's doing his bit for England.'

Mary's father had been one of the many veterans of the First World War to stand to attention with tears welling up in their eyes as the band had played the very last tune of the night at the benefit. Mary herself had found it hard to get the emotional wobble out of her voice as she sang the words to 'God Save the King'.

As she sang, she had turned and found Alex Craig's brooding eyes on her. Something in his expression touched her heart, reaching into her innermost being. She felt a deep sorrow for all the men and boys who were going out to fight for their country in a foreign land. Many of them, she knew, would never come back. But what she felt for this young doctor was something she could not explain, except to say that when she regarded Walter, that special feeling wasn't there.

'And you say Walter's not going to join us today, pet?' Jenny asked for the umpteenth time. 'There's nothing wrong between you and him, is there?'

Mary blanched, picked up two plates without looking her mother in the eye, and headed for the table.

'Of course there isn't, Mam,' she said over her shoulder. 'He just felt he should spend his last Christmas with his mother before going off to Catterick.'

'Here, come back. You've forgotten the sprouts.'

She went back for the missing vegetables and saw her mother looking at her in an oddly wise and penetrating way.

'What's up with you, our Mary?' Jenny said. 'You've been acting funny ever since the benefit. I know you were a bit put out because Walter came so late and then wouldn't dance with you, but . . . No, there's something else, isn't there? You're not getting all het up over that Dr Craig, are you?'

'Mam! You do say the daftest things.'

'Do I?' Jenny was wearing her concerned mother's expression. 'Maybe it's daft, maybe it's not, but I saw the way he looked at you on Saturday night.'

'Oh, Mam, stop it. He was just being pleasant.'

'Aye, and you were lapping it up, my girl. I don't want any daughter of mine going out of her way to flirt with a married man. Do you hear me, Mary?'

'Yes, Mam, but you don't have to worry. Anyway, Alex comes from a very different background.'

'So, it's Alex now, is it? And never mind the different background. Men are men the whole world over and if a girl shows herself to be willing, well . . . you know what can happen. Just look at that Sadie Hurst. What a disgrace. Saddled with a bairn and no man to support her because he was already married with a family of his own. Just you think about that, hinny.'

'Yes, Mam.' Mary felt her cheeks burning hotly. 'Is that it? Can I take these plates in now before everybody starves with hunger?'

'Oh, go on with you.' Jenny tapped her daughter's behind as she walked away. 'I know you're a good girl, really. You'll always do the right thing.'

'I hope so, Mam,' Mary muttered under her breath as she handed out the plates and went back for more to shouts of 'Where's mine?' and 'That

Walter doesn't know what he's missing, the daft begger!'

Mary joined them at the table as they pulled their crackers, donned silly paper-hats, blew on plastic whistles and generally acted like children. She enjoyed the fun, but her mind kept wandering. She didn't think that Walter would ever excite her the way Alex Craig had in that briefest of moments. And she couldn't suppress the burning desire to do something more challenging than keeping the ledgers up to date at the War Pensions Office. Both issues would have to be addressed, and soon.

In the Graham household the atmosphere wasn't quite so jovial. Alex did his best to pretend that all was well, but he wasn't fooling anybody, least of all himself. A part of him couldn't wait to leave. The sooner he removed himself from his flawed marriage the better. He regretted leaving his uncle in the lurch, alone to cope with a busy practice; and Aunt Maggie was like a second mother to him. Neither of them wanted him to go, although they said very little on the subject, which meant they probably understood more about his situation than he had given them credit for.

Fiona had said little to him, other than 'Brave old you!' when he told her he had enlisted. They hadn't spoken of it again in private. In the company of others she tended to keep her own counsel and replied to enquiries on how she felt with a resigned shrug and an acquiescent smile. At a guess, she would be glad to see the back of him. There was already someone waiting to slip conveniently into his shoes – in fact, already had, if Alex's suspicions were correct. Fiona hadn't admitted to having an affair, but it didn't take a genius to work out what was going on.

'Are you all right, son?' Maggie Graham gave him a searching look as they stood in the kitchen together, drying dishes. Fiona was lying down on the spare bed with a migraine. 'You seem a little quiet.'

'I'm fine, Aunt Maggie,' Alex assured her. 'Don't you go worrying about me.'

'Do you really think the war will go on for much longer?'

'Quite honestly, I think it's only just beginning.'

Maggie shook her head, her eyes clouded with troubling thoughts. She put the last of the dishes away and relieved him of his tea-towel.

'You shouldn't be in here with me,' she said gruffly. 'Go and spend some time with your wife.'

He gave her a wry smile. The rupture in his marriage, he felt sure, was such a tangible thing it must be obvious to all and sundry that things were not going well. Nobody liked the idea of divorce and the stigma that was attached to it. Alex hoped it would not come to that. Perhaps an enforced separation was all that was needed to get them back on track again.

'I think, if you don't mind,' he said, kissing his aunt on her warm cheek, 'I'll go out for a wee walk and breathe some good fresh Felling air. My head's full of things that need sweeping out.'

'Alex. . . ?' she said, but when he raised his eyebrows, she shook her head again. 'Go on, then. Things do always seem better for a walk. But mind you come back in time for tea. I've baked all your favourite things.'

'Custard tart?'

'Aye, and lemon-meringue pie,' she said. 'And there's a salmon salad to start with.'

'I'll be back, don't you worry,' Alex grinned.

He stood on the doorstep for a few moments, breathing in the crisp December air, then decided to head for the park. Usually, it was quiet down there, but this was Christmas Day and there were a number of fathers and grandfathers with young children on new toboggans.

He listened to their elated laughter as they were dragged over the ground or skimmed screaming with excitement down the frozen slopes, narrowly missing the trees and falling off and rolling around as they stopped. Perhaps he would have a child of his own, one day, to buy a toboggan for, though he doubted it somehow. Fiona had made her views on the subject crystal-clear. There was, of course, the possibility that she would see things differently after the war.

An unexpected tightening of his throat surprised him. He quickened his step almost to a march as he headed back up the hill, but went a different way towards Victoria Square. The place was deserted except for one or two old miners sitting around the memorial fountain in the centre, putting the world to rights. They nodded across to him, called out seasonal greetings, which he returned automatically. He was experiencing a tremendous feeling of belonging, yet did he really think he was coming back here? Was there a life here for him after the war? Would there be a life anywhere? Even if he survived it, what would he come back to? A wife who didn't want him. But then, Fiona wasn't entirely to blame, was she? To be honest, they had never been an ideal couple. After the first flush of passion had died, they had been left with nothing on which to build a marriage or a future.

As he started to turn back towards his uncle's house, Alex caught sight of a familiar figure trudging cagily through the snow that had deepened overnight and showed no sign of melting, regardless of the fact that the sun was shining down from a blue sky.

'Hello, there!'

The girl must have been deep in thought, for she pulled up so sharply that she skidded and would have fallen if she hadn't grabbed hold of a nearby gatepost. Her soft hazel eyes blinked at him, then her expression became like that of a startled deer as she recognized him.

'Oh . . . .Dr Craig! H-hello! Merry Christmas!'

'Merry Christmas to you, Mary . . . and it's Alex, remember?'

'Alex . . . yes . . . only it feels funny calling my doctor by his Christian name.'

'If it makes you feel uncomfortable, then don't,' he said, walking up to her and taking her arm, for she was still looking unsteady as her feet struggled to gain purchase on the patch of ice beneath her.

'Oh, it's all right . . . I mean. . . .' Mary clamped her lips together, then gave a shy laugh. 'It's just unusual, that's all.'

'We're living in unusual times, Mary,' he said, helping her to walk a few steps away from the ice and on to less precarious ground. 'Where are you off to?'

'I've been invited to my friend's for tea,' she told him. 'Iris and I work together at the War Pensions Office.'

'You're not spending the day with your fiancé, then?'

He detected a small hesitation and she averted her eyes, though it might have been because the afternoon sun was blinding her. 'No. Not today. Walter's planning to join up and his mother's upset about it. He thought it would be best staying at home today.'

'I see.' Alex cupped her elbow in his hand as they moved forward, away from the square and down The Drive, where his uncle lived. 'Do you mind if I walk with you, Mary?'

'Of course not.' She looked up and frowned. 'When do you leave?'

'In a few days.'

'Oh, I see. How awful.'

'I wonder . . . could I ask you a favour?' They had come to a halt and he turned to face her, telling himself that he was crazy to expect anything of this rather nice young woman who would probably marry the local butcher, have numerous children with him, and be a faithful and loving wife. 'Would you write to me, Mary?'

'Write to you? But won't your wife be—'

'She hates writing anything, especially letters. Please say you'll write to me, Mary . . . unless you would find it too much of a chore.'

He saw her swallow and ponder on what he had requested. It obviously bothered her in some way, and yet her eyes were bright and keen.

'No, really, I'd love to write to you. My address—'

'I know your address, Mary.' He wasn't going to tell her that he had already noted it and it was at this very moment sitting in his wallet, in his inside breast pocket. 'I'll drop you a line once I get settled. Letters have to go through the British Forces Postal Office. They're censored, apparently, so don't worry if you can't read all the words. And I might not always be able to reply straight away.'

'Don't worry,' Mary said with a bright smile that gave a lift to his heart. 'I'll wait.'

He wished it were his wife telling him that she would wait, not just for his letters, but for him to return. He wished that his wife could be more like Mary and less like the girl he should never have married.

'I enjoyed dancing with you on Saturday night,' he said, his voice roughening slightly in his throat.

'Me too,' she said and took a step away from him. 'Well, I'd better get along or they'll think I'm not coming.'

'What about the black-out? It'll get dark pretty soon.'

'It's all right. Iris says I can stay the night.'

'That's all right then. Take care, Mary.'

'I always do, Alex.'

The street was deserted, except for the two of them. He knew it was a damned foolish thing to do, but suddenly she was there in his arms and he was kissing her. Oh, it was a tender kiss, at first. Tender and, almost, innocent. Then, when there was a sudden rise of heat between them, he felt her pull away, heard her gasp.

'Oh, God, Mary, I'm sorry. I don't know what made me do that, but we may never see each other again. I just felt impelled to . . . .well, never mind. I apologize. Are we still friends?'

She was staring at him, her eyes as big as dinner plates swimming with light, her mouth slightly open and her breath coming in gusts with every rise and fall of her chest. She swallowed hard before she could get her words out.

'It . . . It's all right . . . really. I . . . I'm glad you did it . . . I . . .' Her forehead creased and then she gave a wan smile that twisted his heart. 'It is Christmas, after all, and you're going off to the war and . . . I *will* write to you, I promise.'

And with those words she hurried away, leaving him standing there feeling cold and empty, and utterly ridiculous.

In between the clicking of knitting needles and the hiss of a copper kettle on the old gas-ring in the church hall kitchen, the ladies of the Social Services Club chatted spasmodically. They were there for a variety of reasons, but mostly to help the war effort, turning up come rain or come shine ever since war had been declared.

Mary's mind, however, was wandering. Alex's leave had been cancelled. She had seen him only once since he joined up. It was a short, stolen moment and she felt guilty about it, though they had done nothing to be ashamed of; just walked, talked and laughed a lot.

She sighed, thinking how she longed to have him back with her now, have him touch her, kiss her. But he always kept at a respectable distance, even though she sensed that he saw something in their relationship that was more than casual.

Mary had come along today with her mother, who was a founder member of the Social Services Club. The women had given her a grand welcome. All help, they told her, was gratefully received since they weren't too numerous. Two of their ladies were expecting babies and not up to hours of non-stop knitting on hard kitchen chairs and church benches. Four other young women had joined up. One was with the ATS, two had gone to the Land Army and the fourth was now with the FANYs.

'I've heard of the FANYs,' Mary said. 'Anne Beasley's with them.'

'It's voluntary, of course,' said one woman. 'But I hear they do a grand job.'

'They used to wear red jackets when they were first formed,' said another and everyone laughed. 'That must have made it easy for the enemy to spot.'

'That Miss Croft up Cube Pit way used to be one, so I hear.'

'Good gracious! Maybe that's why she's so miserable and crotchety. I always put it down to her being an old maid.'

'Aye. Men do tend to drive you mad, one way or another. It seems to me that being without one is just as bad as t'other way round, if you know what I mean.'

There was more laughter, then the vicar's wife presented Mary with a pair of knitting-needles and a ball of grey wool.

'It's nice to see that even a young, single woman can find the time to support us, Mary,' she said and there was a murmur of agreement.

'There aren't many young people around any more, these days,' said one stout lady in a floral frock, a black, squashed, felt hat and a skein of wool in her outstretched hands.

'No, you're right there,' said a thin, sticklike creature with horn-rimmed glasses. She stitched away at some garment or other, her needle flying in and out and missing the earlobe of the woman next to her by a fraction of an inch. 'They think war's something to enjoy – you know, gives them something exciting to do.'

'They'll find out it's not like that,' said a morose woman dressed in black who had lost her husband in the First World War. 'You stay at home with your mam as long as they'll let you, Mary, love.'

As Jenny West went to scald the tea in the big brown teapot, the needles came to an abrupt halt at the wail of the air-raid siren. As always, Mary's skin crept with the fear the sound instilled in her, but she no longer felt sheer panic. They all knew that most of the warnings were for the coastal areas. A scattering of German bombs had been dropping on the north of England since May, but, except in freak circumstances, they felt pretty safe where they were.

'Should we go to the shelter, then?' A jolly-faced woman with strands of wool spilling out of voluminous pockets in her wraparound pinny, looked at her companions, who didn't show any signs of moving.

'Is it worth it?'

'It's a damn sight colder down in that shelter than it is up here. We're more likely to die of pneumonia than a bomb.'

'I read in the paper this morning that this winter's been the coldest winter since 1881. Can you believe that?'

'Aye, I can. The water froze in the tap last month and we had to scrape the ice off the inside of the bedroom windows.'

'I wish I'd seen the River Thames when it froze over. I bet that was a sight for sore eyes, eh?'

'Well, if the Tyne ever freezes I'll be able to skate over to Newcastle instead of catching the tram.'

'Once we get this month over things should start getting better.'

'Aye, I hate February. Always have.'

Mary watched and listened to the conversation carried on through the warning cry of the siren. Then it stopped and all, including the women, fell silent. Only the click of the knitting-needles continued, some slowing down to a soft swish, others going fast enough to strike sparks.

Distant aircraft droned, followed by a loud explosion that made the building shiver and the floor beneath them vibrate. The *rat-a-tat-tat* of ground fire followed immediately. Mary caught sight of her mother, pouring tea and passing it around with hands that weren't quite steady, but only her eyes betrayed the fact that she was really scared. They were all scared, but none of them wanted to show it.

Woooooo-ooooo! There were sighs all around as the all-clear blew. The knitting and the sewing were put to one side and the women relaxed, drank their tea and ate the rock buns that the vicar's wife had so generously provided for them.

'I wonder if they got them?'

'Who?'

'Those blinking Gerries, that's who? How dare they think they can get the better of us? They lost the last war and, by God, they'll not win this one.'

'You going to go over there and give them what for, are you, Minnie?'

'I hear one of them crashed the other day. Our lads shot him down just off Whitby.'

'Aye, I read about that. It was a handsome young lad that did it. Flight Lieutenant Peter Townsend, he was called. Comes from a posh background, but it makes no difference, does it, when you're faced with kill or be killed. They're all just canny lads when it boils down to it, and some poor mother's sons. Bairns, the lot of them.'

The conversation had taken up where it left off, almost as though the air-raid had never happened. Mary looked down at her knitting and groaned when she saw the mess she had made of her stitches. And she was only knitting a scarf, too.

'Eeh, our Mary!' her mother came and stood beside her, taking the needles from her and holding her work up for all to see, which produced a ripple of kindly laughter. 'This lass of mine can sing and dance like an angel, she's good at English ... we won't mention arithmetic ... can speak fluent French and a bit of German ... and just look at the way she knits.'

'Leave the bairn alone, Jenny. With all those talents and a face like one of them Leonardo da Vinci portraits, she can be forgiven for not being a good knitter.'

'Aye, pet, come on. Never mind the knitting. Give us a song to cheer us up. I remember you at that Christmas benefit. No wonder you got a kiss from Dr Craig.'

'And don't forget the dance. Didn't they make a lovely couple!'

'Stop encouraging her,' Jenny West said stiffly, giving them all a chastising look. 'We don't want any involvement with married men.'

'Aye, ye're right, Jenny. Pity that stuck-up wife of his wasn't there to give him the last waltz. She doesn't deserve a nice man like Dr Craig.'

'I wonder what he's doing right now. Eeh, I don't know how they can do it. Be a doctor, I mean. And they say there are a lot of nurses out there in France too. Better them than me, I can tell you.'

'Did you never fancy being a nurse, Mary?'

Mary shook her head. No, she had never thought about it. All she had ever wanted to do with her life was work in an office, get married and maybe have a couple of children. Get married to Walter. It was strange how the thought of it no longer inspired her. When she had said no to a quick register office wedding, he had wanted her to sleep with him before he went off to Catterick. She hadn't done that either. She felt bad about it, too, because it was a purely selfish act to refuse him. Walter had looked so sad, like a little boy whose first toffee apple had been taken away from him before he'd had a lick.

'I hope you won't forget me, Mary,' he had said, his voice thick, as she waved him off at Central Station in Newcastle.

'How can I do that, silly?' she said. 'We're engaged, aren't we?'

'Are we?'

He didn't seem so sure, but she was saved a reply because at that moment the guard called for everybody to be on board. There was an owl-like hoot, steam hissed, and the train put out a trail of acrid blue smoke as it started to pull out of the station. All she had time for was to blow Walter a kiss.

' 'Bye, Walter. Take care. Keep safe.' She shouted all the usual phrases she could think of as she trotted beside the carriage, waving and blowing more kisses, along with dozens of other young women doing the very same thing.

By the time the tail end of the train disappeared from sight, the platform was practically deserted. But already Walter no longer occupied Mary's thoughts. He had been replaced by Alex Craig as he had been the last time she saw him, when he had taken such a liberty with her and kissed her in the middle of the street on Christmas Day. She hadn't slept a wink all that night because of it.

'Penny for them, love?'

Mary's head shot up and she blushed, remembering where she was, with a group of industrious housewives working feverishly and apparently enjoying every minute. She wondered what they would think if they knew what was going through her mind at that moment. They would be shocked, no doubt, especially her mother. Some might laugh, call her all kinds of fool. And they'd be right, of course.

'Let's have another go at that knitting,' she said, picking up her needles and pulling the stitches off so she could make a fresh start. 'Now, how does it go again?'

*

'What do you think?' Iris linked her arm in Mary's as she put her question and gave a squeeze.

'I'm game if you are,' Mary told her and each gave a nervous laugh as they stared at the mobile recruitment office parked in Victoria Square in front of the Wool Shop. On the side of the van were painted the letters F.A.N.Y. and below it, in brackets: First-Aid Nursing Yeomanry.

'Well, it was your idea, Mary,' Iris said, still hanging back. 'If it doesn't work, we'll almost certainly lose our jobs at the Pensions Office, just for being late in this morning.'

'Oh, Mr Hornby's not that bad. He's quite a sweetie, really.' Mary licked her lips and wondered if it had been such a good idea after all to come here, for her courage was suddenly failing her. 'You know what he's like. He'll roll those wobbly eyes of his and quiver all over—'

'All that pink blancmange quivering,' Iris butted in with a shudder. 'I could have nightmares about that.'

'Well, are ye's gannin in or not?'

The coarse but highly recognizable voice behind them made the two friends jump. A figure pushed past them and stood on the wooden steps of the recruitment van with a small, but challenging grin twisting her face.

'Effie? Are you joining up, then?'

'Aye, if they'll have us. Ye divvint have to talk posh to drive and I've driven everything from a kiddie car to a hearse, including that thing there.'

Effie Donaldson pointed to a rather scruffy Norton motorbike parked at the kerbside. It had been there when Mary and Iris arrived, but they had assumed that it belonged to one of the local men.

'You ride a motorbike, Effie?'

'Aye. It's me brother Joe's, but he's not going to be needin' it no more. We got the telegram yesterday.'

'Oh, Effie, I'm so sorry.' Mary stepped forward, full of sympathy, but the girl backed off stiffly.

'Don't be,' she said. 'He was always a bleedin' idiot, our Joe. Well, now, he's a dead hero and folks are sayin' what a good lad he was. Maybe they'll say the same about me when I catch a Gerry bullet. At least it'll be better than laying oot the dead.'

She turned on her heel and marched into the van, her back as straight as a ramrod. Mary and Iris exchanged looks and followed her.

'If she can do it . . .' Iris said.

'So can we,' Mary finished for her.

Inside the van, there were two uniformed girls, much the same age as Mary and Iris. They were directed to take a seat on a long, leather-upholstered bench, where they would have to wait their turn to be interviewed. The interviews were conducted in a closed-off section and only a muffled murmur of voices could be heard through the hardwood partition. Once interviewed, the girls left the van by another exit, probably to stop them exchanging notes about the system.

Mary was the last to go through and she was surprised to see that one of the two interviewing officials was Anne Beasley who stood stiffly to attention by the desk and said nothing, keeping her eyes to the front all the time, just like a regular soldier.

'Sit down, please,' the older woman behind the desk said without looking up. 'Now then, I'm sure you want to know all about our corps, the F.A.N.Y. We are, of course, an old established institution, founded in 1907—'

'Good heavens!' Mary exclaimed. 'It's Miss Croft, isn't it?'

The woman recoiled slightly, her eyelids fluttering. It was obvious that she had not recognized her old pupil. She looked at Anne Beasley for information, her thin eyebrows raised.

'It's Mary West, ma'am,' Anne said deferentially. 'You taught us both . . .'

'Ah, yes, indeed. Mary! What on earth are you doing here, child?'

'I want to help my country,' Mary said, gazing with mixed memories on the face of this woman who had aged so considerably in the years since she had tutored in French and German. 'I didn't know you were in the FANYs.'

She saw Miss Croft's chest rise and fall beneath the khaki tunic, heard a soft sigh, but the face that had always been and still was melancholy, remained bland.

'It wasn't something I talked about,' Miss Croft said. 'I became a commanding officer during the First World War, but in those days we were involved more in a nursing capacity as well as driving ambulances for the Red Cross. Now, I have been asked to help recruit the new FANYs.'

She went on to explain the essentials of being a member of such an illustrious corps and the rigorous training that was required.

'Do you have any questions up to now, Mary?' Miss Croft asked eventually.

Mary looked back blankly and glanced up at Anne Beasley to see if she could see any kind of signal from that direction, but Anne continued to ignore her.

'No, I don't think so.'

'Good, good.' Miss Croft continued, talking over tented fingers and making it all sound more like a Women's Institute lecture on economizing in the home. 'We are looking for drivers mainly on this recruitment operation. Drivers and radio operators. You will, of course, be given some training. However, in view of the pressing circumstances of war, these could well be basic and you might find yourself thrown in, as it were, at the deep end.' She glanced down at the form Mary had filled in while waiting and tapped her pen on it. 'Are you a particularly nervous person, would you say?'

'Not particularly,' Mary said, not really sure, but she didn't leap a mile, as her mother and her grandmother did if something went *phut* beside them.

'Neat handwriting and, as I recall, you speak French fluently and can get by in German. I needn't tell you how invaluable you could be to any unit you join. It is highly likely that you will end up by being sent to France because of your linguistic ability.'

'It's a long time since I spoke either language,' Mary informed her.

There was a slight clearing of the throat from Anne, who was beginning to rock slightly on the balls of her feet, her arms tucked neatly behind her back. Miss Croft looked at her and gave an almost imperceptible nod. Anne suddenly bent over the desk and gave Mary a mouthful of rapid French, to which Mary responded without thinking. When Anne switched to German, Mary replied in the same language, but her German was halting and flawed.

'Thank you, Beasley,' Miss Croft said and Anne returned to standing stiffly to attention.

'That was very impressive, Mary. Your French, at least, is still excellent.'

'I don't get much opportunity to practise foreign languages here in Felling,' Mary said with an amused smile, wondering what Harry Hornby would do if she suddenly addressed him in German. Faint, probably.

'Quite,' Miss Croft almost smiled back at her, but checked herself and returned to the papers before her. 'Now, just one or two formalities . . .'

A few minutes later Mary emerged from the van, her cheeks scorching with excitement. Iris was waiting for her and she could also see Effie Donaldson hovering in the background.

'Well?'

'I think I got accepted, but I have to wait for official confirmation. You?'

'Me too,' Iris squeaked. 'I think my dad must have pulled some strings with his Masonic pals.' Iris's father was an engineer at Swan Hunter's shipyard.

'He must have pulled some for me too, then.' Mary laughed. 'I thought you had to come from a better background than mine. Mind you, it is wartime.'

'They're probably glad of anything they can get.' Iris raised her eyebrows, then grinned. 'Just joking, Mary. Anyway, you're cleverer than me.'

Behind them they heard the spluttering cough of the motorbike engine revving up, then Effie rode off, her tyres kicking up gravel as she swerved perilously around the corner, her skirt riding up to her skinny thighs.

'They must have turned her down,' Mary said, feeling quite sorry for the poor girl.

Iris pulled a face and laughed.

'Well, they do say that the FANYs come from all walks of life, but I doubt if they'd want to dig down as low as Effie Donaldson, even if her father is an undertaker.'

'Even so,' Mary felt the need to defend Effie. 'She can die for her country as well as anybody else.'

'Yes, I suppose you're right,' Iris allowed. 'I'm sorry I said that.'

'So you should be. Come on, let's go and break the news to Mr Hornby . . . and our families.'

'You've done what, our Mary?' Jenny West's eyes were out on stalks and already filling up with tears as she took on board what Mary was telling her.

'I've joined the FANYs, Mam.'

'What in the name of God did you do that for? Frank, did you hear our girl?'

'Aye,' said Frank through the open door between the kitchen and the scullery where he was standing in the tin bath washing off the coal-dust of the day. 'Here was I wishing I had a son to be proud of and me daughter's proved herself to be a man.'

'You what, Frank?'

'Well, ye know what I mean. I'm proud of ye, Mary, lass.'

'But Frank! She . . . she's joined up, for goodness sake. Doesn't that mean anything to you?'

'Aye,' came the reply through grunts and much splashing. 'They turned me down, but now this family can hold its head up high, thanks to our Mary.'

'I didn't know you wanted to be a FANY, Dad,' Mary joked. 'Oh, Mam, stop looking so worried. It's not as if I'm going to be fighting or anything like that. They just want drivers and mechanics and such.'

'But they're all volunteers, that lot,' Jenny said. 'What are you going to do for money?'

'I'll manage, Mam,' Mary said. 'I've got all my savings.'

'But I thought that was for when you got married.'

'Yes, well . . .' Mary wrinkled her nose and avoided her mother's eyes. 'There's plenty of time for that. Right now, helping my country's more important.'

'And where will they be sending you? Not overseas, I hope?'

'We're going on a crash course at York. After that we'll be billeted out wherever we're needed.'

'Oh, aye?' Jenny's chin was wobbling and her eyes were full to the brim with tears. 'And who's "we"?'

'Iris and me,' Mary told her. 'And a few others that were taken on today. I saw Pamela Richardson in the queue, and Nancy Walters. I think poor Effie Donaldson probably got the thumbs down, though, the way she rode off without a word.'

'Who's Effie Donaldson when she's at home?' Jenny said, trying to mask the fact that she was broken-hearted at the thought of her favourite daughter leaving home and doing something other than knitting for the war effort.

'She's from Donaldson's Funeral Parlour, Mam.'

'Oh, she's feisty, that one,' Frank said, stepping into the kitchen in clean long johns and still drying behind his ears. 'When she was born I think the midwife must have rubbed her down with sandpaper. Rough as they come, but she's good at her job. It's not everybody that can lay out a corpse.'

'Well, I'm glad they don't take the likes of her on,' Jenny concluded. 'I wouldn't want you rubbing shoulders with common tarts, and may God forgive me for speaking so bluntly and using such language.'

'Oh, Mam!' Mary laughed and moved to the door; she hadn't even stopped to take off her outdoor things.

'Now where are you off to?'

'I thought I'd just slip over to our Helen's and tell her my news.'

'Well, before you do, and before I forget to tell you, this letter came for you this morning.' Jenny took an official-looking envelope down from the mantelpiece and handed it to her daughter.

Mary looked puzzled as she stared at the unfamiliar writing and the

BFPO postmark.

'Aren't you going to open it? I thought you'd be excited, getting your first letter from Walter, wherever he is, bless him.'

'It's not Walter's writing, Mam,' Mary said, sliding her thumb under the seal and pulling out the single piece of paper that was folded inside.

'Well, who's it from, then?'

Mary stared at the short letter, written in a bold, slanting hand that seemed to have been unsteady at the time of writing. She read it quickly, not believing what she saw there, then blinked at her mother.

'Oh, just a friend,' she said hastily, aware that her cheeks were colouring up furiously.

Murmuring her excuses, she stuffed the letter in her pocket and rushed out into the darkening night. She knew her way blindfolded to her sister's and she headed there now, but her mind played over and over again the few words she had read in Alex Craig's letter.

'My dear Mary, I had hoped to write to you before now, but things are a bit hectic over here. As I take a moment to scribble these words, men are dying all around me, but I have done my best for them. They say we're to move on soon and I don't know where I'll be or if I will ever be able to contact you again. Forgive me, but I carry the memory of your sweet face with me and it gets me through the long days and endless nights. Perhaps it is foolish, but being able to write to you like this helps enormously. I hope you and the good people of Felling are still safe and will remain so. Things are not so good on this side of the Channel. With fondest thoughts, Alex.

By the time she stumbled through Helen's door, she had so many conflicting emotions rushing around inside her she burst into bittersweet tears and nearly frightened her poor sister to death.

'Mary! What on earth is wrong?'

'Everything!' was all Mary could say.

Three months later, in a windswept field hospital in northern France, Alex was washing the blood of a young soldier off his hands, wondering if he would ever manage to get a proper night's sleep. The lad was just twenty years old and talking volubly about how lucky he was to be among the wounded. He couldn't wait to get back home and take his girl-friend ice-skating. They hadn't told him yet that even if he survived surgery he would never walk again, for he had spinal damage and had lost the use of both legs in the explosion that had blown out the brains of his best pal, whom he had tried to save.

Alex had lost track of the time he had been in the field hospital. It felt like a lifetime. During the first couple of days he thought he would never get used to seeing so much human destruction. He did what he could. It was never enough. On the fourth day something took over inside him, an anger like an inner strength that shut down his nervous system and put his emotions on hold. From that moment on he was able to cope and do his job almost like an automaton.

He grabbed what little sleep he could get between batches of injured servicemen being brought in by the Red Cross ambulances. It was never enough, but during those precious minutes of sleep or half-sleep, his mind turned to pleasanter things. Memories of his childhood home on the west coast of Scotland, the happy days spent there before he went to medical school, the short time he had spent in his uncle's Felling practice.

He forced himself not to think of Fiona. He did think, however, about Mary West and wondered what she was doing, what she thought of his unforgivable behaviour that night of the benefit when he had lost his head and kissed her. Had his profound sense of loss and loneliness driven him to do such a thing? It seemed like the right thing to do at the time and she had responded, oh, so sweetly. He saw her gentle face and bright eyes and smiling mouth, not only in his dreams, but in flashes as he cared for his patients, trying desperately to remain impersonal.

The sound of vehicles, struggling with deep, throaty roars over the rough terrain outside penetrated his thoughts, together with his ward sister running between the tightly packed beds calling his name.

'There's another batch of wounded arriving, Captain Craig, sir,' Sister Grace Forsyth told him.

'Where the hell are we going to put them, Sister?'

'We've got a spare ambulance. The FANYs are kitting it out to take the walking wounded to the next field site. Orders to break camp are expected at any minute. It'll be a crush, but until we can get an extension for this circus tent, it's the best we can do.'

'How many moves have you made so far, Sister?'

'Four, including this one,' she replied.

'In how long?'

'In almost as many weeks.'

'Good Lord, Sister. Does Hitler have a crystal ball or something? Is there a spy in the unit perhaps?'

Grace Forsyth shrugged her shoulders and stared at his Adam's apple.

He noticed how her hands bunched into fists and that she stuck them behind her back as if to hide them from sight.

'The Germans are strong in this part of France, sir. They're on the march and they're knocking our units out as fast as they set up camp. It's a war, Captain Craig. Somebody wins, somebody loses.'

'And at the moment it would seem that the Germans have the upper hand and all we medics can do is patch up the suffering they inflict on our boys.'

'Yes, sir. I'm afraid that's the way it is.'

Alex doused his face with cold water and scrubbed his skin dry as Sister Forsyth went on giving him the latest progress reports on the more seriously ill and wounded in their care. The tent hospital was an expedient affair and could be dismantled and moved easily enough with the help of the troops who were attached to the unit. He wondered how long they could keep one step ahead of the advancing Wehrmacht. Things already seemed too close for comfort.

The hospital was draughty and never warm enough and the surgeons often had to work with hands that were blue with the cold, warmed only by the blood of their patients. There was never enough space, staff, instruments or medicines. Equipment was basic and very often archaic, and there was insufficient food to go around.

'Damn the bloody Germans!' he spat out, then, turning, he got his eye on a blond-haired boy as young as the private soldier he had just finished patching up.

The lad was shivering convulsively and muttering to himself, fingers plucking at his coarse army blanket. Alex imagined that the eyes behind the soiled bandage, oozing with gangrenous smelling pus, had once been a clear blue. He probably had a girlfriend back home too, and a mother weeping for him, and a proud father.

'*Horen Sie das Lied?*'

'What's he saying?' Alex asked, wondering why he had not noticed the German soldier before now.

'He's asking if you can hear the song,' Grace said, her expression giving nothing away of how she felt inside, if she felt anything at all.

'What song?'

'I don't know. He keeps humming a tune, trying to sing the words. He's been like that ever since they brought him in.'

'How long has he been here?'

'Three days.'

'And no one has changed the dressings on his eyes?'

'There were other priorities.'

Alex felt a red rage rush through him, but half the fury was directed at himself. He should have noticed this boy. He, at least, had eyes to see.

'Do it now,' he said and when the sister started to object he yelled at her: 'That's an order, Sister!'

An icy current of air swept through the hospital as orderlies brought in the newly arrived consignment of wounded. Once more the place was ringing with the sound of men's voices, cries of agony, moans, delirious ramblings, sobbing for their mothers and calling out for their wives.

Alex swallowed, took a deep breath, then marched forward, issuing sharp orders to orderlies, medics and nurses alike. Already, they feared and respected him enough not to disobey, for he had proved that he was capable of doing all that they could do and more. He saved lives, and to those he could not save he gave as much comfort as was in his power to give. There was no time, either for grief or for prayers. He would leave that up to the hospital chaplain.

CHAPTER FIVE

WHEN Mary first donned her FANY uniform she thought she had never felt or looked so smart as she did in the snug-fitting, tailor-made, khaki barathea tunic and skirt, with a Sam Browne belt and buckle, and buttons that had to be cleaned daily to a meticulous shine.

'I don't think I'll ever get used to this,' Iris complained on the second day when she spilled a tin of Brasso over her jacket and got a scolding from their training officer, a poker-faced individual who took everything so seriously.

'It's not so bad, really,' Mary said, glancing around at the bunch of girls they were training with. 'Everybody's very friendly. I just wish the training was over and we could do things for real. At least I'd feel as if I was helping.'

Iris raised her eyebrows and nodded. 'Yes, it's not as if we don't know how to drive and both of us can cook.'

Mary laughed. 'The pair of us would do well driving a canteen on wheels, wouldn't we? They used to do a lot of that in the First World War, apparently, as well as nursing, though I think it was just helping out, rolling bandages and such.'

'Handing out sticking plasters and Aspro tablets,' Iris added with a giggle.

'Holding a fighter pilot's hand and stroking his brow,' Mary said, dreamily.

'Lovely,' said Iris. 'I'll settle for that.'

'Not if I see him first!'

'Mary West, you're engaged. What about poor Walter?'

'Oh, yes, I forgot about him,' Mary sighed, glancing down at the ring on the third finger of her left hand and then, on seeing Iris's shocked expression: 'Just joking. How could anybody forget Walter?'

But to herself she had to admit that Walter was not exactly uppermost in her mind. She had been on the verge of breaking off their engagement, but she had put it off, thinking it would be cruel to do it just then, and especially at Christmas time. Then, of course, he had been spirited away by the Army to Catterick and was now, like Alex Craig and so many other British servicemen, located somewhere in France as part of the British Expeditionary Force.

Only part of the girls' FANY training was to be here at Penn House in York, where they spent a day in the kitchen cooking for around thirty-five people, but it was fun. They did quite a bit of driving, too, going from York to Newcastle and very often further afield, transporting anonymous personnel to meetings. Both Iris and Mary were adept drivers, but it was Iris who got most of the driving jobs because of her navigational skills, Mary was given lessons in handling radio equipment and learning about radar tracking, but she wasn't exactly the best in her group.

'Do you know, Iris,' Mary said one day, after she had spent the afternoon coding and decoding mysterious messages. 'It's all a bit cloak-and-dagger, if you ask me.'

'Don't complain,' Iris said with a huffy sniff. 'You get all the interesting jobs. Me? I get to deliver medical supplies, transfer patients from hospital to hospital and play chauffeur to anonymous individuals who can't be bothered to pass the time of day with me. And all without lights or signposts.'

'We're not supposed to be chatty,' Mary reminded her. 'You never know who you're chatting to. It could be a spy.'

They stared at one another for a long second, then fell about laughing. Neither of them found it easy to take things seriously. It was like playing at being soldiers and neither of them was any good at parading in step. Iris invariably turned right when she should turn left and Mary had bother concentrating, so she often ended up marching into the back of the girl in front.

After a month, they were transferred to Camberley where the training was more intense as they learned how to handle bigger vehicles, then it was back to Yorkshire to await their postings. It was while they were waiting, in their billets, a small lodging house in Redcar, that life became more interesting.

As soon as they had some free time Mary and Iris had decided to take a stroll along the beach, sucking in the bracing sea air as if it were nectar. The hard winter was now behind them, but it was still chilly. Dodging the wavelets rippling up the corrugated beach and swirling around the lines of concrete tank traps, the girls were relaxed for the first time since leaving home. That was, until the air-raid siren went off, filling the air with its deafening, heart-stopping wail.

'Oh, lor'!' Mary shouted as they both covered their ears and looked about them for a place to take cover. 'The Germans aren't great on timing, are they?'

'No, they always like to spoil our fun,' Iris agreed as they joined hands and ran full pelt towards a dark hole in the cliff face, well known to the locals as a place where pirates of old stored their plunder from ships wrecked on the rocks.

The cave was deep and they ventured in as far as they dared, hoping that the expected enemy plane wasn't planning to bomb that particular stretch of coastline today. However, it wouldn't be the first time an enemy plane had bombed the Yorkshire coastline. The girls were getting used to dealing with the real thing. The false alarms and practice drills had soon become a part of the past. So far, however, bomb damage had not been too extensive.

'You do realize, Mary,' said Iris, as they hid themselves among the rocks, 'that if they do drop a bomb here, we could be buried alive.'

'I'll take my chances on that,' Mary said, wishing she hadn't because her stomach turned over the minute her words were out of her mouth. The sound of plane engines humming, then growing loud like angry hornets, grew closer.

'Blooming heck!' Iris exclaimed breathlessly, moving closer to Mary. 'It sounds like the whole of Hitler's air force is coming.'

'I think it's only two or three,' Mary told her, listening carefully, her hands cupped behind her ears. 'Let's hope that one of them's ours. Yes, listen to that.'

The sound of gunfire, probably from a British Spitfire, went on and on and then there was a moment before the awful dying note of an aircraft could be heard diving into the sea. The girls continued to huddle together, listening to the second aircraft's departing drone.

'I'm not moving until I hear the all-clear,' Iris whispered fearfully.

'No,' Mary agreed. 'That was as close as I ever want to be to armed warfare.'

She tried to laugh, but her heart was pounding too much and she could hardly breathe. How ridiculous, she thought. Here she was, wearing the uniform of the brave, stiff-upper-lipped First-Aid Nursing Yeomanry, and she felt like an absolute coward.

Just as the all-clear blasted out its welcome call, another sound made the girls freeze and hold their breath. The heavy resonance of an engine vibrated the ground at their feet, then it was right there with them in the cave in a gritty spray of sharp, damp sand, and a choking smell of oil and petrol fumes.

Mary froze and Iris screamed before they saw what was the cause of the commotion. A full-sized motorbike with what appeared to be a child riding the broad saddle roared into the cave. At least, it looked like a child until the rider stopped the engine and hopped agilely off.

'Well, who'd 'ave effin' believed I'd find you two hidin' in a cave down here at Redcar? Gawd, ye look so scared I bet ye've both dropped yer buckets and spades and wet yer knickers.'

'Effie Donaldson!' Mary cried out with relief. 'What are you doing here?'

'Same as youse two. I've joined the FANYs. I'm in the motorcycle unit. Now, where's the action, eh?'

'They let you in!' Iris burst out, then spluttered as Mary dug her painfully in the ribs.

'We thought you were part of the enemy action,' she said, then laughed helplessly because the whole situation was so ridiculous.

'What's so funny?' Effie's face creased into a disgruntled frown and she looked ready for a fight.

'You are,' Iris said, joining in with Mary's laughter, tears running down both of their faces.

'Aw, I get the message,' Effie said, struggling to turn her bike around. 'Just cos I talk common, like, ye think they wouldn't want us, eh? Well, I can tell ye that it don't matter no more, cos they need everybody they can get . . . even the likes of me. Anyway, I can afford to pay me way.'

'Really?' Iris said, receiving a second nudge from Mary.

'Aye, I can an' all. Anyway, can either of youse ride a motorbike, eh?'

'You're right, Effie,' Mary said as all three of them emerged into the afternoon sun and shaded their eyes, scanning the seascape for the fallen German plane.

'Look! Over there!'

As Mary pointed to a cloud of smoke and some floating wreckage, a fishing boat zoomed in on the scene.

'They're not goin' to rescue the bliddy Gerries, are they?' Effie swore and threw a pebble into the sea with so much vigour it skimmed the waves and bounced before plunging down out of sight like the plane itself must have done.

'I think there are two planes down,' Iris said, squinting through her glasses, and Mary, whose eyesight was better, concurred.

'Poor sods,' said Effie, revving up the engine of her bike and starting off along the beach. 'See youse back at the base.'

And then she was gone in a puff of smoke and more sprayed sand, and the two friends were left gazing after her with open admiration.

There was a buzz of excitement in the training centre that night that could hardly be contained. One of the girls, Kate Holland, had been in the CO's office when an important telephone call came in. She had been immediately dismissed, but had hovered curiously behind a door that she hadn't quite closed.

Just as everybody was getting ready to sleep, she burst into the long Nissen hut that housed the unit's dormitory of twenty pallet beds. Some of the girls were already in their pyjamas and warming themselves around the cast iron stove at the far end of the building, prior to jumping between the cold sheets.

'Everybody gather round!' Kate shouted as she banged the door shut behind her. 'I've got news!'

'Well, don't keep it to yourself, Holland. Spit it out, girl.'

'Yes, Holland, don't stand on ceremony. We could all do with a bit of jollying up.'

'Well. . . .' Kate approached the stove and held her hands out towards it, shivering because the night was cold and wet. 'I only heard one side of the conversation, but it sounds like our postings have arrived at last.'

'By telephone?'

'No, apparently by that dreadful creature on the motorbike, but the CO in London was checking to make sure she'd got here safely with them.'

Mary and Iris exchanged glances. Neither of them had dared open her mouth when they first arrived, for fear of encountering snobbery, but these young women who, for the main part, came from wealthy, middle-class backgrounds had not minded their northern accents. However, Effie spoke broad Geordie with a thick, guttural accent that turned the English language into something resembling a foreign tongue. Especially when she was roused, which she seemed to be most of the time.

'Do you mean to say that common trollop was trusted with highly important documents,' Sally Ferguson tossed her bobbed blonde hair and made a "tch" sound with her tongue. 'How bizarre!'

'Well, she is a messenger,' Mary said, feeling she had to defend poor Effie. 'And she's been riding motorbikes since she was about fourteen, which is more than any of us can claim.'

'That's true,' said Alice Leatherby, the mild-mannered daughter of a Wiltshire clergyman. 'And she certainly knows how to control the thing. The way she rode in here today frightened the life out of me.'

'She swears like a trooper,' Kate said, wrinkling her nose, 'but I suppose, in a state of war, we can't be all that choosy about who does the dirty work.'

'What makes you think she'll get the dirty work to do, Holland?' Mary asked, suddenly incensed and ignoring Iris's warning jerk of the head. 'Unless you mean stripping down engines? Donaldson's pretty good at that too, I hear.'

'Oh, leave it, West! Just because she comes from your neck of the woods, you don't have to stand up for her all the time.'

'Know where we're all going, then, Holland?' one of the other girls called out loudly; and happily, the question acted like oil on troubled waters.

'No, of course not, but I think we'll get to know tomorrow morning.' Kate Holland grimaced. 'Oh, and there's another thing. A new lance-corporal's just arrived. I gather she's going to be in charge when we do move out. I've met her. She came into the dining hall as I was helping clear away the dinner dishes.'

'What's she like?'

'I suppose you could call her pretty.' Holland was enjoying her importance as news bearer. 'Blonde pageboy, tall, slim . . . and definitely in love with her own power. She had the cheek to make me mop up the floor again because she said she could see muddy footprints on it.'

'God, not one of those iron maidens!'

'I wanted to tell her that the mud was from her own shoes, but I thought I'd leave it until we know what we're dealing with. She might be the CO's niece or something.'

'What's she called?'

'Beasley. And I think she's connected.'

Mary smiled at that, though she wasn't sure that Anne's presence in the ranks was going to be a pleasant experience for any of them.

'She is, actually,' she told them and all eyes were riveted on her. 'Her father's a brigadier, and her brother's a captain in the Northumberland Fusiliers.'

'Lord, West, you're full of surprises! How do you know that?'

'Anne and I spent most of our childhood together.'

'You were *friends*?'

'Sort of . . .' Mary frowned, because although she had spent most of her childhood at Anne Beasley's side, she had never truly felt that they were friends. There was always that feeling that they belonged to two very different worlds, and Anne made sure that their worlds never really met. Just overlapped a little.

'So, she's not a snob, then?' Sally Ferguson asked quite innocently.

'I think, Ferguson,' Mary said, looking the girl directly in the eye, 'that you'll have to find that out for yourself.'

The next morning everyone was up earlier than usual, most of the girls complaining that they hadn't slept a wink all night because of the excitement of being posted and wondering just exactly what they would be doing in a few days, and where.

After breakfast, which they hardly touched, their appetites cut by anticipation, there came a fluctuation of moods as the postings were given out. Not all the girls were happy with their lot. Kate Holland and Alice Leatherby were to be billeted in Northampton and were to drive ambulances, while Sally Ferguson was to go back to Yorkshire, where she would drive for the big brass officers. A few were given postings in Plymouth and Liverpool, but the rest, they were informed, would go to London, where help was needed more than anywhere else in Britain.

'Just to make sure, I'll read out the names allocated to our London postings,' the officer in charge said, having to raise her voice to be heard over the sudden burst of conversation and girlish giggles. The list was long and she read it alphabetically, Mary's name coming next to last.

'Hey, what about me, then?'

There was a subdued groan as a gruff voice called out from the back of the crowded training hall. Mary turned her head, but couldn't see Effie, whose voice it was. The CO looked slightly ruffled and waited patiently for a lull, watching incredulously as the tiny figure of Effie Donaldson pushed her way through to the front.

'I have read out every name on this list,' said the CO. 'You must have missed yours. Weren't you listening?'

'Aye, I was, and you never mentioned us.'

'Us? There are more of you?' The CO was getting decidedly hot under the collar and glancing about for support.

'No, just me, but ye didn't mention us,' Effie insisted.

'She's right, ma'am,' Mary stepped forward and took up position at Effie's side. 'And the word "us" is just her way of talking. It . . . it's like dialect. It's the way some Geordies say "me".'

'Goodness gracious, whatever next?' The CO turned back to Effie. 'What is your name, girl?'

'Effie Donaldson,' Effie told her, puffing out what little chest she had. 'And I *am* a FANY, just like this lot here. I've got all me papers and that.'

The officer searched the list in front of her, reading the names under her breath as her finger traced each one in turn.

'Charlton, Crow, Dawson ... ah ... Donaldson, Eunice? But I called out that name. Didn't you reply? I've got you ticked.'

'But I'm not Donaldson, Eunice, miss ... er ... ma'am.' Effie pouted and her eyes shrank to slits. 'I'm Donaldson, Effie.'

The older woman's eyes returned to the list, then widened perceptively as her finger stabbed the page. 'I see! There are two Donaldsons. I must have missed one.'

'Aye. That's what I thought, an all.'

'Donaldson ... oh, but this is Donaldson, Euphemia. . . ?'

A loud sniff emanated from Effie and she stared down at the toes of her brown leather brogues, which were already scuffed and lacking in polish.

'Aye, well, me mam called us that. She had fancy ideas. But everybody calls us Effie.'

'I see ... yes, well . . .' the CO cleared her throat loudly and folded away her list. 'Donaldson ... Effie ... you are to go to London too. There is a great need for messengers around the dockland area.'

'Gawd, that's a bit too near the bliddy Jerries for my liking.'

There was a titter of laughter, well hidden behind hands and disguised by polite coughs and sneezes, but even the CO was having difficulty keeping a straight face.

'That's one way of putting it, Donaldson,' she said. 'I'm sure you will carry out your duties with the utmost efficiency. Having seen the way you ride that motorcycle of yours, I do believe you could easily dodge any bomb that came your way.'

For the first time, Mary saw Effie really smile, then the smile became a grin and the girl looked almost happy. She turned and gripped Mary's arm, then punched Iris's shoulder, making her wince with pain.

'Did ye's hear that? I'm comin' to London wi' ye's. Eeh, do ye think we'll get to see the King and Queen?'

As it turned out, the girls were sent home on a forty-eight hour pass to allow them to spend some time with their families, but Effie opted not to take advantage of this. She went off on her motorbike, a canvas haversack on her back containing her dress uniform and some spare under-clothes, saying she was going directly to London. She wanted to make sure she saw Big Ben and Buckingham Palace before the Germans dropped bombs on them.

'See youse down there, mebbe,' she told Mary and Iris as she roared off in a black cloud of exhaust fumes.

'Good luck, Effie!' Mary called after her.

'She's crazy,' Iris said with a shake of her head.

'Maybe that's not such a bad thing,' Mary said. 'I sort of envy her, you know? I wish I had her courage.'

Two days later Mary and Iris met again at the station. There was a brisk wind blowing in from the north, driving rain clouds before it, so that there were periods of sunshine alternating with showers and no real warmth to the day.

Or was the cold shiver that kept running amok through Mary's body simply a case of nerves, she wondered? She hadn't felt too badly about going down to London, until her parents heard about it. Her father had been characteristically silent and broody, but her mother was distraught and pleaded with her not to go.

'I have to go, Mum. I've joined up for the duration. How would it look if I backed out now?'

Jenny West was not persuaded. Unlike her husband, the West family pride was less important than having her girls safe at home.

'We might never see you again, Mary,' she said. 'If the Germans do invade, London's the first place they'll head for. They shouldn't be send-ing innocent young girls to places like that. It . . . it's criminal, that's what it is.'

'Mam, I volunteered,' Mary said, trying to sooth her mother's fears. 'We all did. The FANYs are a wonderful bunch of people. I would hate to let them down by letting them think that I don't have what it takes. Besides, for the first time in my life I really feel as if I'm doing something worthwhile.'

'Why don't you ask them to let you stay up here in the north-east? Let them send somebody else to London.'

'I'm not the only one going, Mam,' Mary told her. 'Anyway, I've never felt so passionate about anything in my life.'

'You could help your country here, where you belong, down at the munitions factory, or back at your old job with the Pensions Office.'

'Yes, Mam,' said Mary, thinking how boring it would be making nuts and bolts or inking in ledgers day after day, and being constantly on the alert for the few men left at home who thought they were the answer to every woman's prayer because men were in such short supply.

The station porter's call of "all aboard" and his final whistle jerked Mary back to consciousness. Iris was gripping her arm, squeezing it tightly.

'Do you think it's too late to change our minds, Mary?' she whispered as the train gave a few short jolts forward, then stopped again. 'Look, we could jump off right now, if we wanted to. You don't want to, do you, Mary?'

'No, I don't, Iris Morrison!' Mary scolded her. 'And neither do you, so don't say such daft things.'

'I'm not sure that it's daft. Up here in the north it's dangerous enough driving around ferrying medical supplies and patients, without having to do it in the London black-out.'

'I don't think . . .' Mary started to tell her friend that she didn't think things would be as bad as the newspapers reported, but she stopped at the sight of a figure racing down the platform. 'Goodness me, I do believe they're holding up the train for her!'

'Who?' Iris leaned over Mary to see whom she was referring to.

Anne Beasley, her newly styled blonde hair disarranged as she ran, cap in hand, followed by a red-faced porter carrying her heavy baggage, reached their carriage and hauled herself in, pulling in her valise after her and throwing the porter a few coins for his trouble.

'Oh, hello!' She let an elderly gentleman help her push her valise up on to the luggage rack, then fell into the seat opposite Mary, breathlessly blowing out her cheeks. 'What a coincidence! You going down to your London posting, are you? Jolly good. Me too!'

'Yes,' Mary said, eyeing Anne's insignia. 'I see you're a lieutenant now. Congratulations.'

Anne gave a short laugh. 'Daddy fixed it. It's a jolly good thing to have a father who's a brigadier and a brother who's a major. Alfred got his promotion last month.'

'Very useful,' Iris remarked through gritted teeth, and studied her toes with a tight grimace.

'She's not going to be sick or anything dreadful, is she?' Anne asked, indicating Iris with a jerk of her chin.

'Of course not,' Mary said, hoping that she was right, because Iris did, in fact, look rather pale.

Happily, Iris was not sick, but she remained silent for most of the journey and Mary suspected that she had been quite serious about wanting to get off the train. And to be honest, though she didn't like to admit it to her friend, she too had felt a rise of panic as the train started off. It was like going on a journey to the unknown where danger awaited them in many guises. She wondered whether Anne's careless bravado was genuine or merely a camouflage for how she really felt. Or, Mary wondered, watching the pretty blonde girl from her childhood, would she still be the bossy but naïve girl she had always been? She was now, after all, an officer, even if she had arrived at that level with little or no real experience.

The train shrieked as it pulled into King's Cross Station. Carriage doors banged as they were flung open. There was the sound of whistles blowing, steam hissing, metal clanking and, horror of horrors, the wail of an air-raid siren.

'Oh, not already!' Iris complained as they joined the crowds of travellers stampeding out of the station and dashing down behind sandbags and into air-raid shelters like rabbits diving into burrows.

Mary and Iris dived with them, and the ground shook beneath them as bombs fell on London. They had become separated from Anne the minute they got off the train. Mary shouted to the girl to go with them, but Anne simply stared back with a blank expression and didn't move.

'I should have grabbed her and brought her with us,' Mary said, as much to herself as to Iris.

'Who are you talking about?'

'Anne Beasley. I thought she was just being snobbish and stubborn, but now I'm not so sure. I think, maybe, she was scared.'

'I know I am,' Iris said in a hoarse whisper and she stuffed her fingers in her ears as another explosion rocked the whole shelter.

Shards of wood and stone showered down on their heads. The temporary lighting in the shelter stopped working and they were plunged into darkness, except for the glowing ends of cigarettes. Women screamed, children cried, men shouted, but until the lights came back on nobody could do anything.

Five minutes passed, then everything went quiet. The lights were restored as the all-clear sounded, loud and jubilant. Outside, people were rushing here and there, or moving in dazed slow motion. Ambulances screamed and fire-engines jangled as they raced about the urgent business of rescuing the injured and dowsing the flames leaping from a variety of buildings.

'Well, don't just sit there, you two! What do you think those uniforms stand for, eh?'

The old woman next to Mary was glaring at her angrily.

'What's she getting at?' Iris said in a shaky voice as she brushed herself down, raising clouds of dust.

'You're soldiers of a sort, aren't you?' the woman went on, and others in the shelter turned to look at the two uniformed girls.

'She's right,' Mary told Iris. 'We're here to help people.'

'But, we're not on duty yet . . .'

'Does it matter? Come on. Let's see what's to be done, then we'll try and find our way to our billets.'

'Go on then,' Iris said. 'You first.'

As they stumbled over a jumble of sandbags and rubble, Mary caught sight of Anne Beasley. The girl was curled up, just inside the entrance of the railway station, her hands over her ears, her eyes tightly shut and her face crunched up into a fearful mask.

Mary had been right. Officer or not, Anne Beasley was terrified. The training they had received had not really prepared any of them for the real thing and, Mary suspected, this initiation into the day-to-day life of wartime London was only the tip of the iceberg. She had an awful feeling that from now on it was going to get very much worse.

The fear in Anne's eyes when she looked up to see who was tugging at her arm quickly turned to humiliation.

'Come on, Anne,' Mary said, ignoring the fact that she was addressing an officer. 'There are people who need our help.'

'I . . . I can't . . .' Anne was stuttering, her whole body quivering.

'You haven't even tried yet.' Mary was aware that she sounded hard and unsympathetic, but she knew that if she treated Anne with gentleness the girl might collapse altogether. 'Come on. Iris, take her other arm and let's get her to her feet.'

'Helping your own first, are you?' The same old woman clambered by them, unaided, though there was blood pouring from a cut in her forehead. 'You're a right good example, aren't you?'

They ignored her and got Anne upright and walking. The street was a mass of smoky rubble. The ARP wardens were already on the job, as were the Red Cross and the police. Mary approached a warden and asked what had happened.

'A couple of sticks of bombs got us, miss,' he told her. 'Bloody Gerry was probably looking for the airfield and got lost.'

A burly police sergeant pointed a thick finger at the three girls as they emerged into the late afternoon sunshine and bawled at them in a loud voice.

'Here! You lot there. You're FANYs, aren't you? Well, get your bloody fannies moving. You can take the walking wounded to the first-aid posts. That's them, over there.'

He indicated a couple of vans bearing Red Cross signs and left them to it. Mary gave Anne a shake and she seemed to come out of her stupor, though Iris looked as if she was about to faint away at the sight of all those bleeding bodies strewn about the road, moaning and mewing and calling for help.

'Iris!' she shouted. 'You'll feel better for having something to do. Come on.'

'What about Anne,' came the weak response. 'We can't just leave her, can we?'

'She's not hurt, but those people are. Leave Anne here and come and help me. We'll pick her up later.'

Iris followed Mary meekly, clamping her mouth shut and closing her eyes at the sight of the wounds that presented themselves before her, but she managed not to faint. Between them, they moved a dozen or more people into the first-aid stations where the nurses went about their business with calm, cool efficiency.

'You've got to admire them,' Mary said, looking about her to make sure that there were no more injured members of the public to deal with. 'They say the nurses across the Channel are putting up with a lot worse than this all day long. And here are we, afraid of a few bombs in our own country.'

'Better them than me, Mary,' Iris muttered through clenched teeth. 'I never could stand the sight of blood.'

'Me neither,' said Mary with a wry smile. 'However, I have a feeling that we're going to get used to it, and very soon.'

'Oh, Lord!'

'Come on, let's get Anne. I don't fancy being abroad in London when the blackout starts.'

All three of them were conveniently billeted together in the same lodging house near the docklands of the East End. It was shabby and lacked even the first basics of home comforts. With thirty FANYs packed into the eight rooms available, there wasn't room to swing the proverbial cat. Mary, Iris and Anne, being the last to arrive, considered themselves fortunate in being allocated a small converted sitting-room on the ground floor. It had a gas fire that still worked and a small hob on which they could heat things, two bonuses they were more than grateful to have.

By the next day Anne seemed to have recovered her equilibrium and her spirit as she faced her unit for the first time.

'It really is quite simple,' she lectured them. 'We report to HQ, pick up a fleet of ambulances, and then it's up to you to transport the sick and the injured to and from the hospitals. You'll be issued maps with all medical locations marked clearly as well as alternative routes to take in the case of roads being blocked.'

Mary and Iris's ambulance turned out to be a converted laundry van. They took it in turn to drive. Their expertise in first-aid had been gained in a few short lessons in how to dress wounds, apply a tourniquet and take down personal details so that next of kin could be informed of the situation.

Mary's short training in communications was not, at present, to be put to the test. Drivers were more in demand in the dockland area of London. She often wondered what Anne was doing, other than organizing the unit and taking care of necessary clerical duties, for she was often absent and never dirty or dishevelled like the rest of them, but it wasn't her place to pose any questions. In any case, she had enough to do, keeping up Iris's morale and blocking out her own fears.

And when Mary felt her own morale sink to its lowest ebb, she thought of Dr Alex Craig, though she knew it was wrong to do so. And she hoped he was still thinking of her, still safe, still alive wherever he was.

And just occasionally, her mind would turn to thoughts of Walter.

CHAPTER SIX

'WILL it ever stop, Mary, do you think?' Iris said.

She was lying on her back in her bed, staring up at the cracked, discoloured ceiling. Her face was pale and lined with fatigue and Mary, as she looked at her friend, thought that it was probably like looking into a mirror, which they didn't have, except for the fly-blown job in the bathroom on the first floor. She didn't look at her reflection much, except to make sure that her hair was neatly rolled up at the back and tucked into her cap at the sides.

'It has to stop one day,' she said, pondering over the letter she was trying to compose, though she spent more time gnawing the end of her pen than writing. 'And when it does, Iris, we'll probably miss it. You know, the thrill of the action.'

'I hope you're joking.' There was a long pause, then Iris lifted her head and looked across to where Mary sat near the window, writing by the light of the dawn filtering through a tear in the blackout curtain. 'Mary? Aren't you tired of it all?'

'I try not to think about it,' Mary replied without looking up from the page that had so many smudges and crossings out that a child of four might have written it.

'Are you writing to Walter again?'

'No.' Mary threw down the pen and sighed. She had been trying to compose a few innocent sentences to send to Alex Craig, but everything she said seemed laden with hidden meaning.

'Has he ever written to you?'

'Who?'

'Walter, of course. Goodness, Mary, you must be more tired than you look. Well, has he?'

'No, he hasn't, but then he's not good with words.'

'Still, you'd think he'd make the effort. You're his fiancée, after all.'

'Yes, but he's probably . . . you know . . . busy.'

There was another long silence, then Iris was probing again.

'So who *are* you writing to?'

'Nobody.'

'If you don't want to tell me, that's all right, but we're supposed to be friends. From the look on your face just now, it's somebody pretty special.'

'Yes, well . . .' Mary got up and stretched, eyeing her bed and wishing she could snuggle down inside the blankets, no matter how uncomfortable it was, and sleep for a week. 'It's just . . .'

She had been on the verge of telling Iris of her very strange and distant relationship with Alex Craig, doctor; Captain Alexander Craig of the Royal Army Medical Corps. Alex Craig, married man.

However, there was a commotion in the entrance foyer that was guaranteed to wake up the whole house. Even through the wall the girls could hear a barrage of expletives that would have made a sailor wince.

Iris sat up, her eyes wide and frightened, clutching the blankets tightly in both hands beneath her chin.

'Relax, Iris,' Mary said calmly. 'It's only Effie.'

Effie Donaldson had turned up a week after they had settled into their billets.

They waited for the commotion to die down, but it didn't. Voices called one on top of the other and feet thundered on the stairs.

'What is it, do you think?' Iris asked, one leg out of bed, her hands fumbling to take out her curlers.

'Well, not even Effie makes that much fuss for nothing, so it must be a call-out.'

'But we've just got back. They can't expect us to be out there all the time, surely?'

'I suppose it depends on how serious it is.' Mary was climbing into her uniform. 'Come on, Iris. Never mind your curlers. Shove them under your cap. They'll act as a safety helmet.'

As she crammed her own cap down tightly over her thick hair, a fist hammered on their door and Effie burst in on them without waiting.

'I've been sent,' she announced breathlessly. 'You've got to come quick and it's all hands on deck. All hell's broke loose down on the docks. There's been an explosion at an oil-depot and everything's going up in flames.'

Out in the street the FANYs were assembling and piling into their various modes of transport, mainly converted vans and lorries that doubled as ambulances when they weren't delivering supplies or setting up soup kitchens alongside the Salvation Army. Mary caught sight of Effie, once more astride her bike, heading towards the disaster area.

'West! Morrison!'

Through the noise, Mary and Iris heard their names called out as they emerged into the chilly night and saw Anne Beasley at the wheel of a Humber car. 'Get in! You're coming with me.'

'Yes, Beasley!' They gave a fleeting salute and moved forward.

Mary jumped into the vehicle, her heart pounding as Iris crushed herself beside her, then they held on for dear life as Anne set off at a breathtaking pace. Their way was lit by a full moon. Before long even the moon was outdone by the rosy glow from fires raging for about a mile all the way down to the docks.

'Sorry!' Anne, who was not driving well at all, had mounted the pavement a second time as she careered around a corner, following the other vehicles. The car teetered and almost turned over.

Mary could hear Iris muttering beside her and saw Iris crossing herself over and over again. She bit down on her smile and refrained from reminding her friend that she wasn't a Catholic. Iris, she knew, had done a lot of praying since their arrival in London weeks ago. All she could talk of, these days, was the end of the war and how, the next time, she was going to get married and get pregnant, and not necessarily in that order. Anything, she kept saying, rather than join up again.

'Say one for me, Iris,' Mary said out of the corner of her mouth as they approached the barrier line where the first officials on the scene were giving instructions and doing their best to put some order into the obvious chaos.

A red-faced ARP warden stepped out and banged on the driver's door of the car. Mary felt Anne jump nervously next to her. They had never seen their CO in action. It was, therefore, somewhat worrying, though not entirely surprising, to see pure apprehension ooze out of Anne's pores. Her neck muscles strained as she swallowed with apparent difficulty.

'Sorry, ladies,' the warden said, giving them all a curious once-over. 'You'll never make it down this way. You'll have to go around and approach it from the south. You lot Army, are you?'

Anne froze and just stared ahead of her, her eyeballs protruding and wobbling in her head. Her knuckles on the steering wheel showed white bone.

'We're FANYs,' Mary explained as another explosion went off and Iris started praying again.

'Oh, I see. That's what that crazy female on the motorbike said she was. Wouldn't take any notice of me. Rode straight on as if she had some kind of guardian angel sitting on her shoulder and knew it.'

'That's got to be Effie,' Mary said, her heart turning over. 'Did she get through?'

The man shrugged, then looked at where a new column of smoke and leaping flames were reaching for the sky from a large building a couple of hundred yards down the road.

'I'd like to say yes, miss, but that there building was where she was headed. It's a hostel for the blind. I daresay not many of them will need their white sticks now. Sorry about your friend, miss.'

Mary gulped and turned to Anne, who hadn't changed her expression at all and showed no inclination to do anything but sit there, unmoving, clinging to her wheel.

'Beasley!' Mary shouted and shook the girl's shoulder. 'Anne! Come on, we've got to do something. Drive on.'

There was a rattling sound as Anne blinked and continued to stare ahead. The noise was her teeth clattering with fear and her skin, pale and grey-tinged, seemed to be covered in goose pimples and was damp with glistening perspiration.

'Can't!' Anne uttered through the rattling teeth. 'I can't do it! I can't!'

'What did she say?' Iris wanted to know, her own teeth chattering slightly.

'She's in shock,' Mary told her, leaning over Anne to open the car door and calling out to the ARP warden, who was still standing there on the street: 'Can you help her out? I need to get to the wheel.'

The man hesitated fractionally, not used to taking orders from a female, then he nodded and lifted Anne bodily from the vehicle and set her down on the pavement. Anne's legs buckled under her and she sat down abruptly on the cracked concrete.

'Look after her, will you?' Mary said, slipping into the driver's seat and easing the car forward, ignoring the man's warning shouts. 'We'll come back for her.'

'Oh, God, Mary, what are you doing?' Iris cried out, hanging on to the side of the car as it veered this way and that, avoiding the pitted ground and the lumps of stone and brickwork from the damaged buildings on either side of them. 'You'll get us both killed!'

'Get out if you want to, Iris,' Mary shouted back. 'I don't mind, but I'm going in there to look for Effie.'

'She's not worth the effort,' Iris said unkindly. 'Anyway, they say the Devil takes care of his own.'

'What makes you think he's on Effie's side?'

They had almost reached the hostel when more flames shot up from its roof and black plumes of smoke writhed out of the blasted windows. Rescue teams around the building backed off with urgent shouts as a wall collapsed.

'It's no good, Mary,' Iris whimpered at her side. 'She's had it. Nobody's going to get out of that building now.'

Mary drove forward as far as she could get, but left the engine running. It might have been seconds later, or minutes, she would never know, but suddenly there was a shout and somebody pointed. She followed the pointing finger, squinting towards the entrance of the building where she could see a movement through the curtains of smoke that billowed out into the street.

'I don't believe it!' Mary's eyes were burning and streaming and the smoke was attacking her lungs and making her cough.

'What? Mary, what's happening?' Iris was rubbing her own eyes and coughing too.

'Look for yourself, Iris. Now do you think that Effie Donaldson isn't worth a kind thought?'

As the wind became blustery and blew the smoke away, a figure emerged. Effie, as black as a chimney sweep, having difficulty putting one staggering foot before the other, advanced with great determination. Behind her, there was a man of indeterminate age, his hand resting on her shoulder. And behind him, another, and another. In all, there must have been twenty blind men, walking in a long, linked chain, all following Effie Donaldson as she led them to safety.

An ambulance pulled up and started loading the blind men, and Effie sank to her hunkers and watched, calling out to them.

'Ta-rah, lads!'

They lifted sightless eyes and shouted their heartfelt thanks.

'Aw, man, it was nowt!' she called back. 'We was bliddy lucky, that's all. You take care now.'

Mary, with Iris following like a shadow, approached carefully, watching where she placed her feet.

'Effie?'

Effie looked up, wiped a sooty hand across her eyes and grinned.

'Well, just look what the wind blew in.'

As Mary got closer she saw that the dirt on Effie's face was streaked with blood and her uniform was torn in a variety of places.

'Are you all right?' she asked, thinking it was a ridiculous question, for the girl was obviously injured.

'I'll mend, but there are some poor sods in there that won't,' Effie told her. 'I don't suppose you've got a fag, have ye?'

Mary shook her head, but then a burly policeman stepped forward, a packet of Players in his outstretched hand.

'Here you are, luv. Have one of mine.' He even lit it for her and watched her inhale, wincing slightly as she did so. 'Keep the pack, eh? That was a brave thing you did back there.'

'Aw, gan on, man. Anybody would have done the same. Ta for the fags.'

He turned to Mary and shook his head as if he couldn't believe Effie's words.

'She's one of your lot, isn't she? I see you're all wearing the same badge. ATS is it?'

'We're in the FANYs,' Mary told him proudly.

'Well, I suppose the F must stand for "fearless". Take my advice now and get your friend seen to. There's a first-aid station a couple of streets away. I expect they'll also need a helping hand down there. That is, unless you're all off to a dance?'

He laughed and strolled off down the devastated street, giving them a brief, backward glance and a wave.

'Come on, Effie. He's right. Let's get you seen to.'

'Gawd, that sounds like I'm a dog and ye're gonna have us put doon.'

Mary hooked a hand under Effie's armpit and helped her to rise. She had difficulty standing, for her legs appeared to have turned to rubber.

'Hang on to me, Effie.'

'Aye, I think I will, if ye don't mind, but don't let anybody see.'

Iris hesitated a split second, then went to the other side of the injured girl and between them she and Mary walked Effie back to the Humber. They had to lift her in and only then did they see the blood-soaked trouser-leg where something jagged had pierced the material and torn the flesh.

'Don't worry,' Mary gripped Effie's cold hand. 'We'll just pick up Anne and take you both to the first-aid station.'

Anne had not shifted from the spot where they had left her, but the rigidity of the initial state of shock had seeped away, leaving her huddled and crying silent tears.

'It's all right, Anne,' Mary said, putting a tight arm about the girl's shoulders. 'None of us knows how we're going to react to situations like these. Not even the men, so there's an excuse for us not being too brave, isn't there?'

Anne simply hung her head and climbed into the back of the car with Effie. Nobody spoke as Mary drove around the bomb craters at about twenty miles an hour. She couldn't have driven any faster, even if Hitler himself had been after them. Her insides shook, but she didn't dare show it.

*

'What are youse three going to do with yer leave, then?' Effie sat scratching the healing scar on her injured leg.

Mary lay back against the leather upholstery of the King's Cross to Newcastle train and let out a long, low, sigh. Two whole days of being back in Felling. It seemed like sheer luxury, though she knew it would be over all too soon.

'I don't know, Effie,' she said, stretching and yawning. 'I'd like to spend some time on the sands at South Shields. And maybe I'll go dancing at the Palais. And I can always lend a hand to the social services, as long as they don't ask me to knit or sew. Maybe I'll go up to the hospital and do something there . . . write letters for servicemen or something.'

'I'm going to enjoy doing absolutely nothing,' Iris said. 'That is, unless I can find myself a sweetheart and then, who knows?'

'Gawd, listen to the pair of ye's,' Effie said with a smirk. 'What d'ye think ye can do in two bliddy days, eh?'

'Effie,' said Iris from behind closed lids and a Cheshire cat grin, 'if you have to ask, I feel sorry for you.'

'Nah, divvint dee that, man! I figure we're all better off without a man. They cause nothing but problems. I know. I lived with plenty of 'em.'

'But they were your brothers and your father, Effie,' Mary said. 'It's not quite the same, is it?'

'Isn't it?' Effie sniffed then gave her nose a good blow on a grubby hankie. 'Tell us about it some day.'

'What are you going to do, Anne?' Mary said, looking across at Anne Beasley, who had remained silent for most of the journey, pretending to be interested in the book she was reading.

'Just spend some time with the family,' Anne said, her pale eyes lifting, then she returned to the page she hadn't turned for the last fifteen minutes. 'I believe my father's going to be there for a few days. His old war wound's playing up, He was wounded at the front during the First World War, you know.'

'Eeh, that must be painful,' Effie said as she nibbled on a fingernail. 'My brother was wounded at the back. He couldn't sit down for weeks. Them French farmers all protect their daughters with shotguns and our Ted's got a back end on him that's not easy to miss, even when he's in full flight.'

Anne stared at her uncomprehendingly, while Mary and Iris fell about laughing, enjoying the release it gave them.

'What did I say, then?' Effie asked, her eyes opening wide.

'Oh, Effie, you're priceless,' Mary told her. 'Don't ever change, will you?'

'Fat chance of that. Hey, we're coming into Newcastle.'

A whistle bleated, the engine coughed and metal clanked loudly as the train slowed down to an unsteady crawl, pulling into the platform where travellers waited to go on to Edinburgh. There were a lot of uniforms, a lot of anxious women saying goodbye, and children looking lost and pensive. The gaiety seemed to have gone out of the city.

After London, Mary knew it would be pretty quiet back home. Quiet, but blissful. It would make it all the more difficult to get back into the swing of things once they returned to the Capital. It would take a great deal of courage. Perhaps more than she possessed. But she would do it somehow. She might be only a tiny cog in a very large wheel, but it had to help. It had to! And she wasn't alone. There were so many people with the same fears, doing their best just as she was, even if their best wasn't good enough.

Iris was scared all the time, but she managed to rise above that fear. Anne went rigid with shock, but she still went on, more disturbed by being thought a coward than giving in to her fears. As for Effie, she seemed to be completely fearless. Some of the girls in the unit thought her stupid and brainless. Mary would rather trust her life to that girl's bravado than to any other person she had ever met.

By the time the girls hopped on to a tramcar for Felling dusk was falling, and the blackout became effective, with all the buildings turning into dark silhouettes. As they crossed Sunderland Road and headed for the High Street, a special constable with a muted torch hailed them and demanded to see their identity cards.

'Is that you, Fred Gibbons?' Effie squinted as he shone the torch-beam into her face. 'Take that thing away, will ye. It'll give ye nightmares.'

'Effie Donaldson? Well, I'll be damned!'

'You will be if you don't let us get home soon.'

'And here was me thinkin' you was dead!'

'I'm flattered that you thought of me at all, Fred. Come on, bonnie lad, let us pass. These are friends of mine.'

There was a snicker of a laugh, then the fellow swept his torch-beam across the other three faces and looked suitably mollified when he saw their uniforms.

'Well, I never! So, it's true. You did join the Army.'

'The FANYs, Fred.'

'Oh, aye? Whatever. Off ye's go, and don't hang about. Ye nivvor know, there might be an air-raid th' night.'

'Hitler wouldn't dare. Not th' night, Fred. It's our first night back home.'

True to Effie's word, Hitler did not attack that night. Mary sat in her parent's home, trying to read the letters they had saved for her, while fielding her mother's questions on the quality of her accommodation and the food, and her father's questions on the state of the docklands in London.

'Eeh, love, it's so good to have you back home,' her mother said for the umpteenth time, pushing forward plates of biscuits and wedges of custard tart that she had baked specially for the day, probably using all her sugar allowance to do so.

Mary smiled. There was a limit to how many times you could give the same response to the same statement. There was a letter from Walter. Just the one. She opened it, trying to feel something other than concern for his safety. Like her mother, Walter seemed incapable of saying anything new. He talked of the weather that wasn't being too kind to them; of the "canny lads" in his unit and the old French homesteads he had seen. The French, he thought, were a funny lot who made a lot of noise when they talked, and had no manners. They ate anything that moved and the villages usually had open drains that stank to high heaven in the afternoon sun.

And he ended with: "Not much action yet, but they say we might see some Germans soon. I'm looking forward to it. Hope you are well and thinking of me and us. Home soon. Love, Walter.'

'Is that from Walter, love?' Jenny looked inquisitively up from her sewing. 'How is that fiancé of yours?'

Mary put Walter's letter back on the table.

'He says he's looking forward to meeting the Germans soon.'

'Oh, dear God! Poor lad.'

'Yes.'

'Who are your other letters from? They all seem to be from the same person. Nice handwriting.'

Mary looked at the three envelopes, swallowed, gathered them up and smiled at her mother.

'It's just a friend, Mum. A . . . a soldier, you know. Lots of the girls write to servicemen serving abroad. It's good to make them feel as if they have somebody back home. Letters are important when they're away from home.'

'Aye, I can see that, poor souls. But Mary, you wouldn't . . . I mean . . . don't forget that you're marrying Walter, now, will you?'

'Oh, Mam, stop going on about Walter and me getting married. Now, if you don't mind, it's late and I'm tired, so I think I'll go to bed.'

Jenny gave her a funny look. 'All right, love. See you in the morning, eh?'

There were three letters from Alex Craig. She couldn't believe it. They were friendly, chatty letters – the kind a brother might send, but he wasn't her brother. He asked her questions, too. Where was she, what was she doing, was she safe and happy? And, why didn't she write? He would value a letter from her so much.

Mary started to crumple the letters up, then straightened them out again and hid them beneath the blotter of her leather writing-set that Helen had given her last Christmas. She picked up her pen and wrote: 'Dear Alex . . .' Even the act of writing to him seemed like a betrayal. That would be how Alex's wife would see it, no doubt. But Mary swallowed her guilt and gave way to the compelling desire to reach out to him, even if it were only a matter of a few hastily scribbled words on a scrap of paper.

As it was, her renewed thoughts of Dr Alex Craig uppermost in her mind, she found it impossible to sleep. However, she told herself, it was because it was so quiet up here, not like the constant hustle and bustle of the great city.

The following morning, she was up early, just as the blackout was lifted. Her mother, always an early riser, was already in the kitchen preparing scrambled eggs from the chickens they kept in the back yard. It would be a welcome change to the powdered egg they had forced upon them in London. You could taste the stuff for hours after eating it.

'You're not going out already, are you, our Mary?' Jenny said when Mary pushed her empty plate away from her and gulped down the last drop of tea.

'Yes, Mum. I need to get out and walk about a bit. You know, see the place.'

Her mother laughed. 'Well, Felling hasn't changed much, love, war or no war. But you enjoy your walk. The fresh air will do you good. You look thin and pale. I hope I can pamper you while you're home. Fatten you up a bit.'

Her mother fattening her up used to be the bane of Mary's life. It had turned her into a well-built girl who could have easily lost a few pounds to look and feel better, but Jenny would never see it that way. If people didn't eat three square meals a day, she thought they were sickening for something.

These days, people were lucky if they could get one square meal a day, now that food was rationed. There was never enough to go around, unless, of course, you paid through the nose to the black-market men who were popping up everywhere.

There had been a lot of that kind of thing in London. Spivs, they called the men who were able to provide just about anything, at a price. Spivs and wide boys. In other words, barrow-boys who were on the make and ready to twist their own grandmothers out of their last penny in order to make money. They usually wore broad brimmed trilbies, jackets with wide shoulders and those awful loud ties. And they had a very persuasive way of speaking.

Mary took a slow walk down to Victoria Square. It looked much the way it had always done, apart from the absence of iron railings. These had been melted down and were now helping to build ships or making guns or plane parts. There was no bomb damage that she could see. Her mother had told her that the nearest they had so far come to being bombed was when they were virtually shaken out of their beds by an explosion in Gateshead a few miles away.

She looked around her at the people who went about their everyday business and wondered if they knew how lucky they were not to be living in the south-east corner of England, which would undoubtedly be the main target area if the Germans ever got through.

Women in headscarves, clutching shopping bags, were queuing outside the Co-op. Their faces were serious, their eyes had a faraway glaze to them, their normal chatter was now reduced by the thoughts and the experiences of war.

Mary acknowledged one or two smiles and nods from people who recognized her. She was giving a wave to Walter's father through the window of his butcher's shop when she collided with a woman coming out.

'Oh, I'm sorry!' Mary apologized, bending to pick up a package the woman had dropped.

It was in doing so that she noticed the large flat dress box the woman was carrying, which hid the fact that she was pregnant. The woman muttered something, and adjusted her coat and the box so that her condition was again well hidden. Without a further word, she hurried off, leaving Mary frowning after her, wondering where she had seen her before and why she should behave so oddly.

There was a rapping on the glass window beside her and Mary looked up to see Mr Morgan beckoning. The shop was almost empty of customers, the last one being attended to by Walter's mother, who looked red-faced and flustered, but pleased to see Mary all the same.

'Hello, lass,' George Morgan patted her shoulder. 'You home on leave, are you? I hear you've been in London. What's it like down there, then?'

'Oh, George,' his wife said, pushing by him so that she could give Mary a hug. 'Let the girl be. I'm sure she doesn't want to talk about London, do you, pet?'

'Not really,' Mary said with a wry smile. 'I was just thinking that you would hardly know there's a war on here in Felling. It's lovely.'

'Aye, well, don't let folks hear you say that. They think they're hard done to, some of them. Have you heard from our Walter, pet?'

Mary nodded. 'Yes, there was a letter waiting for me.' She hesitated, not wishing to impart any information before knowing how much Walter had told his parents. With his father's bad heart and his mother's nerves, it was probably best they didn't know too much.

'He's going to be fighting the Germans soon,' Mrs Morgan said, drawing her mouth in and rolling anxious eyes to the ceiling. 'Our Walter's not a fighter. I mean, what's he going to do out there with all the bullets flying and the bombs going off? It's not right, it isn't.'

'I don't think Walter has a choice, Maureen,' her husband said with a look at Mary. 'None of them have, poor souls.'

Mary thought it was time to change the subject and recalled the woman she had bumped into.

'That woman who went out just now,' she said. 'The one carrying the big box. . . ? I seem to know her face, but can't put a name to it. Who is she, do you know?'

'Oh, her!' Maureen Morgan tilted her chin up and gave a disdainful sniff. 'That's the doctor's wife. Young Dr Craig, I mean. They say the higher you jump the further you have to fall, and didn't she fall flat on her snooty face!'

'Oh . . . but. . . .' Mary remembered Alex's wife now and her heart sank. He had not mentioned the baby in his letters, but surely he must know. 'I didn't realize she was . . . expecting.'

Mr Morgan moved off to leave the two women chatting about domestic matters. Mrs Morgan gave a smirk and her fingers dug into Mary's wrist.

'No, and I doubt her husband does either, but when he gets back, he's going to have a surprise waiting for him, isn't he? And you'd be right in your calculations, though she's trying to pass it off as his, the brazen hussy.'

'Do you mean. . . ?'

'Aye, pet. If that poor lad's the father of her child it would be some kind of blooming miracle.'

CHAPTER SEVEN

'Is this the first time you've been on board ship?' the young purser asked Mary.

Mary was leaning on the ship's rail, gazing out in wonder at the heaving sea as Plymouth and the shores of England disappeared behind them. A few feet away Iris was leaning over the same rail, but not for the same reason. Her face was almost as green as the undulating waters beneath her. She had not been able to utter a word without retching since they embarked on their most exciting posting since joining the FANYs.

The purser had caught Mary's eye the moment she had ventured outside their cabin, making sure he was always within speaking distance, smiling shyly and looking as if he was desperate to find a way to get to know her without being too obvious. This was the exact opposite to what she had expected, being on a ship full of naval personnel. They had a certain reputation with the ladies that she was hoping to avoid, but the purser had a nice face, so she turned a beaming a smile on him.

'I've been on a ferry boat on the River Tyne,' she told him, 'but this is a bit different.'

'You're not scared, are you?' he said, moving closer to her so that their elbows touched.

'Scared? No. I find it exhilarating.'

'Not like your friend over there, eh?' He nodded in Iris's direction. 'I hate to think what she's going to be like when we really get out to sea.'

'Poor Iris, yes.'

'She's not the only one. A lot of the sailors who come on board for the first time spend hours puking, just like that, until they find their sea-legs.'

He gave her a wide-eyed stare that made her feel self-conscious, but it wasn't entirely unpleasant to have a good-looking young man to talk to.

'Well, that's encouraging, I must say,' she laughed. 'So, how long are we going to be on board before we get to France?'

He gave a shrug. 'That depends on whether or not we meet trouble. These days we have to sneak in by the back door, and even then the Gerry U-boats manage to intercept some of our ships. They've got ruddy crystal balls, if you ask me.'

'Well, let's hope their fortune teller is on leave today.'

'You're a FANY, aren't you? We've shipped a couple of units over to France lately. They're great girls. You going to the Polish camp?'

He was referring to Coetquidan, where hundreds of Polish soldiers were camped, having escaped capture by the Germans and had managed somehow to make their way to France. They were assembled around the Breton town waiting for transportation to England. In the meantime, FANY units were employed to keep the men happy and sane, so far away from their homeland. Ambulances and mobile canteens manned by FANY girls were much in demand. They brought with them not only the spirit of the Corps, for which they were already famous since the First World War, but also a goodly supply of home comforts.

'We'll get our orders when we land,' Mary said carefully, her training in close-mouthed security coming to the fore.

'Right.' The purser straightened and glanced over his shoulder at the sound of the captain's voice calling him from the steps to the bridge. 'Looks like I'm needed. Maybe I'll see you later? There's a film on in the officer's mess, if you're interested.'

'That's nice. Yes, I'm sure we'll all be there.'

'Yes . . . right . . . well . . .' He looked slightly crestfallen and Mary wished they had met somewhere on land, on a pier perhaps, with the only things likely to dive-bomb them were the seagulls. 'Enjoy the trip.'

Mary went to stand by Iris, whose colour was changing slightly from green to grey and pink-tinged around the edges.

'Oh, God, Mary! This is awful. They didn't warn us about . . .' She clamped her mouth shut and swallowed with difficulty.

'I must have the blood of an old sea dog in me somewhere.' Mary laughed gently and gave her friend a hug. 'I'm really enjoying this. It's so exhilarating.'

'We're not here to have fun,' Iris said and managed a grin, for she had repeated the words their CO had instilled into them. 'We're here to help our country win the war, or so the boss says at every opportunity.'

'Exactly! But nobody said we couldn't do both.'

The boss of their unit, this time, was not Anne Beasley, but a rather stern, older woman, who was a stickler for military precision and was sadly lacking when it came to a sense of humour.

'I'd give anything to be back home right now.'

'Don't let our raw recruits hear you say that, Ensign Morrison. You don't want a mutiny on your hands.'

'I can't think why they promoted me like that, Mary.' Iris looked puzzled. 'I mean, I'm just an ordinary girl like the rest of our unit, and not all that bright, really.'

'Go on with you.' Mary shook her head. 'You drive that canteen of ours like a demon and you have a photographic memory when it comes to maps. Don't you realize how valuable that is, to be able to memorize a route like that? I get lost if I turn round in Oxford Street.'

'Don't look now, but we're not in Oxford Street, Mary,' Iris said, doing her best to keep the conversation light-hearted, despite her innermost feelings. 'But I am glad we're still together, you and me and . . .'

'And Effie,' Mary finished for her. 'Yes, me too.'

'Oh, God, that Effie will be the death of me.'

'I hope not, Iris. Where is she, anyway?'

'Last time I saw her she was sitting on her bunk swearing she wouldn't budge for hell or high water until she could get away from all those men in uniform.' Iris gave Mary a hard look. 'And by the way, Mary, I saw you chatting to the purser as if that ring on your finger didn't mean anything.'

'Don't be daft, Iris. He was the one flirting, not me.' Mary glanced down at her left hand and spread the fingers. 'In any case, I don't wear Walter's ring any more.'

'Oh, Mary! Why ever not? You haven't broken up with him, have you?'

Mary gave a slight shake of her head and concentrated on the foamy white wake of the ship streaming out behind them like a fluttering bridal train. She didn't know if she would ever be a bride, but one thing was certain. Walter would never be her husband. It had taken a kiss from Alex Craig and a long separation to finally make up her mind, but made up it was.

'Don't let's talk about it,' she said, and Iris knew from the tone of her voice that it was time to change the subject, so they talked about the cinema on board and how they would enjoy watching Clarke Gable and Claudette Colbert in *It Happened One Night*.

A few hours later, almost silently, and under cover of darkness, HMS Dolphin docked at St Malo. Iris, Mary, Effie and the rest of their unit assembled until the call was given to mount their vehicles and drive off the ship. During the short voyage their CO, Captain Mountford, had been taken ill with appendicitis and was to be returned to England, leaving Iris in command. With some trepidation, she took the wheel of the leading van, which they had christened Phoebe. Beside her, Mary and Effie sat mute, sharing the same tingling anticipation as everyone else. At long last, they were going to see a different side of the war and the excitement was tangible as if it wrapped itself around them like a thick army blanket. There was underlying fear too, but none of them dared dwell on that.

Iris drove carefully, following the waving hands that guided her down the ramp and on to the dock. From there, more hands waved, beckoning her forward, until one white palm halted their progress and someone approached the driver's side of the vehicle.

'Eeh, what is it now?' Effie complained, then her eyes popped out on stalks as the man in strange, civilian dress, threw them a string of words in rapid French.

'Mary?' Iris glanced over at Mary and raised her eyebrows. She knew some French, but the man's accent was heavy with a patois.

Mary leaned over and answered him. There was a short exchange, then she nodded and patted Iris's arm.

'It's all right,' she said. 'This is our guide, Gaston Frébus. He has orders to ride with us to the Polish camp.'

'That's going to be cosy,' Iris muttered out of the corner of her mouth. 'Couldn't we have brought your purser along? This one's not so pretty to look at.'

Mary saw the Frenchman's face twitch. Above the large Breton moustache that hung down like a black curtain, his dark eyes twinkled.

'Tell your friend,' he said, in perfect English, 'that it is not how we look, but how we behave that counts in this life.'

'He's bloody English!' Effie swore loudly.

'And tell your other friend,' the man said, 'that we are not necessarily what we appear to be, including the Germans.'

'I think she's already finding that out, *monsieur*,' Mary said, returning his twinkling smile.

'Permission to come aboard, *mademoiselle*?' He was again addressing Iris.

'Permission granted . . . er . . .' Iris looked flustered.

'Just call me Gaston,' he said. 'I'll need to sit up front.'

'I'll go in the back,' Effie decided, already scrambling over into the back of the van. 'And you drive carefully, Iris. I don't want me bike to fall over or to have crockery landing on me head.'

'It's all very informal,' Gaston said as he settled himself on Mary's left.

'That's only when the three of us are on our own,' Mary told him. 'We come from the same small town in north-east England.'

'Ah! I thought I detected a regional accent.' He slapped his hands on his knees and slipped back into French. '*Alors, mes braves! On y va!*'

'What did he say?' said Iris, and Mary could tell from the tone that her friend's jaws were tightly clenched.

'He says let's go.'

'Well, what are we hanging about for, eh?' came from Effie in the back. 'Go on, Iris. On yer var . . . or whatever he said.'

Gaston's forehead creased slightly, then a wide grin spread over his face and he laughed.

'I think I'm going to enjoy the journey, *mesdames*.'

It wasn't such a long journey in terms of miles, but it was slow because of the narrow, winding country roads and the fact that they could only drive with tiny slits in the heavily masked headlights. At one point Iris stopped the van at a crossroads and frowned at Gaston, who had instructed her to go straight on.

'No, we go right here, surely,' she said confidently. 'Right, left, then straight on until we reach Rennes.'

'You could be mistaken,' Gaston said, a half quizzical smile showing beneath his moustache.

'But she's not,' said Mary. 'Is she?'

There was a short hesitation, then the Frenchman shook his head. 'Well done. I thought I might catch you out. They told me you were good, Ensign Morrison. I just didn't appreciate how good. Right it is.'

After a few miles they had to stop when one of the vans ended nose first in a roadside ditch, having skidded on a patch of mud. It took a while to locate the local farmer, who came to their rescue with a team of Percherons and a handful of farm workers. While they waited, the farmer's wife gave them all a taste of home made red wine. It was so rough it almost stripped their tonsils, but they appreciated the gesture and the woman's tears as she pleaded with them to help keep France free.

'Mary?' Gaston came to chat to her while they waited for the toppled van to be pulled back on to the road. 'I may call you Mary?'

'Yes, of course. Are you French or English, Gaston?'

'We have to be adaptable in this job,' he said, without really answering her question.

'The Resistance?'

'You know better than to ask.'

'I don't need to. I was told to expect contact from you as soon as we arrived in France.'

'I see. Your French is excellent, by the way. Only a slight accent that could be taken for Belgian. Where did you learn the language?'

'I had a private tutor,' Mary told him, 'and I spent a lot of time in France with her and a friend when we were children.'

'Very convenient. And you speak German, too, I hear.'

'Not fluently, but I can get along all right.'

'That's good, because the Poles tend to speak either Russian or German. I imagine you will be very popular with them. They don't understand much English, yet they are destined for England, when we can get them out.'

'How long will that take, do you know?'

'Hard to tell. It could be weeks. On the other hand, if we're unlucky, it might only be a matter of days.'

'Always nice to hear good news!' The words were muttered behind them and they spun around to find Effie standing there, her shoulders slumped and her hands deep in her pockets. 'Couldn't you think of anything better to greet us with?'

Without waiting for a response, she marched off down the line of ambulances looking for her usual handout of cigarettes.

'What a strange creature,' said Gaston, himself drawing deeply on a strong-smelling Gauloise.

'Effie's all right,' Mary told him, smiling fondly after the other girl. 'I'd trust her with my life.'

'She is so full of anger, that *petite garce*!'

'That's just her way. I suspect there's a soft place deep down somewhere inside her heart. She just doesn't like it to show. I suppose it makes her feel vulnerable.'

'Are you always so understanding, Mary?' He flicked the ash from his cigarette and picked a shred of tobacco from his tongue.

Mary blinked at him, surprised at his words. 'I didn't realize I was being particularly understanding,' she said.

'Well, you are. I know now why they sent you.'

'I'm trained in communications,' she said with a little laugh. 'There's not much call for understanding when you're dealing with dots and dashes.'

'I think you'll find you'll be deployed among the refugees rather than wasting your talents behind a machine. I assume there are others in this unit who can handle Morse code?'

'All of us, to some extent,' she said and he looked impressed. 'That, and driving and a bit of mechanical engineering. It was all very hurried, so we're not what you might call experts, but we muddle through.'

'And what about your friend?' He was watching Iris through half-closed eyes. 'Does she muddle through?'

'Iris passed muster with higher grades than the rest of us when it came to driving and orienteering, as you've already noticed. She can't add two and two, but she has a photographic memory.'

'She's afraid, but she copes with it well.'

'We're all scared, Gaston.' Mary was beginning to get irritated with the mysterious man from the French Resistance. 'We'd be fools if we weren't. It's what keeps us on our toes.'

'But *you're* not scared,' Gaston flashed her a look, then turned back to study Iris. 'Neither is the little spitfire you call Effie . . . but Ensign Iris . . .'

He sucked air through his teeth and shook his head. Mary felt her hackles rise slightly.

'As you yourself indicated,' she said quickly, 'people aren't always what they seem. Don't worry about Iris. She can function, even through her fear.'

'Well, we shall see.' Gaston threw his cigarette down and extinguished it with his heel. 'Come on. The van has been returned to the road.'

The small column of vans and ambulances bearing the sign of the Red Cross as well as the insignia of the FANYs, set off once again. This time, Gaston placed himself between Mary and Iris, which might have been coincidental, or strategic planning on his part. Mary wasn't sure, but when he placed an arm behind Iris's back, she saw her friend's cheeks glow surprisingly pink as the dawn light crept over the land.

The Polish holding camp south of Rennes, just outside the town of Coetquidan, was one of several based in Brittany. There were, nevertheless, over a hundred Polish refugees housed there. At first sight of the fragile, emaciated creatures who stood or sat outside their Army issue huts, the FANY unit felt profound shock.

'Eeh, gawd, look at them,' Effie exclaimed in a horrified whisper, for it would have been unseemly to speak out loud about the state of these men who watched them with gaping mouths and staring, haunted eyes.

'We've heard about their suffering,' Mary said, her voice hoarse with emotion, 'but I never thought it would be as bad as this.'

'Are they sick?' Iris asked and Gaston shook his head.

'Not in the way you mean,' he said. 'They are sick with fear and exhaustion and loneliness, just like every soldier who has been removed from his homeland and dropped behind enemy lines. That goes for the German soldiers too. They are not all Nazis, you know. Don't ever forget that.'

'What will happen to these men?'

'They will stay here until Britain decides to move them. They have refused to retreat and give themselves up to the Germans. They would rather die first.'

'Brave men,' Mary said.

Gaston gave a nod. 'Yes. Britain can make use of them, if we can get them over the Channel.'

Mary gulped back the question that rose like a lump in her throat. Did that mean, she wondered, that there was a risk that the Poles would not make it to England? And if that were so, what of the FANY units that were now here, supposedly to make things better for them? Would they, too, be trapped like rats in a cage?

The girls were shown to a long, corrugated-iron shack that would have housed ten comfortably, but they were nearer to twenty women and beds had been pushed together so closely that there was hardly any room to walk around them.

There was a Major Moorcroft in charge, who welcomed them apologetically to their cramped quarters, then handed them over to a sergeant who explained the workings of the camp, where everything was to be found and, lastly, instructed them on how to light the wood-burning stove that stood in the centre of the building.

'She's a temperamental bitch, this one, but a good kick in the arse . . . beggin' yer pardon, ladies . . . usually does the trick.'

'That works with men, too,' Effie said, which raised a laugh, especially when the sergeant's mouth dropped open as he took a good look at who had spoken.

'Gawd luv us! I ain't seen no FANY like you, luv. They usually talks posh like a lot of Princess Elizabeths.'

'Well, if Princess Elizabeth had been born in Gateshead, she might talk like me an' all.'

'You, I've got to get to know.' The soldier rocked on his heavy boots and grinned from ear to ear.

'Don't bank on that, hinny,' Effie said, two rosy spots appearing on her cheeks, but there was the hint of a smile. 'Cheeky bugger.'

'So, Sergeant,' Iris had stepped forward before Effie could start a slanging match, 'now that we're here, what do you want us to do?'

'Basically, it's household stuff. And a bit of social life for the Poles. You know what I mean. . . ?'

'If he means what I think he means, I'm off.' Effie's smile had been replaced by a thunderous expression and her bony elbow was digging into Mary's ribs. 'I might be common as muck, me, but I'm no flamin' whore.'

The sergeant looked taken aback, then embarrassed as he realized how his words had been misconstrued.

'Nah, I didn't mean that kind of thing! 'Course I didn't. We've got a gramophone and a few records, but fellas dancing wiv other fellas isn't kosher, like. Not even where the Poles are concerned. The major . . . it was his idea, so don't go blamin' me . . . thought it might be a good idea to organize some kind of dance . . . or concert. Boost morale, sort of thing. Does anybody here speak Polish?'

There was a deathly hush as Iris looked at each girl in turn and they all shook their heads.

'German's not my favourite language at the moment,' said the sergeant, 'but some of these soldiers speak it. And Russian.'

'Well, I can speak some German.' Mary spoke out and three others said they could too, but no one spoke Russian.

'Right,' said Iris, squaring her shoulders and looking as if she meant business; she was obviously enjoying her new role as the acting CO. 'Let's split ourselves up into groups. Some of you on the domestics . . . cleaning and cooking and the likes. Others, like West here, and you three . . . Hart, Marshall and Waring . . . conversation, writing of letters etc., We were all briefed on what would be required before we left England, so let's get to it.'

'Hang about a bit.' The sergeant held up his hands, then pointed at Effie. 'You . . . the poisoned dwarf. What can you do, eh?'

'Not that it's any of your business, but I do a good job of laying out dead bodies,' Effie answered him and he did a double take.

'Yes, well . . .' The soldier's face twisted and he scratched his head as he stared at Effie in disbelief. 'That could come in handy, I suppose.'

'Yes, but make sure you don't lie down when she's around,' shouted out one of the girls. 'She'll have you embalmed quicker than you can say "cor blimey".'

'Might improve his looks,' said another.

'All right, all right, that's enough!' Iris clapped her hands and her unit jumped smartly to attention, but the smiles were still evident; Iris Morrison was well-liked, despite her northern accent. 'We have our work cut out. I suggest we start straight away by going around and getting to know the Polish soldiers. Shut up, Donaldson!'

'I nivvor said a word, me!' Effie's eyes widened to their full innocence.

'No, but you were going to,' Iris said, her mouth twitching at the corners. 'I could hear the rust stirring in your brain.'

'Eeh, I don't know,' Effie said with a grumpy sniff. 'She's always gettin'' at us, that one.'

'Just say "Yes, Morrison", Effie,' Mary said, prodding her from behind.

'Wot? Oh, aye . . . .I mean, yes, Morrison. I'll go and give Joe a bit of spit and polish.' Effie looked at the sergeant, who was scratching his head and looking perplexed. 'That's me bike, just so you don't get any wrong ideas.'

It was to be Effie's job to transport messages between camps, by far the most reliable method of communication. The old Norton was still going strong, despite its delapidated state. She couldn't bear to be parted from it, and had even named it after her dead brother who had owned it before her. Joe had been her favourite brother. A bit of a rough diamond, by all accounts, but as gentle as a lamb with Effie, which was more than could be said for the other men in the family, including her father, who treated the corpses he encountered with more respect than the women in his life.

Mary and the three other girls who spoke some German divided the soldiers between them, which meant they had, on average, twenty-five men each. She found, disappointingly, that most of the men spoke Russian, but only a handful were fluent in German.

One, a major, spoke some English, though it was with difficulty because he had a bad stammer and seemed inordinately shy. The unit had been in the camp only a few days when he approached Mary's table, where she had set up a kind of outdoor office, the weather being so warm and fine.

Jan Berwinski was thirty years old and came from a small town called Poznan. He had pale blond hair and clear blue eyes and was the tallest of all the Polish soldiers in the camp. He must have been handsome once, but the war had taken its toll, lining his face and giving him that terrible, haunted regard that all the men here had, even when they smiled. Laughter was rare. Somehow, they didn't seem to have the strength for it.

Although Major Berwinski was not in Mary's section, coming from the opposite end of the camp, he gravitated towards her on every possible occasion. He even found enough courage to dance with her when the FANYs organized a social gathering on the first Saturday after their arrival. She had felt him shaking like a leaf against her through his heavy uniform, his face red, his brow glistening. At first, he didn't even try to speak to her, but as the evening wore on his nervousness abated. When the dance came to an end, the major introduced himself and asked, with the utmost politeness, if he could come and see her sometime.

She had been a little hesitant, not wishing to offend Waring, in whose section he was. However, Elizabeth Waring seemed to have her hands full with soldiers who spoke neither English nor German, so Mary agreed, and the young Pole looked very relieved.

Mary looked up now from her letter writing at the sound of a throat being cleared. It was a small, self-conscious sound, so it was no surprise to her to find Major Berwinski standing a few yards from her table. She had set up her station beneath the spreading branches of a huge oak-tree since the sun was particularly hot that afternoon.

'Hello, Major Berwinski.' She smiled at him. 'Did you want to see me about something?'

'I . . . I . . . yes . . . I . . .' He took a couple of faltering steps forward, then stopped. 'You have w-work . . . yes? M-m-much w-work?'

Mary put down her pen and pushed the pile of papers she was working on aside. She had been transcribing her own notes, taken down from the soldiers, and turning them into official documents so that the Poles could be more easily assessed and registered when they were eventually transferred to England. It had been a slow and exacting task, extracting the required information from the men in order to trace their families and their military and medical backgrounds.

'I'm not too busy to talk to you, Major,' she said, beckoning to him. 'Please . . . sit down.'

He nodded and slid thankfully into a rickety, farmhouse chair that creaked beneath his weight. Mary smiled and waited. She knew better than to try and force these men to speak about their problems. Already it was painfully obvious that even the fittest among them were psychologically bruised; a condition that was as debilitating as any physical injury.

'I talk with you . . . Miss. . .?' He spread his hands, indicating with embarrassment that he had forgotten her name, which wasn't surprising, given the number of new English people they had been thrown together with over the last few days.

'My name is Mary,' she said and saw his eyes light up.

'Mary? *Ja*! Is name of my woman in Poznan. Maria she is called. Look!'

The inevitable wallet full of photographs from home came out and, with hands that shook somewhat, Jan Berwinski spread his life in black-and-white images on the table before her. Mary picked up one photograph of a pretty young woman with fair hair, which hung over her shoulder in a long plait.

'Is this your wife?' she asked. 'Maria?'

'*Ja* . . . and this . . . my . . . how you say . . . *kinder*. . . ?'

'Children.'

'*Ja* . . . children. *Danke*.'

He pushed a small snapshot towards her. It showed two small children playing in the sunlight by a twinkling river. They were smiling happily up into the camera. The little girl was barely two years old.

'Oh, they're lovely, Jan. You must miss them a lot.'

'I wait to hear news, but n-nothing . . .' He swallowed with difficulty and gazed off into the distance. 'I fear for them.'

'How long is it since you saw them, Jan?'

'Is eight months. If I go to England . . . I do not know when I see them again.' He sucked in a great gulping breath and wiped a hand over his eyes. 'I go now. You work . . .'

'Jan, no . . . just a minute . . .' Mary stood with him, went around the table and took hold of his hand, squeezing it and trying to give this poor man some of her own inner strength. 'Why did you come to talk to me?'

He shook his head. With a brief sweep of his arm he indicated the whole camp stretching out before them.

'I s-speak badly . . . .I cannot speak with them . . . the others. With you, Mary, I do not speak badly. With you I speak like normal person.'

Mary gave him a warm smile and dropped his hand. She had noticed how his stammer had quickly abated each time they had spoken together.

'You can come and talk to me any time, Jan.'

He nodded, then stood to attention before her, clicking his heels with military precision. A tremulous smile lit up his face and he took his leave of her. Mary watched him walk back to his hut, feeling a rush of sympathy that tore at her heart.

'Now, now, Mary.' Iris's voice next to her made her jump. 'No fraternizing with the refugees, even if he did dance with you and go all gooey-eyed when you sang the other night. And he wasn't the only one.'

'Well, they're a long way from home, Iris.'

'So are we, but I suppose it's harder for the Poles, isn't it?'

'Yes, poor souls. They may never see their loved ones again,' Mary said, frowning. 'We really don't know how lucky we are, Iris. These men have lost everything. The major's just been showing me pictures of his wife and children and the place where he lived in Poland. It was beautiful. Heaven only knows what state it's in now, or if his family are still alive.'

'What's his name?' Iris was sifting through a series of official looking messages that had just come in.

'Berwinski,' Mary replied and Iris looked up and blinked, her expression becoming suddenly very serious.

'Major Berwinski? Wife, Maria, two children, Piotr and Anya? From the town of Poznan?'

'Yes, that's right. Why?' Mary's eyes swept over the telegram attached to the government form that Iris handed her. 'Oh, Iris!'

'You'd better tell him.'

Mary wanted to refuse. She couldn't bear to think of the suffering this news was going to inflict upon the young Pole. Hadn't he suffered enough?

'Yes, all right,' she said, straightening herself up and smoothing out the wrinkles in her uniform. This was no time to be overtaken by soft, feminine emotions. She had volunteered to do a job, and this was part of it.

She knocked on the open door of hut number four. When she entered, a group of Poles smoking and playing cards together looked up and saw the telegram clutched in her hand. They had been there long enough to know that it was bad news for one of them. She could see the fearful anticipation shining in their eyes.

'Major Berwinski,' she said, and he turned from the little primus stove where he was making himself a cup of tea. 'Jan. . . ?'

She saw his chest heave. His mouth opened, but no words issued forth. The other men withdrew tactfully, each touching their comrade lightly as they passed. There was no standing on ceremony because of his rank. He was one of them, a man in anguish, and there but for the grace of God they all would go.

As she approached him, Mary saw Jan swallow over and over again, saw his eyes protrude uneasily from his gaunt face, which became more drawn as he waited to hear what she had to say to him.

'It's bad news, Jan,' she said softly, reaching out to steady him as he staggered weakly and clutched at the back of a chair for support.

Almost as if he knew it was on its way, he had been compelled to speak of his wife and children, show her their pictures, trying, perhaps, to ward off the terrible moment by some magical turning of fate.

He shook his head vehemently and put his hands over his ears.

'I do n-not w-w-wish to know!'

Backing away, he collided with the wall, then slid slowly down to the floor. Mary lowered herself down beside him, stroked his bowed head, rubbed a hand comfortingly up and down his rigid spine. Her heart was bursting, but she had to keep her voice steady.

'You have to know, Jan,' she said gently. 'Word has just come in. Maria . . . and the children . . . they've been taken . . . they're not sure where . . . but . . .'

Mary choked on her words. They had almost certainly been transported. Maria Berwinski was a Jew.

'No . . . no . . .' Jan cried out, his head rocking from side to side. 'Dead is better! In a camp they will p-perish . . . s-slowly. Ah . . . my Maria . . . my Piotr . . . my little Anya!'

Mary took him in her arms and held him close. One by one the other men returned to the hut and gathered around. One touched her on the shoulder and nodded, saying something in Russian, which she took to mean that they would look after him now. The soldier helped her to her feet, smiled and nodded again. Mary left them to their shared grief, hoping she would not have too many more incidents like that, though her hopes were probably futile.

She did not have too much time to dwell upon Major Jan Berwinski's sad news, for the moment she stepped out of his hut into the warm, late-afternoon sun, she heard the familiar throb of Effie's motorbike as she rode into camp to deliver another batch of messages from the main base on the other side of Coetquidan.

Within minutes, the CO called an urgent meeting in the staff mess. France was about to fall to the Germans, he announced. Because of the huge enemy advances, they were being forced to strike camp and move north to Normandy where the only remaining British and Canadian stronghold existed.

'These are dangerous times, my friends,' the colonel said, his face tired and drawn. 'Some of us will not survive them. We can only retreat and pray that we make the coast without too much loss of life.'

'Then what do we do?' Effie whispered in Mary's ear. 'Swim across the Channel?'

'If we have to.' Mary smiled grimly, pressing her hand over her heart, which was beating so irregularly that she was finding it difficult to breathe.

'Well, if that's the case, I might as well surrender right now,' Iris said. 'I can't swim.'

'Ye'll not catch me surrendering to the Jerries,' Effie grunted. 'I'll walk on the bliddy water first.'

And, Mary thought, of all of them there, Effie was the one most likely to do just that.

On a cold, wet day in May, Jenny West stood peering through the cemetery railings at the funeral party gathered about the newly dug grave. There was a simple coffin and a single wreath of waxy-white lilies. Not many people were in attendance, she thought, but then it was a very private burial and, given the circumstances, she guessed that the family would be glad to see an end to the affair without too much fuss.

Not that a death in anybody's family should be considered bothersome, she thought. Especially the demise of someone as young as Fiona Craig. The news had seeped through the town on a whisper. Some heads nodded as if they were agreeing that death had served as some kind of justice, but Jenny couldn't bring herself to think so cruelly. A young woman was dead, and her unborn child with her. Complications had set in. A heart defect, apparently, that no one knew about.

Jenny wiped the rain from her spectacles and tried to make out the mourners around the grave where the gravediggers were in the process of lowering the coffin. She could make out Dr Gordon and his wife, and she assumed the grief-stricken couple beside them were the girl's parents, come down from Scotland for the occasion. Another man stood a little way off, looking grey-faced and very much alone. That, she would put money on, was the man who was at the bottom of all the family's troubles. Fiona Craig's fancy man and the father of her dead child. There wasn't a person in Felling who doubted it. The girl had been seen too many times flaunting her affair in public.

Well, she thought with a sigh, they do say we reap what we sow, but this seems harsh justice to me.

She was just about to move away as the group around the grave broke up and people filed out through the cemetery gates. Dr Gordon saw the family members to his car, then got his eye on Jenny and called to her to wait.

'Oh, Dr Gordon, I'm so sorry. I didn't want to disturb you in your time of grief.'

'Not at all, Mrs West.' Dr Gordon was, as ever, polite and friendly. 'I've been thinking about you lately, so I'm glad to have this opportunity. Tell me, have you heard from Mary recently? I heard she joined up.'

'Yes, that's right, Doctor.' Jenny smiled proudly, but inside she was still fearful for Mary's safety. 'She's with the FANYs.'

'That's very admirable. I hear they're extremely well thought of. Where is she stationed? It seems a while since I saw her.'

'Well, she was in London for a while, but she's been moved.'

'So, where is she now?'

'They shipped her off to France, Dr Gordon.'

'Dear me.' Seeing Jenny's anxious expression, Dr Gordon put a hand on her shoulder and smiled reassuringly. 'Let's hope she's not in too much danger. They say the fighting's getting worse and worse as the Germans advance. They're already evacuating servicemen from Dunkirk because there's nowhere for them to retreat to.'

'Dunkirk? Where's that, Dr Gordon?'

'It's next door to Calais – just across the channel.'

'Oh, that's all right, then. Mary's in Brittany. Lovely place that is. She went there once with the Beasleys. She went all over France with them as a bairn, you know.'

'Yes, I see.'

Jenny couldn't understand why he should look so grave, but she put it down to young Mrs Craig's funeral and all that that entailed.

'Your nephew couldn't be here for his wife's funeral, then, poor soul?'

'No, I'm afraid not, Mrs West. We don't even know if he has been informed of her death as yet. It's a difficult situation, you see.'

'Well, yes, that's understandable. But then, we mustn't dwell on the lassie's indiscretions, eh? Best soon forgotten.'

He frowned and gave a little shake of his head.

'No, Mrs West. I wasn't speaking of that silly business . . .' Dr Gordon scraped a large hand over his face. 'Actually, we don't even know if Alex is still alive over there in France. All communication seems to have broken down.'

'Oh! Oh, I see! Oh, I am sorry,' Jenny said, trying to hide her embarrassment. 'Well, let's hope the poor lad gets out.'

'Yes, indeed. Let's hope that . . . and Mary too.'

Jenny nodded and they said their goodbyes. She walked away, feeling a little dazed. Surely Mary couldn't be involved in all that fighting over in France. She was just an innocent volunteer after all. Her job was to drive people about and do a little clerical work. She was teaching English to Polish refugees, for goodness sake, not shooting at Germans.

'Helen!' She banged on her eldest daughter's door and thanked God that the girl was there. She had been allowed time off from her job in the munitions factory because the baby was sick with the measles. 'Helen,

I've just been down to the funeral . . . you know, that poor Dr Craig's wife. I've had quite a scare.'

Helen took her mother by the arm and led her to a chair in the sparsely furnished accommodation she was renting. The place smelled musty and the linoleum that covered the floor was scuffed and cracked. Even in summer it was going to be cold, but Helen seemed happy enough living there.

'What is it, Mam? You're as white as a sheet.'

'It's our Mary. Dr Gordon seemed to think she might be in some kind of danger. She will be all right, won't she? Oh, God, Helen, tell me our Mary's going to be all right!'

'Of course she is, Mam.' Helen sat down by her mother on a worn, leatherette sofa with tired cushions and tufts of horsehair escaping through the cracks. 'She's a FANY. They don't get involved in the fighting.'

'No?' Jenny wiped her eyes and smiled shamefacedly. 'Oh, you're right, lass. It's just me being silly.'

'You're not silly, Mam, but you do worry too much. Our Mary'll be fine, you'll see.'

'Aye. Aye, she will. Now, I'd better go and see if I can get a rabbit from the butcher's for the tea. You know how your dad likes my rabbit-pie.'

CHAPTER EIGHT

A LEX had lost track of how many times the field hospital had been moved. He functioned mostly on automatic pilot these days, too tired to think, too exhausted to sleep. The senior MO was too sick with dysentery to do much else than sit behind a desk handing out advice and the only surgeon in the unit had died from a heart attack a month ago.

The wounded were coming in thick and fast. There wasn't time to care, to indulge in emotion of any kind. He did what was necessary, passing from one man to the next. Most of them were dying and he could do nothing about it. The *Wehrmacht* kept on advancing, forcing the British troops to retreat until all that was left to them was the thin strip of Dunkirk coastline.

Orders had come in an hour ago. They had to move, yet again, but this time it was to be final. They had to get the wounded to the wharf at Dunkirk and wait for the boats that were able to approach the great breakwater under cover of darkness to lift them off. Embarkation under enemy fire was to be expected. Difficult choices were going to have to be made and it went without saying that only those servicemen who could survive such an operation would be able to go.

That meant only about half the patients he had in his care as things stood. The others wouldn't even make it to the coast. The journey would kill them. There was to be no second chance for those who didn't make it to the boats this time round. Word had it that this was to be the final evacuation. Those who stayed would either die or be interned in the German prisoner-of-war camps.

'Go with them, Craig.' Major Williams's voice was weak and he looked years older than his age, which wasn't much above forty.

Alex shook his head. 'You know I can't, sir. I have to stay behind to look after the men who are too ill to travel.'

'There's no need for both of us to stay.'

'That's true, which is why I'm advising you to get on one of the ambulances and get the hell out of here. Dammit, man, you're sick.'

'It'll pass. Besides, I don't have anything to go home for, do I? They say things aren't too bad in the POW camps if you play your cards right. I'm also pretty useful, being a doctor.'

He gave a small laugh that was intended just for show. Alex knew that the major had very little to go back home to. Maybe it was some kind of suicide bid, this insisting on staying behind. He hoped not. Williams was a good man, a strong man. If he survived the camps he would still have the opportunity of a long life before him.

'You can't look after fifty men on your own, sir. Not in your state.'

'There won't be fifty of them by the time it takes you to get the others to the beaches. They're dying like flies back here. Now, get yourself along, Captain. That's an order.' He took a faltering step forward and placed his hands heavily on Alex's shoulders. 'Go on, Alex. I'll be fine. Say hello to Blighty for me and . . . well, good luck.'

'You too, David.' Alex saluted smartly and watched as Major Williams staggered back into the hospital. For a moment, he hesitated, feeling guilty for the flood of relief that was coursing through him. It would be good to see England again, but was it good to do so at the other man's expense?

'Captain Craig,' Grace Forsyth's voice made him start.

'What is it, Sister? Not more wounded? We don't have room.'

'No, sir, but there's a man asking for you. He was brought in yesterday with a mild case of shellshock. He says he comes from Felling, in the north-east of England.'

Alex pressed his hands over his eyes and sighed.

'What's his name?'

'Private Walter Morgan, sir, of the Royal Northumberland Fusiliers.'

Alex's brow creased as he strove to remember the name. 'It . . . doesn't . . . mean . . . anything to me, but I'll go and see him. Where is he?'

'Between the German prisoner and the young amputee.'

'Fit enough to be moved?'

'I would say so, yes, sir.'

'Very well, Sister. I'll go and see him now.'

Sister Forsyth placed a restraining hand on his shoulder.

'Alex . . . Captain Craig . . . you must try to get some rest.'

'I haven't seen you take much time off, Grace.'

'No, but then I'm not quite so much in demand. If you don't get some sleep soon you won't be capable of performing the lancing of a boil, let alone major surgery.'

Since the resident surgeon's death and Major Williams's illness, Alex had been coping with every medical condition thrown his way. His knowledge of surgery was minimal, but he was all these poor devils had. He could swab their wounds, extract the shrapnel, clean, disinfect, and stitch them up, hoping that they would survive long enough to reach a more experienced surgeon before they died.

He had not trained as a surgeon beyond medical school basics. It wasn't his chosen field of expertise. He deplored what war had made of him. What he did was little short of butchery at times, but for many he was their last chance, their only hope between life and death.

'Private Morgan?'

The man in the low pallet bed, near the entrance to the large tent hospital, lay shuddering uncontrollably. Above sunken cheeks a pair of haunted eyes stared up at the ceiling. In rapid rhythm his fingers plucked relentlessly at the blanket that covered him.

'Sir?' The man stirred, raised his head slightly and gave Alex a look that mirrored so many of the men who appeared before him.

'You wanted to see me,' Alex said, bending over the soldier and trying to recognize him, though there was nothing familiar about the long, heavy jawed face. 'I'm Captain Craig. Sister Forsyth tells me you're from Felling.'

'Aye, s-sir. S-sorry I c-can't salute you, sir, but. . . .' Private Morgan gave a huge gulp and shuddered some more. 'C-can't s-seem to l-lift me arms.'

'That's all right, Private. Take it easy. We don't stand on protocol here.'

'Me name's Wa-Walter Morgan, s-sir.' The soldier's eyes rolled. He swallowed with difficulty and gave another great shudder. 'You d-danced with my f-fiancée last Christmas . . . Mary?'

'Good Lord!' Alex felt his heart trip and miss a beat at the mention of Mary's name. 'Yes . . . yes, of course. What can I do for you, soldier?'

There was a poignant pause while Walter struggled to get his words out. Alex leaned on the instrument trolley that was parked alongside the soldier's bed, wondering what Mary saw in this nondescript young man. Then he told himself not to be absurd. What business was it of his anyway, even if he did consider Mary to be his own personal angel of mercy?

'Is it t-true . . . ? We're to m-make a break f-for it soon, s-sir? They're c-coming to get us?'

'That's what I've heard,' Alex said, trying to keep the visit professional by taking the young soldier's pulse as he listened.

'In case I d-don't make it, sir . . .' Walter Morgan said, speaking now through clenched teeth and trying desperately to control the terrible trembling that had his whole body in its grip, '. . . tell Mary . . . I love her . . . you know . . . s-sir?'

Alex straightened and looked down upon the supine figure that seemed so solid, yet so vulnerable.

'Don't worry, soldier,' he said, gripping the younger man's shoulder and giving it a reassuring squeeze. 'You'll get out all right. And then you'll be able to tell her yourself.'

'I d-don't know, sir.' Walter closed his eyes and squeezed out two fat tears that slowly trickled down his face. 'Sorry . . . don't know what's wrong with me . . . c-can't stop sh-shaking and crying like a b-baby.'

'Have you taken your medication?' Alex asked.

'I swallowed something the nurse gave me and I feel a bit fuzzy.'

'That's just a sedative, soldier. It'll relax you.'

'She'll think I'm a c-coward.'

'Nobody's going to think that.'

'She will. They all w-will.' Walter's trembling surged with renewed vigour. 'Look at m-me. Like a blooming j-jelly. I'm s-scared, sir.'

'We're all scared, Private Morgan, but our minds and our bodies deal with it in different ways.'

'Maybe Mary won't want me any more. I wasn't much of a fiancé. And I've not written to her . . . I'm not one for writing letters.'

'Has she written to you?'

'Aye . . . yes, sir, but . . .'

'Well, then?'

'She's changed. It was like getting words from a stranger.'

'Not everyone can express themselves well on paper, Private Morgan.'

Alex spoke gently, feeling a turmoil of emotions stirring beneath his ribcage. Mary's vibrant personality had shouted out from the letters he had received. Reading them had been the next best thing to having her there with him in person.

'If I get back to England,' Walter continued, his voice strangled as he fought back the tears. 'If I get back, sir, I'll be the best damned husband on God's earth, because I couldn't bear it if I lost her. I really couldn't. She's so special, you see. There'll never be anybody but Mary for me. Can you understand that, sir?'

'Oh, yes, Private Morgan,' Alex said with a tightened jaw. 'I can under-stand that very well. Get some rest now. You're going to need all your strength once we get the word to break camp and head for the beaches.'

'That'll be nice,' Walter said, already sinking into a drug-induced sleep as the sedative kicked in. 'Always liked the seaside, me . . . Mam! Mam, where's me bucket and spade? Got to . . . got to . . . build . . . a castle . . . for Mary . . .'

With one final shudder, Walter Morgan fell into a deep sleep. Alex covered him with the blanket that had come adrift. The man had a fifty-fifty chance of being fit enough to join the walking wounded when they eventually did move out. His chances of survival after that were anybody's guess. Word was coming through all the time now about troops being lifted off the Dunkirk beaches. Apparently, there was a fleet of small boats, as well as the warships, both commandeered by the government and volunteered by their owners. These little craft were darting in and out like minnows in order to save the troops who were trapped along the coastline.

'We've had orders to move out.' Grace's voice was gentle beside him and she was handing him the message she had intercepted from their resident signalman. 'I'm sorry, sir, but I thought it might be something I could deal with without bothering you.'

'That's all right, Grace,' Alex scanned the scribbled words. 'So this is it, at last.'

Grace Forsyth's eyes met his for an uncomfortable instant, then she cast them down as if her head were too heavy to hold up. 'Yes, sir,' she said, already moving away. 'Excuse me. I have things to do.'

She walked away, calm and erect, with no sign of panic. It was amazing how she coped so efficiently. One day, he hoped, he would find out just exactly what made the woman tick.

'Bloody suspicious, don't you think, Captain?'

Alex turned to the orderly who had addressed him. Private Grundy was a wiry little fellow and possibly the most conscientious of all the field hospital staff. A man of few words, he got on with the job without complaint. Alex felt he could always be relied upon, although he wasn't too popular with the nurses, and was definitely not Sister Forsyth's favourite person.

'What's that, Grundy?'

'How do the ruddy Jerries know where we are all the time, eh? It's as if we're giving off signals.'

'I suppose it's just that the Germans have the upper hand at the moment,' Alex said, but he was frowning thoughtfully into the middle distance.

'A *helping* hand, more like, if you ask me.' Grundy nudged Alex as they took a breath of air together outside the main entrance of the tent hospital. 'What's she at, then?'

He indicated, with a jerk of his head, the figure of Sister Grace Forsyth disappearing into the patch of woodland at the far end of the camp. In the shadow of the trees she stopped and looked about her, then seemed to beckon. No one else appeared and, after a moment, the nurse slipped completely from view.

Alex rubbed the back of his neck where he felt the hair rise in a sort of *frisson* that made him shiver. He told himself not to be foolish. It was nothing more than the cool breeze touching him. Grace Forsyth was a highly valued nursing sister. She regularly performed tasks far beyond her duty. Since his arrival in France, she had worked religiously at his side. He could not fault either her expertise or her courage.

'It's probably a case of not wanting to visit the latrines,' he said to the orderly. 'Don't worry, Grundy. Sister Forsyth always has a good reason for everything she does.'

'That's what I'm afraid of, sir,' Grundy said.

'What does that mean?'

Grundy shook his head. 'Wouldn't like to say, sir, but I'd keep your eyes and ears open, if I was you. It isn't the first time I've seen her acting peculiar like.'

Alex gave the man an enquiring look, but Grundy was not to be drawn. He gave a brief salute and went back to help clear out the oper-ating-theatre. Alex would join him later to see just how much in the way of medical supplies they could conveniently take with them on the jour-ney to the coast. But first, he would have a word or two with Grace.

She reappeared as he reached the edge of the wood. At first sight of him, she looked taken aback as if he had caught her out doing something forbidden. Then she recovered herself and walked towards him, but her smile was unsteady and her eyes were dull.

'Did you want something, Captain Craig?' she asked and he thought that her voice seemed unnaturally high.

'I'm sorry, Grace,' he said, the smile forced because of the tightness of his jaw. 'I saw you go into the wood and wondered if there was anything wrong.'

'No, nothing wrong. Why should there be?'

'You seemed to be . . .' he hesitated and saw a shadow of anxiety flit over her face like a cloud scudding over the sun. 'Were you talking to someone?'

Grace blinked furiously and he saw the tip of her tongue run over her lips before she relaxed and gave him his answer.

'I'm embarrassed to be found out,' she said, smiling bashfully. 'Yes,

Captain Craig, I was talking to someone . . . someone I am driven to talk to from time to time. It keeps me sane.'

Alex's mind was racing on wheels, trying to remember whether he had ever seen Grace fraternizing with any of the soldiers in the unit. Was she indulging in some kind of liaison? He knew so little about her. She wasn't the kind of woman who spoke of her private life. Affairs were inevitable for a lot of people, married or single, when they were separated from those whom they loved by a war and the death and destruction that surrounded them. They lived for the moment, in the knowledge that each day might be their last.

'Oh?' He regarded her, his head to one side; it obviously disturbed her, for she threw her hands in the air and issued a long, loud sigh.

'All right,' she said. 'I'll confess.'

'Confess?' Alex's stomach lurched. He didn't think he was going to like what he was about to hear.

'Yes, Captain . . . Alex . . .' Grace glanced from left to right and then behind her as if checking that nobody was within hearing distance. 'You may not understand, but . . . I was talking to God. I talk to him all the time. I have to, you see. I really have to.'

'Oh, Grace I didn't mean to pry, but . . .' Alex took a step towards her but she held up a hand, warding him off.

'Captain Craig!'

There was a shout from the hospital tent as a commotion broke out. Alex gave Grace one last apologetic look, then rushed to see what was happening. As he ran through the ward towards a group of patients and nursing staff grappling together in a heaving, grunting, shouting mass, a pistol shot rang out. The group fell apart. Alex pushed through and found a man standing over the young German soldier, his gun still smoking in his hand. There was a spreading red stain in the centre of the boy's chest.

'Sergeant Forbes!' Alex called out, trying to keep his voice steady. 'Put down your weapon.'

Forbes remained rigid for a moment, then his shoulders hunched and his chest heaved as he tried to control his anger.

'Drop the gun, man!' Alex repeated the order and the weapon fell with a dull thud to the ground where a nurse quickly stooped to whisk it away.

'Dirty Jerry bastard!' Forbes resisted hands that tried to pull him away.

'What happened here?' Alex demanded and there was a stony silence. 'What?'

Grundy stepped forward and put himself between Alex and the

sergeant, giving the man a push so that he was obliged to step back.

'Anybody see what happened?' Grundy asked.

'It was the cigarettes.' A young nurse with frightened eyes spoke up at last. 'Sergeant Forbes found the German helping himself to his cigarettes . . . he accused him of stealing . . . you know, told him to put them back.'

'And?' Alex fixed the girl with a stern eye and she winced as if he had hit her. 'What then?'

'Nothing, sir.' The nurse looked close to tears. 'The German looked puzzled. He still had the cigarettes in his hand when Forbes shot him. Look . . .'

They all looked and there was the packet of cigarettes in the dead soldier's hand. Alex retrieved them, turning them over and over.

'He nicked them from me!' Forbes spat out. 'Rotten thieving Nazi!'

'The cigarettes, Sergeant, would seem to be German. Since when have the British Army been issued with German cigarettes?'

'He didn't have any rights. He shouldn't have been here among decent folk, nicking things like the filthy bloody pig that he is . . .' Forbes surged forward again, but this time was successfully restrained.

Alex stood over him, squeezing the offending packet of cigarettes to a pulp in his hand, wishing it was the fellow's neck.

'This man whom you call a Nazi, was a boy of eighteen, serving in the German Army. The war was not of his making. Like all of us, he was hoping to go back home to his family. For Christ's sake, Forbes, he had no eyes! He couldn't see.' With a sound of disgust, Alex threw the remains of the cigarettes in the sergeant's face. 'You're on Standing Orders, Sergeant. Get out of my sight.'

Alex expected him to protest loudly, but Forbes went as meekly as a lamb.

'What about the German lad, sir?' Grundy asked.

'Give him a decent burial, Grundy. Make sure you keep his personal belongings. One day his family will be glad to have them.'

'Yes, sir.'

'Right.' Alex drew himself up, pulled in a gulp of soured air and returned the gaze of the group of patients and medical staff that had assembled around him. 'We're moving out at dusk, ready or not. Let's get sorted out, shall we?'

Mary was worried about Iris. For a few days now she had seemed lethargic and reluctant to chat, which was not at all her usual behaviour. At first, Mary wondered if her friend might be sickening for something.

There had been a few cases of gastritis in the camp, probably due to unclean water. Iris, however, claimed that there was nothing wrong with her.

Today, Gaston had brought word that thousands of troops were being lifted off the beaches around Dunkirk. He had spoken briefly to Iris, who was always uneasy in the Frenchman's presence, then he had strolled over to Mary's table, now under a canvas awning since the weather had taken an uncharacteristic turn for the worse.

'*Bonjour*, Gaston.' She greeted him with a smile and got a flash of white teeth in return, but then the muscles of his face tensed up again and his eyes regarded her darkly.

'*Comment vas tu*, Mary?'

'*Ça va, et toi?*'

They often lapsed into French when they were together. Mary couldn't help wondering whether Iris resented her ability to speak so well in Gaston's mother-tongue, for it gave them a certain amount of intimacy. Mary's rapport with the Resistance worker had been good, after the rather shaky start, though she did not personally find him physically attractive. On the other hand, she had caught Iris watching the man when she thought she was not being observed, a faraway expression on her face.

'I have asked Iris to drive into Rennes with me. It is not far. There are supplies to be found for the camp.'

'I thought the shops in France were empty these days,' Mary said, leaning back in her chair and watching the rainwater form a cascade as it ran from the canvas in glistening streams.

'*Ah, oui!* But there are ways and means to obtain anything, for a price.'

'The black market, do you mean? Yes, we have that in England too.'

'Do you hate the black marketeers for making money while their people starve?'

Mary shook her head uncertainly. 'I'm not sure what to think about it. We're all struggling to survive this war the best way we know how. The hardest thing to understand is the selfishness of those who have plenty, but who don't share it with those in desperate need. But then, it's too easy to sit in judgement.'

'That is true. None of us knows what forces people to act the way they do. When I was young . . .'

He stopped suddenly, glanced at her, then at the rain. Mary knew he had been about to reveal something very personal about himself. She raised her eyebrows and waited, but he just smiled and shrugged and slapped the table between them.

'It is not important. In a very short time, Mary West, you will be back in England and you will soon forget Gaston Frébus. You . . . and *chère* Iris. Does she have a good life waiting for her?'

'I hope so, Gaston.' Mary watched him as he got up and stretched; like everyone else he looked tired and old beyond his years. 'Do you have a family back . . . wherever you are from?'

He smiled wistfully at her and she thought there was a moist glistening in his eyes, but it could have been a trick of the light.

'Not any longer. My mother, that's all. The others . . .' He gave a shrug that spoke volumes.

In the circumstances, Mary felt that it would have been indiscreet to probe further. Gaston was a very private man, doing a dangerous job. Death must stalk him routinely, wait for him around every corner.

'You're wrong, you know, about us forgetting you,' she called out after him as he stepped out into the rain. 'I certainly won't. And neither will Iris.'

He gave her a weary wave and walked away, his feet being sucked down by the mud at every step. Across the central reservation, where they had danced and sung around a barbecued wild boar only last night, she could see Iris climbing into Phoebe. She saw how her friend watched Gaston as he approached, and then Mary knew what was troubling her. Iris was in love with the short, grizzly Frenchman, which explained the number of times she had seen them walking together, or talking with heads bowed over a cup of tea.

No fraternizing, indeed. Such an impossible rule. How could any of them put a halt to love once it attacked such a vulnerable organ as the human heart? She was happy for Iris, although a part of her, the sensible part, could not believe that there was any likelihood of the relationship having any kind of 'happy ever after' ending.

Mary heard the van's throaty cough as Iris started the engine, then it was moving off in a cloud of exhaust fumes. She mused on what kind of supplies Gaston and Iris would come back with. Or was it just an excuse to spend some time together away from camp? She didn't mind. Let them have this small pocket of happiness in the middle of wartime mayhem, she thought.

But Mary's musings came to an abrupt end when she suddenly saw a group of Polish soldiers heading her way, heads bowed under the beating rain, feet jumping and dodging the puddles as they came for the day's English lesson.

*

The small convoy carrying Alex, patients and staff came to an abrupt halt. They were sandwiched between the vehicles of an RACO army field workshop that had come successfully through enemy lines all the way from Belgium. Now, the order to halt was given, even though they were still a few miles from the coast.

Alex, sitting up front in the unit's only remaining staff car, with Private Grundy and Sister Forsyth, felt the tension growing as it spread down the line. Behind them, ambulances, full of injured soldiers packed like sardines, were queuing up. And not so far behind the straggling column the horizon was a mass of black smoke-clouds with shells going off and gunfire echoing through the evening air, making the ground vibrate beneath them.

In front of them the sky was full of flames, rising high. They could feel the heat, hear the crackle and the occasional dull explosion.

'What the hell. . . ?' Alex was half out of the car, but Grundy jumped down before him.

'I'll see what's going on, shall I, sir?'

Before Alex could stop him, the orderly was running down the column to the leading vehicles. Beside him, Alex felt Grace give an involuntary shudder. Throughout the whole journey she had remained silent, her hands clasping and unclasping in her lap. He reached out and gripped her wrist, noticing how cold she was, despite the warmth of the summer night.

'Are you all right, Grace?'

'Yes . . . yes, I'm fine.' It was such a small, weak voice and not at all the voice of the strong-willed, efficient nursing sister he had come to know.

'We're all a bit jittery,' he said with a sympathetic smile. 'Soon be over now.'

He could see Grundy sprinting back to the car. The orderly was breathless by the time he skidded to a halt, but he looked excited, so it had to be good news rather than the bad they had expected.

'It's all right, sir. The fires are ours. Brits and Canadian, so I'm told. They're demobilizing all the lorries and the cars and setting fire to the fuel. The Jerries are just behind us, but the beaches are only a mile away. Anyway, we've got orders from the Beach Master to get the ambulances through to the wharf. Most of the troops have gone ahead on foot. They say there are columns of them stretching right up from the water's edge.'

'All right, Grundy.' Alex nodded with a wry smile. 'Let's not waste time. Get these ambulances moving.'

'Yes, sir!' The orderly grinned broadly and did his mock salute, which he had picked up from a Canadian airman they had treated for burns. The airman had had one good finger remaining on his right hand, with which he insisted on saluting as best he could.

It was a matter of minutes before they reached the quay where the wounded were to be picked up by the bigger rescue ships. There were good-hearted grumbles and a few groans as the walking wounded stepped down from the ambulances, some of them supporting or carrying the more severely wounded.

'Come on, you lazy lot.' Grundy's voice could be heard over the mumble of hushed voices. 'On yer feet, them as can. Them as can't . . . crawl! You're used to that, aren't you?'

'He's a good man,' Grace Forsyth said at Alex's side.

'None better,' Alex replied, then gave her a curious look. 'I thought you didn't like him.'

'Maybe I've had reason to change my mind,' Grace said, then rubbed her hands up and down her arms with a shiver.

Alex nodded and studied the lines and the shadows on her face. She had become very thin over the last few weeks, and yet she had never fallen down on her duties. He liked her a lot, but there was always something he felt she was hiding from him, something mysterious lurking in those dreamy, faraway eyes of hers.

'Organize your nurses, Sister.' He gave the order, but the tone of his voice was gentle.

'Yes, Captain Craig.'

By the time the command came down the line to start towards a grey hospital ship cagily docking, they were ready. And none too soon, for there was a growl of plane engines and a squadron of German Stukas came screaming over their heads, strafing the beaches and the quay with bullets.

Whole columns of men dived for cover as sand and sea were scuffed up in explosive bursts. Some of the men did not get up again. All Alex could do was watch helplessly and thank God for those who remained unharmed. He could see, mirrored on every face, the turbulent emotions that were going on in his own heart. The hopes, the fears of the men around him, and excitement mingled with terror.

'I'll bring up the rear, Captain Craig, sir,' Grundy shouted in his ear.

'What about the vehicles?'

'The lads from the RACO will see to all that as soon as we're clear. By all accounts the Jerries aren't far behind. Either that or they're using ruddy cannons to shoot the sparrows.'

'Let's hope our boys have a few cannons to keep them at bay until we get everybody on to the boat.'

'Yes, sir.' They both ducked as the Stukas turned and strafed the wharf and the beaches yet again, but this time there was return fire from the ground and two of the aircraft burst into flames, coming down a few miles inshore.

'I hate to think what chance the men on the beaches have in this,' Alex said.

Grundy blinked and gave a huge gulp. 'It's every man for himself, sir, once they get into the water. The boats don't have time to hang about. It's going to be tough, sir.'

'Medic! We need a medic back here!' The cry echoed out from a hundred yards up the beach as the sound of the remaining aircraft engines faded.

Alex looked about him and decided that he was probably the only qualified doctor within range of the group of men gathered about a prostrate figure.

'You can't go back there now,' Grundy complained, seeing what was going through Alex's mind. 'Come on, Captain Craig, sir. If you miss this chance you might never get out of this bloody country.'

'I don't like it any more than you, Grundy, but I have no choice,' said Alex, then he thumped the orderly on the shoulder in a friendly gesture. 'And Grundy . . . in case I don't make it in time, I want you to know that I couldn't have got through all this without you. Thank you, for everything.'

'Oh, gawd, sir, don't say that!' Grundy's eyes glistened in the dark, lit up by the distant fires. 'You'll make it, Captain. We'll all make it. Even him.'

Alex looked over his shoulder to see the staggering figure of Private Walter Morgan wandering past with arms outstretched like a sleepwalker, mumbling things about the seaside, his mother and his bucket and spade. And then he cried out a name and a ghostly hand traced an icy line down Alex's spine.

'Mary! I'm coming, Mary.'

Grundy grabbed hold of the confused soldier and guided him back on to the breakwater.

'Go on, sunshine,' he shouted, giving Walter a push in the right direction. 'Straight ahead.'

'Look after yourself, Grundy,' Alex called out.

'See you on the other side, sir ,' came Grundy's voice from behind as he now made his way to the rear of the line.

Alex headed off towards the men calling for a medic and found them grouped around a young private with a gaping wound in his stomach.

'You got to save him, sir,' one of the men said. 'He's me brother.'

There was little that Alex could do but close the lad's eyes and watch as a group of grown men cried real tears over their comrade-in-arms.

As he walked back to the wharf, he could see Grace struggling beneath the weight of a soldier walking with one leg and a crutch. Alex was about to go to her aid, thinking she would never make it, but at that moment she was joined by a bulky soldier with only one arm, who still had enough strength to take the weight of his compatriot.

Despite the number of troops still clambering up and over the dunes in front of him, Alex was aware that an uncanny silence had fallen. Between him and the oily black sea, there was little movement as men crouched together in organized columns, ready to get into the water the minute the boats came into view. Through the darkness, he could hear groans and coughs and vague mutterings. The next few hours were going to be the longest of all their lives, he was sure, but there was little choice. He would do what he could to help and direct the newly wounded to the wharf where they could join the long queue slowly moving on to the boats.

An hour or two later – he had lost track of time – there was a change in the atmosphere. There were subdued cheers and a surge forward as the last remaining men on the beaches saw the heartening sight of a small flotilla of boats approaching with the first silvery rays of morning light. At the same time the hospital ship was sliding slowly out into the Channel with its precious cargo.

Moving carefully along the lines, carrying out basic first aid where it was necessary, Alex was suddenly aware of a familiar figure stumbling down the beach towards him. It was Grundy. The idiot had stayed behind after all. He was carrying on his back a young soldier bigger than himself with bandaged eyes and bandaged stumps where his feet should have been.

'You'll never make it, Grundy,' Alex said, striding alongside the younger man. 'Save yourself, man!'

'We don't know that we won't make it until it's all over, sir,' Grundy replied, his face and neck running with perspiration from the effort he was having to put into his impossible task.

'There are others. You can't save them all.'

'Yes, sir, I know. I had to make a decision. This fellow got my vote. He lied about his age. I'd like to think we could help him see his eighteenth birthday, even if he won't be able to see or dance to celebrate it.'

'Grundy, has anybody told you that you're one crazy fool?'

Grundy gave a sheepish grin and nodded. 'Aye, sir. More times than I care to remember.'

'I don't want to lose you, Grundy.'

'Don't you bother yourself none about me, Captain Craig. Only the good die young, as my old granny used to say. She said that as she buried me grandad. He was ninety-five and I take after him, apparently.'

Alex smiled and saluted Grundy smartly, his throat too tight to speak. He watched the private struggle down to the shoreline where columns of men were wading out into the water towards the boats that looked as if they weren't fit for anything more than hauling fish.

The evacuation had been quite orderly, until it became obvious that there would not be sufficient space in the boats for all the troops who were left. Panic was breaking out in pockets all along the beaches. It was a heartbreaking sight that would have moved any man to tears, but there was no time to stop and weep. Alex looked about him frantically, his eyes searching for Grace Forsyth, sure that she must still be there somewhere. She, like Grundy, had stayed behind and was not, he was sure, on the hospital boat with her patients. He couldn't afford to spend time looking for her. It would be like looking for a needle in a haystack.

He could see men wading out into the water, swimming towards the first boats where helping hands were waiting to drag them aboard. Grundy passed him at a lunging gallop, the young injured soldier still riding on his back.

'Come on, sir,' the orderly shouted. 'It's now or never.'

Alex took one last look around him. Men were still streaming over the sand-dunes, heading for the beaches and the lapping waves. They wouldn't all make it. They would have to stay behind and take their chances with the Germans. He started forward, his natural instinct to save his own life, even while he felt guilty for doing so.

He plunged into the briny water, feeling the thrust and suck of the waves rising to his knees, dragging him into the surging tide. He collided with a figure that was floundering up to his waist in water and shouting that he couldn't swim. Alex recognized Mary's fiancé, Walter Morgan.

'What the hell are you doing back here, Morgan?'

Walter stared at him vaguely, but his eyes no longer seemed to register anything. He kept shaking his head and beating the water with his fists.

'Can't s-swim! C-can't swim!'

'If you'd stayed with the rest of the unit you wouldn't have had to swim, you idiot!' Alex bellowed in the private's ear. 'Why the blazes didn't you stay in line?'

He knew that anything he said to the man was useless. Morgan was beyond comprehension of any kind. Alex took hold of the man's shoulders and gave him a shake, then pushed him towards the milling broth of bodies in the water just as more German aircraft started strafing the beach. 'Go, go, go!'

Walter clung to him as they advanced further into the sea, his face stricken with terror. Alex could feel the man trembling as if he had an engine inside him running on full throttle. If he weren't careful, Morgan would drown them both.

With one hand clasping the private's collar, Alex struck out, heading for what appeared to be the last boat, a fishing-smack by the look of it, with men on board calling urgently that they could wait no longer. A net was thrown down for them to haul themselves up. He saw Grundy up ahead trying to climb it with his heavy cargo clinging around his neck. Arms stretched out to reach him, but as the orderly reached the boat's undulating rail, a shell sang past Alex's ear and found its target. Grundy and the young boy fell backward without a sound and Alex knew they were already dead before they hit the water.

Private Morgan was still clinging on, restricting Alex's movements. Alex kicked out with his feet, holding on to the man with both hands now. Walter was swallowing water and gagging, and when he wasn't doing that he was mumbling incoherently, all the effects of his shellshock rushing back to take him in its grip.

Alex's strength was waning, but the boat was within reach and he heaved Walter towards it. A fisherman leaned over and pulled the semi-conscious soldier on board, then was coming back for Alex, but Alex felt himself pushed aside and felt a fist drive itself into his midriff.

Winded, Alex sank down and swallowed a mouthful of the choppy sea before fighting his way back to the surface in time to see the boat drift away out of his reach. The last man on board the fishing-smack, the one who had fought to take his place, was hanging over the rail, and as he lifted his head, Alex saw that it was Forbes, who had murdered the young German soldier in his care.

The man pulled back his lips in an evil sneer, then something exploded very close. Alex felt an indescribable pain, and the world retreated.

CHAPTER NINE

IT was the middle of June when the order came for the Polish soldiers to be moved north and on to England. It was no longer safe to remain where they were. Thousands of troops had already been rescued from the Dunkirk beaches. Now it was their turn to be taken off from St Malo.

With the vans and ambulances loaded up with the displaced Poles, the cortège made its way quickly in the direction of the sea, taking the shortest route possible. Almost at the outset, the Army contingent of officers in charge found themselves in trouble. A bomb from a lone Stuka hit the rear vehicle, killing all on board. Then the leading truck, carrying the CO and his driver, broke an axle and went off the road. Both men were badly injured as a result. It was therefore down to the FANYs, led by Iris and Mary, to find a way through on their own, leading a band of men who, if captured, would almost certainly be shot or incarcerated in Nazi concentration camps.

Mary didn't like to think what could happen to the twenty FANYs in the unit if capture did come about. She knew that all the girls must be doing their best to think positive. It was what they did best when there was nothing left to do.

Beside her, Iris was shedding perspiration like water as she took the lead, manoeuvring her vehicle over rough terrain and narrow, winding roads. Mary put her trust in Iris's ability to remember the network of French roads she had been required to memorize, but even Iris's photographic memory was beginning to flag in such stressful conditions.

'We're not lost, are we?'

Effie leaned over the back of Mary's seat and peered out through the mud-spattered windscreen. The wipers were almost impotent against the driving rain, and the road they were on had turned into a river of mud some miles back, so that the worn tyres of the ambulances were in danger of skidding if they did not progress with care.

Iris slowed down to a stop and applied the handbrake with both hands as though she had no strength left. Exhausted or not they all knew that they couldn't afford to waste time. Their orders were to get to a small fleet of fishing boats just off St Malo, and time was of the essence.

Gaston Frébus had told them that the German lines were closing in fast. He escorted them as far as Rennes, then reluctantly said goodbye.

'I can't go any further with you,' he had said, speaking softly, his eyes fixed on Iris. 'I'm needed elsewhere.'

'But Gaston . . .' Iris started to speak, but the Frenchman touched a finger to his lips, his eyes wandering fleetingly over to Mary.

'I must leave you. You know I must. Keep heading north on this road and it will take you to St Malo. There, the boats will be waiting. Go with God, my dear brave FANYs.'

He kissed the tips of his fingers and touched them to Iris's trembling lips. Mary saw tears form and glisten on Iris's eyelashes, saw the tensing of her cheek muscles. She looked away and when she looked back, Gaston was gone, blending with the darkness that enveloped them. Iris's wretchedness at their separation was like a palpable aura all around her.

Mary wanted to say something comforting, but what could she say that would make Iris feel better? Gaston was going back underground with his Resistance fighters. His chances of coming out of the war alive were minimal. Come to that, Mary thought, their own chances weren't all that good if they messed up and didn't reach St Malo in time. Or, worse, got captured by the Germans.

'Hey, what's up with her?' Effie demanded with an unaccustomed anxious edge to her voice.

Mary looked at Iris, who had slumped in her seat, her head in her hands, her shoulders shaking as she wept copiously. It was the first time she had ever seen Iris in tears, but love, as she well knew, did strange things to the emotions. Things that very often ran out of control, even in the coldest of hearts.

'I'm sorry,' Iris sobbed. 'I don't know what's wrong with me. I just . . . I just can't go on . . .'

Mary put an arm about her shoulders and hugged briefly. Her throat contracted and her heart squeezed and wanted to break. On the outside, however, Mary knew that she had to be strong enough for all of them.

'Come on, Iris. This is not the time to go soft on us. Plenty time for that when we get back to England.'

'I can't help it, Mary.' Iris swiped frantically at her tears and blinked through red-rimmed eyes at the dark road ahead. 'I can't remember any of it. It . . . it's all gone. All the roads . . . they look the same. I don't know whether we're going north or south or . . . or in any direction. I'm sorry!'

'Aw, gawd,' growled Effie. 'This is a fine pickle we're in and no mistake.'

Mary jumped out, aware of eyes watching curiously as the drivers of the vehicles behind pulled up and waited anxiously.

'Move over, Iris.' She barked out the order and, after a small hesitation, Iris slid into the passenger seat and Mary took the wheel.

She started the motor, glancing up at the dark, velvety sky with its sprinkling of stars. Directly overhead, the Milky Way could be clearly seen, like a powdery, muslin veil.

'Gaston said it was a straight route from here, so that's what we're going to take.'

'Just a minute,' Effie said. 'What if I get on me bike and ride on ahead. If I come up against a problem I can double back.'

'Do you have sufficient fuel, Effie?' Mary asked, not at all sure whether it was a good idea or a bad one, but she was open to any suggestion, since her navigational prowess was not terribly sound.

'Aye.' Effie nodded, already clambering through the van at the back and unchaining her beloved motorbike where it was fixed for safety. 'Enough until it runs out, anyway. By then we should be where we're headed.'

'You're a brick, Effie!'

'Aye. Bricks for brains, me ma used to say. Just like our poor Joe. A lot of good it did him, didn't it?'

'Be careful, Effie.'

'Aw, gan on. It'll give us something to do. Better than sittin' here bitin' me nails while you two twiddle yer thumbs.'

They saw her cheeky grin as she rode past the van, the sound of the motorbike engine disappearing into the distance. Mary followed, keeping in a straight line, heading due north. Twenty minutes later, Effie appeared again, giving the thumbs up.

'We're all right for the next ten miles,' she said and was off again.

And that was how the unit managed to find its way to the harbour of St Malo. It wasn't too difficult a journey after all, though later, all the girls admitted that they hardly breathed the whole way.

On Effie's last trip she arrived back breathless, her eyes shining with hope and enthusiasm. 'I've seen the sea!'

'Marvellous, Effie! How far, would you say?'

'Only a few minutes. The moon came out just as I got there and I could see small boats just sitting there, bobbing in the water.'

'Let's get going then,' Mary said. 'Effie, pass the word back that we're almost through. It'll be good for morale.'

'Aye.' Effie touched a finger to her forehead and revved up her bike. 'Then I'll ride on and make sure they know we're coming. I'd hate to have them go without us.'

It was the typical, fatal last ride. They drove up over a rise, then started down the other side where the road was clogged with mud. Mary saw Effie veer off to the left, taking a short cut down on to the beach. She was halfway there and men were beginning to appear, emerging from the dinghies and rowing boats that were lined up at the water's edge. A couple of them waved. Then it happened.

Effie must have hit something. She and her bike were thrown high into the air before coming crashing back to earth. The explosion that followed lit up the beach and shook the ground beneath the vehicles following, their wheels sinking into the soft sand. Mary, her heart heavy and hollow, sat behind her wheel and watched the scene, not believing what she had just witnessed. Iris whimpered uncontrollably beside her.

The fishermen had things under control by the time the FANY unit and the Polish soldiers assembled around their vehicles. One of them called out in French and it was some time before Mary could bring herself to answer him.

'All right, everybody,' she shouted after a brief discourse; pale faces turned her way, eyes wide and staring, mouths trembling. 'Make your way to the boats as quickly as possible.'

'Oh, Mary!' Iris said, her voice a hoarse whisper. 'Poor Effie! What happened? What was it?'

'They have no idea, but he says she's still alive,' Mary told her, desperately trying to keep her emotions under control. 'She's badly hurt, but she's still alive. Come on. Let's get her.'

'Get her? But how badly is she hurt?'

'I don't care, Iris. I'm not leaving Effie behind.'

'I will help!'

Mary hadn't seen him in the confusion, but there was Major Jan Berwinski and two of his comrades beside her, looking in the direction of the heap of smouldering black metal that had once been so much a part of Effie. They ran forward to where the fishermen were staring down at Effie's still body. Using a fisherman's waterproof jacket as a makeshift stretcher, they carried the injured girl carefully.

'Bloody Nora!' Effie's pain-racked cry could be heard half-way along the beach, but it had strength and instilled hope in all of them.

'*Vite, vite!*' The Frenchmen urged, beckoning and herding everybody in the direction of the boats.

No one needed to be told a second time. Dinghies were already filling up and setting off towards larger vessels lying further out to sea. Mary pushed Iris towards the nearest boat where an elderly fisherman pulled them aboard and sat them down amidst ropes and nets stinking of fish. Jan and his companion gently passed Effie over into Mary's arms and pushed the boat off, jumping in themselves at the very last minute.

Effie groaned slightly and Mary could see that she was in a lot of pain. She held her close and saw Effie's eyes flicker open.

'Gawd, what a fuckin' awful smell! I hate fish, me!'

'Effie Donaldson, stop complaining and watch your language. For once in your life just lie still and let us get you safely home.'

'What about me bike?' Effie was so traumatized she had forgotten to swear.

'Never mind your bike. What about you?'

'It hurts, Mary,' Effie whispered back through clenched teeth. 'Eeh, dear God, it hurts.'

'I know, Effie.' Mary held the girl as best she could, trying not to cause her more pain than was necessary. 'I know. This is going to be rough, but you've got to hold on.'

'Aye, Mary. I'll hold on . . .'

Effie gripped Mary's hand. Her eyes closed, she gave a grimace of pain and her head dropped back as she lost consciousness. It was best that way.

Alex was aware of being in a different place at a different time. Things were a little confused in his head, as if he were walking through the blurry veils of a bad dream. A dream he was anxious to be rid of, yet he was afraid of what he would wake up to. He remembered the thud of the bullets that had hit him, recalled the pain, then the salt water washing over him, his body being carried this way and that by the surging tide.

Before he passed out completely, there was the sensation of hands grappling with his clothing, pulling him out of the water, through the clinging sand. Then there was nothing. Only a black, mindless floating with hollow, distant voices, first loud, then fading into nothingness.

He was unaware of how long this state had lasted, but now there was movement beneath him, and all around. The air went from warm and stale to cool and fresh. There was the purring of an engine and a vibrating that rattled his bones. There was pain, but it was masked by his half-conscious state. He held on to the dream as long as he could, slipping in and out of it over a long period of time that could have been hours or days, or even weeks.

He awoke at last to muffled voices that echoed strangely in his ears. The air was now cold and dank and he was shivering convulsively beneath a thin, coarse covering, lying on a hard surface. There were men's voices, low and mumbling, then a woman spoke his name.

'Can you hear me, Alex?'

'Mary?'

He called out her name, thinking that he was still dreaming that he was back in England, walking hand in hand with Mary West, and his heart was light and happy and full of love. It wasn't the first time he had dreamed of Mary. Sometimes, though, someone else was there in the dream with him, walking away, never looking back, fading into the distance.

Please don't leave me, Mary!

Someone was gripping his shoulder, shaking it slightly. He heard himself groan, though the sound seemed to come from another world. His hand, when he lifted it to his forehead, weighed a ton, while his head was light and spinning dizzily.

'Where am I?'

'Oh, Alex, thank God!'

His eyelids were sticky. They didn't want to open. He rubbed at them with fingers that seemed only vaguely his. At last his eyes were open, but all he could see was shadowy darkness. He turned his head and was blinded by a light coming down a long tunnel, bringing with it a cool breeze and the smell of the countryside.

His eyes closed again and he drifted off, but awoke to someone taking his pulse. Alex squinted through slits and saw an oil lamp on a rustic oak table. It was shedding amber light into a rustic room that was largely wattle and daub and smelled of generations of country living. He tried to rise on his elbows, but a firm hand pressed him back into his pillow.

'You must rest for now,' the voice belonging to the cool fingers said, then he turned his head to look at her, knowing now who she was.

'Grace! What's happening? What are you doing here? Where are we?'

'Later. Go to sleep now.'

'Sleep? I feel as if I've been asleep for a hundred years.'

'Well, not quite as long as that.' Grace smiled sadly. 'You've been in a coma, Alex. We dug two bullets out of you. One in your hip and another in your shoulder, but the real damage was done by the shrapnel that got awfully close to your brain.'

'In that case, I'm lucky to be alive, but . . .' Once more Grace held him down as he tried to rise, the look on her face telling him that she didn't exactly agree with what he had just said.

Someone spoke from the shadows and Grace glanced over her shoulder, but she didn't reply. She touched the back of her hand to Alex's cheek, then started bathing his face.

'I persuaded them to bring you with us,' she was saying in a low voice. 'They didn't want the responsibility, but when I told them you were a doctor, they agreed to get you to a safe house where your medical skills will be much needed. That's the best I can do, Alex.'

Alex frowned, trying to make sense of what she was saying, then the truth dawned on him.

'They are Resistance fighters?' he asked and saw a glint in her eyes as she started sponging down his body. 'If that's the case, then you must be. . . ?'

'I'm nobody, Alex,' she said. 'And tomorrow you must forget that you ever saw me. Lives depend upon it. I was your nursing sister and perished on the beach at Dunkirk, along with so many others.'

It was another few days before Alex felt some strength seeping back into his body. On the fourth day, Grace bade him farewell.

'Tomorrow, they will take you to a safe house,' she said. 'I can't come with you, Alex.'

'Where will you go?' he asked, watching her restless movements as she paced the earthen floor in front of him.

For reply, she gave a small shake of her head and rubbed her upper arms as if she were cold, though the room was hot and airless.

The next morning she was gone and Alex was on the move again, lying beneath a dirty tarpaulin that smelled of pigs or sheep. He was wedged in among sacks of vegetables. There was the *clip-clop* sound of a plodding horse and a low rumble of French conversation. He stirred, but heard a quick warning.

'*Non, monsieur. C'est trop dangereux. Restez là.*' It was a deep, male voice, thick with a regional accent that he did not recognize.

They stopped the cart some miles down the road at the edge of a forest and allowed him to sit up. Which was when he realized he had been stripped of his uniform and dressed in rough country clothes that gave off as much smell as the tarpaulin. The men driving the cart in which he was riding looked like farmers, but he guessed they were members of the newly formed French underground movement.

One of them gave a wide grin and pointed across the valley that was opening up before them. In the distance there was a chateau. The man nodded, then indicated that Alex should hunker back down out of sight. He gave a click of his tongue and the old horse started up again.

Alex was surprised to find that they had brought him right up to the chateau, where they were greeted loudly by an elderly French couple and a group of excitedly yapping dogs. There was a loud conversation, but there were also a few words conducted in guarded whispers. Suddenly the tarpaulin was whipped off and one of the Frenchmen pointed to a sack of cabbages and jerked his head towards a large shed to the side of the chateau.

Alex wasn't sure that his legs would support him, but he lost no time in grabbing the sack, limping, staggering with it to the shed, where another man was waiting.

'Take off your clothes,' the man ordered in perfect English and Alex blinked at him, seeing that the fellow was already scrambling out of his own outer garments. 'Go on and be quick about it.'

They exchanged clothes. Alex was pleased that he got the best of the bargain, for the clothes the young man had given him were at least clean, even if they were not very comfortable, being on the small side.

'What happens now?' Alex asked.

'You'll find out. Stay out of sight. There are collaborators everywhere.'

The man sauntered out into the sunlight, whistling. He joined the other two men at the cart and they began carrying in the other sacks of vegetables, but before they reached the shed, Alex felt a light touch on his shoulder and an old Frenchwoman indicated that he should go through a gaping trap-door in the ground. As the trap-door shut above his head, Alex heard the sacks of vegetables being placed over it.

'Welcome to our hospital, sir!'

He had come through a long passageway that opened up into a large, vaulted cellar. There were makeshift beds, some of them occupied, a table with basic surgical instruments and a Primus stove on which bubbled a large cauldron full of onion soup, a plate of grey-looking bread and strong-smelling cheese on a stool beside it.

The young man who spoke was bare to the waist and wore only a pair of bloodstained shorts. He appeared to be in mid-surgical procedure.

'What the hell is this place?' Alex asked, wavering about like a drunkard and wishing he could sit down, but he couldn't see a vacant chair, just vacant-eyed airmen, some of them wearing the Canadian Army insignia.

'Underground hospital, sir. Men get shot down. The Resistance chappies bring them here to be patched up. We keep them until they're well enough to make their own way to the Pyrenees, then they have to walk over the passes into Spain. Some of them actually make it.'

'Where are we, exactly?'

'It's a safe house. Just outside Toulouse.'

'I see. And you are a doctor? A surgeon?' The lad didn't look old enough to be either.

'A medic, sir. Trained in the field, you might say. Needs must when the devil drives and all that. You any good with the needle, sir? This man needs stitching up. I think I got all the shrapnel out, but stitching isn't my forte. Never could stand the sight of a needle.'

Alex looked down at the young medic's hands and saw that they were shaking so much it was unlikely he would be able to hold the needle, let alone stitch up the wounds.

'It's been a long night, sir,' the young soldier said by way of explanation. 'I've been on my own since the last doctor went out for a smoke and never came back. Don't know what happened to him, sir.'

'If I could sit down to it, I'll manage,' Alex said, flexing his stiff fingers. 'What's your name, son?'

'Jenkins, sir. Private Arthur Jenkins. They tell me you're the real thing.'

Alex gave a weak laugh as the young man pushed a broken chair behind his knees and he sank down on it. 'Right now, I'm more patient than doctor. Name's Captain Alex Craig. I was a general practitioner back in England, but since I've been in France I've done everything but deliver babies and pull teeth.'

Jenkins nodded, then his boyish grin became serious. 'I don't know how to tell you this, sir, but we're up the spout, so to speak. You see, the chateau's just been commandeered by the Gestapo. They tend to come and go a bit and never stay too long. Word has it that a party of them are arriving tomorrow.

'So what are we supposed to do?'

'We carry on pretty much as before, sir, but even more in secret. With a bit of luck they won't stay too long. It's pretty isolated out here.'

'What if somebody gives us away?'

'You don't have to worry about that. Old Monsieur Laroque and his wife are on our side, and so are all their staff. Most of them work for the Resistance.'

Alex gave a resigned sigh.

'It looks like we're in for an interesting time, then,' he said, rolling up his sleeves and making a start on stitching up the cleaned wounds of the man lying face down on the bunk in front of him.

Private Jenkins placed a brown paper parcel down at his feet. 'That arrived for you yesterday, sir. You might be needing it if we get caught.'

Alex frowned as he fingered the coarse string holding the package together. He couldn't imagine what it might be, or who could have sent it.

'Open it, would you, Jenkins?'

It turned out to be Alex's own uniform, cleaned and pressed. Where there had been bullet holes they were carefully darned. Grace Forsyth, he thought. It had to be her handiwork. She had already saved his life once. It looked as though she was continuing to be his guardian angel. Without his captain's uniform he would quite likely be shot as a spy.

'It won't be the same without Effie, somehow,' Iris said, staring through the train window at the passing scenery.

'Poor Effie,' Mary said. 'This war has destroyed so many lives already. I hate to think where we'll all be by the time it's finished.'

None of them liked to contemplate the future too much. The girls had been allowed a home visit before going to their new postings. This time they would be looking after Polish soldiers in special holding camps up in the north-west of Scotland, prior to retraining in the British Army. The place was, reportedly, as bleak as Siberia in winter, but at least it was safe. Despite its still being summer, Mary made a mental note to pack some winter clothes.

The brief visit to the family had been torn with mixed feelings. It had been wonderful to see the family again, but Mary had been forced to break off her engagement with Walter once and for all. She thought she would carry the guilt of it right through her life, especially since he was no longer a well man. He had survived the escape from Dunkirk, but the shellshock he had brought with him persisted, resulting in his needing hospital treatment. She would never forget the day she went to visit him in the hospital.

It had been quite a shock seeing him sitting there in a wheelchair, shaking like a jelly, eyes staring and mumbling to himself. He had cried like a baby at sight of her, then again and again at short intervals all the time she was with him. The doctors were doubtful that he would ever recover totally, and might even go further into a vegetative state.

'What did Walter say when you broke off your engagement?' Iris said suddenly, making her start. 'Was he upset?'

'I couldn't tell him,' Mary said with a sigh. 'I told his parents. . . . Goodness, Iris, how did you know what I was thinking?'

'You had that awful sad face on you,' Iris said. 'I knew it had to be either Walter or . . . well, you know.'

Mary knew only too well what Iris was getting at. The worst news of all had been blurted out quite innocently by her mother. Jenny West's words rang constantly in Mary's head. She couldn't seem to get rid of them. *That poor Dr Craig's been reported missing, believed dead. He was supposed to be with the Dunkirk lot, but he didn't make it, apparently. Someone saw him get a bullet, then he went down in the sea, poor soul.*

'It wasn't meant to be, Iris,' Mary told her friend, blinking furiously to stop the tears that were stinging her eyelids. 'You know . . . me and Alex Craig.'

'Did you and he actually . . . you know. . . ?'

Mary bit down on her mouth and stared at her hands that were clasped tightly in her lap. She shook her head. 'We had feelings for each other right from the start. I know it was wrong, but . . . Oh, Iris, if only he had lived . . . I'm sure we could have been so happy.'

'Stop it! Stop it this instant, Mary West.' Iris gave an agonized cry and searched for her hankie. 'I haven't stopped thinking about Gaston and wondering where he is and if . . . Oh, hell, now you've got me blubbering.'

Mary gave a sniff, dabbed at her eyes and blew her nose, feeling ashamed. Here she was in her brand new FANY uniform and she was behaving disgracefully. There was more to life than dwelling on the bad things, like Iris and her Frenchman, and Effie who might never walk again. Walter might end his days as a gibbering idiot. And Alex . . . dear, sweet, gorgeous Alex, whom she had fallen in love with on such short acquaintance – he was lying under the sea, or mangled on a beach at Dunkirk and it was all for nothing. So many lives destroyed. *For nothing.*

Put an end to all this self-pity, Mary West. Get hold of yourself, girl, and get on with your life. You don't stop fighting until there's nothing left to fight for.

There was a great reunion when Mary and Iris met up again with their unit in Glasgow before going further onward to the Polish camps on the west coast of Scotland. It was a case of laughter and tears as they did a head count to find out who was still attached and who was missing. Kate Holland and Sally Ferguson were there, but Alice Leatherby had mysteriously disappeared, her absence explained in couched terms such as: *I think she was going to be married. Damned good job, too, since she was so-so, if you ask me.*

Everyone was sad to hear about Effie Donaldson. She had never integrated with the unit, but her reliability and her bravery had astonished them all. And then there was Anne Beasley. No one seemed to know anything about her.

'There was always something not quite right about Beasley,' said one girl, her face twisting. 'Couldn't quite make her out.'

'She thought herself a bit above the rest of us, I think,' said another. 'I don't know why, just because she'd lived in France and spoke French and German like a native.'

'I think she was just reserved,' Mary said, needing to be loyal to her childhood memories of times spent with Anne in France. 'Not a people person.'

'You can say that again. Not FANY material either, I would say. Got the jitters at the mere whiff of trouble.'

Mary saw Iris glance warily her way and guessed that she was remembering how she had fallen foul of her nerves leading the unit to St Malo. She said nothing, but gave an encouraging smile. Nobody knew what had happened that day and there was no reason for them to be made aware of it now.

They picked up the new transport from the FANY HQ and started off on the journey up the north-western coast of Scotland. Getting away from towns and the eastern coastline had brought back to them all just how beautiful Britain really was without the brutal scars of war.

The camp to which they were allocated was indeed a bleak, God-forsaken place, but the Poles gave the girls a warm welcome. It was good to see them all again, Mary thought. Especially her old friend, Jan Berwinski.

'Mary!' He stood before her, his arms open wide, his smile genuine and his eyes betraying the fact that he believed they had already enjoyed a special kind of relationship.

'Hello, Jan! Oh, it's lovely to see you again.'

The kiss was unexpected. His soft lips caressing her cheeks, his hands squeezing hers in the way that people do when there is something going on between them. Mary wasn't disappointed, but she couldn't put her whole heart into it. Jan still had a wife and two children somewhere, as far as she knew. The attraction was no doubt born of mutual loss and loneliness.

'He's in love with you, Mary,' Iris said later that night as they sat warming themselves around a peat-stove.

Mary held her hands out to warm them, wondering how much colder it would get before winter actually set in.

'It's what happens to people when they are thrown together in tragic circumstances or when they share danger,' she said, wishing she could feel more for the Polish soldier who had latched on to her as if she were some kind of guardian angel.

'He's really nice,' Iris persisted. 'You're lucky. I don't know if I'll ever meet up with Gaston again. Hell, I don't even know if Gaston Frébus is his real name!'

No, Mary thought, gazing into the glowing stove, nothing seemed real any more. It was like walking through a dream that was sometimes good, sometimes bad. The trouble was, when you woke up, one day in the future, you would find it wasn't a dream at all, but terrifyingly real.

The next few weeks were something of a respite for the FANY girls while they tended the Polish soldiers, boosting morale as best they could. There were many social occasions when a dance would be organized and the girls would dance with the men and they would sing together around camp-fires in-between the rigorous Army training programme aimed at rehabilitating the soldiers for a return to a war that still showed no sign of coming to an end.

During the freezing days of Christmas, Mary received the most precious gift of all. It came in the shape of a greetings card from Dr Gordon and his wife.

' "My dear girl," Mary read the message out aloud to Iris, hardly able to contain her absolute joy. *"Just had word. Alex is alive. No details as yet, but he wanted you to know. All best wishes . . ."*

Oh, Iris!' was all she could say.

Alex found it difficult to believe that he had been running the underground hospital at Grovignac for over a year under the noses of the Gestapo and the Vichy collaborators. French Resistance workers came and went, bringing in fresh patients, transporting others down to the Pyrenees and guiding them to freedom over the high mountain passes to Spain.

Alex waited for orders to get out, to rejoin his unit, but none came. No doubt he was too useful where he was. He was certainly kept busy and up to now, it was a miracle the hospital had not been discovered.

The Germans could often be heard engaged in ribald fun when they entertained their important guests. Fortunately, it didn't happen all that often. However, it was, he was sure, only a matter of time before their cover would be broken.

He often wondered whether he could trust the local Resistance man who carried messages to and fro, acting as a liaison between French and British agents.

'Your orders, Captain Craig, are to continue your work in this hospital for the time being,' the fellow had said when Alex tried to pump him for information. The Frenchman was pleasant enough, but he gave nothing away, appearing and disappearing with proficient ease like a ghost.

The 'hospital' had once been a cave, hollowed out generations ago by the then owners of the chateau, and used as a wine cellar. There was a hidden door that led through into the existing wine store and Alex and his patients had often to maintain a difficult silence when footsteps resounded on the stone stairs and there was a clink of wine-bottles only a few feet away as the Germans chose the wine for their dinner table.

Food for the hospital inmates was provided from the chateau kitchen by way of a refuse bin, which was kept clean, but where everything left over from the Gestapo meals was thrown in, supposedly to be disposed of or fed to the pigs or the dogs.

Last night the Germans had got more exuberant than usual and a few gunshots had rung out, followed by the agonized screams of Madame Laroque, who was quickly and effectively comforted by her husband, though she could be heard sobbing well into the night. In the early hours Alex allowed himself a rare breath of fresh air. He found Serge Martin, the old gardener, sitting smoking on a broken stone wall near the shed. It was a dark, moonless night and, since it was evident by the silence that the Germans had retired and would likely be comatose until morning, he ventured out, eager to stretch his aching limbs and exercise his legs.

'Ça va, Serge?' he whispered from the shadows behind the old man.

Serge gave a slight nod and continued to suck on his pipe. They had become friends on Alex's few words of schoolboy French and the old man's limited English. It was a relief, sometimes, to talk to someone who wasn't sick or injured or scared.

The old Frenchman lowered his pipe and turned his head and Alex saw that a tear glistened on the lined cheek.

'Bâtards!' Serge hissed, jerking his chin in the direction of the chateau. 'You hear their pistols, monsieur? They kill Madame Laroque's dogs. They do it for fun . . . like sport. Boum, boum, boum! They laugh. It is big joke.'

He lowered his pipe and spat furiously at the ground, then shook his head sadly. Alex could feel the weight of his sorrow. He was an old countryman. He lived off the land and in his eyes animals were creatures that worked and earned their keep as well as any man. There was no sentimentality attached, and yet here he was moved at the senseless killing of four innocent lapdogs, the much loved pets of his employers.

Alex had been worried that the dogs would give something away to the Germans, but they had been kept very much under control and only one, the tiny one they had named Chiffon, had insisted on finding her way somehow into the hospital. She was little more than a pup, only a few months old. In normal circumstances, Alex could well have adopted the wee creature. However, that was over. The dogs were no more. How long, he wondered, before the Gestapo started shooting people for fun?

The two men sat side by side a few minutes more, then, not wishing to chance his luck, Alex pressed the old gardener's shoulder and went back down the tunnel to the hospital. He checked on his patients, but all was well. They were breathing evenly, except for one large Canadian pilot whose snoring had worried them all in case it could be heard through the thick cellar walls. Alex turned the man on to his side and wedged a shoe under his back, then slipped beneath the prickly wool blanket on his own bunk.

As he put his feet down he jumped as he touched something warm and moving. Flinging back the blanket, he could see from the light of the near-gutted candle at the bedside a shaggy face emerge, with silky butterfly ears, a black nose and huge shining eyes.

'Good Lord!' he exclaimed in a hoarse whisper. 'Chiffon, is that you?'

The tiny terrier gave a squeak of delight, pounced at Alex and proceeded to lick him all over.

'What's up, sir?' Private Jenkins sat up in his bunk at the other side of the room, rubbing bleary eyes.

'It seems we have an escapee in our midst,' Alex said, smiling down at the dog and ruffling its soft head.

'Lucky dog,' Jenkins said with a frown. 'Not so sure how it leaves us, sir. She could be trouble.'

Alex appreciated Jenkins's point, but he didn't have the heart to do what Jenkins obviously thought was necessary. He could no sooner put his hands around the dog's neck and squeeze the life out of her than he could kill a human being.

'We'll see. I think she deserves a second chance, don't you?'

*

In December of 1942 Mary was called into the office of the commanding officer, a Major William Haugh. The major was a bit of a stick-in-the-mud, didn't have much to say for himself and kept well away from the social gatherings, and the girls.

'First of all, West,' he said, looking at Mary sternly so that she half expected to be taken to task for some rule that she had possibly broken, 'I'm instructed to tell you that your services are terminated at this camp.'

'Really, sir?' said Mary, standing stiffly at ease, hands behind her back the way she knew Haugh liked it.

'Secondly, you are to return home for a few days' leave.'

Mary's brow creased into a complex frown. 'Might I ask why, sir?'

'I am not at liberty to say anything to you at this moment, West, except to congratulate you on being promoted to captain. Word is you have carried out exceptional duties above and beyond your status. Well done, my dear.'

'Oh!' Mary exclaimed, still none the wiser, but she knew better than to question Army personnel, and especially the officers, when they issued an order from HQ. Why they had pushed her rank up to captain was beyond her. All she had done was her duty.

Not knowing whether to be excited or disappointed, Mary said goodbye to her fellow FANY members. Iris was tearful and claimed that the war would not be the same without her. And she said a special goodbye to Jan, who was more than a little perturbed at losing her, although he, too, was due to leave the camp very soon in order to join an Allied unit, having done a long stint counselling and helping to train his fellow Poles. Their relationship had remained pretty much platonic, though it was clear that Jan would not have objected if it progressed on a more personal level.

'Mary,' he said with a break in his voice, 'one day, I hope we will meet again. I pray that it will be so.'

'That will be nice, Jan,' she told him, gripping his hands and giving him a brief kiss on both cheeks. 'In the meantime, I wish you all the luck in the world.'

'I will carry you here, for ever,' he said, patting his heart. 'May God keep you safe, Mary.'

'And you too, Jan,' she responded sincerely, adding: 'And your family.'

They both knew that the likelihood of Jan's wife and children still being alive was minimal, but neither one of them could bear to voice these thoughts.

*

It was a total surprise, to Mary when she received an invitation to Sunday lunch at Anne Beasley's home. It was waiting for her on her arrival in Felling and Jenny West was more than a little put out, and understandably so.

'I've hardly seen you since this damned war started, our Mary. How dare they think that you'd rather be eating with them on your first Sunday home?'

Mary grimaced and kissed her mother on the cheek. It was unusual, she had to agree, but something told her that it might be important to go. Besides, she was curious to know what had happened to Anne.

'Don't worry, Mum. You'll have me here for Christmas.'

Jenny rolled her eyes to the ceiling. 'Don't expect the usual roast turkey and stuffing, love. There aren't any to get any more. I've ordered one of Mrs Halyard's ducks, but how I'm going to make that stretch to six people I don't know. Your dad's hoping to get his hands on a joint of pork, so we might have a roast with crackling. One of his pals from the pit runs the pig club, but nothing's certain these days.'

'Never mind, eh? We'll be together and that's the main thing.'

When Sunday came around Mary presented herself at the front door of Anne Beasley's home, but was puzzled to find that Anne was not there. She was even more puzzled to find that the other guests were a rather mysterious looking man, who was introduced as Mr Smith, and Miss Frances Croft, looking thin and gaunt and even more unsmiling than ever. Mrs Beasley fussed over her guests with a worried frown and seemed as if she couldn't wait to be dismissed. When Brigadier Beasley suggested that she had things to see to in the kitchen she rushed off with an expression of profound relief.

'Perhaps I can help you, Mrs Beasley?' Mary called out after Anne's mother, but the woman took no notice and the brigadier got up immediately to close the door.

'Mary,' he said, fixing her with a beady eye. 'There isn't time to beat about the bush. This is quite out of the ordinary and you would normally be required to do a few months' training, but we're hoping to waive that in order to expedite things.'

'What things, sir?' Mary said, feeling an uncomfortable shiver touch her spine.

'You have, no doubt, heard of the Special Operations Executive . . . the SOE?' the brigadier said, with a swift glance at Mr Smith who was studying Mary carefully.

'Yes, of course,' Mary replied, feeling the hairs on her arms and the back of her neck stir alarmingly. 'Some of the FANYs have been enrolled, I believe.'

'Well, Mary, we would like to know if you would volunteer to go into France in order to do some very important work for us.' He cleared his throat noisily before going on. 'We wouldn't ask, but quite frankly, my dear, you are the best candidate available to us at this time.'

Mary had been aware of an uneasy atmosphere ever since she stepped over the threshold. Mrs Beasley looked very tense and the brigadier had an over-anxious look in his eyes. Mr Smith, on the other hand, looked like a man who did not possess feelings of any kind. And it was Mr Smith who now took over and addressed her.

'Miss West . . . Mary . . .' He hesitated. 'This interview must be kept strictly confidential. I am connected to MI6 and to the SOE. The thing is, we know of a traitor who has been causing us lots of trouble by giving important information to the Germans. The brigadier's daughter went in some weeks ago, but we have not heard from her after her first message saying she had reached her destination. She was going in as a German, you understand.'

Anne was in the SOE! Mary couldn't believe it, yet it would explain her apparent disappearance from the FANYs and the fact that no one appeared to know her whereabouts.

'I have a horrible feeling,' Mary said, 'that I know what you are going to ask me to do.'

'You can refuse, of course,' Brigadier Beasley said quickly. 'You are, after all, a volunteer.'

'There's an underground medical unit operating a safe house under the nose of the Gestapo, who are using Chateau Grovignac as a kind of holiday home.' Smith eyed her speculatively. 'You know the chateau, I believe?'

Mary's eyes grew wide. 'Yes, that's right. I spent a lot of time there with Anne when I was a child.' She glanced at Miss Croft, who was look-ing anything but happy. 'It belonged to relatives of Miss Croft. A French couple by the name of Laroque. They were always very kind to me.'

'An aunt and uncle . . . yes.' Miss Croft nodded gravely, then cast her head to one side as if trying to shed the burden of guilt for what was about to descend on Mary. 'I'm so sorry about this, my dear.'

'Mary, if you are willing,' said Smith, with a caustic glance at Frances Croft, 'you will be sent to the chateau as Monsieur and Madame Laroque's granddaughter, Marie-Jo Laroque. You will have the necessary identity. The girl did exist until she was killed a year or two ago in a motor-car accident. The Germans would not know this and the only photographs the elderly couple have are of Marie-Jo when she was very young.'

'But this traitor, Mr Smith,' Mary wanted to know. 'How do you know he is in that vicinity?'

'Because our contacts in the Resistance tell us he has almost certainly moved down there from the north. He was feeding information to the Germans throughout the Dunkirk landings. The field hospitals seem to have been the source.'

'You think it's someone connected with the hospitals?'

'That's what we believe, though all we have to go on is a nondescript message from an agent very close to the chateau, but before we could ascertain more on the identity of the traitor our communications were wiped out. We haven't been able to make contact since. Whoever this traitor is, he does seem to know about every strategic move before it happens. That can only mean that he's one of ours . . . or someone very close.'

'And you want me to go in and winkle him out?' Mary laughed drily. 'I'm no spy, Mr Smith . . . or whatever your name is.' He flinched at that. 'I'm trained in basic engineering skills and communications. I haven't done much more than drive an ambulance, man a mobile canteen and teach English to a few Polish refugees all the time I've been in the FANYs. What makes you think I can help?'

'Firstly, you speak fluent French, according to Miss Croft here. Secondly, you speak sufficient German to understand what's going on, although we must impress upon you not to show that you understand. Thirdly, you know Anne Beasley, who has had SOE training, but is probably in a tricky situation right now. Lastly, we think you have already shown that you can keep your head in a difficult situation. Your CO has recommended you highly, Miss West.'

Mary blew out her cheeks, her eyes sliding from Smith to Brigadier Beasley to Miss Croft. The two men were staring at her hopefully. Frances Croft seemed detached, her eyes melancholy, the corners of her mouth turned down. She plainly did not want to be there.

'I think you're expecting an awful lot of me, quite frankly,' Mary said at last.

'Yes, we are, but we wouldn't ask if we didn't think it wasn't absolutely necessary.' Smith was pacing the lounge, his hands clasped behind his back.

'If it's any help, we believe you will be absolutely safe,' said Brigadier

Beasley. 'You just have to behave like any young Frenchwoman visiting her grandparents, keep your eyes and ears open and wait to be contacted.'

'Normally, you would have been interviewed and trained in London or Scotland before being sent into France, but we don't have time.' Smith watched her closely as he spoke. 'Evacuation plans for a lot of these safe houses were issued some time ago, so the Germans must already be aware of them by now. We no longer trust our communications system at this point, so we would be asking you to deliver a message by word of mouth. It is of utmost importance that the message gets through. We believe it's only a matter of days, or hours, before the hospital's cover is completely blown. There are many lives at stake here and you could help save them.'

'Whom would I contact?' she asked, steeling herself against the fluttering butterflies that were invading her stomach. 'And how?'

'A French Resistance worker,' Smith said. 'Codenamed *Le Blaireau*. He's a local wine-grower and his vineyards are in the vicinity of the chateau. We will put you down near Paris under cover of darkness. It will be necessary for you to take a train to Toulouse. From there you must make your own way to the chateau.'

'As Marie-Jo Laroque.' Mary nodded. She closed her eyes tightly and held her breath for just a few seconds. She wasn't convinced that she was the right person for the job. 'What message am I supposed to give *Le Blaireau*?'

'You must tell him to look for the nightingale with the loudest song. He will know whom you mean and act accordingly.'

'The French shoot nightingales, don't they?' Mary said with a wry smile.

Smith ignored her remark. 'You must deliver your message, then wait for your next contact, which will be about your lift out of France. *Le Blaireau* is head of a large band of Resistance fighters. They will get you safely out of the danger zone. But if you can't deliver the message, many lives will be lost.'

'One of those lives could well be my daughter, Mary,' Brigadier Beasley said, nervously fingering his moustache. 'The last we heard was that she was due to visit Chateau Grovignac sometime soon.'

'I really don't think I'd be good enough for this job,' Mary said, shaking her head. 'It's far too important.'

'We do not agree, Miss West!' Smith's patience was wearing thin.

'Smith. . . ?' The brigadier looked at the MI6 man for permission to continue and received an almost imperceptible nod. 'The thing is, Mary, there's a British serviceman there whom we think you know. He was reported dead, but turned up at a safe house and has been very active ever since the Dunkirk evacuation. He's been working under cover for a long time, running the hospital at Grovignac.'

'Who is that, sir?' Mary steeled herself for his answer, hardly daring to hope.

'Captain Alexander Craig.'

'Alex!' She felt her blood run cold, then boil inside her veins. 'You're speaking of Dr Craig of Felling? Dr Gordon's nephew?'

'The very same. The thing is, Mary, we know there's a spy – someone either working with him or who knows him. Unfortunately, our contact has not been in touch for some time and we fear that . . .'

'When do I leave?' Mary asked, not waiting for the brigadier to finish speaking.

She saw him relax, though Miss Croft maintained her rigid posture, closing her eyes, her lips moving as if in prayer.

'Thank you, Mary,' the brigadier said, his voice thick with emotion. 'Thank God for people like you. We will leave immediately. Your family will be informed. Shall we go?'

CHAPTER TEN

THE drone of the Lysander light aircraft reverberated in Mary's head. At the same time, her heart reverberated in her chest. Her mouth was dry and every nerve in her body was screaming with panic. Breathing was difficult and she thought that any minute now she was going to pass out. But she kept telling herself that she was doing the right thing. Now was not the time to get cold feet. It was far too late now to change her mind.

Inside the plane, it was freezing cold, and although Mary was shivering, she was also burning with anticipation at what she was about to do. Someone tapped her on the shoulder, making her start. She looked up into the face of a young, rosy-cheeked airman.

'We're there,' he said and Mary's stomach churned. 'Get ready.'

There was a sinking feeling as the plane landed, bumping along on uneven ground. As it slowed, Mary got to her feet, her legs feeling rubbery. She moved slowly into position. The airman opened the aircraft door, revealing the dark, empty land and she felt a blast of icy air like needles pricking her skin.

'Now – quick!' A voice hissed urgently in her ear, but she couldn't let go. Her hands had become paralysed, her brain numb.

Whether she jumped or was pushed, she couldn't remember, but suddenly she was stumbling down the fixed ladder and jumping the rest of the way to the ground. Someone threw her bag after her. She grabbed it and ran, bent double, for cover towards a copse of nearby oaks and pines. The Lysander had already gone, flying off with hardly a sound.

Mary stood up and looked around her, glad there was a moon and enough light for her to see her way, although it could be tricky if there were any Germans about who might spot her. Not even genuine Frenchwomen would be abroad in the middle of the night.

She checked that she had everything she needed. The clothes, the bag and the papers were all authentic French. Before she boarded the plane they had stripped her of anything that might be construed as English, even her underwear. Ever since she had agreed to come on this mission, she had forced herself to think in French whenever possible, and now she muttered in French under her breath as she made her way towards the city of Paris.

By the time she reached the outskirts, the morning sun was beginning to rise. She enquired from a street-sweeper where *la gare* was situated and he pointed her in the right direction, warning her that there were checkpoints everywhere and hoped she had all her papers intact. She assured him that all was well and continued on her weary way.

The railway station was empty but for a few early morning travellers, some of whom wore German uniforms. All she could do was imagine herself as Marie-Jo Laroque, on her way to visit her grandparents for Christmas. It wasn't too difficult, since the Laroques had treated her as one of their own. They were a delightful couple and she could remember exactly what they were like and how they lived in the grand chateau.

'Your papers, *mademoiselle*?'

Had she reacted like an ordinary citizen of France, or like a British spy? She looked up at the tall young Gestapo officer, standing proudly erect in his smart black uniform. He was smiling at her. Automatically, she returned the smile.

'Yes, of course,' she said, delving into her bag and producing the papers she had been provided with.

He seemed to take a long time inspecting them, but that was possibly because Mary was nervous and struggling to present a calm exterior.

'*Merci, mademoiselle*,' he replied after a slight hesitation and returned her papers with a smile.

He looked as if he wanted to converse some more with her, but at that moment the early-morning train for Toulouse approached and his comrades called out to him to rejoin them. He saluted Mary smartly with yet another charming smile and left her to board the train without a backward glance.

It was a long, tedious journey. Mary slept most of the way, which was surprising, considering the mission she was on, but the stress of the whole venture was taking its toll. Besides, the carriage was empty for a good part of the way with nobody to hear her if she spoke in English in her sleep.

At Toulouse she changed for Foix, where there seemed to be some confusion on the platform. She gritted her teeth and presented her ticket and her papers to the German soldier who was keeping the guard company. They were, fortunately for her, too busy searching a family of travellers who were acting suspiciously to bother about a single young woman, plain-faced and shabbily dressed.

'*Allez-y vous!*' The guard waved her through and she emerged on to a dark street with people scurrying about, anxious to get home before the evening curfew. She found a small hotel and put up for the night. Very early the next morning she ascertained from the hotel concierge that there was a wagon going in the direction of Grovignac and she could hitch a ride for a few francs. The man in charge of the two magnificent Percheron horses pulling the wagon was pleasant enough, but after asking her where she was headed, he kept himself very much to himself, for which she was grateful.

When they arrived at Grovignac, the village that took its name from the chateau, Mary waited until she recognized the scenery before she got out in order to go the rest of the way on foot. Thereafter, she found it surprisingly easy. Chateau Grovignac, with its widespread vineyards, had not changed over the few years since she and Anne used to play in among the vines in summer and eat the semi-sweet black grapes, which often resulted in griping stomachs.

She remembered the winding track, the avenue of tall plane trees with their marbled bark, and the huge, solitary oak with the branches like outstretched, welcoming arms, and a hole in it big enough for a child to hide in.

The small farmhouse at the top of the hill above the vines looked deserted, though most French houses did after dark, even in times of peace. No dog barked, for which she was grateful, but there was a disturbed cackling of geese and hens as she walked through the forecourt, keeping well into the side of the wall so that she was hidden from view.

Mary was only a yard or two away from the door when it creaked open and the long barrel of a rifle poked out. She sucked in air and held her breath, her heart thudding loudly in her chest. They had warned her that the place had changed hands in recent years, the previous occupants having retired, so the tenants would not recognize her.

'*Il y a quelq'un?*' It was a gruff, female voice. '*Qui est-ce?*'

'*Je cherche Le Blaireau, madame,*' Mary called out softly, giving the phrase she had been instructed to give. Literally, 'I'm looking for the badger'.

She heard a gasp, then the door was opened more fully, though no light shone out. The rifle was withdrawn and a pale, thin hand beckoned.

'*Entrez, mademoiselle . . . vite!*'

With the door shut and bolted firmly behind her, Mary stood hesitantly, waiting for her eyes to adjust to the complete lack of light. Then the woman opened an inner door and there was the flickering glow of a fire and the smell of meat stew and garlic, mixing in with the usual odours of damp and mould, and other things that Mary did not ponder on, so glad was she to be inside and warm.

The woman was elderly, brown-skinned and lined like old leather. She ladled out some *cassoulet*, tore off a chunk of bread from a huge round loaf and put it down on the rough wooden table in the middle of the room.

'Eat!' she said, pouring a large glass of red wine and pushing that, too, in Mary's direction. 'Eat now. We talk later.'

Mary had no appetite, but she managed a few mouthfuls just to please her hostess. The thick bean stew was surprisingly good, but the wine was typically rough. It did, however, warm her and revive her spirits.

'Madame,' she said, as soon as she felt the time had come to talk. 'You know who I am and why I am here?'

'I know nothing, mademoiselle. Only that my husband . . . the man you call *Le Blaireau* . . . told me there could be a visit.'

'He's here?'

'I regret . . . no. Jean-Pierre died three days ago. Shot through the head by collaborators. His men too . . . all of them. They fell into a trap.'

Mary felt the blood drain from her face and her hands begin to shake. Who would she deliver the all-important message to now? She reached for her glass and drank down a good third of the disgusting liquid, but it helped calm her.

'I'm sorry, madame.'

'It is war, no?'

'Your husband was my contact. He was to . . . to help me . . .'

'You arrive too late, mademoiselle . . . you cannot stay here . . . you understand? Each minute you are in my house puts my life in danger.' Mary nodded, for the moment rendered speechless. 'It will be morning soon. You must go then. There is a bicycle in the barn. Jean-Pierre will not be needing it any longer.'

'Thank you.' Mary gulped and cleared her throat. 'You're very kind.'

'You speak excellent French,' the old woman said. 'But you have the proud and haughty look of an Englishwoman. You must learn to be a little more humble if you want to fool the Germans.'

'Thank you, madame. I'll remember your advice.'

The woman nodded, then went to the window, opened it and threw open the heavy shutters. There was a lilac light in the sky, though there was still darkness all around. Somewhere close by a rooster proclaimed itself.

'Go now,' the woman said. 'Wait an hour in the barn, then leave. It would not be prudent to arrive too early at the chateau.'

'An hour . . . yes . . .' Mary licked her lips, gave a final glance of longing at the glowing pieces of timber in the grate and went to the door.

'And remember. You do not know me. I have never seen you. That is also the advice you would have been given by my husband.'

'Yes, madame. I understand. Thank you again.'

'Go safely, *ma petite. Adieu.*'

Daylight was bathing the hillsides in gold as Mary cycled along the narrow, winding road that led to Chateau Grovignac, which was situated on a hill, its towers protruding from dense woodland. Typical of winter in this part of France, it was a beautiful day with a wide expanse of blue sky and there was warmth in the sun that bathed the landscape in mellow gold. She began to relax, though it was not to be for long. The road veered sharply to the right and there, a few hundred yards on, was the chateau, in all its glory.

There was a car blocking the road, surrounded by uniformed figures speaking in voluble German. From what they were saying, the car had broken down. The driver was peering under the bonnet, red-faced and perplexed.

Mary's first impulse was to do an immediate about turn and head for cover, but that would appear suspicious. In any case, it was too late. One of the German officers, alerted by the squeak of her bicycle wheels, looked over his shoulder and saw her. Her heart immediately sank.

'*Alors, mademoiselle!*' He spoke in French, heavily laden with his German accent. 'Come here. Quick, quick! Don't worry. I am not going to eat you.'

The others laughed at their commandant's attempt at humour. Mary dismounted and approached them on foot, wheeling her bicycle and hoping that they couldn't see how her knees trembled beneath the long woollen skirt she was wearing.

'Is there a problem?' she asked, giving them all an uncertain smile.

'There is, indeed, *mademoiselle*. This idiot here has driven like a madman for the past hour and now we have broken down. We are already late for our rendezvous at the chateau. Are you from there?'

He was looking her up and down as he spoke, the thick lenses of his spectacles glinting in the sun so she couldn't see his eyes, but she knew they would undoubtedly be wary, not to say suspicious.

'No, *monsieur* . . . .at least, not exactly. I have come to visit my grandparents, Monsieur and Madame Laroque. They are the proprietors of Chateau Grovignac.'

'Name?'

'Marie-Jo Laroque.'

'Papers?' He held out a gloved hand and she once again presented her forged papers, praying that whoever had created them was a master at his craft, for this man did not look like anybody's fool. 'Thank you, *mademoiselle*. Now, perhaps you would be so kind as to ride up to the chateau and inform Oberleutnant Hauptmann what has happened.'

He was obviously satisfied and handed the papers back to her after only a cursory glance.

'Yes, *monsieur*.' Mary climbed back on her bike and set off towards the chateau, desperately trying to ride without wobbling.

'I hope to see more of you in the next few days, *fräulein*,' he called after her in German.

Mary stopped, put a foot to the ground, then remembered that she was not supposed to understand German.

'*Comment, monsieur?*' she said, furrowing her brow at him, but he simply smiled, nodded and waved her on.

Perspiration was pouring from her as if it were midsummer by the time she dismounted at the steps to the chateau. She jangled the bell on her bike, thinking that it might well be the kind of thing a visiting grandchild would do. Almost immediately the door opened and two immaculately dressed people appeared. The old couple came out on to the steps and stared at Mary uncomprehendingly. Behind them, a third figure appeared. Yet another German officer.

Mary ran up the steps, smiling broadly, and threw herself first into the old woman's unsuspecting arms.

'*Mamie!*' She kissed the woman's cheeks, then passed on to the man, whose wise old eyes were betraying nothing of what must be going on through his mind. '*Papie! Surprise!* I have come to you for Christmas. Are you not pleased to see me?'

'You are always welcome here, child,' said the man, taking her by the arm and turning her so that he could be sure she had seen the German standing behind him.

Mary smiled up at the handsome, blond-haired lieutenant, who was regarding her curiously.

'*Bonjour, monsieur.*' She dipped a tiny curtsy and saw his eyes narrow. 'I am Marie-Jo Laroque . . .' There was the faintest gasp of astonishment from Madame Laroque. '. . . and I have come to visit my grandparents for Christmas.'

'Indeed?' He inclined his head and gave the faintest of smiles.

'I haven't seen them for so long and . . . well, it's Christmas . . . nearly . . . and . . .' She stopped rattling on and took a deep breath. 'Oh, are you Oberleutnant Hauptmann? I passed a group of . . . of military gentlemen just down the road there. Their car has broken down. The one in charge asked me to tell you. I think they have an appointment and are afraid of being late.'

'Ah! Very well . . .' He turned to someone standing in the shadows behind him. 'Will you excuse me, my dear. I must go and pick them up. Perhaps, Monsieur Laroque, you could send somebody to repair our visitors' car?'

'Marie-Jo.' Madame Laroque took Mary by the hand and started leading her up the steps towards the big, iron-studded door. 'I hardly recognized you. Come inside, child, before you freeze. Leave your bicycle there. It will be quite safe.'

Mary stepped inside the hall, which looked no different from how it had been all those years ago when she visited as a child, though it seemed smaller and shabbier. Perhaps it had always been that way and she was now seeing the place as an adult, rather than an impressionable teenager with stars in her eyes.

'So, you have come to spend Christmas with your grandparents?'

The voice that addressed her spoke in German, but this time it belonged to a woman. The wife or companion of the Oberleutnant Hauptmann, no doubt. Mary's head jerked around so that she could see the woman more clearly as she stepped out into the light shining through the open doorway. She registered the long, platinum-blonde hair, the mascara and the rouge and the blood red lipstick, then her jaw sagged and her heart leapt alarmingly.

'I'm sorry, but I do not speak German,' she said, careful not to let the shock of recognition show on her face.

'Of course, how silly of me,' Anne Beasley said, switching now to French. 'How pleasant to have someone of my own age to talk to while the men are at their business.' She held out a limp hand, which Mary grasped. She felt a warning squeeze. 'My name is Anna. Anna Kraus. Come, you must tell me all about yourself.'

Five minutes later, Mary found herself sitting beside Anne on a *chaise-*

longue in the high-ceilinged *salon*, with its huge oak beams and chande-
liers and wide, open fireplace. The heat from the burning pine-logs in the
grate warmed the place and cast dancing reflections on the faces of the
two young women. They were alone, Madame Laroque having excused
herself in order to check on refreshments for the new arrivals.

'For God's sake, don't give me away, Mary,' Anne whispered urgently.
'The Laroques haven't recognized me up to now as far as I know. Now,
what the hell are you doing here?'

'Looking for you, basically,' Mary told her, sticking to French, feeling
it was safer than English in the circumstances. 'Communication has
broken down between the French Resistance and England – at least for
this part of the world. They seem to think that there's a spy in the
network, passing on information as soon as it's received. It has to be one
of our own people . . . or someone good enough to pass himself off as
one of our own.'

'We suspected as much. That's why the safe houses are constantly on
the move.'

'Except the safe house here, apparently.'

Anne blinked at her and Mary felt as though she had betrayed a secret.

'But, surely, you knew?'

'No.' Anne shook her head. 'I've been playing things safe for the last
few months, worming my way in on the German side of things. It wasn't
so difficult at first, but now I'm in it's not as easy as I thought to get information. Heinrich is a good man, but he's also a good German officer.
Besides, he doesn't like talking about war with me.'

Mary felt a surge of heat starting from her neck and rushing to the
roots of her hair. She didn't like what Anne was telling her, but this was
neither the time nor the place to criticize her old friend's morals. Besides,
Anne was a British SOE agent and acting under orders.

'Don't look at me like that, Mary,' Anne said, reading her thoughts.
'We're all making sacrifices for our country. Some do it with their lives.
Besides, nobody's forcing me and . . . well, he's nice. He's actually *very*
nice.'

'Are you in love with him?'

There was a brief moment when it looked as though Anne was going
to say yes, but then she shook her head.

'Of course not. He's German.'

Alex was in place at the arranged time. It was the fifth failed rendezvous
at which he had waited for *Le Blaireau* to bring him news about the

proposed transfer from the chateau to a point nearer the Pyrenees so they could be on hand for British and Canadian troops escaping into neutral Spain. The old man had told him a week ago that the Germans were wiping out every safe house between Paris and Lourdes. This was to be the last move before Alex could be lifted out and returned to England.

But *Le Blaireau* hadn't come and now Alex was beginning to worry. With the chateau being full of Germans for the last few days, none of them had been able to come and go as usual. Not even to steal a few necessary gasps of fresh air. The vault was stinking because they couldn't get rid of the sewage and there had been no fresh food for forty-eight hours. This last party of Germans were intent on having a good time and, consequently, they seemed to be awake and roaming about at every hour of the day and night.

There had been music and dancing. The noise had filtered through to Alex and Private Jenkins. Two Canadians, their wounds all but healed, had jigged around the stone floor while those still recovering sat up in their beds, clapping their hands to the rhythm. Alex felt mean when he ordered them to be silent, but this was not the time to get careless. Not if they wanted to get out of the place alive.

'*Monsieur*!' From the darkness, Alex heard Serge's whisper. He stiffened and listened intently to what the gardener had to say, conscious that the old Frenchman was risking his life every time he spoke to him. '*Le Blaireau est mort* – dead, *monsieur.*'

Damn! Alex's blood turned to ice in his veins as he saw all his hopes of escape dashed. Without *Le Blaireau* and the help he had promised, they were all condemned.

'Thank you, Serge,' he whispered back, but he knew that the Frenchman had already gone.

A scratching noise from inside the exit of the vault attracted his attention. It was followed by a whimpering sound and more scratching. Chiffon! As usual, she was desperate to run free in the open air, but Alex was determined that she would not end up slaughtered like her brothers and sisters. She was a dear little thing and was never far from his side. At night she curled up in the discarded helmet of a dead soldier, but quite often, Alex would wake up and find her snuggled in beside him.

'Chiffon?' He tiptoed back into the shed from his hiding place between two huge lime trees. 'Be quiet!'

He started to lift the trap-door, which had recently been camouflaged in such a way that it was hidden, yet could still be lifted from inside without the weight of the vegetables on top. He didn't see the dog emerge, but was suddenly aware that she was skittering away over the gravel drive with a joyous yelp. She had not barked since the day she had escaped the German bullets that killed her brothers and sisters, but recently she had been showing a certain amount of agitation.

'Blast!' Alex stood up and took a few paces forward. He didn't dare call out or whistle. Not even Chiffon was worth the lives of the dozen men holed up beneath the chateau waiting to be rescued.

Because everything was so silent in the chateau grounds, the noise being contained inside the building where he could hear yet more music and stamping and clapping of hands, Alex stepped further out than he should have, hoping to attract the dog and bring her back. Too late he heard the crunch of gravel, saw Chiffon hesitate, then turn and rush, not towards him but towards someone standing in the shadow of the terrace wall. Someone who, like him, obviously didn't want to be discovered.

Mary, tired from dancing with the stomping, heavy-footed Germans in their jackboots, wondered whether they slept with them on and thought that they probably did, and to attention. A very small part of her envied Anne her German lover. They had already retired for the night, to a chorus of bawdy cheers. Heinrich was young and good-looking and, yes, possessed all the necessary charm that the others plainly lacked, especially when they were drunk, which was what they were now.

Making her excuses early, Mary pleaded a migraine and told them she was going to bed. They had complained amicably enough, but because they had so much drink in them, it being Christmas Eve, she was at last dismissed with little more than a wave of the commandant's hand.

On the upstairs landing where her bedroom was, a door creaked open and Anne appeared, barely clad, holding the edges of a flimsy housecoat together. She beckoned to Mary, then tiptoed out to meet her.

'He won't sleep for long, so I've got to be quick,' she whispered frantically, her eyes darting in every direction as if the woodwork might be growing ears. 'They know about the safe house beneath the chateau. Heinrich let it slip. They were supposed to move in tonight, but they're all too drunk, so they've postponed it until tomorrow.'

'It's Christmas Day tomorrow!' Mary exclaimed, not believing that any human being could plan such a coup that would almost certainly result in more than one death on Christmas Day.

'They're holed up underground, apparently. This chateau was built over a series of caves. Do you know where the entrance is, Mary?'

Mary shook her head. They had never been allowed down in the cellars as children.

'No, but I've seen the gardener disappear into a shed at the back with bins of food and the odd bottle of wine, but that was only once and could mean nothing at all.'

'You've got to try and warn them, Mary,' Anne said, her eyes bulging and two angry red blotches appearing on her high cheekbones. 'I don't care how you do it, but it's up to you now. I can't get away.'

'But you can't stay here, Anne,' Mary whispered frantically. 'Come with me now.'

Her eyes pleaded, but something told her that Anne was reluctant to leave, even if she could. Mary had seen how her old friend interacted with her German, seen how they looked at one another, how they touched and spoke so fondly together. He was the enemy and Anne was skating on thin ice by going with her heart rather than her head.

For Mary, it had been a nerve-racking few days living with a houseful of Germans. They had been surprisingly polite and far too involved with their own pressing business, not to mention their merrymaking at the expense of the chateau's good wine cellar, to pay much attention to the owner's mousy granddaughter. Only once had one of the men made advances that unnerved Mary, but Oberleutnant Hauptmann had put him firmly in his place. Anne's German, as Mary always thought of Hauptmann, reminded his fellow-countryman that although they were the conquerors, they must at all times conduct themselves with dignity.

'Leave the girl alone!' he had bellowed. 'You should have better things to do, Franz, than be unfaithful to your wife.'

There was the creak of bedsprings and the two women stiffened as a slurred voice called out.

'Anna? Anna, where are you? Come back to bed. I'm lonely.'

Anne pressed a finger to her lips and ran back into the room. Mary could hear her telling Heinrich that she had just slipped to the bathroom. She wished she had been able to say something to her, other than stare like an imbecile and feel so totally helpless.

Mary went to her room and donned a thick coat and scarf, then slipped down the back stairs and made her way slowly and carefully around the chateau until she was in sight of the old shed. She had been standing there, wondering what to do next, when she heard the dog. Suddenly, she was cornered. The dog rushed at her from one direction, while someone was watching her from the shadows on the other side.

Mary took a step forward and so did her observer. There was only a short gap between them. The dog was dancing excitedly around her, mewing like a kitten, patting her with soft, gentle paws. Sure that it must be one of the Germans watching her, Mary decided to brazen it out and bent to pick up the tiny creature, which immediately fell silent, nuzzling her neck and licking her face.

'*Bonsoir*,' she called out softly, then continued to speak soothingly to the dog in French. There was no reply from the person standing there like a statue, then the place where they were was lit up like a stage as the moon appeared from behind a dark cloud. She gave a strangulated cry. 'Alex!'

He jumped forward, grabbed hold of her and dragged her back into the pitch-black of the shed. His hand clamped down over her mouth and she felt his fingers, steely hard, digging into her arm.

'Tell me it's not a dream,' he whispered, his mouth close to her ear. 'Oh, my God, Mary, what are you doing here?'

'Oh, Alex, is it really you?' Mary mumbled as her body sagged against him.

A pair of strong arms encircled her as he held her close to his chest, making the little dog between them gasp and wriggle. She felt his mouth press into the top of her head, then he was kissing her on the lips, tasting the tears that rolled down her cheeks.

'This is crazy,' he said thickly. 'It can't be happening.'

'Alex, you've got to get out,' Mary said, struggling to keep her composure. 'They know about you. You've got to get out now.'

'What?'

'The Germans in the chateau. They're planning to raid the safe house tomorrow.'

'So, we've finally been rumbled, eh? But how are you involved, for Christ's sake? You should be safely back in England doing what you FANY girls do best.'

'I was sort of enlisted in the SOE,' she told him. 'I don't think they had anybody else at such short notice. Are there many of you?'

He took her down into the cave hospital, where eight pairs of eyes looked at her with mixed reactions. Mostly disbelief.

'This is Mary, everybody,' was his short introduction. 'No time to explain. We need to pack up and get out immediately. Leave anything that's not absolutely necessary and let's get out of here.'

'There are two German staff cars in the drive,' Mary said. 'I noticed yesterday that the keys had been left in. It'll be a tight squeeze, but they should get us far enough away. We could be in the Pyrenees in a few hours.'

Alex was slinging a canvas haversack on to his back. The other men were looking nervous and confused, but they seemed ready enough to follow orders, even if it was Mary giving them.

'Well, I won't say that I'm going to miss the old place,' said one young man with a grin and Alex slapped him on the back.

'Me neither, Jenkins,' he said, then indicated the tunnel down which he had just brought Mary. 'Shall we go?'

They were cautious as they lifted the hatch and climbed out, one after the other, some of the men not so agile because of their injuries. However, they had existed together for so long in close proximity to one another that they had become a family. Help and support was forever at hand.

A high-pitched, canine yap pulled Alex up as they crept down the wide, sweeping drive, keeping close in to the high laurel hedge that circled the chateau grounds.

'Oh, hell!' he said and Mary turned to see the little dog, Chiffon, standing in the middle of the gravel forecourt, all aquiver, her tiny stump of a tail wagging. 'Chiffon, go! *Va-t-en!*'

He picked up a pebble and threw it at the dog. It landed in front of the terrier's nose, making her leap back with a startled, whimpering cry. Mary's heart contracted. She was an animal lover and she could see from Alex's expression that it pained him to be so brutal towards the dog, but they couldn't take the risk of her revealing their presence. A barking dog, even one as minute as this one, could arouse the deepest, alcoholic stupor.

'Let's go,' Alex ordered, his voice rasping low in his throat.

'Just a second, sir.' Jenkins ran over to a third, smaller car and they saw him fiddling under the bonnet. 'That fettles him. He won't be going anywhere in a hurry.'

'Into the damned cars, now.' Alex was beginning to sound impatient. 'Go, go, go!'

He grabbed Mary's hand and ran across the courtyard with her, the other men following. They ran, she noticed, on bare feet, with their boots strung around their necks. There was less noise that way. There was a moment's panic as they struggled to fit a large airman into one of the cars. He had a broken leg encased in bulky splints, but they made it by having him lie across the back seat. As soon as he was installed, they released the handbrakes and let the cars cruise soundlessly down the long, curved drive towards the big wrought-iron gates.

Not until they were through the gates and on the road did they start up the engines. Alex swore again as he fumbled with the ignition and the car he was driving coughed apologetically and refused to start. However, it must only have been nerves, for it started immediately after and everyone breathed sighs of relief.

'I was beginning to think that our cover was invincible,' he said through gritted teeth. 'I might have known that our luck would run out eventually.'

Mary found some maps of the region in the glove compartment, which was good news indeed. Better news still was the fact that Private Jenkins, who was squashed in beside her, claimed to be a dab hand at map-reading, so she gladly handed over the navigation to him.

Only a couple of hundred yards from the chateau, Alex glanced in his rear mirror.

'Oh, no!' he groaned and slowed the car down to a walking pace.

'What is it?'

Mary strained her neck so she could see what he was looking at, afraid that it was a problem with the second car. Apart from almost running into the back of them at the unexpected slackening of pace, the other car appeared to be fine. But there was something moving in the road behind. Ears flopping, long pink tongue curled up over her nose, the little dog, Chiffon, was racing to catch up, short legs going like pistons.

'I can't leave her,' Alex said with an embarrassed smile.

'Never thought you would, sir,' said Jenkins, grinning as he pored over a map with the aid of a torch. 'Well, I mean to say, she is our lucky mascot, isn't she?'

The dog was running abreast of them now, running tirelessly and glancing at two-second intervals at Alex through the driving seat window. She made no sound until he swore again softly, opened the door with the car still moving, and the dog leapt in over his knees and landed on Mary with an ecstatic yelp.

'Right,' said Alex, giving Chiffon a quick stroke and Mary's hand a squeeze. 'Now that we're all here, let's go for real. How long before we get to the Pyrenees, Jenkins?'

'Depends which roads we take and how fast we drive, sir,' Jenkins answered him, 'but I reckon on three hours, stopping for nothing.'

'Hmm.' Alex moved up in the gears and put his foot down on the accelerator 'Well, let's hope we don't have to stop . . . for anything. Keep us to the country roads, Jenkins. We can't afford to meet a German patrol.'

'In that case, better take this next left turn,' Mary said, pointing as the almost hidden turning came up.

'Hold on, everyone!' Alex managed the turn without landing them in the ditch, but only just. 'How did you know that was there, Mary?'

'I've been here before, remember? The trouble is, in the dark and without signposts, it all looks so different.'

'We'll make it, Mary,' he said, gripping the wheel and leaning forward to concentrate on the rough track. 'It looks like a bumpy ride, but next stop the Pyrenees.'

Anne Beasley sat with Monsieur and Madame Laroque in their smart *salon*, while the Germans searched the grounds for the missing fugitives. They had discovered the underground cave hospital twenty minutes ago, having failed to make any of the old French people who lived there tell them where it was.

She sat stiffly erect in her chair, looking coldly upon the battered faces of the two French people who had been so kind to her as a child. Miss Croft's *Tante* Adèle held up her head proudly, though it was evident that she could no longer see through her black, swollen eyes. Her lip was split and bleeding and, Anne knew, there had to be unseen injuries to the poor woman's torso. *Oncle* Didier was slumped on the sofa beside her, bleeding from a vicious blow to the head. One arm hung limply down and she wasn't sure whether they had broken it or simply dislocated the shoulder. With difficulty, his good hand reached out and touched the hand of his wife. Their fingers intertwined.

'*Ça va, Adèle?*' he whispered.

'*Ça va, chéri,* she replied.

The servants, Madame Dufore, the housekeeper and, Monsieur Martin, the gardener, and his simple-in-the-head assistant, sat at the back of the room. The housekeeper wept noisily. Anne wished she could afford to shed the tears that were falling inside her, but she could not. She had been given a pistol and told to shoot any one of the occupants of the room, if they so much as moved. She prayed she would not have to carry out the order, but she was prepared to do anything to protect her true identity. As far as she could tell, the Laroques had not recognized her as the child they had known as Anne Beasley.

A clump of jackboots crossing the hall made her jerk to attention even more rigidly. The sound of the telephone dial spinning round seemed extra loud, but the one-sided conversation was muffled. When it was over, Heinrich entered the room, came over to her and took the pistol out of her sweaty grip.

'They have taken the kommandant's cars,' he said. 'And disabled mine. Did you not hear them in the night?'

'No, of course not, Heinrich. I was asleep like you. We all had too much to drink. It is Christmas, after all.' Anne could feel her heart dipping and tripping along erratically. 'Have you phoned for some taxis?'

He was a long time in replying and Anne had a sinking feeling in her stomach. Something was not right. Heinrich had lost his smile, his charm. He looked more than worried. He looked furious.

'If I asked you about the British safe house at Agen, would you lie and tell me that you don't know what I'm talking about?'

Anne smiled sweetly up at him and made to take his hand, though her insides were quaking.

'Heinrich, darling, what is all this about? Of course I don't know . . .'

His hand flew out so quickly she had no time to see it coming. His signet ring cut a weal across her cheek and sent her flying back into the cushions of the chair.

'Traitor!' he yelled out as the room filled with angry Germans, humiliated at having been tricked and robbed into the bargain.

'What is this?' Kommandant Heffner demanded. 'Please explain, Oberleutnant.'

'I have just spoken to my . . . my contact, Herr Kommandant. It appears that the lovely Anna here is not German at all. She's English.'

'How very interesting. Can one assume that you have not been indiscreet during your . . . shall we say . . . love trysts?'

'No, Herr Kommandant . . . I mean, yes, you may assume that. There have been no indiscretions. You have my word on that.'

'Very well, then. We will leave you to deal with the problem as you see fit. You know what I mean.'

'Yes, of course.' Heinrich's face had turned to stone. 'You are leaving, Herr Kommandant?'

'As soon as I acquire two new cars,' the kommandant said, glancing at his watch. 'Which should be very soon now.'

They waited almost an hour until cars were brought from the village. Each hollow tick of the ormolu clock on the marble shelf above the fireplace gave Anne the feeling that her life was slipping away. She had failed miserably in her duty. Somehow, she had revealed herself to an enemy spy, but who could it be? It could only have been someone at one of the safe houses she had visited after her drop into France. Her job had been to winkle out the traitor, but it hadn't been as easy as she had imagined. And then she had met Heinrich and everything went topsy-turvy.

A cold finger of fear traced its way down her spine. There was, she thought, only one person it could possibly be, but it was too late now to do anything and Mary was going to walk right into a trap if she made it to the safe house in the Pyrenees, if that was where they were headed, and she was sure they were.

'Come, Anna,' Heinrich said, hauling her to her feet and dragging her with him to the door. 'It is time.'

He turned at the door and waved his pistol at the four old people and the boy with the scared eyes and a dribble of saliva on his chin.

'Nobody moves, do you hear? You stay where you are and you will keep your miserable lives.'

Nobody moved. Nobody spoke. What was the use? He was going to execute Anne no matter what they did. The blessing was that he was not going to do it in front of them.

'Where are you taking me?' Anne demanded, suddenly realizing that they were walking down the hill from the chateau and that he had not yet used his pistol on her as she had fully expected.

'Damn you, Anna!' He spat the words at her, his grip not losing its power for one second. 'Why did you choose me as your pawn, eh? Why me? We had something good . . . I thought you felt something for me. Something genuine.'

'I did, Heinrich,' she said, suddenly feeling the sobs and tears that she had been holding back, welling up and choking her. 'I do care for you. I do!'

'That's the problem,' he said, stopping so suddenly that she almost fell and he caught her to him in a tight embrace, his mouth seeking hers hungrily; and just as suddenly, he let her go. 'I know you care, Anna. *I do know.*'

'So?'

'So that's why I must give you a chance.' He raked impatient fingers through his fair hair. 'My superiors expect me to put a bullet in your head, but I cannot do it. I cannot be the one who pulls the trigger. I am too damned weak.'

Drawing in a ragged breath, he marched her into the village where people were out in the streets, making feeble attempts at celebrating the festive season, though there was little in the way of festive food to enjoy. At the sight of the tall German officer with his arm around the pretty blonde woman, they stared curiously and even gathered round when he called out to them, kissed the girl fully on the mouth, and she showed little resistance.

There were titters of subdued laughter, no one knowing exactly what the spectacle was supposed to be, or how they were supposed to react to it. Some drew back, while others surged forward, forming an uneven ring around the couple.

'Ah, I see I have your attention!' he called out to them in fractured French. 'You see this woman? She thinks she is in love with me. I have shared my bed with her. Does this not shock you, my fine friends?'

Eyes were beginning to exchange wary glances. This was new. A German officer of the *Wehrmacht* baring his soul in public?

'I have heard what you people do to your compatriots who have affairs with German soldiers. So, I place her in your hands. She is not French, but English. Perhaps that makes a difference, eh?'

With that he gave Anne a push into their midst. She turned to plead with him not to leave her there, but he was already walking away and the circle of people had tightened around her. At first it seemed that they were simply stunned, not knowing what to do with her. Then a shout went up and hands came at her, touching her, pinching her, punching her. She went down on her knees and a boot sank itself into her stomach.

As she folded over with the pain of the blow, more heavy blows rained down on her, then they lifted her and carried her away and she prayed for death to come quickly.

The journey had taken longer than anticipated because they travelled at night. As they made their way cautiously through the foothills of the Pyrenees looking for a possible route where the frontier wasn't guarded by the enemy, they almost fell foul of a group of French partisans mistaking them for Germans.

The danger, however, soon passed. From that moment on, the German staff cars were discarded and the partisans guided them to an isolated house on the outskirts of the town of Saint-Girons. The woman who lived there welcomed them warmly, giving them the traditional hearty *garbure* soup and wild rabbit that she cooked on a spit over the open fire. She did not seem at all surprised to see them and explained that there had been many refugees before them, and would no doubt be many more to follow.

'My house is small,' she told them as they sat elbow to elbow at her kitchen table, passing the wine and the bread and thinking they had not tasted anything so good for a long time. 'If the Germans come, you must hide in the roof space. Eat now, then I have clothes for you.'

'Clothes, madame?' Mary looked at their hostess quizzically.

'*Oui, mademoiselle.* It is winter and there is much snow on the mountain. If you are to walk over the passes into Spain you will need more than those things you stand up in now.'

'But you couldn't possibly have enough spare clothing for all of us,' Mary said with a quick, anxious glance at Alex, who was following the conversation closely.

'Not all, that is true. Some must go. The others must stay, until the next passage.'

'That lets me out,' said the airman with the broken leg. 'I suppose I'll be holidaying here until the spring.'

There were murmurs of sympathy, but the man simply shrugged and got on with the business of eating. When there was no choice, he seemed to say, what was the good of arguing? Best go with the flow of things.

'How will we find our way across the mountains, madame?' Mary asked.

'My son will take you. He knows these mountains, every rock and stone. Every blade of grass. He grew up here. You will be safe with him.'

After the meal, when the men were bedding down for the night in every available space, arguing good-naturedly over who should guard the fire and who should keep a look-out for Germans, Alex touched Mary on the shoulder and jerked his chin towards the door.

'Mary and I will take first watch,' he told the others. 'We will take it in turn, two by two in one hour stretches.'

Outside, wrapped in blankets against the cold December air, they sat side by side, pressing as close together as they could get. It was the first time they had been alone since leaving the chateau, though they had not stopped touching, even when it could be no more than their arms and shoulders pressed together as they drove. Their raw emotions were palpable even through the layers of clothes.

Mary could feel Alex breathing deeply beside her. There was so much she wanted to say, so much to tell him, yet she couldn't bring herself to put it all into words. Not just yet awhile. She stared mutely at the purple sky, its clouds reflecting the pale snow that covered the ground and rose in breathtaking peaks for miles beyond the valley.

After a minute or two, she felt him move, felt his hands on her, felt him pulling her so close that they might be one entity.

'My dear, sweet Mary,' he whispered, his breath comfortingly warm against her forehead. 'I thought I would never see you again.'

'I thought for a long time that you were dead,' she told him. 'I still can't believe that we're here together. I can't believe what's happening.'

She slid her arms around him, hugging him tightly. Nothing mattered any more but this moment. Even if they only had this night, it was worth everything she had been through.

'You know I love you, don't you, Mary?' He looked deeply into her eyes and she nodded. 'I fell in love with you the first moment I saw you. There's a wonderful sense of peace about you. It shines out of you like some incredible inner beauty. It's quite, quite magical.'

'Well, you weaved your own magic spell around me, Alex, the night of the talent contest when you danced with me, then later, when we kissed.'

'I was wrong to do that, but I couldn't stop myself. A married man shouldn't be carrying on like that . . . like this, but . . .' He lowered his head and found her lips and she surrendered herself selfishly to his kiss before pushing him gently away. 'What is it? What's wrong, Mary?'

'Alex . . . don't you know . . . about your wife?'

'Fiona?' He blinked at her, the muscles in his cheeks tensing. 'What about her? What's happened? I've had no news from home since Dunkirk.'

No, she thought. It had probably been withheld. They couldn't afford to have Alex affected by personal matters. His work was too valuable.

'Oh, Alex.' There was no easy way to tell him what she knew to be true. 'Fiona . . . she was pregnant and . . . and . . .'

'Pregnant? No, she couldn't have been . . .' She saw him gulp as he guessed the truth of the situation. 'Oh, I see. Yes, I suppose it was always possible, seeing the company she was keeping.'

Mary bit down on her lips. 'The thing is, Alex, something went wrong . . . very wrong. They died . . . Fiona and the child.'

He was immobile for a long moment, then his face contorted and he dropped his head in his hands. 'Oh, God!'

'I'm sorry, Alex.' What else could she say? He must have loved Fiona once, had some happy times with her.

As she reached out to comfort him, there was a sound that carried like an eerie echo across the valley. A dog howling, long and low, then rising in a sharp, ear-splitting crescendo. Alex looked up, his eyes full of pain. They got to their feet simultaneously just as the door behind them creaked open and the old French woman appeared.

'*Ah! C'est Le Loup! Enfin!*'

'What did she say?' Alex asked.

'She says it's the wolf, but . . .' She turned to the woman who was still in the doorway, nodding her head and smiling. 'Madame, what is it? That sound. Is it really a wolf?'

'No, *mademoiselle*. That is my son letting us know that he is coming. All will be well now. You will see. By this time tomorrow you will be across the frontier into Spain.'

A few minutes later there was the rattle of stones as someone left the shadow of the sparse scrubland and sprinted, bent double, to the house. Beneath the overhanging porch roof he straightened up and a shaft of moonlight shone on his face. A pair of dark eyes twinkled at Mary and although she could hardly see his mouth for the large black moustache that covered his upper lip, she knew he was smiling.

'Gaston Frébus!' she gasped, delightedly giving herself up to his brief hug and the customary *bisous* on both cheeks. 'Oh, Iris will be pleased to know that you are safe.'

'Iris is here?' His eyes lit up with anticipation.

'No, Gaston. She's still looking after the Poles in Scotland. This is Alex, by the way . . . I mean—'

'Captain Craig and I are old friends,' Gaston told her and laughed at her look of surprise. 'I travel around a lot in my job. We have shared the same safe house on more than one occasion.'

Alex gave an enigmatic smile. 'I don't know whether you're good news or bad, Gaston,' he said. 'Every time you turn up I have to decamp.'

Gaston frowned, then gave a short nod. 'I have been giving this some thought,' he said slowly, fingering his moustache and staring at the ground at their feet. 'For the moment, I will keep my ideas to myself. Come inside, my friends. You must rest if you are to be strong enough for the journey ahead.'

CHAPTER ELEVEN

'F IRST of all,' announced Gaston as they got ready to leave the farm-house, 'we go to the last safe house on our route, where there are more refugees waiting. Not all will make it over the mountains. We can take only the fittest. *Le Chemin de la Liberté* is high and we must make the ascent in darkness.'

No one liked the idea of splitting up, but they all knew that the Frenchman was right. For one, the airman with the broken leg was burning up with fever from an infection in his wound. Another was still too weak after a bout of dysentery.

'Where is this safe house, Gaston?' Alex queried.

'Not far from here. In the ruins of an old monastery. There is a fully equipped hospital there in the old cloisters. It's small but effective.'

The monastery he had described was well hidden and could only be reached by a steep climb up a rocky path. They did it in easy stages, resting when necessary, forever on the look-out for German patrols. At first glance, the buildings looked no more than piles of rubble, but this acted as an efficient camouflage. Beyond the innocent-looking rocks and stones, a whole world thrived.

Mary was amazed at what she found inside the dilapidated stone edifice. How they had managed to get beds and equipment up there without detection was a miracle. And there were nurses, English and French, bustling about cheerfully under the direction of a rather pretty but severe ward sister.

'Gaston!' The sister-in-charge came forward as Gaston led his weary group into the main building. 'I didn't expect to see you again so soon.'

Mary heard a small gasp from Alex, though it was unclear why he should look so perplexed.

'I've brought you some more house guests,' Gaston said with a laugh. 'A few are going over the frontier with me, but the others, I'm afraid, will have to stay with you for a while.'

'Yes, I see . . .' The woman's eyes wandered over Gaston's shoulder and came to rest briefly on Mary before flickering away and widening as she recognized Alex. 'Captain Craig!'

'I didn't think we would ever meet again, Grace,' Alex said, remaining stiffly by Mary's side.

Mary felt a curious pang of jealousy that seared her heart. How long, she wondered, had Sister Forsyth and Alex been colleagues, sharing the dangers that had possibly thrown them together, physically and emotionally. The woman seemed to be doing her best to hide feelings that drained her face and made her breathe unevenly.

Alex was regarding her through half-closed eyes, and it was impossible to read his thoughts.

'This brave woman saved my life, Mary,' he explained softly. 'She stayed behind at Dunkirk when she could have escaped. She was the one who dragged me out of the sea and got me to Chateau Grovignac. I still don't know how she did it, but I owe her more than I can possibly repay.'

Sister Forsyth looked embarrassed. Her eyes avoided contact as she fussed over the little band of servicemen, ordering her staff to change dressings and find clean clothes for the new inmates of *La Citadelle*, which was what the hospital was fondly known as.

'How is our new patient, Sister?' Gaston asked and she looked somewhat confused until he reminded her. 'The woman I brought in two days ago.'

'Not very well, though it's nothing physical that I can find. I've had to sedate her heavily. Perhaps, Captain Craig would examine her while he is here . . . Alex?'

Alex nodded and followed a young nurse down a long, dark corridor, leaving Sister Forsyth to organize accommodation and food for the newcomers.

'Have you been here long?' Mary asked the woman, who ignored the question.

'I'm afraid you will have to share the nurses' accommodation,' Sister Forsyth said stiffly. 'But still, if it's only for one night . . .'

'I'm sure it will be fine.' Mary smiled, but the gesture wasn't reciprocated.

'For the moment, if you would like to wait here, I'll have some tea brought to you.'

But Mary did not get her tea. A few minutes later, as she waited in a communal sitting area for the tea to arrive, Alex reappeared and headed straight for her.

'I think you are better suited to deal with the patient I've just seen, Mary,' he said. 'Come with me.'

He led her to a small square cell where there were four beds, but only one occupant. At first, Mary took it to be a young man lying flat on the hard, uncomfortable pallet bed, but as she approached, the head, with unruly tufts of hair sprouting from a roughly shorn skull, turned in her direction. Two large, pale blue eyes, flat and lifeless, stared up at her.

'Anne! Oh, my God, Anne, what have they done to you?' Mary knelt down by the bedside and took Anne Beasley's limp hand in hers. She pressed the cold fingers to her cheek and couldn't prevent her eyes from growing moist.

'Mary?' Anne's voice was a feeble croak and suddenly her face was flooded with tears. 'Oh, Mary! You got away! You're safe!'

Mary couldn't believe that in so short a period of time any person could look so tortured. She sat there for a long time, holding Anne's hand, listening to her drugged ravings, piecing together the fragmented story of how she had been turned over to the villagers at Grovignac. How they had beaten her and shaved off her hair. Whether they would have done worse was debatable.

'But how did you escape?' Mary asked gently and Anne shook her head.

'I thought I was going to die,' she said, her voice only just audible. 'I was prepared to die, Mary . . . but someone came . . . a Frenchman . . .'

'That was Gaston Frébus,' Mary said.

'He yelled at them . . . carried me out of the village . . .' Anne licked her dry, cracked lips. 'I don't remember anything after that. They keep giving me tablets . . . I can't seem to think straight . . . can't remember anything . . .'

'Don't worry about it, Anne. We'll soon get you out of here and back home.'

Anne's head was thrashing about from left to right. 'There's something . . . something I have to tell you,' she kept muttering over and over, but she didn't seem capable of recalling what that something was.

Mary waited until Anne drifted into a peaceful sleep before she rejoined the rest of the group. As she sank down in a sagging old armchair, Chiffon jumped up on to her lap and licked the salty tears from her cheeks. She cuddled the little dog to her and looked across at Alex.

'It was Anne who saved our lives at the chateau,' she said. 'She thought she had failed in everything she did . . . and she lost the man she loved because she wasn't a German. When he found out he was supposed to . . .

to kill her, he couldn't do it. Instead, he left her to the mercies of the French villagers. Oh, this damned war! What it's doing to people. . . !'

'Sssh, Mary, ssh, my love.' Alex came to sit on the arm of her chair. He stroked her head gently, soothingly. 'Don't let it get to you. You're going to need all your strength to get over these mountains.'

As she had sat with Anne, so Alex sat with her. She must have fallen asleep where she was and they left her there, covering her with a blanket. When she awoke in the early hours, she still had the little dog curled up on her stomach like a hot water bottle, snoring gently like a baby.

The place was not entirely in darkness. There were candles in iron brackets all along the rough-hewn stone walls. They cast long, eerie shadows as the draughts of air caught them and played with the dancing flames. At first, Mary didn't know what had awakened her, then she heard a noise. The scuff of a soft leather slipper on the slate floor. At the far end of the hall she saw a figure creep stealthily across from one side of the corridor to the other and disappear through a narrow doorway that creaked stiffly.

Why she felt the need to go and quietly investigate, she did not know, but there was something about Sister Grace Forsyth – for that was who it was – that bothered her. She had saved Alex's life and for that she was to be commended, but who was she, really? Why was she creeping about her own hospital like a thief in the night? Like a vague echo somewhere in her heart, she could hear the voice of Smith, the MI6 man, giving her the coded message she had been unable to deliver. '. . . *the nightingale who sings the loudest . . .*'

Mary gave a small gasp. Perhaps, after all, it was nothing to do with a bird. It was hardly a code at all, if her thoughts were correct. The nightingale could also mean a nurse. And the one who sings the loudest? That would be the matron, or sister in charge. Not Florence Nightingale, but Sister Grace Forsyth!

Chiffon stirred with a small whimper when Mary left her, still curled up, on the chair she had just vacated.

'Ssh!' she told the dog in a whisper, tucking the blanket around it. 'Stay, Chiffon! Good girl!'

The door had been left slightly ajar. Mary squeezed through the gap. Immediately inside, a steep stairway led up to another floor with ancient beams through which slivers of light filtered. The beams creaked as someone paced, disturbing the light with its dark, moving shadow. There was a woman's voice, low and guarded. It was Grace Forsyth, but she was speaking in fluent German, although she appeared to be alone.

It didn't take Mary long to work out that she had stumbled on the spy in the network. No wonder they hadn't been able to catch the person who had caused the Allies such grief. Who would suspect a dedicated nursing sister of such treason?

Treading cautiously, Mary mounted the last few stairs and peered through the crack of a half-open door. It was an ancient oak door, grey with age and rotting around the edges, so there was a good view into the room beyond. There were more candles and a rickety table with a chair. On the table there was what appeared to be a radio set. Mary was familiar enough with communications to know that this was no British radio. Almost certainly, it was German. And what Sister Forsyth was saying proved without a shadow of a doubt that she had been responsible for exposing a string of safe houses including this one.

Mary leaned forward, holding her breath, wanting to see more of the room and Sister Forsyth herself, but as she shifted her weight the floorboard beneath her gave a loud creak and the door was pulled back with such force that she almost fell into the room.

Grace Forsyth blinked at the interruption. Her face remained bland, but her eyes swivelled to the side and that was when a pair of strong hands grabbed Mary by the shoulders. Before she could make any sound, a hand clamped itself over her mouth and she was dragged bodily into the room.

As the door slammed shut behind them, her attacker loosened his grip on her. Mary bit down on the suffocating hand and managed to open her mouth to scream, but found that she was looking down the long barrel of a German Luger pistol. She could smell the oil on it, taste it almost.

'So! We have a little English mouse in our midst.'

He was not the prettiest of men, but thickset with a pudgy face and soft pink lips. He wore no uniform and his clothes were that of a country person, but he looked dangerous enough to Mary.

'Tie her up!' he ordered. 'Gag her. We do not need her getting in the way of things at this stage.'

'What are you going to do with her?' Sister Forsyth looked on the edge of hysteria. 'You can't kill her. They'll hear the shot.'

As she spoke, Grace tied Mary's wrists together and, with shaking hands, pulled a knitted scarf tightly around her mouth. Mary felt her teeth grind on the wool, smelled the sweat of the German who had unwound it from his thick bull-neck.

When he was sure she was secured, the man pocketed his revolver and, with a greasy, wet-lipped smile, he pulled out an evil-looking knife.

'There are many ways to silence people,' he said, savouring every word.

Mary tried to cry out, but the wool in her mouth was too thick. The scream turned into a cough and she thought she would choke if she couldn't get some air into her lungs soon. But the German was not going to take pity on her. He placed a foot in the centre of her chest and pushed her flat to the floor.

As she felt unconsciousness beckoning, Mary heard the frantic scratching at the base of the door and an anxious whimper. Oh, no, she thought. It was Chiffon. The dog had followed her.

'What have we here?' Distracted by the commotion, the German pulled open the door and Chiffon bounded in. No sooner had she entered than she let out a squeal of pain as the man's foot caught her a hefty kick, sending her flying back out of the room.

'Little rat!'

However, Chiffon wasn't going to give up. With courage that outstripped her six pounds in weight, she came back and tried to get past him in order to reach Mary. Silently, Mary prayed that the poor creature would get the message and run off and hide, but Chiffon danced all round the room, barking and yipping and whining pathetically.

The German once more had his pistol in his hand and Mary saw that he was fixing a long silencer to it. He aimed it at the dog, fired and missed. But it had the required effect of sending Chiffon racing back down the stone stairs. And then the gun was once more pointing directly at Mary, aimed between her eyes.

'No!' Grace Forsyth cried out and took a step forward, putting herself between Mary and the German. 'No more!'

Mary felt consciousness beginning to slip away from her. There was a dull thunk and Grace fell heavily to her knees, grasping at her midriff where a bloodstain was spreading and oozing out through her fingers. At that moment, Alex and the two big Canadians erupted into the room, followed by Private Jenkins and the brawny Scot, Jock McCulloch.

Within seconds the German was overcome and locked securely in a cell. Mary followed Alex back into the infirmary. He carried the limp body of Sister Forsyth in his arms and his face was stricken with the horror of what had just passed. He laid the woman gently on a bunk with the other shocked nurses and patients looking on.

'Hold on, Grace!' Alex said, taking the dying woman's hand, squeezing it, and stroking her forehead.

He dressed the wound as best he could, but even Mary could see that it was useless. Swallowing hard, she took a cool, damp cloth from a young nurse and began to wipe it over Sister Forsyth's face, which was contorted with agony and damp with perspiration.

'I don't understand,' she said, glancing at Alex, feeling his pain. 'She was giving information to the German, revealing our position here. *She* must be the one they call "the nightingale".'

'The nightingale?' Alex shook his head uncomprehendingly. 'It doesn't seem possible that it could be Grace. She worked tirelessly with me in Normandy. I could never fault her work as a nursing sister. She was a little strict with the staff, but they respected her for that. Hell, Mary, she saved more lives than I did. How can she be a traitor?'

As he spoke, Grace Forsyth stirred and groaned.

'Alex,' she muttered weakly. 'Alex, you must get away from here. You must save yourself . . . and the others.'

Her eyes, glazed with pain, now lit on Mary and she gave a fleeting smile that ended in an agonized gasp as she tried to form the words that were in her head.

'Don't try to speak, Grace,' Alex said. 'It will only make it worse.'

'I must . . . I must tell you . . . why . . .'

'Why?'

'Why I did it . . . betrayed so many people . . . my own country.' She sucked air into lungs that were barely functioning, but she was determined to go on. 'My husband is a German Jew . . . my Erich. They are holding him . . . and my son, Johann . . . in Le Vernet concentration camp . . . .though I think they are both dead now. They promised to keep them alive as long as I passed vital information to them . . . the Nazis . . . the d-damned Nazis . . .'

'Grace, I'm so sorry . . .'

Alex bent over her, the better to hear her words, but the rattle in the woman's throat told them all that the end was near.

'Forgive me . . . Alex . . .'

Alex straightened and stared down at the woman with whom he had spent a great deal of time since he arrived in France. She had pulled him from the sea, saved him from the enemy, and taken him to a safe place. And now, she had taken the bullet that was meant for Mary.

'It's over,' he said, closing Grace's eyes for the last time as the nurses around the bed wept.

'And now we must do as she said, Alex,' Gaston Frébus joined them and laid a hand gently on Alex's arm. 'There is no time to waste. The German she was with was a member of the Gestapo. We got him to talk.

Our situation is already known. The Germans will be arriving very soon.'

'How soon?'

'Who knows? Two hours, two days? More than that he would not say. We must leave immediately.'

Alex shook his head. 'We can't all leave. There are still sick and injured patients here. They can't travel.'

Gaston nodded gravely. 'There are some caves near here. They are well hidden. I will take you there with your patients, but the others must then come with me over the passes to Spain.'

'I'm not leaving,' Mary said stubbornly. 'Not as long as Alex is still here.'

Alex raised his eyebrows and gave her a stiff smile. 'I'm sorry, Mary, but I must insist that you go with Gaston. I can function better if I don't have you to worry about.'

'But Alex—'

'No, sweetheart. Apart, we stand a chance of surviving . . . at least, one of us will.'

'Alex is right,' Gaston said. 'Come, Mary. There is no time to argue. Get dressed quickly. It is going to be very cold on the mountain passes.'

In the end, only six patients and a small handful of nurses formed Group A and undertook the long trek over the soaring massif of Mont Valier. There had been a heavy fall of snow overnight, rendering the journey difficult, so that only the very fittest were eligible to make the trip. There were the two Canadian airmen, and four British soldiers. Private Jenkins elected, selflessly, to stay behind to help Alex look after Group B until their time came to be rescued, though no one could say how or when that would be.

Mary's heart was breaking at the thought of leaving Alex behind. They had only just found one another. Surely she could not lose him now? She tried to understand. There were men who needed him, lives he could save. But it was difficult to accept such a decision, even if she knew it to be the right one. She couldn't question his bravery, but she was selfish enough to want him with her. She wanted to walk into safety with him, the two of them hand in hand, like lovers. But maybe it was not meant to be.

Alex kissed her all too briefly. She clung desperately to him, but there was no time to linger. Gaston was anxious to be off. He led the way, with the Canadians bringing up the rear, Mary roped safely between them. After the first few hundred yards, Mary heard a high-pitched yelp. She turned and saw Chiffon bounding towards them, bouncing like a rubber ball over the snow-covered ground, long fur flying. Half-way, the dog stopped, turned and gazed back to where Alex was still standing, one hand raised in a wave of goodbye.

At first, the dog clearly did not know where she wanted to be, but then they heard Alex's shout, telling Chiffon to '*va-t-en*!' She spun about, gave another yelp and raced on to where Mary was waiting. Mary dropped to one knee and caught the dog as she leapt into her arms, kissing her and cuddling her, laughing and crying at the same time. When she looked up again, Alex was gone.

'Here, Mary,' said Brad Shaw, the biggest of the two Canadians. 'Give the little lady to me. I'll tuck her inside my shirt. That snow up ahead looks deep enough to bury her.'

It certainly was difficult walking, even with the rackets Gaston had provided for them, together with warm mountain clothes and ski sticks. In parts, as the foothills gave way to the steeper climbs up into the passes, they often found that for every three steps they took forward, there was one back. The darkness made it doubly difficult; the wind buffeted them, burning their skin and making their eyes water. But behind every scarf-wrapped head there was a grim smile of determination.

The ascent up to the highest pass was a strenuous one, but once at the summit, the party of fugitives were relieved to find that there were no German guards at this point of the frontier between France and Spain.

'This is the last free passage left,' Gaston remarked as they all fell exhausted in the snow, not caring how cold it was and simply glad not to have to be climbing any more.

After the pass, it was downhill all the way. They continued to march through the night, marvelling at last at the spectacular sunrise that lit up the snowy peaks like pink-and-gold icing on a cake. They sheltered in a deserted village in the Spanish foothills in order to recuperate their strength. No one spoke. There was no need for words. The atmosphere seemed alive with emotion. Mary thought that she would be able to reach out and touch it like something good and solid.

'I will leave you now,' Gaston told them as they assembled to begin the next step of the march. 'I must go back to the others. I have heard of a group of Resistance workers still active just back over the border. They will help me, I am sure.'

'Gaston,' Mary said, tucking her arm in the Frenchman's and giving it a squeeze. 'I'm so grateful to you for what you've done. Please be careful, but I'm going to ask you to get Alex out for me . . . and Anne Beasley.'

Too many good people have died for their country already. I don't want that to happen to either of them.'

'I'll do my best, Mary, and . . .' Gaston hesitated, his face creasing into a frown. 'Please tell Iris when you see her that . . .' He sucked in a deep breath. 'Tell her . . . perhaps we will meet again . . . when the war is over.'

'I'll tell her, Gaston.'

She kissed his cheek, called to Chiffon, and started walking with the others in the direction he had instructed them to go.

It felt as though the journey would never end as they traversed miles and miles of rough tracks, the frozen land stretching out continuously before them. Some of the nurses complained that their feet were covered in blisters and bleeding from the chafing of the ill-fitting boots. Mary's feet were no better, despite an extra pair of socks that Alex had insisted on her having. Even the men were beginning to be despondent, believing that they were heading in the wrong direction.

Then Mary, her sharp eyes scanning the misty horizon, gave out a cry and pointed to a high pinnacle of rock that rose vertically out of the ground like a finger pointing to heaven, just as Gaston had described it.

'Brad! Where are your binoculars? Look over there.'

The big Canadian was at her side in an instance, the glasses up to his eyes, following the direction of her pointing finger.

'Yeah! That looks like it, all right, Mary,' he said with a wide grin, then turned to the others. 'Right, you feeble bunch of ramblers. We're on track, so pull up that last ounce of God-help-you and let's get going.'

The thought that the end of their long journey was in sight set the adrenalin coursing through their veins. They were able to shrug off the exhaustion as morale lifted and they strode out purposefully towards their goal.

Within an hour, they had reached the cliff on which the village of Santa Engracia perched. It was not as vertical as it had at first appeared. There was a rough track winding round it, steep, and at times treacherous for feet that were unsure and numb with the cold and fatigue. Darkness was falling fast when they limped blindly into the silent village, 1,000 feet above the valley.

But it was not the village they were heading for. It was the ancient hotel, the Casa Guilla, towering from the highest point of the cliff, which was their final destination. The foundations of the *casa* had been there, so Gaston had told them, for ten centuries and, judging by what they could see of the place, it hadn't changed much from the time of its construction.

'Do you think there's anybody here?' Mary asked shakily, hanging on to the stone portal at the entrance and listening intently, but the place was as silent as the grave.

'If there isn't, lassie,' said Jock McCulloch, 'we're in a good bit of trouble.'

'Well, we'll soon find out,' Brad said, banging loudly on the door with his fist.

Silence. Brad knocked again, then suddenly an upper window was opened and a head appeared, speaking in voluble Spanish.

'Anybody speak Spanish?' Brad asked; nobody did.

'*Le Loup nous a envoyé*!' Mary cried out, guessing that people who lived so close to the French border must know a little of the language.

The window snapped shut, but two minutes later there was the scrape of shoes on stone and the huge, iron-studded door opened with a loud groan. A man appeared, a flickering candle in hand, and behind him a dark-haired woman. Both were smiling.

'You are welcome,' the man said in English and the woman nodded eagerly. 'Come in.'

Once everyone was inside and the door shut and bolted behind them, more candles were lit and they found themselves in a long, low-ceilinged cave dwelling that was evidently used as a bar, for there were barrels and bottles lining the walls, a counter and a row of high stools. Old farm tools were displayed, rusty and decorated with cobwebs, in hewn out alcoves, and hanging from broad, rustic oak beams. Nothing had altered, it seemed, since the seventeenth century when marauding bandits had used it for storing their contraband.

'Well, this is my kind of place,' Brad declared, rubbing his hands at the sight of so much alcohol just waiting to be drunk.

'Please, all of you . . . sit. My wife will prepare a meal, but in the meantime . . .' The Spaniard placed a collection of glasses on the bar counter and started pouring from a dusty bottle.

When Mary tasted the contents of her glass she spluttered a little and the top of her head seemed to soar up to the low ceiling. But it was good and they all needed this medicinal dose of raw, Spanish brandy.

'We are known to your people as the Eyrie,' the Spaniard said, refilling the men's glasses and encouraging the women to drink up, even if they didn't like the taste. 'You can call me Diego. Now, if you will excuse me, I will contact Flying Fox . . . they will come for you.'

None of them could remember what they ate that night, but they felt better for the food and drink, if a little intoxicated. After the meal, with everyone falling asleep at the long, communal table, their host took up position on a precarious balcony that hung out from the dining-hall over a deep gorge.

'Come . . . look!' He called out, but only Brad and Mary went to join him. 'I want to show you my view. This is what our peaceful world looks like now. Perhaps it will not stay that way for long, but I look at it every day and every night and my heart breaks at the thought of having it taken from me.'

They looked out at a wide expanse of inky blackness, the stars twinkling above them, and below, clusters of lights joined like a pretty necklace, diamonds on a chain.

Mary felt the pain of nostalgia break loose inside her as she thought of how England had looked before the war and the blackout. And how, God willing, it would look again sometime soon.

They moved back into the warmth of the old building. Everyone was clustered around a crackling log-fire that was filling the air with the smell of burning pine. Their bodies sagged wearily into soft-cushioned chairs and sofas, heads dropped on to chests; eyes closing as they drifted off to sleep.

It was in the early hours of the morning, just before dawn, that the Spaniard awakened them.

'We go now, please,' Diego said and they hurriedly struggled into their outdoor clothes. 'We will take the trucks to the coast, then you will board a boat for Gibraltar. After that, England is not far away.'

Mary carried Chiffon in a soft leather bag slung across her shoulder. Only the tip of the dog's pointed nose showed, sniffing the air as they hurried after Diego. At the bottom of the steep slope, where the rock seemed to grow out of the plain, two ancient trucks, complete with Spanish drivers, awaited them.

'Vaya usted con Dios – go with God, my friends,' said the Spaniard, gripping their hands, each in turn.

As Mary climbed on board the second truck and it took off with a rattling jerk and a dry grating of gears she experienced a terrible sinking in her stomach. Taking the little dog out of the bag, she buried her face in the long, silky fur. Chiffon gave a whimper and nuzzled into her neck.

'He'll be all right, Chiffon,' she whispered, dashing away two tears that had found their way on to her cheeks. 'He'll come back to us. He's got to.'

She looked out at the scenery racing by and her heart cried out: 'Live, Alex! Please live!'

*

Alex had not been able to watch Mary walking away from him for more than a minute. When she turned and waved, it was all he could do not to run after her. But his responsibility to his patients and the handful of helpers who had elected to stay behind was too great. Personal feelings had to be put aside. If he was going to survive the next few days he would need all his stamina and all his wits about him. He needed to put Mary out of his mind.

'Captain Craig, sir,' Private Jenkins was hurrying towards him, I can't find that English woman . . . Miss Beasley. She's gone.'

'Gone? She can't have, Jenkins. There isn't anywhere to go, for goodness sake.'

'Well, I've looked everywhere.'

'The silly woman didn't have the strength to walk out, surely!' Alex looked around him, but the cave they were sheltering in was basic. There were no passages off or nooks or crannies where anyone could hide. 'Leave it to me, Jenkins. She can't have gone far.'

Alex stood at the entrance of the cave for a moment, then climbed up to a higher level and surveyed the land all round. At first there seemed to be nothing but boulders and scrub and patches of frozen snow. Then he saw it. The flash of white that wasn't snow, and it was moving. Anne Beasley had been wearing a heavy white woollen jacket when Gaston had brought her in. It must be her, but what the hell was the woman playing at?

Grabbing the leather flying-jacket that Gaston had provided for him, Alex took off in the direction from where he had seen the movement. It didn't take him long to reach her. Anne was crawling along on all fours, her battered face rigid with determination. She even tried to fight him off when he grabbed hold of her, but her strength was all spent.

'Leave me alone,' she cried in a voice too weak to contain any threat. 'Let me go. I have to go . . . have to . . . to do something . . .'

'What have you to do, Anne?'

'Stop them,' she said. 'I have to stop them, tell them . . . not here . . . not this way . . .'

'You're talking gibberish, woman,' Alex said, his patience thin with the urgency of the situation. 'If you go this way you'll only run into German lines.'

'Yes . . . yes, I know.'

He pulled her to her feet, but she sank against him, then her legs gave way and she slid to the ground and sat there, looking dazed. The heavy sedation she had been under since her arrival at *La Citadelle* was still making itself felt. Why Grace had seen fit to give her such a hefty dose was beyond him, but as always, he had given the senior nurse the benefit of the doubt. She had worked too long under tremendous strain. Lots of women would have cracked, given the same situation.

'Come on, let's get you back to the cave. We stand a chance there, but not out here in the open.'

'But they'll think I'm German,' Anne persisted, her voice strident as she fought off his hands. 'I can tell them . . . Oh, I don't know, but I can give them false information . . . send them in another direction. You'll be safe . . . you and the others. Mary . . . you'll tell her . . . please tell her I'm sorry. I feel like such a traitor. She got into this mess because of me. She can't die . . . I won't let them get her. . . !'

As Alex hoisted her up into his arms, a droning, like an angry hornet, buzzed in his ears. He struggled on, with Anne's limp body, slipping and stumbling on the stony ground. They were almost halfway back to the cave when he saw it. A German bomber. And it was heading his way.

'Dear God!' he shouted as he started to run drunkenly under the weight of his burden, heading for a rocky outcrop, which was the only place close enough to give them some cover.

The line of rocks seemed to get further and further away from him at every step as the Heinkel approached. His legs felt heavy and paralysed. As the bullets started strafing he fell on top of Anne, and they rolled together down into a narrow gully. He felt the bruising force of rocks and stones pummelling his body and hated to think what they were doing to the already fragile girl.

Wedged in the V of the shallow ravine, icy water running beneath him, penetrating his clothing, Alex opened his eyes and looked to where Anne was lying a few feet away. The force of their fall at the end had separated them. She made no sound and didn't move. It wasn't clear whether she was alive or dead, but Alex was powerless to do anything, one way or another. His left foot was firmly wedged between two boulders and from the feel of it, his ankle was broken.

Wincing with pain, he breathed out a curse. However, a broken ankle was the least of his worries. The lone Heinkel had been joined by others. Bombs were falling, shaking the ground like an earthquake. It went on for some minutes, then the noise subsided and there was an eerie silence, broken only by the echoing sound of trickling dust and shattered fragments of stone pouring down into the gully. He had no doubt what the target had been. The old monastery, and probably the cave too, had certainly been reduced to rubble, and the people inside buried in it, patients, nurses – and the courageous Private Jenkins.

Alex wanted to cry out as rage welled up in his throat, his whole being fired with fury against war and warmongers, and even God, for letting it happen. But he had to swallow his anger if he was to get out of this alive.

'Anne? Anne, can you hear me?' he called out, keeping his voice just above a whisper.

There was no response. She was, he could see, half-buried beneath rubble, her fair hair no longer glinting in the sun, her skin as pale as death shining through the dust.

He struggled to sit up, every move an agony. Somehow, he had to free his foot. He had to get out of there, get back to the cave. But how? He cast about for something to help him, then got his eye on a stout tree branch that had been blasted from the trunk and was lying a few feet away. It was a long stretch, but he was just near enough to grip the end of it, his fingers curling around the rough bark.

Slowly, he tugged and pulled, ignoring the sharp splinters that punctured his skin and drove themselves into his flesh. At last the branch moved and started to slide his way.

Holding it firmly in his two hands, he advanced it towards the boulders that were trapping his foot, but it was the wrong shape. Each time he tried to prise one of the boulders free, he ended up jabbing the thing into his injured ankle. It was useless.

'Damn!' he swore aloud, thinking that it was a pitiful thing for a man to come this far through a war and end up dying like a rabbit caught in a hunter's snare.

Alex lay back, panting, trying to hang on to consciousness. The situation called for clear thinking. It was no good waiting meekly for death to come. Somehow, he had to get out of here.

He dug around in his pockets, searching for something, anything, that might help him. There was nothing of any note. A scarf, a pair of gloves, a notebook, a pencil and a small penknife. He had used the knife more than once in emergency to removed shrapnel and bullets from patients in the field when there were no other instruments to hand. Well, perhaps it would serve him well, for if the worst came to the worst, he would have to try and amputate his own foot.

First things first, he thought, gripping the pencil and opening the notebook. After some moments of reflection, he began to write:

My dearest Mary, I am writing this in the full expectation that I will not be coming back, that my life is about to end, here in the Pyrenees. Perhaps, if this letter does reach you, it will bring you some comfort and the knowledge that, whatever happens, I do love you and will go on loving you through death and beyond . . .

Alex's head jerked up at the sound of heavy footsteps approaching. There was more than one pair of feet. He reached for the knife, opening it clumsily and suppressing an intake of breath as the sharp point cut into his palm. Ever nearer the footsteps marched and then, suddenly, two figures were silhouetted black against the sun and Alex looked up into the blinding light.

He knew before he heard their astonished voices that they were German. He knew, also, that they had pistols and were levelling them at his head. Alex made one last frantic effort to free his foot and stand, not wishing to be shot like a mangy dog, scrabbling in the dirt. But his efforts were in vain; the pain too much. The world suddenly tilted on its axis and became a very dark place.

'. . . *whatever happens, I do love you and will go on loving you through death and beyond . . .*'

Mary read Alex's words again and again. Her heart was torn apart, but she dared not let the emotion out or it would engulf her and she would be lost for evermore. She had cried bitterly when she first held the scrap of paper in her hands, smoothing out the folds, touching the stains that were undoubtedly Alex's blood.

'But where did it come from?' she demanded of the CO who had handed it to her.

'It came with some official papers and personal effects of soldiers killed in battle. Someone recognized Captain Craig's name and it was already known that he was last seen in the Pyrenees. And, of course, he had written your name and address at the top, almost as though he expected it to be delivered to you.'

The woman frowned and patted Mary's hand with genuine sympathy. Mary was breathing shallowly, holding on to her grief until she could be alone.

'Oh, Alex!'

'I assume that the letter has got to its correct destination,' the CO said gently. 'I'm so sorry, my dear.'

'Gaston Frébus was supposed to be going back for him . . .'

'Frébus, you say? Ah, yes. Something came through about him the other day. Apparently, he has had to go underground. His cover was blown. It's not entirely sure that he is still alive either.'

Mary closed her eyes, her own grief temporarily pushed to one side as she thought of Gaston, and wondered how she was going to break the news to Iris.

'He was a very brave man,' she said and the CO nodded, then shuffled papers around her desk, signalling that the interview was over. 'Do I have a fresh posting?'

The CO nodded again, obviously more comfortable dealing with the business side of things.

'No more SOE work for you, West. We thought perhaps we could use you as an instructor for the new intake of FANYs. You'll be an excellent example to the raw recruits.'

Mary nodded numbly. 'Thank you, Miss Fellows. I'd like that.'

'Take a few days' leave, West. Go and see your family, then report back to HQ in London. And West . . . I've put you forward for a medal. Jolly well done.'

Mary looked astounded. She muttered her gratitude. A medal, indeed. She didn't want a medal. She would trade in all the medals in the world, if only Alex could be with her right now.

CHAPTER TWELVE

A FTER the bombs, the silence. It was an eerie sound, that first sound of peace in 1945. Then came the singing in the streets, and the dancing. The war was over and people the length and breadth of Great Britain were going crazy. Words could not describe how they felt. War had been a way of life for so long. Now, they had to get used to another, new life, for there was no going back to normal. Not for any of them.

Frances Croft was no exception. The previous World War had ruined her life and she had never recovered from the invisible scars it had left her with. The Second World War had brought her almost to her knees, then a faint glimmer of light had shone through. She wasn't quite sure when or how it had started.

That day when she was feeling so terribly low, so miserable that she was, indeed, contemplating taking her own life – that was when things began to get a little better. That young doctor. His words, his kindness and understanding, had made a difference. The feeling of being needed, too, helped her back from the dark hole she had fallen into. She had sworn never again to get involved with the FANYs, but they had approached her, begged her to help find girls who would do them proud. She had even taken to wearing the FANY uniform again, pleased that her worth had been recognized, if only in a small way.

She had provided the Corps with girls who were worth their weight in gold. In particular those two she had tutored as children. Anne Beasley and Mary West. What gems they had turned out to be and both of them in line for a medal. As was the unfortunate Donaldson girl. What bravery. If she had her way, Frances would award medals to every one of the FANYs. The fact that three of the bravest souls she knew came from this small town alone made her doubly proud, though at the time, she had suffered terrible pangs of guilt and remorse, sending them to a life filled with so much danger.

Frances's fingertips smoothed over the sheet of paper she was holding. The action caused the tears that had fallen on the paper to smudge the bold black handwriting, but it didn't matter. They were tears of happiness. Nearly a quarter of a century had gone by, but here at last was the letter she had so often dreamed of receiving. Such foolishness, those dreams, she had thought at the time. And yet, as if by magic, the man she had loved all those years ago, was writing to her as if their affair had happened only yesterday. He was in the north of England and wanted to know if he could come and see her.

She read and re-read his words, already knowing them off by heart.

I hope, my dear Fanny, that this letter will not cause you problems. You no doubt have a full life by now, a husband, a family. I am on my own. My marriage broke down some years ago. It would mean so much to me if we could meet. I'm afraid I've become old and set in my ways, but I thought it might be pleasant to share a few nostalgic memories of those days we spent together in that Belgian Field Hospital . . .

Frances jumped at the sound of sharp rapping on the front door. She got up, quickly mopping her eyes and hurried to see who it was, for she didn't receive visitors very often.

'Mary!' she exclaimed on opening the door and seeing the young woman, resplendent in her FANY uniform, standing there. 'Why, Mary! How wonderful to see you. Do come in, my dear.'

Mary smiled broadly and stepped inside. Frances showed her into her cosy sitting-room, frowning slightly at the girl's demeanour. It had always bothered the rather straight-laced Miss Croft that Mary West could always dredge up a smile, no matter what had happened to her. Here she was, having experienced the atrocities of war at first hand, seen close friends injured and killed and, rumour had it, lost the man she loved, and there was still enough joy inside her spilling out like a ray of blessed sunshine.

'How are you, Miss Croft?' Mary asked, thrusting a bunch of glowing marigolds into her hands. 'These are for you. My dad grew them in the allotments to keep insects away from his vegetables.'

'Oh, how lovely, but to what do I owe this pleasure, Mary? The last time I saw your mother you were still in London.'

Mary nodded. 'Yes, she said you were in the habit of calling in. That was kind of you. Mam really appreciated your visits.'

'So . . . the war's over, Mary.' Frances indicated that they should sit down. 'And thank God for that.'

'Yes. I came back from London as soon as I could. It's a madhouse down there, as you can imagine. Anyway, being a Geordie, I wanted to be here for the Victory parade at St James's Park.'

'Ah, yes. It will be an emotional occasion.'

'More than you know, Miss Croft. Anne's mother has been in touch with me. She has asked for our help. Me and Iris Morrison and . . . and you, if you're agreeable.'

'Our help? In what way?'

And when Mary explained the problem, Frances knew immediately that her days with the FANYs were still not quite at an end. Not yet. There was one very important job she had to see through before she could get on with the rest of her life, wherever that would take her.

It was the 14 May, 1945 and it was a day that would remain embedded in the hearts of the people, not least the people of the north-east. A huge Victory parade was due to take place in the football stadium of Newcastle United. St James's had never witnessed such a gathering, nor such a spectacular performance. The parade was to be made up of elements of the armed forces and civilian organizations, marching to massed bands. The atmosphere for miles around was electric as spectators and participants flocked to the venue.

'We'll never make it,' Iris said as she and Mary sat in the back of Miss Croft's old black Humber car, heading for Central Station in Newcastle. There was a tight jam of traffic at a standstill on the Tyne Bridge, every vehicle packed with eager or anxious faces, all wanting to be in on the grand finale.

'We've got to make it,' Mary told her calmly and caught sight of Miss Croft's worried eyes in the rear-view mirror. 'I promised Anne's mother that we would do this for her. We started out together, you and Anne and me . . . and Effie, of course.'

'Poor Effie!' Iris let out a heartfelt groan.

'I'm not going to give up on any of us, do you hear, Iris?' Mary's hands were clenched into sweating fists, her nails digging into her palms. 'Remember what Effie used to call us when we were together? The Glory Girls of Felling.'

'Oh, goodness, yes, though she sometimes changed it to the Gory Girls to fit the occasion. Oh, don't remind me. I couldn't go through all that again.'

Mary fell silent. Like Iris, she wouldn't want to repeat the last few years, but one thing was sure. During that long expanse of time she had felt more alive than ever before. Every last blood corpuscle had shouted out, every nerve had given its last to do something worthwhile. She wouldn't say that it had been easy. Sometimes, she had wanted to sink down in the mud and the bloody gore and cry her heart out. She had cried over lost friends. But of all the experiences she had suffered during the entirety of the war, walking over the Pyrenees into Spain, leaving Alex behind had been the hardest to bear.

Mary lowered her head now as tears sprang to her eyes, which they did each time she thought of Alex. She rubbed her cheek against the silky coat of Chiffon, Alex's little dog, who was sitting on her lap. She had brought the dog back to England with her and they had become inseparable companions.

Chiffon stirred, lifted her head and licked at the salty tears that were falling on her from above. The dog had been as restless as Mary during the last few days, the two of them sharing the excitement, the unbearable anticipation of this special day.

'Oh, dear,' Mary said, a croak in her voice. 'This is no time to give way, is it?'

She felt a squeeze from Iris's hand and knew that Iris was feeling every bit as emotional as she was. There had been no news of Gaston Frébus, and the likelihood of there ever being any was, Iris had long ago accepted, extremely thin. She had been bravely philosophic about it. It was, she had told Mary, the last time they spoke of Gaston, never meant to be. Their worlds were too far apart.

'This is useless!' Miss Croft banged her hands on the steering wheel. 'I'm afraid we're not going to be in time to meet that train, girls.'

'Damn!' Mary looked out of the window and saw how impossible it was to move the car inch by agonizing inch across the bridge. 'Look, even if we miss the parade, I'm not going to miss that train. Come on, Iris. Get out.'

'What are you doing?' Miss Croft asked, her thin eyebrows shooting into her hairline.

'We'll run ahead on foot. It's not that far. Just to the end of the bridge and turn left into Neville Street.'

'Well,' Iris groused as she clambered out on to the pavement. 'At least there aren't any land-mines to worry about this time. Come on. Race you, Mary!'

Mary started to tell Chiffon to stay behind in the car, but the little dog, seeing her beloved mistress departing in such a hurry, could not bear to be left behind. She gave her customary, high-pitched yip! and leapt out after Mary, running alongside her and in and out of the legs of other hurrying pedestrians, a doggy smile of excitement on her face and the tip of a tiny pink tongue characteristically curled up over her black button nose.

They made the station just in time to see the King's Cross train wheeze into its platform with a puff of steam and sulphurous smoke. The platform itself was packed with people, most of them families meeting husbands, brothers, sons. Out of every train window, pale-faced, weary servicemen hung out, grinning, waving, shouting. As the train came to rest with a huge breathy sigh, doors opened and the servicemen tumbled out amidst kit bags, crutches and flags.

'Oh, God, how will we find them in this lot?' Iris said as the girls fought their way through the milling crowd.

'That's not as difficult as you might think, Iris,' said Mary, pointing. 'If I'm not mistaken, that's Mrs Beasley's best Sunday hat over there.'

The hat in question was indeed spectacular with its fuchsia silk cabbage roses and purple ostrich feather. And Mrs Beasley was tall, so even in a crowd of men that ridiculous hat could be seen bobbing along from quite a distance.

The departing passengers were thinning out, having been met and fussed over by those waiting on the platform. Mary held her ground, Iris pressed close by her side, neither of them really knowing what to expect. Mrs Beasley had told them that Anne had eventually been released from hospital, where she had been in the psychiatric ward for some time, having been liberated from a prisoner-of-war camp.

Brigadier Beasley had died two years previously, leading his unit into a heavily mined battlefield. Mary often wondered how Anne's mother had coped until now, but the woman had shown considerable courage and strength. She had, however, pleaded with Mary to meet the train that morning.

'Anne is very depressed, you see,' she had told Mary. 'She thinks everyone will see her as a traitor, especially her friends in the FANYs. It will mean so much to her if you are there and . . . well, you know . . .'

Mrs Beasley had thrown up her hands, unable to find the words, but Mary had understood. If anything, Anne had suffered more than any of them. She had been hurt physically and mentally. She had lost the man she loved, been marked as a traitor by people who did not understand the truth of the situation. She had been interned and could so easily have lost her life, but she had survived it all. Most of all, she had risked her own safety to save others, Mary included. The least Mary could do now was to help make things easier for her from now on.

Standing on tiptoe, Mary looked over the heads of the remaining servicemen who straggled behind the main group of passengers. And then she saw her. Anne, with close-cropped hair glinting in the rays of light filtering down from above. Her mother had her clasped firmly to her side, talking to her all the while, urging her on.

'Here!' Mary shouted at last, when the two women were near enough. 'Here we are!'

Mrs Beasley looked enormously relieved, but Anne's face seemed to grow even paler, if that were possible. Her slow steps faltered and her mouth set itself into a grim, thin line.

'Oh, you made it,' Mrs Beasley breathed, her eyes welling up with tears and she sniffed into her hankie. 'I didn't think . . . oh, thank you for coming. Isn't this wonderful, Anne? Your friends have come to meet you, darling.'

Mary saw Anne's throat contract as she swallowed hard. She looked painfully thin, like a skeleton covered in faded parchment. The eyes that rose to meet hers were sunken into purplish hollows and seemed colourless, without life.

Squaring their shoulders and tugging at the hems of their FANY tunics, Mary and Iris executed a smart salute, their faces cracking into beaming smiles of welcome.

'It's so good to see you, Anne,' Mary said, reaching out and hugging the girl tightly, but there was no noticeable response and when Iris did the same, all there was was a slight frown creasing Anne's forehead, which still bore a scar from her ordeal in France. It would be a constant reminder to her for the rest of her days.

The small group of women stood there staring at one another, in suspended animation. None of them knew what to say, what to do. In the end, it was Anne herself who made the first move. Her chest heaved and she turned to her mother.

'Please . . . I want to go home . . .'

'She's very tired, you see,' Mrs Beasley said by way of excuse.

'So are all these other soldiers and airmen and sailors,' Mary said, trying to keep a level tone in her voice and she saw Anne flinch, saw the girl's jaw set as she clenched her teeth. 'But they all have one last duty and they're proud to carry it out . . . and you will be too, Anne. Come on . . .'

'What. . . ?'

'We're all taking part in the Victory parade up at St James's,' Mary told her. 'And we're not doing it without you, because you helped win this damned war, Anne Beasley, as much as any one of us. And if Effie were here, she would probably tell you . . . in her words . . . that we're *bliddy* proud of you, girl.'

'That's right, Anne,' Iris said with a broad smile that quivered ever so slightly around the edges. 'We started out together and that's how we'll end.'

Anne blinked from one to the other of them and then looked at her mother, whether for support or confirmation of what they had just told her, it wasn't clear, but Mrs Beasley's head was up and her expression proud.

'You can't let them down now, Anne,' she said. 'If you do, you're not the daughter I took you to be.'

A nerve twitched in Anne's pallid cheek. She took a shaky step forward, hand outstretched. Mary took it and gave it a squeeze.

'I've been ill,' Anne whispered, not letting go of Mary's hand. 'But I think I'll be all right now . . . if you'll be there for me, Mary?'

'You don't have to ask,' Mary said, then turned to see what was making Chiffon bark so excitedly.

The dog had been erratically dancing about their feet, but now she took off and was flying down the platform in her customary bouncing run, short legs hardly touching the ground.

'Chiffon! Come back here!'

They all watched curiously as a lone figure emerged from the last carriage. A tall man, immensely smart in a new captain's uniform, leaning on a cane and walking with a slight limp. The peak of his cap shaded the dark eyes that scanned the station platform as if he was drinking in every inch like nectar.

Then Chiffon was upon him, leaping ecstatically into the air. He let the cane fall, bent low and held out a hand. The dog licked his fingers, then he picked her up and cradled her, looking about him again, his eyes searching eagerly.

Mary moved forward. She had hardly dared believe it when she received news of his capture by the Germans. It had come through long after she had given up hope of his being alive. And then there came the letter which she carried constantly close to her heart, reading it over and over, fingering it, scared it might disappear, taking her hopes with it.

'*My darling Mary, I'm coming home. . . .*'

Alex's eyes had alighted on her. Her heart pounded, her mouth was dry, yet still she could not believe that what she was seeing was not merely a hallucination. They might, at that moment, have been the only two people left in the world. There was nothing between them now except the hazy dust prisms slanting from the glass panels in the station ceiling.

He returned the dog gently to the ground, removed his cap and flung it away from him as he bounded towards her a little unsteadily, but that didn't matter. It didn't matter at all.

'Alex! Is it really you?' She choked on her words.

'Mary! Oh, my God, Mary, what a sight for sore eyes!'

He came to a halt, then held out his arms to her and she rushed into them with a cry that broke like brittle glass in her throat.

'I didn't think I would ever see you again,' she told him through racking sobs as he smothered her face with kisses.

'Well, they tried to kill me off, but I kept thinking of you and . . .' Alex took her face between both his hands and gazed down at her, all the love inside him spilling out of his eyes. 'Oh, my lovely Mary. You've no idea how good it is to be back home and holding you in my arms.'

'We . . . we're on our way to the Victory Parade at St James's Park,' she said, thinking how every word she uttered, every emotion she felt, would pale into insignificance from this moment on.

A rush of feet and loud, eager exclamations made the group turn around. Miss Croft had arrived. And Dr Gordon and his wife were hurrying breathlessly down the platform with her, faces beaming at the sight of the prodigal nephew they had twice thought was lost to them.

They threw themselves upon Alex, including Mary in their warm embrace. When they calmed down, Alex looked long and hard at Mary.

'I don't want to be apart from you so soon, Mary,' he said, 'but I have a feeling that what you were planning is very important – to all of us.'

'Oh, Alex!' Mary felt herself torn in two different directions, but she knew he was right.

'Go on,' he said, kissing her gently. 'Later, when today is over, we'll have the rest of our lives to enjoy together. Besides, I fully expect to be part of the show.'

'Quite right, Captain Craig.' Miss Croft was the first to recover her equilibrium with a cough and a quick wipe of her eyes and nose. 'The pair of you will have all the time in the world to talk in private, but right now, we are expected to take part in the Victory Parade and I'm determined that we'll do just that.'

As Alex and his aunt and uncle waited, the others took Anne into the station washroom and helped her change into a brand new FANY uniform, which they had obtained especially for her. It was too big, because she had lost so much weight, but if she thought it looked ridiculous, she made no comment and neither did her proud mother. Mrs Beasley was too happy to see her daughter alive again to complain about ill-fitting garments.

A few minutes later they all walked proudly into the big football arena where the various units were being organized, ready for the biggest spectacle ever to have been performed there.

Although Mary was loath to leave Alex's side, they were obliged to split up as they each joined their own units. Miss Croft marched proud and erect in front of her three Felling FANY girls, following the direction the organizers had given her to find their unit.

'Oh, I do wish . . .' Iris started to say, then her lip quivered.

Mary knew that Iris was thinking about Gaston and wishing he were there with them.

'I know, Iris. Me too,' she said sympathetically. 'I'm sorry Walter can't be here either, but they say he's very poorly and I . . .'

She stopped as a sudden disturbance broke out behind them.

An official held up a hand, ordering them to stop and also gesticulating to the cause of the interruption. They turned to find a motorbike and sidecar rattling up towards them, its engine roaring, coughing and spluttering out black exhaust-fumes as it covered the churned up turf and came to a halt beside them in a noxious cloud.

'Eeh, would ye look at that! Gawd luv us! It's the bleedin' Glory Girls of Felling! Were ye thinkin' of enjoyin' this effin' parade without me, eh?'

The minuscule figure in the sidecar took off its helmet and goggles and there was Effie Donaldson, as bold as brass, grinning at them as if she was on a works' outing. People stared at the rough-tongued young woman with the scarred face, but she took no notice of them. She grinned even more widely as Mary, Iris and Anne surged forward, laughing at their amazed expressions.

'Effie,' cried Mary. 'What on earth are you doing here? I thought—'

'Doesn't matter what you thought,' Effie said, her forehead creasing like a paper concertina. 'Nobody's going to make me miss this parade. Here, grab hold of me legs till I can get meself out of this here pram . . .'

Effie was holding out a pair of false legs, thrusting one at Mary, the other at Iris. The man on the bike was already coming round to help, hauling the legless Effie up so that she could sit on the top of the sidecar in order to fix the false legs to her two stumps.

'Oh, lor!' Iris took half a step back. 'I don't think I can take this.'

'Jesus wept, girl,' Effie said, fixing Iris with a sharp eye. 'Ye've been all through the war and this still makes you want to throw up? This is me brother, Billy, by the way. He's the only one of me brothers left now. Got caught the minute he landed in France and spent the whole of the war in a POW camp, would ye believe? The other silly sods all got theirselves killed, God rest their souls. Come on, Billy. On wi' me legs. I'd hate them to hold up the parade just for me.'

Mary exchanged glances with the others as Billy Donaldson strapped on the prostheses to what was left of his sister's legs. It didn't take long before Effie was standing before them, a little unsteadily, but nevertheless upright.

'Where's yer sticks, our Effie?' Billy said, but Effie threw a hand up, giving him the victory sign, though it looked a lot ruder when she did it.

'I didn't bring them,' she said, fixing her eyes on Mary. 'I thought maybe me friends here would give us a hand. I'd like that fine.'

Mary glanced at Iris, whose eyes were growing larger by the minute.

'Yes, Effie,' she said, her smile wobbling slightly. 'We'd like that fine too, if you're sure you can manage.'

'Can I effin' manage! Come on you lot. Let's show 'em.'

'Just a minute!' Billy was on her again. 'Where's yer medal? Ye canna gan on parade without yer medal, our Effie!'

Effie sucked air in through her teeth and wrinkled her nose. 'Aw, man, Billy. Give over about that silly medal.'

But Billy was rummaging around in the sidecar and he came up, exultant, the medal in his hand. He thrust it at her and she looked embarrassed.

'Go on, Effie,' Mary said. 'You were the one who said "let's show 'em". Well, now you've really got something to show, haven't you?'

Effie scowled, then the corners of her mouth turned up. 'Where's yours then?'

'Oh. . . .' Mary gave a wry smile, then pulled her own George Cross out of her pocket. 'All right, Effie. I'll wear mine if you wear yours.'

'Gan on then but watch what you do with that pin.'

They grinned at one another and Iris insisted on doing the honours for both of them, ignoring Effie's remarks about not liking the shade of blue of the ribbon on which the medal hung.

There weren't so many FANYs there in the parade, so the small group from Felling stood out and there were heartrending cheers as they took their cue and marched on to the field as the bands struck up one of Elgar's famous *Pomp and Circumstance* marches.

Anne took her place at the side of Frances Croft, walking as weakly as a newborn lamb, but moving determinedly under her own steam, with her head held high. Behind her, sandwiched between Mary and Iris, Effie rocked perilously on her false legs. Not once did she show signs of giving up, even though the grimace that was set like concrete on her face told them that she was in considerable pain.

Mary felt awash with multiple emotions as she and Iris helped keep Effie in step, but she didn't care how they were marching and, judging by the roar of the crowds looking on, they didn't care either. Every last person on the Newcastle United football field was a hero and this was a moment of glory they would never shed, no matter how long they lived.

The street parties that followed the Victory Day Parade were small and quiet by comparison, but they too were filled with unforgettable moments as families joined together, eating at long tables, singing and dancing around big bonfires to scratchy records played on gramophones that had to be kept wound up or the music would go down in a wavering, distorted spiral.

Felling held its own Victory Day, with the Salvation Army Band playing in Victoria Square and songs belted out by the Felling Male Voice Choir, which they considered to be as good as any of their Welsh counterparts any day.

Mary was spending the day with Alex, having persuaded her family to let her out of their sight, and promising that she was not going to run off anywhere. The whole place was festooned with paper decorations and colourful balloons, as gay as any Christmas, though the sun was shining warmly and the girls were all in their pretty summer frocks and cheeks were rosy from the electrically charged atmosphere.

She called first at Dr Gordon's house, where Alex was living temporarily. The doctor and his wife made her very welcome and it was evident that she had their approval.

'Well, are you ready to join in with the celebrations, Mary?' Alex asked, taking her hand in his and squeezing it, before planting a kiss on her temple.

She nodded. 'I'm ready for anything, Alex.'

Mary caught sight of Stuart and Maggie Gordon, standing close together, smiling warmly at them.

'Now isn't that a wonderful sight?' Dr Gordon said, nudging his wife.

'Aye, Stuart,' Maggie replied with a great sigh. 'It's really good to see you so happy, Alex. You too, Mary. Heaven knows, you both deserve some happiness.'

'Shall we go, then?' Alex was still clasping Mary's hand as they stepped out on to the street and joined the milling throng of locals in the square. 'Just look at this. I'm betting on the surgery being full of headaches and upset tummies in the morning.'

As they made their way through the long trestle tables groaning with food and great brown pots of tea, all freely donated from everyone's meagre rations, people laughed and joked with them. At every other step there was someone to shake Alex's hand or salute him. And a few even remembered that Mary had once worn the khaki uniform of the FANYs and gave her the same respect, which greatly embarrassed her.

'You know, Mary, you're ever so pretty when you blush like that,' Alex said as they paused by the fountain in the middle of Victoria Square to listen to the band playing yet another rendition of Auld Lang Syne and grown men joined the womenfolk, weeping into their hankies.

'Oh, dear!' Mary sighed and blushed some more as tears filled her own eyes.

'I didn't upset you by that remark, did I?'

'No, don't be silly, Alex. Of course you didn't.' Mary slid her arms about his waist and hugged him so tightly he could hardly breathe. 'I was just thinking how lucky we are and . . . and that song . . . you know . . . *should old acquaintance be forgot.* . . . It reminded me of the people I got to know, who will never see a day like this. People like Gaston Frébus, old Monsieur and Madame Laroque, and Jan Berwinski. And the German Anne fell in love with, who saved her life by turning her over to the French when he should have shot her. And . . . my goodness, who is that with Miss Croft?'

Mary pointed across the square to where Frances Croft was standing chatting to a rather nice-looking man in his fifties. Their conversation was quite animated and both were smiling broadly. Mary could see that Miss Croft must have been quite striking as a young woman and even though her face was now lined and her hair drab and streaked with grey, she appeared to have shed twenty years.

They pushed through the crowd, Mary waving and trying to attract Miss Croft's attention. At last the older woman saw them and spoke quickly to her companion. He nodded genially and led Miss Croft forward most carefully, his hand placed protectively at her back.

'Mary, my dear! And Dr Craig. I'm so glad to see you here today.' She turned to the man by her side and her expression softened to one of pure love as she introduced him. 'This is my good friend, Mr Temple. We haven't met for many years, but now . . . today . . . he has come to see me and . . .'

'Mr Temple?' Alex said, shaking the man's proffered hand. 'Mr John Temple?'

'Yes, that's right. Have we met before?'

Alex shook his head. 'No, but I think I saw your name once . . . forgive me, Miss Croft, but I'm afraid I was guilty of reading one of your private letters . . . that day I visited you, at the beginning of the war.'

'Oh, I see. Yes.' Now it was Miss Croft's turn to blush and she turned a bashful smile on John Temple. 'That must have been your goodbye letter to me, John.'

'You kept it?'

'Kept it and cried over it . . . many times.'

John Temple looked uncomfortable for a moment, then he shook his head and patted Miss Croft's hand, which was resting on his arm.

'War changes us so much, doesn't it?' he said. 'It changes people, and it changes their lives. When I wrote that letter, Fanny, I didn't know how much things had changed. I found out too late, but I still couldn't do anything about it.'

'Anyone who's been through a war would understand that,' Alex said.

'Didn't you ever get in touch with Miss Croft later?' Mary asked and saw the older man's wistful smile.

'No, my dear, and not a day passed that I didn't regret my silence, but pride and guilt rule our lives to a great extent. I tried to stay true to my vows, true to my beliefs. However, I do intend to make up for lost time, don't I, Fanny?'

Frances Croft dimpled and gave a girlish laugh. 'He's even more romantic than I took him to be when we met in that horrid old field hospital more than a quarter of a century ago.'

'And you love every minute of it, or am I very much mistaken?'

Miss Croft shook her head and laughed again, embarrassed, but clearly enjoying the occasion. 'Am I correct in thinking that you two are . . . well, you know . . . going out together?'

Now it was Mary and Alex's turn to laugh. Mary thought how easy everyone found laughter suddenly, after all the years of hardship and worry and being serious.

'Alex and I . . .' she hesitated and glanced up at Alex as if begging confirmation of what she was about to announce. 'We're going to be married just as soon as it can be arranged, Miss Croft, and we want you to come to the wedding. You will, won't you? And . . . and Mr Temple too, of course.'

Frances Croft clasped her hands together under her chin and looked delighted.

'Oh, Mary, I'm so pleased. You know, I felt so guilty about putting your name forward to the SOE. I tried to get you withdrawn, but . . . oh, my dear, do forgive me. It must have been horrendous for you.'

Mary shook her head and smiled kindly. 'No more so than for any of the others,' she said. 'I don't regret any of my time spent over the last five years. I'd like to think that I've come out of it a better person. I didn't do so much, really, but I did my best.'

'That's all any of us can do,' Alex said, the fingers of one hand ruffling her hair as he pressed a kiss on her forehead.

They were standing there, regarding one another when someone hailed them and Mary looked up to see Iris pushing her way through the crowd. She held one arm aloft and a sheet of paper fluttered in her grip.

'Mary!' She came to a breathless halt, acknowledging them all with a swift glance before pushing the letter in Mary's hands. 'You won't believe it, but I've heard from Gaston!'

'Gaston! He's alive?'

'He was when he wrote this,' Iris prodded the paper; her eyes welling with tears and she sucked in a sobbing breath of air. 'Oh, Mary, it is from him, isn't it?'

The letter was cryptically written in a bold, almost indecipherable hand and it was unsigned, but Mary was more than convinced that Gaston Frébus had written it.

Do not worry for me, the letter said. *I have gone to earth for now, but this wolf will bay to the moon again one day. In the meantime, I will think of you, my English flower. It will warm me in the long days that lie ahead. Say a prayer for me occasionally, never forget me, but go on with your life and make it a good one.*

'Maybe one day I'll see him again, Mary,' Iris said. 'Do you think so?'

'Anything's possible, Iris,' Mary told her. 'Especially when you're Gaston Frébus, it seems to me.'

She didn't like to dampen her friend's hopes by suggesting that this was perhaps the last they would ever hear of the man known in the High Pyrenees as *Le Loup.* Men like Gaston tended to disappear, leap-frogging from one identity to another, one life to the next. They thrived on danger. An ordinary life would hold no appeal.

'Yes, my dear,' said Miss Croft with a swift glance at her companion. 'Just look at me. I gave John up many years ago – at the end of the First World War – and here we are planning a new life together. The same could happen for you and your Frenchman. Who knows?'

Yes, Mary thought, a little sadly. Perhaps it was best that Iris did not know the truth, whatever that truth was. Not yet awhile. Perhaps in a year or two, she might not be so vulnerable, not so much in love with her French Resistance fighter. Time might have faded the memory of him. She might meet a nice young man here in her own home town, settle down and be happy.

'Let's go, Mary,' Alex said in her ear, tugging at her arm; she had sensed that he was somewhat twitchy and she thought she knew what the problem was, for her own feelings were running along the same lines.

They said their goodbyes, promising to be in touch and suddenly Mary was being almost dragged along the street. In his impatience, Alex's limp from the badly broken ankle he had suffered just before he was captured, and which had not healed properly, seemed much less noticeable.

'Alex, not so fast,' she complained breathlessly as they left the mêlée and started down an almost deserted lane. 'Where are we going at such a speed?'

'It's no good, Mary,' Alex gasped, stopping before a garden gate. He opened it and almost pushed Mary up the path to the dull brown painted front door. 'If I can't have a few minutes alone with you I'm going to explode.'

There had been no time since his return for them to be completely alone, apart from a stroll through the town, hand in hand and a quick, furtive embrace behind trees and corners, not wishing to share their feelings with the curious eyes of the rest of the world.

She heard the jingle of keys and saw that his hand shook slightly as he fitted one in the lock. It turned easily and he pushed open the door.

'Alex?'

'Mary, please don't feel badly about this. It was never really Fiona's home. She never put her mark on it, like most women would. I swore I would never bring you here, but I can't stand sharing you with so many people. I hate the darting into doorways so nobody can see us.'

'What are you trying to tell me, Alex?' Mary smiled with infinite wisdom, but she wanted to hear him say the words.

'I want to make love to you, Mary,' he said quite openly, his eyes fixed on hers so intensely that she felt hypnotized. But she was not afraid. She would never be afraid of Alex. 'Do you mind?'

'What would you do if I said no?' She was playing cruelly with his emotions, but she needed to spin out this precious moment. She didn't think for one moment that his dead wife might be haunting the walls of this house, waiting to spoil their new-found happiness. Nothing could ever do that, ever again.

'I might beat my chest, fall prostrate at your feet and weep more tears than an Indian monsoon,' Alex said, an amused twitch lifting the corner of his mouth. 'It would not be a pretty sight, I assure you.'

He was drawing her inside, closing the door behind them, leading her into a plain, almost bare living-room. She took the room in with one swift glance and felt relieved. There was no visible sign of Fiona Craig. Not an ornament, not a photograph nor a relic of any kind of the marriage that should never have been. Either he had removed them, or they had never existed in the first place.

The house was cold and smelled slightly damp, but it hadn't been lived in for a long time. Mary shivered and Alex took off his jacket and draped it about her shoulders.

'I'm afraid the gas has been switched off, so we haven't any light,' he said, looking bleakly at the two gas-mantels on either side of the fire-place. 'However, there should still be some coal in the cellar. There's an open grate in the front room. We'll soon get the place warmed up, unless . . . .is it too soon, Mary? Am I rushing you? You must say.'

She smiled up at him, then reached up and hooked her hands behind his neck, not caring that his jacket slipped to the floor or that she was pimply with the cold.

'I don't think six years is rushing things, Alex,' she told him. 'And if you don't make love to me soon I will die right here in your arms and you'll never forgive yourself.'

Alex wasted no more time. He made sure, during the blissful hours that followed, that there would be nothing to forgive himself for. And for that short time at least all memories of the war, not to say the whole of the outside world, ceased to exist. There was only the love of two people, who had always been meant for each other, melding together as one.

EPILOGUE

THE cemetery was surprisingly full on the day in 2007 when Felling buried one of its best-loved inhabitants. Although she had outlived most, if not all, of her friends and contemporaries, there were few people who did not know or have great respect for Mary West Craig.

There were uniformed representatives from the Army and from the FANYs, but one uniformed figure in particular stood out, proud and erect and, everybody thought, might well have been Mary herself stepping out from the past, were it not for the young woman's bright, Titian-red hair.

'Nearly over.' Matt Feathers squeezed her hand as he glanced surreptitiously at his watch for the umpteenth time.

Sarah Craig smiled patiently. Matt was a nice young man and she loved him dearly, but she didn't think he would ever understand her link with the past, and in particular with her grandmother.

'That wonderful woman is my hero,' she told him with a shake of her tawny mane. Rain droplets were captured in the natural curls that glistened there like diamonds on fire as they were now touched by the sun. 'I don't care how long it takes to wave her off to her next big adventure.'

'What is it with you Craig women?' Matt frowned at her and she wished he wouldn't, because he looked far nicer when he smiled. 'You're never happy unless you're dashing off in search of excitement and danger. I mean to say, why can't you see some glory in settling down to marriage and raising a family? Preferably with me.'

Sarah buried her face in the bunch of handpicked marigolds she was clutching. She had picked them from her father's garden at the last minute. Matt had wanted to know why she wasn't spending money on a proper wreath or bouquet, if she thought so much of the old lady. But money didn't come into it. Marigolds were Mary's favourite flowers. She had planted them herself all around her own private seat on the terrace of the nursing home where she had spent her last few happy years.

As for marrying Matt, Sarah wasn't at all sure about that. There was plenty of time and they both had careers to sort out. They had met at medical school. Sarah had quickly swapped people for animals and was now a fully qualified vet looking for her own practice. She had joined the FANYs five years ago, following in the footsteps of Mary, not to mention her own mother.

'Your grandfather would be so proud of you,' Mary had told Sarah, then added the words that were so familiar to all the family: 'Alex was such a brave man. He saved a lot of lives, you know, back in the war. We must never forget him.'

Mary never seemed to see that she had been every bit as courageous as her dear husband, whom she had worshipped with the kind of fierce love that nothing could ever undermine. They had been everybody's idea of the ideal couple, right up until his death. He had died peacefully, holding Mary's hand, while the family celebrated the birth of the new millennium, a contented smile on his still handsome face.

'I'm not sure that old Mary West Craig approved of me as husband material for her precious granddaughter,' Matt muttered in Sarah's ear as mourners lined up to throw their flowers on to the coffin, which had just been lowered into the grave.

Sarah gave a small laugh. 'Well, you should never have made that remark about the FANY being a girl soldier's playgroup. Mary was fiercely protective about the Corps and very proud of the part she played during the war. It's a pity that she's going to miss the grand centenary proceedings this year, though. I was really looking forward to taking her down to London with me.'

'You still can, in a way,' Matt said, digging in his pocket and drawing out a somewhat shabby piece of material.

'Ssh!'

The hiss came from behind them and Sarah felt her mother's fingers digging her in the back.

'Sorry!' she whispered back, but she couldn't help feeling that Mary would never have wanted a sombre funeral. In fact, the old lady had taken Sarah to one side not so long ago and told her some remarkable things: *I want singing and dancing when I'm gone, do you hear me, girl? Tell all of them to wear red. I hate black. It's so funereal.'*

Sarah had passed the word, but of course, everyone had ignored her. Old-fashioned respect and tradition dictated that they wear black and appear mournful. Only Sarah herself broke with tradition. She wore her FANY uniform with a black armband and, underneath it, some sexy red underwear. Mary West Craig would have appreciated that.

'What have you got there?' She turned back to Matt and took the morsel of cloth from his hand. 'Oh, it's an old FANY badge. Where on earth did you get that?'

'When they called me in to see Mary she gave it to me. It was cut from her original uniform. Nothing left of the uniform itself, she told me, but she had saved that and she wanted you to have it. Only, I forgot all about it until now.'

'Is that what you meant by still being able to take her to London for the centenary?'

'Yes.'

Sarah drew in a deep breath and blew him a silent kiss as her mother gave her another push from behind and they all advanced until they were standing there in a circle around the grave. All the family together on one rare occasion. And Matt, who was proving to be more sensitive than she had suspected.

'I think I might marry you after all, Dr Feathers,' she whispered in his ear, then threw her bouquet of flowers in a golden shower over the coffin, but retaining four of the blooms.

'Well, that's a relief.' Matt gave a lopsided smile. 'But I hope you're not going to continue running off every time the FANYs press the emergency button.'

Sarah knew what he meant. During her service in the FANYs she had been posted to every disaster zone imaginable. She had spent some weeks with her unit in Sri Lanka helping to track down missing relatives following the tsunami, which struck on Boxing Day 2004. More recently, she had been involved in the London bombings, which had come very close to the work her grandmother had done sixty years ago.

'That depends on how many children we have.' She grinned, warming to the thought of settling down to family life.

'I did actually like the old girl, you know,' Matt said. 'If you're only half the woman she was I'll never be good enough for you.'

'Nonsense!' Sarah choked up as the gravediggers moved into position and began shovelling the loose soil over her beloved grandmother's coffin. ''Bye, Mary. I'll try to make you proud of me . . . you and Gramps.'

She kissed her fingers and touched them to the polished granite stone that bore her grandfather's name, Dr Alexander Craig. Sarah liked to think that the loving couple had been reunited at last and were on the "other side" somewhere, still gazing lovingly into one another's eyes, still holding hands.

'She was quite a character, was Mary,' Matt said.

'She might have been old and fragile in body at the end, Matt, but she had the brain of a young and vibrant woman,' Mary said. 'I think, really, she was more than ready to go, but was holding on. Did I ever tell you, Matt, what her dying words were? She said *I can go happily now, knowing that I'll live on through you, Sarah.*' Then she turned her head as if someone had just walked into the room, but there was no one there that I could see. *Alex!* she said, and smiled so broadly I thought she might live for ever, but she didn't. She went ... *pouf!* ... and was gone in an instant. It wasn't sad, not really. She must have really been happy with Gramps. They were married for over fifty years, you know.'

Matt put an arm about Sarah's shoulders and hugged her to him.

'I hope we can do as well,' he said.

They were the last mourners left standing at the graveside. Sarah was reluctant to leave. She wished Mary were still there, as she had been all her life, calm, patient, full of wisdom. Sarah had been able to go to her with all her problems and Mary always had a quiet word of advice. She was never negative, always looked on the bright side of things and found good in everything and everybody, no matter what.

She had supported Sarah's decision to become a FANY, even when the rest of the family had tried to dissuade her. Like Mary, Sarah was blessed with stubborn determination and usually went her own way. She had never regretted the choice.

Just like Mary during the war, she had handed out blankets and spare clothing. She had made numerous cups of tea, driven ambulances and so much more. Sometimes the tasks were arduous, sometimes horrific, yet she always came out a stronger, better person at the end. And she never stopped thanking Mary West Craig for passing on her indomitable genes that made it all possible. How that great old lady would be missed.

'Excuse me, but are you related to Mary Craig, the old lady they just buried?'

The crunch of gravel on the path and the rather gruff voice had startled them. Sarah looked up to see a pocket-sized figure with black, shoulder length hair and dark, curious eyes.

'Yes,' she said. 'Mary was my grandmother. Did you know her?'

'Aye, I did,' the girl nodded. 'Well, no, not really, but me mam told me all about her. Her aunty Effie and your grandma were good friends it seems.'

'Oh, yes, Mary used to talk about Effie. And the others. There was a regular group of them. Here you are. See, they even managed to get buried side by side. Mary was the last to go.'

'Gawd, they must have been quite something.'

Next to Mary's grave was a stone dedicated to one Euphemia Donaldson, aged eighty; next came Iris Coldwell, née Morrison, aged seventy-nine, beloved wife, mother and grandmother. And on the other side of Mary, lay Anne Beasley, aged seventy-three.

'Aunty Effie lost both her legs in the war, but it didn't keep her down. She never married, of course. They say her sharp tongue used to keep the men at bay more than those false legs of hers. She used to tell everybody that being a FANY was better than sex any day, but the way she looked I doubt she'd have the choice, God love her. Lord knows, I can't talk. They say I'm the spittin' image of her.'

'They were known as the Glory Girls after the war,' Sarah muttered and saw the girl's sharp stare. 'I bet they could tell some stories between them.'

'Aye. Gawd, I'd give anything to have been one of them, wouldn't you? Oh! Bloody hell, sorry, I've just seen the uniform. So, you *are* one of them, eh?'

Sarah laughed lightly. The girl was rough around the edges, but there was something very likeable about her.

'Yes, I am, and you could be too, if you're interested.'

'Nah! They wouldn't want the likes of me in that posh set-up.'

'What makes me think that your Aunty Effie would want to hear you talk like that?'

The girl frowned and knelt by her great-aunt's grave. She pulled up a few weeds and stuck a bunch of daffodils in an old cracked earthenware vase.

'Is it difficult to get in?' she asked, keeping her head lowered and doing her best to disguise the interest in her voice. 'I mean, it's got to be better than what I do, laying out folks for a living.'

'You're an undertaker?'

'Aye. Just like me aunty Effie was all those years ago. It's the family business, you see, but I'd give me eye-teeth to get out and see a bit of life, instead of spending me days keeping dead bodies company.'

Matt was again consulting his watch and itching to get away. Sarah smiled and nodded to him, signalling that she was coming, but first she delved into her bag and produced a business card.

'Here, take this. I'll be going back to London soon to help with the centenary plans, but if you're interested in joining the FANYs, give me a ring or come and see me.'

'Aye, well . . . mebbe.'

'By the way, what's your name?'

The question produced what was probably a rare smile on the serious face of Euphemia Donaldson's great-niece.

'Oh, I got the works when I was born, I did, seeing as how aunty Effie was still alive and kicking. Go on, guess.' She looked at Sarah from beneath dark, heavy brows; Sarah shook her head and the girl took a deep breath before reciting: 'Mary Effie Iris Anne Donaldson, that's what. Only people call me Nora.'

'Well . . . er . . . Nora . .' Sarah said, wondering why 'Nora'. 'That's quite a name, and one to be proud of.'

'Aye, it is an' all. Thanks.'

Sarah smiled, nodded, then regarded her watch. She was anxious to get back to her parent's home where the funeral tea was being held. 'Well, as I say, get in touch.'

She placed a flower on the graves of Iris, Anne and Effie, and hurried after Matt. Nora Donaldson stood by the graves, watching her go, a strange, excited fluttering inside her. She had been feeling down lately and, when that happened, the only place she liked to be was here, tending old Aunty Effie's grave. It was a coincidence, meeting Mary West's granddaughter like that. She seemed an all right kind of girl, too.

'So, Effie, what do ye think, eh? Me, a FANY? What a laugh. Bloody Nora! I wonder if they'll let me keep me Harley Davidson? I bet you'd have loved a ride on that, eh?'

She stood back from the row of graves, pulled herself up to her full five feet nothing, and gave a smart salute. A slow smile spread across her face as she lowered her arm, then punched the air.

'*Yes!*' she shouted, and was sure she heard a satisfying response from the Glory Girls.